P9-DED-225

By Dale Brown

ROGUE FORCES
SHADOW COMMAND
STRIKE FORCE
EDGE OF BATTLE
ACT OF WAR
PLAN OF ATTACK
AIR BATTLE FORCE
WINGS OF FIRE
WARRIOR CLASS
BATTLE BORN
THE TIN MAN
FATAL TERRAIN
SHADOW OF STEEL
STORMING HEAVEN
CHAINS OF COMMAND
NIGHT OF THE HAWK
SKY MASTERS
HAMMERHEADS
DAY OF THE CHEETAH
SILVER TOWER
FLIGHT OF THE OLD DOG

Coming Soon in Hardcover

EXECUTIVE INTENT

DALE BROWN

ROGUE FORCES

HARPER

An Imprint of HarperCollinsPublishers

This book was originally published in hardcover June 2009 by
William Morrow, an Imprint of HarperCollins Publishers.

This is a work of fiction. Names, characters, places, and incidents are
products of the author's imagination or are used fictitiously and are not
to be construed as real. Any resemblance to actual events, locales,
organizations, or persons, living or dead, is entirely coincidental.

HARPER

An Imprint of HarperCollins *Publishers*
10 East 53rd Street
New York, New York 10022-5299

Copyright © 2009 by Air Battle Force, Inc.
ISBN 978-0-06-156088-0

First Harper paperback printing: March 2010
First William Morrow hardcover printing: June 2009

HarperCollins® and Harper® are registered trademarks of Harper-
Collins Publishers.

Printed in the United States of America

Visit Harper paperbacks on the World Wide Web at
www.harpercollins.com

10 9 8 7 6 5 4 3 2 1

Thank you to Kris Thompson for his generosity

CAST OF CHARACTERS

AMERICANS

PATRICK S. MCLANAHAN, Lieutenant-General, USAF (ret.), partner and president, Scion Aviation International

KEVIN MARTINDALE, former president of the United States, silent owner of Scion Aviation International

JONATHAN COLIN MASTERS, Ph.D., chief of operations, Sky Masters Inc.

HUNTER NOBLE, VP of development, Sky Masters Inc.

JOSEPH GARDNER, president of the United States

KENNETH T. PHOENIX, vice president

CONRAD F. CARLYLE, national security adviser

MILLER H. TURNER, secretary of defense

WALTER KORDUS, White House chief of staff

STACY ANNE BARBEAU, secretary of state

U.S. MARINE CORPS GENERAL TAYLOR J. BAIN, chairman of the Joint Chiefs of Staff

U.S. ARMY MAJOR-GENERAL CHARLES CONNOLLY, division commander, northern Iraq

U.S. ARMY COLONEL JACK T. WILHELM, executive officer, Second Regiment, Allied Air Base Nahla, Iraq

ARMY LIEUTENANT COLONEL MARK WEATHERLY, regimental executive officer

ARMY MAJOR KENNETH BRUNO, regimental operations officer

USAF LIEUTENANT COLONEL GIA "BOXER" CAZZOTTO, commander, Seventh Air Expeditionary Squadron

KRIS THOMPSON, president and CEO of Thompson Security, private security company at Allied Air Base Nahla, Iraq

FRANK BEXAR, privately contracted intelligence officer

CAPTAIN KELVIN COTTER, USAF, deputy regimental air traffic management officer

MARGARET HARRISON, privately contracted UAV director

REESE FLIPPIN, privately contracted weather officer

TURKS

KURZAT HIRSIZ, president of the Republic of Turkey

AYŞE AKAS, prime minister of the Republic of Turkey

HASAN CIZEK, minister of national defense, Republic of Turkey

GENERAL ORHAN SAHIN, secretary-general, Turkish National Security Council

MUSTAFA HAMARAT, Turkish foreign minister

FEVSI GUCLU, director, National Intelligence Organization

GENERAL ABDULLAH GUZLEV, chief of staff of the military of the Republic of Turkey

GENERAL AYDIN DEDE, replacement military chief of staff

MAJOR AYDIN SABASTI, liaison officer to U.S. Second Regiment at Allied Air Base Nahla, Iraq

MAJOR HAMID JABBURI, deputy liaison officer

GENERAL BESIR OZEK, commander, Jandarma (Turkish national internal security forces)

LIEUTENANT-GENERAL GUVEN ILGAZ, deputy commander, Jandarma

LIEUTENANT-GENERAL MUSTAFA ALI, replacement Jandarma commander

IRAQIS

ALI LATIF RASHID, president of the Republic of Iraq

COLONEL YUSUF JAFFAR, commander, Allied Air Base Nahla, Tall Kayf, Iraq

MAJOR JAAFAR OTHMAN, Iraqi Maqbara (tomb) Company, Seventh Brigade commander

COLONEL NOURI MAWLOUD, liaison officer to Second Regiment

ZILAR "BAZ" (HAWK) AZZAWI, Iraqi PKK rebel leader

SADOON SALIH, Azzawi's assistant squad leader

WEAPONS AND ACRONYMS

ACRONYMS AND TERMINOLOGY

AMARG—Aerospace Maintenance and Regeneration Group (the "Boneyard"), a U.S. Air Force facility near Tucson, Arizona, that stores, dismantles, and recovers parts from out-of-service aircraft

AOR—Area of Responsibility

AQI—Al-Qaeda in Iraq, an Iraqi offshoot of Osama bin Laden's terrorist organization

"battle rattle"—personal equipment necessary for combat operations

bullseye—a designated point from which range and bearing information to an objective can be transmitted on open frequencies without revealing one's own location

C4I—Command, Control, Communications, Computers, and Intelligence

Çancaya—the seat of government of the Republic of Turkey

CHU—Containerized Housing Unit, a mobile living space resembling a cargo container used by U.S. soldiers in Iraq

CHUville—an area of a large number of CHUs

DFAC—Dining Facility

ECM—Electronic Countermeasures

EO—Electro-Optical, sensors that can electronically distribute or enhance optical images

FAA—Federal Aviation Administration, U.S. aviation regulatory agency

FOB—Forward Operating Base, a military base close to or in enemy territory

Fobbits—slang for staff and support personnel

Fobbitville—slang for the headquarters building

FPCON—Force Protection Condition, a rating of the enemy or terrorist threat level for a military installation (formerly THREATCON)

GP—Geneal Purpose (gravity bomb or vehicle)

IA—Iraqi Army

IED—Improvised Explosive Device

IIR—Imaging Infrared, a heat sensor with enough resolution to form images

ILS—Instrument Landing System, a radio beam system that can guide aircraft to land in severe weather conditions

IM—Instant Messaging, transmitting text messages between computers

IR—Infrared

Klicks—kilometers

KRG—Kurdistan Regional Government, the political organization that administers the autonomous Kurdish region of northern Iraq

LLTV—Low-Light TV

LRU—Line Replaceable Units, components of aircraft systems that can be easily removed and replaced on the flight line if they malfunction

Mahdis—slang term for any foreign fighter

Mission-adaptive technology—system of automatically shaping aircraft surfaces to allow greater flight control capabilities

Modes and codes—settings for different aircraft identification transponder radios

MTI—Moving Target Indication, a radar that tracks moving vehicles on the ground from a long distance

Netrusion—transmitting false data or programming into an enemy computer network via digital communications, datalinks, or sensors

NOFORN—No Foreign; a security classification that restricts foreign nationals from accessing data

PAG—Congress for Freedom and Democracy, an alternate name of the Kurdistan Workers' Party

PKK—*Partiya Karkerên Kurdistan*, Kurdistan Workers' Party, a Kurdish separatist organization seeking to form a separate nation from the ethnic Kurdish regions of Turkey, Iran, Syria, and Iraq; recognized as a terrorist organization by several nations and organizations

ROE—Rules of Engagement, the procedures and limitations for a combat operation

SAM—Surface-to-Air Missile

SEAD—Suppression of Enemy Air Defenses, using jammers and weapons to destroy an enemy air defense weapon, radar, or command and control facilities

triple-A—antiaircraft artillery

WEAPONS

AGM-177 Wolverine—air- or ground-launched autonomous attack cruise missile

CBU-87 Combined Effects Munition—an air-dropped weapon that releases antipersonnel and antivehicle mines over a wide area

CBU-97 Sensor-Fuzed Weapon—an air-dropped weapon that can detect and destroy numerous armored vehicles at one time over a wide area

CID—Cybernetic Infantry Device, a manned robot with enhanced strength, armor, sensors, and combat capabilities

Cobra gunship—U.S. Army second-generation weaponized light helicopter

CV-22 Osprey—a medium transport aircraft that can take off and land like a helicopter but can then swivel its rotors and fly like a fixed-wing aircraft

JDAM—Joint Direct Attack Munition, a bolt-on kit for gravity bombs that gives them near-precision accuracy using Global Positioning System navigation information

KC-135R—latest model of the Boeing 707 family of aerial refueling tanker aircraft

Kiowa—light helicopter that carries advanced sensors used to spot targets for helicopter gunships

MIM-104 Patriot—American-made ground-based antiaircraft missile system

SA-14—second generation Russian-made shoulder-fired antiaircraft missile

SA-7—first generation Russian-made shoulder-fired antiaircraft missile

Slingshot—high-powered laser defensive system for aircraft

Stryker—an eight-wheeled multirole armored personnel carrier of the U.S. Army

Tin Man—a soldier outfitted with advanced body armor, sensors, and strength augmentation systems to increase his combat capabilities

XC-57 "Loser"—a flying-wing aircraft originally designed for the U.S. Air Force's Next Generation Bomber, but converted to a multi-mission transport aircraft when the design lost the contract competition

REAL-WORLD NEWS EXCERPTS

BBC NEWS ONLINE, 30 OCTOBER 2007: . . . Tensions between Turkey and the Iraqi Kurdish region had been rising steadily in the months running up to the current crisis, triggered by PKK attacks which have killed some forty Turkish troops in recent weeks.

. . . In May, Turkey was angered when the three provinces of Iraqi Kurdistan were handed security control by the US-led multinational forces, and promptly raised the Kurdish flag instead of the Iraqi one.

. . . "You don't need 100,000 [Turkish] troops to take their positions," said a senior Iraqi Kurd politician. "What they're clearly planning to do is to stage a major incursion and take control of the major land routes inside Iraqi Kurdistan leading up into the border mountains from the Iraqi side."

. . . There is speculation in Kurdish circles that the Turks might also try to bomb or otherwise neutralize the two Iraqi Kurdish airports, at Irbil and Sulaymaniyah, which Ankara asserts have been allowing PKK fighters to gain refuge.

. . . "The Turks could wipe them out or bomb

them as they have done in the past. What they are proposing is something larger than that. They are talking about a large-scale military incursion, which is getting people extremely, extremely nervous and worried. The concern of many people is that Turkish ambition may stretch beyond taking out the PKK . . ."

BBC NEWS ONLINE, **18 JANUARY 2008:** . . . Turkey has been threatening military action against the PKK ever since insurgents intensified their attacks on Turkish troops, putting the government here under immense public pressure to respond with force. Last month, the government authorized the military to carry out cross-border operations [into Iraq] against the PKK whenever necessary.

The air strikes on Sunday night were the first serious sign of that.

. . . Ankara says it has tacit approval from the U.S. for its operations, under an agreement reached in Washington last month by Prime Minister Recep Tayyip Erdogan and President George W. Bush.

"I believe the USA supplied actionable intelligence, and the Turkish military took action," Turkish foreign ministry spokesman Levent Bilman told the BBC . . .

"TURKISH TROOPS KILL 11 REBELS IN SOUTHEAST TURKEY NEAR BORDER WITH IRAQ—ASSOCIATED PRESS," 12 MARCH 2008—Ankara, Turkey: Turkish troops killed 11 Kurdish rebels during clashes in southeastern Turkey near the border with Iraq, a private news agency reported Wednesday. The fighting comes two weeks after Turkey's eight-day incursion into northern Iraq to flush out the rebels of the Kurdistan Workers' Party, who have been battling the Turkish government since 1984.

. . . Some Turkish nationalists fear that increasing cultural rights could lead to the breakup of the country along ethnic lines. They worry that Turkish Kurds could be encouraged by the U.S.-supported Kurdish region in northern Iraq, which has its own government and militia. . .

SECOND QUARTER 2008 FORECAST, © STRATFOR.COM, 4 APRIL 2008: Regional trend: Turkey is emerging as a major regional power and in 2008 will begin to exert influence throughout its periphery — most notably in northern Iraq . . .

Turkey is feeling strong not only in northern Iraq, but also in the nearby Balkans and Caucasus, where it is seeking to mentor newly independent Kosovo and a newly oil-rich Azerbaijan . . .

" 'IRON MAN' IS THE NEW FACE OF MILITARY CONTRACTORS," JEREMY HSU, SPACE.COM, 6 MAY 2008: When superhero Tony Stark isn't donning his Iron Man armor to personally rough up villains, he's pitching the U.S. military on new gadgets to fight the War on Terror.

. . . Private individuals and companies might not be as visible as UAVs soaring above the skies of Afghanistan and Iraq, yet their role has grown just as dramatically during the recent conflicts.

. . . No one questions that the United States could not fight a war now without outsourcing to military contractors . . . That means military contractors have also expanded beyond just selling military hardware. They now run supply lines, feed troops, build base camps, consult on strategy and even fight as private security forces . . .

"IRAN: U.S.–IRAQI DEAL WOULD 'ENSLAVE' IRAQIS—RAFSANJANI," STRATFOR.COM, 4 JUNE 2008: Iranian Expediency Council Chairman Akbar Hashemi Rafsanjani on June 4 said the Islamic world will try to stop a long-term security agreement between Iraq and the United States, saying the terms of the deal would "enslave" Iraqis, the Associated Press reported. Rafsanjani said the U.S.–Iraqi deal would lead to a permanent occupation of Iraq, and that such an occupation is dangerous for all states in the region . . .

THIRD QUARTER FORECAST, **STRATFOR. COM, 8 JULY 2008:** . . . Regional trend: Turkey is emerging as a major regional power and in 2008 will begin to exert influence throughout its periphery — most notably in northern Iraq . . . Turkey is becoming bolder on the international stage: sending troops into northern Iraq, mediating Israeli-Syrian peace talks, pushing energy projects in the Caucasus and Central Asia, and making its influence felt in the Balkans . . .

"IRAQI PARLIAMENT CALLS SESSION ON KIRKUK," ASSOCIATED PRESS,

30 JULY 2008: . . . Tensions escalated Monday after a suicide bomb attack in Kirkuk during a Kurdish protest against the elections law killed 25 people and injured more than 180.

Kirkuk is home to Kurds, Turkomans, Arabs, and other minorities. After the explosion in Kirkuk, dozens of angry Kurds stormed the offices of a Turkoman political party that opposes Kurdish claims on Kirkuk, opening fire and burning cars amid accusations that their rivals were to blame. Nine Turkomen, or ethnic Turks, were reported wounded.

Prime Minister Recep Tayyip Erdogan of Turkey, which has been defending the rights of Turkomen, called Iraqi authorities to express concern over the incidents in Kirkuk and proposed to send a plane to bring the wounded to Turkey for treatment, the Iraqi president's office said . . .

"TURKEY CONCERNED WITH CITY OF KIRKUK," ASSOCIATED PRESS, 2 AUGUST 2008: Baghdad—The Turkish government has expressed concern regarding the Iraqi city of Kirkuk, where ethnic Turks are locked in a territory dispute, an Iraqi official says.

An unidentified Iraqi foreign ministry spokesman said Foreign Minister Hoshyar Zebari had been contacted by Turkish Foreign Minister Ali Babican regarding the situation in the city, the Kuwait News Agency KUNA reported Saturday.

The province of Kirkuk has demanded the city become part of the Iraqi Kurdistan region, while Turkey has steadfastly opposed such a movement.

While the city holds the largest concentration of ethnic Turks in Iraq, the spokesman said Zebari has maintained that any attempts to solve the dispute will be conducted solely by Iraq.

Zebari said any outside attempts to become involved in the dispute would not be welcomed by Iraq, the spokesman told KUNA.

"LASER GUN'S FIRST BLAST," *WIRED,* **DANGER ROOM, 13 AUGUST 2008:** Boeing announced today the first ever test firing of a real-life ray gun that could become U.S. Special Forces' way to carry out covert strikes with "plausible deniability."

In tests earlier this month at Kirtland Air Force Base, New Mexico, Boeing's Advanced Tactical Laser—a modified C-130H aircraft—"fired its high-energy chemical laser through its beam control system. The beam control system acquired a ground target and guided the laser beam to the target, as directed by ATL's battle management system . . ."

"RECORD NUMBER OF U.S. CONTRACTORS IN IRAQ," *CHRISTIAN SCIENCE MONITOR,* **PETER GRIER, 18 AUGUST 2008:** Washington—The American military has depended on private contractors since sutlers sold paper, bacon, sugar, and other small luxuries to Continental Army troops during the Revolutionary War.

But the scale of the use of contractors in Iraq is unprecedented in US history, according to a new congressional report that may be the most thorough official account yet of the practice. As of early 2008, at least 190,000 private personnel were working on US-funded projects in the Iraq theater, the Congressional Budget Office (CBO) survey found. That means that for each uniformed member of the US military in the region, there was also a contract employee—a ratio of 1 to 1.

. . . Critics of military outsourcing say the real problem is flexibility and command-and-control over private workers . . .

"ANKARA'S S-300 CURIOSITY," STRATEGIC FORECASTING INC., 26 AUGUST 2008: . . . Turkey is in the process of acquiring several variants of the Russian S-300 air defense system, Turkish daily *Today's Zaman* reported August 25 . . .

. . . Should Turkey succeed in this acquisition, Ankara's subsequent work would take two important approaches. The first is reverse engineering, where key components are disassembled and their inner workings closely examined. The second is training in electronic warfare against actual systems . . .

"TURKISH ARMY SEEKS EXPANDED POWERS," ASSOCIATED PRESS, ANKARA, TURKEY—10 OCTOBER 2008: Turkey's leaders met Thursday to discuss increasing the military's powers to combat Kurdish rebels following a surge in attacks, some launched from rebel bases in northern Iraq.

Turkey's parliament already voted Wednesday

to extend the military's mandate to carry out operations against Kurdish rebels in northern Iraq, including cross-border ground operations.

But the military has requested increased powers to fight rebels of the Kurdistan Workers' Party, or PKK. Thursday's meeting was focused on extending the options available to the military and police . . .

ROGUE
FORCES

PROLOGUE

OUTSIDE AL-AMADIYAH,
DAHUK PROVINCE, REPUBLIC OF IRAQ
Spring 2010

The *dilok*, or traditional wedding celebration, had been going on now for several hours, but no one appeared to be tired in the least. Men were dancing on large *defs*, or frame drums, and tap-dancing to folk music performed with amplified *zurna* and *temburs*, while the other guests cheered them on.

Outside, it was a warm, dry, clear evening. Knots of men stood in groups here and there, smoking and drinking small cups of thick coffee. Women and older girls in colorful dresses and scarves carried trays of food to them, helped by sons or younger brothers carrying flashlights.

After serving the men outside the wedding reception, a woman carried a tray down the road beyond the lights, her ten-year-old son leading the way, to two Toyota pickup trucks semihidden in the trees, one on each side of the road leading to the farm. The boy shined the flashlight at the pickup truck to his left, right into the eyes of his older brother. *"Alslam ylikm!* Caught you sleeping again!" he shouted.

"I was not!" the brother retorted, much louder than he intended.

"Hani, don't do that. Now your brother will not be able to see in the darkness for some time," the boy's mother scolded him. "Go give your brother some treats and tell him you're sorry. Come, Mazen," she said to her husband, "I have more coffee for you."

The husband set his AK-47 aside on the truck's front bumper and gratefully accepted the treats. He was dressed for the celebration, not for guard duty. "You're a good woman, Zilar," the man said. "But next time, send your lazy brother out here to do the work for you. It was his idea to place guards outside the reception." He could sense her pained expression. "I see. He is busy recruiting again, no? His own daughter's wedding and he can't stop?"

"He feels very strongly—"

"I know, I know," the husband interrupted, gently placing a hand on his wife's cheek to reassure her. "He is a patriotic and committed Kurdish nationalist. Good for him. But he knows the militias, police, and military monitor such events, take photographs from unmanned aircraft, use sensitive microphones, and tap telephones. Why does he continue? He risks too much."

"Nevertheless, I thank you again for agreeing to take a shift out here for security," the wife said, taking his hand from her face and kissing it. "It makes him feel better."

"I haven't picked up a rifle in years since I left the *peshmerga* militias in Kirkuk. I find myself checking the safety every three seconds."

"Oh, do you, my husband?" The woman stepped toward the AK-47 leaning against the bumper and examined it with her fingers.

"Ah, la, tell me I didn't . . ."

"You did." She flicked the safety lever back up to "safe."

"I'm glad your brothers aren't around to see you do that," her husband said. "Perhaps I need more lessons from a former High Commune of Women commander."

"I have a family to raise and a house to take care of—I put in my time in the Kurdistan independence movement. Let the younger women do some fighting for a change."

"You can put any younger woman to shame—on the rifle range, and in bed."

"Oh, and how would you know about the skills of younger women?" she asked playfully. She placed the weapon back down and approached her husband, swaying her hips seductively. "I have many more lessons I'd prefer to give you, husband." He gave her a kiss. "Now, how much longer are you going to keep my oldest son out here?"

"Not long. Maybe another hour." He nodded toward his son, who was busy fending off his younger brother from the few remaining baklava on the tray. "It's nice to be out here with Neaz. He takes this task very seriously. He—" The man stopped because he thought he heard an approaching bicycle or small scooter, a sort of quiet hushing sound that indicated speed but not power. There were no lights on the road or highway beyond. He frowned, then placed his coffee cup in his wife's hand. "Take Hani back to the community center."

"What is it?"

"Probably nothing." He looked down the dirt road again and saw no sign of any movement—no birds, no rustling trees. "Tell your brother I'm going to roam around a bit. I'll tell the others." He kissed his wife on the cheek, then went to retrieve his AK-47. "I'll be ready to come in after I get . . ."

Out of the corner of an eye, high above to the west, he spotted it: a brief spurt of yellow light, not solid like a searchlight but flickering like a torch. Why he did it, he wasn't sure, but he pushed his wife aside, into the trees beside the gate. *"Get down!"* he shouted. "Stay down! Stay—"

Suddenly the ground vibrated as if a thousand horses were stampeding right beside them. The husband's face, eyes, and throat were choked by clouds of dust and dirt that appeared from nowhere, and rocks were thrown in every direction. The wife screamed as she saw her husband literally disintegrate into chunks of human flesh. The pickup truck was similarly chewed apart before the gas tank ruptured, sending a massive fireball into the sky.

Then she heard it—a horrible sound, impossibly loud, lasting only a fraction of a second. It was like a giant growling animal standing over her, like a house-size chain saw. The sound was followed moments later by the loud *whoosh* of a jet plane flying overhead, so low that she thought it could be landing on the dirt road.

In the space of just a few heartbeats, her husband and two sons were dead before her eyes. Somehow the woman got to her feet and ran back toward the wedding reception, thinking of nothing else but warning the other members of her family to flee for their lives.

"Lead is clear," the lead pilot of the three-ship A-10 Thunderbolt II bomber radioed. He pulled up sharply to make sure he was well clear of the other aircraft and the terrain. "Two, cleared in hot."

"Good pass, lead," the pilot of the second A-10 Thunderbolt radioed. "Two's in hot." He checked the AGM-65G Maverick missile's forward-looking infrared video display, which clearly showed the two pickup trucks at the end of the road, one burning and the other still intact, and lined up on the second pickup with a gentle touch of his control stick. His A-10 was not modified with a dedicated infrared sensor pod, but the "poor man's FLIR" video from the Maverick missile did the job nicely.

Nighttime cannon runs were not normally advisable, especially in such hilly terrain, but what pilot would not take the risk for a chance to fire the incredible GAU-8A Avenger cannon, a thirty-millimeter Gatling gun that fired huge depleted uranium shells at almost four thousand rounds per minute? Besides, with the first target burning nicely, it was easy to see the next target now.

When the Maverick aiming reticle showed thirty degrees depression, the pilot dropped his plane's nose, made a final adjustment, announced "Guns, guns, guns!" on the radio, and pulled the trigger. The roar of that big cannon firing between his legs was the most incredible feeling. In a single three-second spurt, almost two hundred huge shells flew to their target. The pilot centered the first second's worth on the pickup, covering it with fifty shells and causing yet another spectacular explosion, and then raised the A-10's nose to let the remaining hundred and thirty shells stitch up along the road toward a fleeing terrorist target.

Careful not to get target fixated, and very aware of the surrounding terrain, he pulled up sharply and vectored right to climb to his assigned altitude. The maneuverability of the American-made A-10 was amazing—it did not deserve its unofficial nickname of "Warthog." "Two's clear. Three, cleared in hot."

"Three's in hot," the pilot of the third A-10 in the formation responded. He was the least experienced pilot in the four-ship formation, so he was not going to do a cannon pass . . . but it was going to be just as exciting.

He centered the target—a large garage beside a house—in his Maverick missile aiming screen, pressed the "lock" button on his throttle quadrant, said "Rifle one" on the radio, turned his head right to avoid the glare of the missile's motor, and pressed the "launch" button on his control stick. An AGM-65G Maverick missile flew off the launch rail on the left wing and quickly disappeared from view. He selected a second missile, moved the aiming reticle to the second target—the house itself—and fired a Maverick from the right wing. He was rewarded seconds later with two bright explosions.

"Lead has a visual, looks like two direct hits."

"Three's clear," he radioed as he climbed and turned toward his planned rendezvous anchor. "Four, cleared in hot."

"Four copies, going in hot," the fourth A-10 pilot acknowledged. His was possibly the least exciting attack profile and one that normally was not even performed by the A-10, but the A-10s were the new members of the fleet, and their full capabilities had yet to be explored.

The routine was far simpler than his wing-men's: stores control switches set to stations four and eight; follow the GPS navigation cues to the release point; master arming switch to "arm"; and press the release button on the control stick at the preplanned release point. Two thousand-pound GBU-32 GPS-guided bombs dropped into the night sky. The pilot didn't have to lock anything on or risk diving toward the terrain: the guidance kits on the weapons used GPS satellite navigation signals to guide the bombs to their target, a large building near the farm that was advertised as a "community center" but that intelligence sources insisted was a major gathering and recruiting spot for PKK terrorists.

Well, not anymore. Two direct hits obliterated the building, creating one massive crater over fifty feet in diameter. Even flying at fifteen thousand feet above ground, the A-10 was rocked by the twin explosions. "Four's clear. Weapon panel safe and clear."

"Two good *infilaks*," the lead pilot radioed. He didn't see any secondary explosions, but the terrorists might have moved the large cache of weapons and explosions reportedly being stored in the building. *"Muhtesem!* Good job, Thunder-bolts. Check arming switches safe, and don't forget to turn off ECM and turn on transponders at the border or we'll be sweeping you up in the wreckage like they'll be doing with those PKK scum back there. See you in the rendezvous anchor."

Minutes later, all four A-10 Thunderbolts, newly acquired warplanes of the Turkish Air Force, were safely back across the border. Another successful antiterrorist mission against the rebels hiding out in Iraq.

The woman, Zilar Azzawi, groaned in agony as she awoke a short time later. Her left hand was in terrible pain, as if she had broken a finger or thumb when she fell . . . and then she realized with shock that her left hand was *gone,* severed off at midforearm. Whatever had killed her husband and sons and destroyed the truck had almost succeeded in killing her. Her PKK commando training took over, and she managed to tie a strip of cloth from her dress around her arm as a tourniquet to stop the bleeding.

The entire area around her was in flames, and she had no choice but to stay where she was, on the side of the road, until she could get her bearings. Everything around her, except this little patch of dirt road, was burning, and she had lost so much blood that she didn't think she could go very far even if she did know which way to go.

Everything and everyone was gone, utterly blasted away—the buildings, wedding reception, all the guests, the children . . . my God, the *children, her* children . . . !

Azzawi was helpless now, hoping just to stay alive . . .

"But, God, if you let me live," she said aloud over the sounds of death and destruction around her, "I will find the ones responsible for this attack, and I will use all of my powers to raise an army and destroy them. My previous life is over—they have taken my family from me with brutal indifference. With your blessing, God, my new life shall begin right now, and I will avenge all those who died here tonight."

APPROACHING JANDARMA PUBLIC ORDER
COMMANDO BASE, DIYARBAKIR, REPUBLIC OF TURKEY
Summer 2010

"*Canak* Two-Seven, Diyarbakir Tower, winds three-zero-zero at eight knots, ceiling one thousand overcast, visibility five in light rain, runway three-five, cleared for the ILS approach normal category, security status is green."

The pilot of the American-made KC-135R tanker/cargo plane acknowledged the call, then clicked on the passenger address system. "We will be landing shortly. Please return to your seats, be sure your seat belts are secure, stow your tray tables, and put away all carry-on items. *Tesekkur ederim.* Thank you." He then turned to the boom operator/flight engineer seated behind the copilot and shouted cross-cockpit, "Go see if he wants to come up for the landing, Master Sergeant." The engineer nodded, took off his headset, and headed aft to the cargo compartment.

Although the KC-135R was primarily an aerial refueling plane, it was frequently used for both hauling cargo and carrying passengers. The cargo was in the forward part of the cavernous interior—in this case, four pallets filled with crates, secured with nylon netting. Behind the pallets were two twelve-person centerline economy-type passenger-seat pallets bolted to the floor, with the occupants facing backward. The ride was noisy, smelly, dark, and uncomfortable, but valuable force-multiplying planes such as this were rarely allowed to fly unless fully loaded.

The crew engineer squeezed around the cargo and approached a napping passenger seated at the end of the first row on the port side. The man had longish and rather tousled hair, several days' worth of whiskers, and wore rather common street clothes even though anyone traveling in military aircraft had to wear either a uniform or business attire. The engineer stood before the man and lightly touched his shoulder. When the man awoke, the master sergeant motioned to him, and he stood and followed the master sergeant to a space between the pallets. "Sorry to bother you, sir," the boom operator said after the passenger had removed the yellow soft foam earplugs that everyone wore to protect their hearing from the noise, "but the pilot asked to see if you wanted to sit in the cockpit for the approach and landing."

"Is that a normal procedure, Master Sergeant?" the passenger, General Besir Ozek, asked.

Ozek was commander of the Jandarma Genel Komutanliği, or Turkish national paramilitary forces, a combination of national police force, border patrol, and national guard. As a trained commando as well as commander of the paramilitary unit charged with internal security, Ozek was authorized to wear longer hair and whiskers to better slip in and out of undercover roles and more unobtrusively observe others around him.

"No, sir," the boom operator replied. "No one is allowed in the cockpit that is not on the flight crew. But . . ."

"I asked that I not be singled out on this flight, Master Sergeant. I thought that was plain to everyone on the crew," Ozek said. "I wish to remain as inconspicuous as possible on this trip. That is why I chose to sit in the back with the other passengers."

"Sorry, sir," the boom operator said.

Ozek looked around the cargo pallets and noticed several passengers turning around to see what was going on. "Well, I suppose it's too late now, isn't it?" he said. "Let's go." The boom operator nodded and escorted the general to the cockpit, thankful he didn't have to explain to the aircraft commander why the general hadn't accepted his invitation.

It had been many years since Ozek had been inside a KC-135R Stratotanker refueling aircraft, and the cockpit seemed a lot more cramped, noisy, and smelly than he remembered. Ozek was a veteran infantryman, and didn't care to understand what attracted men to aviation. An airman's life was subject to forces and laws that no one saw or fully comprehended, and that's not

the way he ever wanted to live. The re-engined
KC-135R was a good plane, but the airframe had
been around for over *fifty years* now—this one
was relatively young at only forty-five years—
and it was starting to show its age.

Yet aviation seemed to be all the rage in the
Republic of Turkey these days. His country had
just taken possession of dozens of surplus tactical
fighters and bombers from the United States: the
much-loved F-16 Fighting Falcon fighter-bomber,
which was also license-built in Turkey; the A-10
Thunderbolt close air support attack plane, nicknamed the "Warthog" because of its ungainly,
utilitarian appearance; the AH-1 Cobra helicopter gunship; and the F-15 Eagle air superiority jet
fighter. Turkey was well on its way to becoming
a world-class regional military power, thanks to
the United States' desire to relieve itself of battle-
tested but aging hardware.

The boom operator handed the general a
headset and motioned to the flight instructor's
seat between the two pilots. "I know you didn't
want to be disturbed, General," the pilot said
over the intercom, "but the seat was open and I
thought you'd enjoy the view."

"Of course," Ozek responded simply, making
a note to himself to have the pilot removed from
the service when he got back to headquarters;
there were plenty of men and women who knew
how to follow orders waiting to fly tankers in the
Turkish air force. "What is the security status at
the airport?"

"Green, sir," the pilot reported. "Unchanged
for more than a month."

"The last PKK activity in the area was only

twenty-four days ago, Captain," Ozek said irritably. The PKK, or Partiya Karkerên Kurdistan, or Kurdistan Workers' Party, was an outlawed Marxist military organization that sought the formation of a separate state of Kurdistan, formed from parts of southeast Turkey, northern Iraq, northeast Syria, and northwest Iran, all of which had Kurdish ethnic majorities. The PKK used terrorism and violence, even against large military bases and well-defended places such as civilian airports, to try to keep itself in the public eye and pressure the individual states to work out a solution. "We must remain vigilant at all times."

"Yes, sir," the pilot acknowledged in a hushed voice.

"You are not performing a maximum-performance approach, Captain?"

"Uh . . . no, sir," the pilot responded. "The security condition is green, the ceiling and visibility are low, and the tower advised that we are cleared for a normal-category approach." He swallowed, then added, "And I did not want to upset you or the other passengers with a max-performance descent."

Ozek would have berated this young idiot pilot, but they had already commenced the instrument approach, and things would get very busy here shortly. Maximum-performance take-offs and approaches were designed to minimize time in the lethal envelope of shoulder-fired antiaircraft weapons. The PKK used Russian-made SA-7 and SA-14 missiles against Turkish government aircraft on occasion.

However, the probability of such an attack today *was* small. The ceiling and visibility were fairly low, which restricted the time available for a gunner to attack. Also, most attacks occurred against large helicopters or larger fixed-wing aircraft during takeoff phase of flight because the heat signature that the missiles locked onto was much brighter—during approach, the engines were running at lower power settings and were relatively cooler, which meant the missiles had a harder time locking on and could be jammed or decoyed easier.

The pilot was playing the odds, which Ozek disliked—especially because he was doing so just to try to impress a senior officer—but they were in the soup now, and breaking the approach off at such a moment, close to mountains in bad weather, was not an ideal choice. Ozek sat back and crossed his arms on his chest, making his anger apparent. "Continue, Captain," he said simply.

"Yes, sir," the pilot responded, relieved. "Copilot, before glideslope intercept checklist, please." To the pilot's credit, Ozek thought, he was a good aircraft commander; he would be a good addition to some airline's crew complement, because he wasn't going to be in the Turkish Air Force for very long.

This lackadaisical attitude was unfortunately more and more prevalent in the military these days as the conflict between the Turkish government and the Kurds continued to morph. The Kurdistan Workers' Party, or PKK, had changed its name to PAG, or the Congress for Freedom and Democracy, and avoided using the term *Kurdistan* in its literature and speeches in an effort to appeal to a wider audience. These days, they held rallies and published papers advocating more human rights laws to ease the suffering of all oppressed persons in the world rather than advocating armed struggle solely for a separate Kurdish state.

But that was a ruse. The PKK was stronger, wealthier, and more aggressive than ever. Because of the U.S. invasion and destruction of Saddam Hussein's rule in Iraq, as well as the civil war in Iran, the Kurdish insurgents were fearlessly staging cross-border raids into Turkey, Iraq, Iran, and Syria from numerous safe camps, hoping to capitalize on the chaos and confusion and establish a strong base in each nation. Every time Turkish forces responded, they would be accused of genocide, and the politicians in Ankara would order the military to stop pursuit.

This only emboldened the PKK. The latest travesty: the emergence of a female terrorist leader. No one knew her real name; she was known as Baz, or "The Hawk" in Arabic, because of her ability to strike quickly and unexpectedly but seemingly fly away and escape her pursuers so easily. Her emergence as a major rallying force for Kurdish independence, and the Turkish and Iraqi governments' lackadaisical response to her call for bloody war, was disturbing to the Jandarma general.

"Coming up on glideslope intercept," the copilot said.

"Gear down," the pilot said.

"Here it comes," the copilot responded, and he reached over to just above the pilot's right knee and moved the round landing gear actuator switch to the "down" position. "Gear in transit . . .

three green, no yellow, press-to-test pump light checks, gear is down and locked."

The pilot took his eyes off the horizontal situation indicator just long enough to check the gear lights and push to press-to-test "gear hyd" light. "Checks, gear is down and locked."

"On course, on glideslope," the copilot said. "Two thousand feet to decision height." The copilot reached across and discreetly tapped his airspeed indicator, a silent warning for the pilot that his airspeed had dropped a bit—with a general in the cockpit, he didn't want to highlight even the tiniest mistake. Their speed had dropped only five knots, but tiny errors seemed to snowball on an instrument approach, and it was better to catch and correct them right away than let them create bigger problems later.

"*Tesekkur ederim*," the pilot responded, acknowledging the catch. A simple "roger" meant the pilot had found his own mistake, but a thank-you meant the copilot had made a good call. "One thousand to go."

Filtered sunlight began to stream into the cockpit windows, followed moments later by sunlight filtered through widely scattered clouds. Ozek looked out and saw they were dead centered on the runway, and the visual approach lights indicated they were on glideslope. "Runway in sight," the copilot announced. The ILS needles began to dance a bit, which meant the pilot was peeking out the window at the runway instead of watching his horizontal situation indicator. "Continue the approach."

"Thank you." Another good catch. "Five hundred to decision height. Stand by on the 'before landing' checklist and . . ."

Ozek, focusing out the window and not on the gauges, saw it first: a white curling line of smoke coming from a street intersection ahead and off to the left, *inside the airport perimeter fence*, heading straight for them! "*Strela!*" Ozek shouted, using the Russian nickname, "Star," for the SA-7 shoulder-fired missile. "Break right, *now!*"

To his credit, the pilot did exactly as Ozek ordered: he immediately jammed the control wheel hard right and shoved all four throttles up to full military power. But he was far, far too late. Ozek knew they had just one chance now: that it was indeed an SA-7 missile and not the newer SA-14, because the older missile needed a bright hot "dot" to home in on, while the SA-14 could track any source of heat, even sunlight reflecting off a canopy.

In the blink of an eye, the missile was gone— it had missed the left wing by scant meters. But there was something else wrong. A horn blared in the cockpit; the pilot was trying desperately to turn the KC-135 to the left to straighten it out and perhaps even line up on the runway again, but the plane was not responding—the left wing was still high in the sky and there was not enough aileron authority to lower it. Even with the engines at full throttle, they were in a full stall, threatening to turn into a spin at any moment.

"What are you doing, Captain?" Ozek shouted. "Get the nose down and level the wings!"

"I can't get turned around!" the pilot cried.

"We can't make the runway—level the wings and find a place to crash-land!" Ozek said. He looked out the copilot's window and saw the soccer field. "There! The football field! That's your landing spot!"

"I can fly it out! I can do it . . . !"

"No you can't—it's too late!" Ozek shouted. "Get the nose down and make for the football field or we're all going to die!"

The rest happened in less than five seconds, but Ozek watched it as if in slow motion. Instead of trying to wrestle the stalled tanker back up into the sky, the pilot released back pressure on the controls. As soon as he did, and with the engines at full military power, the ailerons immediately responded, and the pilot was able to bring the plane wings-level. With the nose low, airspeed built up rapidly, and the pilot had enough smash to raise the nose almost into a landing attitude. He pulled the throttles to idle, then to "cutoff," moments before the big tanker hit the ground.

Ozek was thrown forward almost into the center console, but his shoulder and lap belts held, and he ruefully thought that he had felt harder landings before . . . and then the nose gear slammed down, and the Turkish general felt as if he had been snapped completely in half. The nose gear collapsed, and mud and turf smashed through the windscreen like a tidal wave. They plowed through a soccer goalpost, then crashed through a fence and a few garages and storage buildings before coming to a stop against the base gymnasium.

CHAPTER 1

Masters Two-Two, this is White Sands." The portable radio squawked to life, splitting the still, early-morning air. "You are cleared for takeoff, runway one-zero, winds calm, altimeter two-niner-niner-seven. Threat condition red, repeat, red, read back."

"Roger, Masters Two-Two copies, cleared for takeoff, runway one-zero, threat condition red."

A large, rather strange-looking aircraft spooled up its engines and prepared to take the active runway. It somewhat resembled a B-2 Spirit "flying-wing" stealth bomber, but it was vastly more bulbous than the intercontinental bomber, suggesting a far larger payload capacity. Instead of the engines embedded inside the fuselage, the aircraft had three engines mounted atop the rear of the fuselage on short pylons.

As the weird "winged guppy" aircraft taxied across the hold line onto the active runway, about a mile to the west a man wearing a cloth cap, balaclava, a thick protective green jacket, and heavy gloves lifted a MANPADS, or Man-Portable Air Defense System, launcher onto his right shoulder. He first inserted a vegetable-can-size device into the bottom of the launcher, which provided argon gas coolant for the infra-red seeker and battery power for the device.

"Allah Akbar, Allah Akbar," the man intoned in a quiet voice. He then got to his feet and aimed the weapon east toward the gradually increasing sound of the aircraft's engines spooling up for takeoff. It was not yet light enough to see the plane from that distance, so the missileer lowered a pair of night-vision goggles over his eyes, carefully adjusting his head position so he could still aim the MANPADS through its mechanical sights. He activated the weapon by pressing and releasing the integrated safety and actuator lever. He could hear the gyros spinning up in the missile's guidance section even over the noise of the airliner rumbling across the desert.

As soon as he centered the sights on the green-and-white image of the retreating jetliner, he heard a low growling sound in his head-phones, indicating that the MANPADS' infrared sensor had just locked onto the jetliner's engine exhausts. He then pressed and held the "uncage" lever, and the acquisition tone got louder, telling him that the missile was tracking a good target.

He waited until the aircraft was airborne, since if he hit it while it was still on the ground, the crew could probably stop the plane safely on the runway and put the fire out quickly, mini-mizing loss. The most vulnerable time was five seconds after liftoff, because the plane was accelerating slowly and its landing gear was in transit; if it lost an engine, the crew would have to react swiftly and precisely to avoid a catastrophe.

Now it was time. He whispered another *Allah Akbar,* super-elevated the launcher so that the target was on the lower left corner of the mechanical sights, held his breath to avoid inhaling any missile exhaust, then squeezed the trigger.

The small ejection motor fired the missile out of the barrel about thirty feet into the air. Just as the missile began to fall, its first-stage solid rocket motor fired, and the missile headed for its target, with the sensor solidly locked on. Then the missileer lowered the MANPADS and watched the engagement with glee through his night-vision goggles as an instant later he saw the missile explode in a cloud of fire. *"Allah* friggin' *Akbar,"* he muttered. "That was *cool.*"

But the counterattack wasn't over yet. As soon as the sound of the explosion reached him a second later, the missileer suddenly felt an intense burning sensation all throughout his body. He threw the spent launcher onto the ground, confused and disoriented. It felt as if his entire body had suddenly burst into flames. He dropped to the ground, hoping to extinguish the flames by rolling around, but the heat got more intense by the second. He could do nothing but curl into a protective ball and cover his eyes, hoping to avoid being blinded or burned alive. He screamed as the flames spread, engulfing him . . .

"Whoa, boss, what happened?" he heard a voice say in his headphones. "Are you okay? We're on the way. Hold on!"

The man found his chest heaving and his heart pounding with the sudden surge of adrenaline coursing through his bloodstream, and he found it hard to speak for several moments . . . but the severe burning sensation had suddenly stopped. Finally, he got up and dusted himself off. There was no evidence whatsoever that anything had happened to him except for the awful memory of that intense pain. "No . . . well, maybe . . . well, yes," the missileer, Dr. Jonathan Colin Masters, replied shakily. "Maybe a little."

Jon Masters had just turned fifty years of age, but he still looked and probably would forever look like a teenager with his thin features, big ears, gangly body movements, crooked grin, and naturally tousled brown hair under his headset. He was the chief operations officer of Sky Masters Inc., a small defense research and development company he'd founded that for the past twenty years had been developing absolute cutting-edge aviation, satellite, weapons, sensors, and advanced materials technology for the United States.

Although he no longer owned the company that still bore his name—a board of directors, led by his ex-wife and business partner Helen Kaddiri, and the company's young president, Dr. Kelsey Duffield, ran company affairs now—and was rich enough to travel the world for the rest of his life if he chose, Jon enjoyed spending time either in the lab designing new gadgets or out in the field testing them. No one really knew if the board of directors allowed him to do things like fire live MANPADS missiles or stay out on the missile range during a test just to humor him . . . or because they were hoping he'd get dusted by his own inventions, something that had nearly happened many times over the years.

Several Humvees and support vehicles—including an ambulance, just in case—rolled up, illuminating Jon with headlights and spotlights. A man jumped out of the first Humvee on the scene and ran over to him. "You okay, Jon?" asked Hunter "Boomer" Noble. Boomer was the twenty-five-year-old vice president in charge of air weapon development for Sky Masters Inc. Formerly a U.S. Air Force test pilot, engineer, and astronaut, Boomer once had the enviable job of designing exotic aircraft spacecraft systems and then being able to fly the finished product himself. Flying the revolutionary XR-A9 Black Stallion single-stage-to-orbit spaceplane, Boomer had been in orbit more times in the past two years than the rest of the American astronaut corps combined had been in the past ten years. "Jeez, you gave us a scare back there!"

"I told you, I'm fine," Jon said, grateful that his voice didn't sound as shaky as it had a few minutes earlier. "I guess we dialed the emitter power up a little too high, eh, Boomer?"

"I set it to the *lowest* power setting, boss, and I checked and double-checked it," Boomer said. "You were probably too close. The laser has a fifty-mile range—you were less than two when you got hit. Probably not a good idea to star in your own tests, boss."

"Thanks for the advice, Boomer," Jon replied weakly, hoping no one would notice his shaking hands. "Great going, Boomer. I'd say the Sling-shot automatic countermissile weapon test was a complete success."

"So would I, Boomer," another voice behind him said. Two men approached from another Humvee, wearing business suits, long dark coats, and gloves to ward off the early-morning chill. They were followed by two more men, similarly dressed, but their coats were open . . . which made it easier for them to get at the automatic weapons slung on harnesses underneath. The man with the longish salt-and-pepper hair and goatee shook his finger at Jon and continued: "You almost succeeded in killing yourself, Jon . . . *again*."

"Nah . . . it went exactly as planned, Mr. President," Jon responded.

The man, former president of the United States Kevin Martindale, rolled his eyes in disbelief. A Washington establishment figure for decades, Martindale served six terms in Congress, two terms as vice president, and one term as president before being voted out of office; he then became only the second man in the history of the United States to be voted back in again.

He also had the distinction of being the first vice president ever to be divorced while in office, and he was still a confirmed bachelor who was often seen in the company of young female actors and athletes. Although over sixty years old, Martindale was still ruggedly handsome, self-confident, and almost devilish with his goatee and long, wavy hair, featuring the famous "photographer's dream" twin curling silvery locks that automatically appeared across his forehead whenever he was angry or emotional.

"He still likes being involved in his own tests, Mr. President—the more outrageous, the better,"

the man beside him, retired Lieutenant-General
Patrick McLanahan, said. Shorter than Martindale but considerably more solidly built, McLanahan was as much a legend as Martindale,
except only in the shadowy world of strategic
aerial combat. He'd served five years as a B-52G
Stratofortress navigator and bombardier in the
U.S. Air Force before being chosen to join a top-
secret research-and-development unit known as
the High Technology Aerospace Weapons Center,
or HAWC, based at an uncharted air base in the
Nevada desert known as "Dreamland."

Led by its audacious and slightly uncontrol-
lable first commander, Lieutenant-General Bradley James Elliott, HAWC was tasked by the White
House to perform secret missions throughout the
world in order to stop an adversary from escalating a conflict into an all-out war, using cutting-
edge experimental technology that wouldn't be
used by any other military forces for many
years—if ever.

HAWC's specialty was modifying older aircraft with new systems and technology to make
them perform unlike anything anyone had ever
seen, and then using weapons brought to HAWC
for classified test programs in the real world to
quickly and quietly suppress a potential foe.
Most of HAWC's missions would never be known
about by the public; the pilots chosen to test-fly
a brand-new aircraft would never know not only
that were they not the first to fly it but that the
plane had *already been used in combat*; the families
of the scores of dead aviators and engineers, both
military and civilian, would never know what
really happened to their loved ones.

Because of Elliott's single-minded determination to dominate, as well as HAWC's incredible capabilities, which far exceeded any civilian or military commander's expectations, the unit often initiated responses to new threats without full knowledge or authorization from anyone. That eventually led to mistrust and finally to outright condemnation by the Washington and Pentagon establishment, which sought to isolate and even undermine HAWC's activities.

As its most experienced and tested aviator and systems operator, McLanahan had been alternately praised, punished, promoted, dismissed, decorated, and disgraced during his fourteen years as a member of HAWC. Although he was widely considered America's most heroic general since Norman Schwarzkopf, McLanahan retired from the Air Force as quietly as he had appeared on the scene, without fanfare, praise, or gratitude from anyone.

As both vice president and president, Kevin Martindale had been HAWC's most ardent supporter and advocate, and over the years he knew he could rely on Patrick McLanahan to get the job done, no matter how impossible the odds. With both of them now out of public life, it was no surprise to Jon Masters to see them standing side by side here in the deserts of New Mexico, on a secret weapon test range.

"Congratulations again, Dr. Masters," Martindale said. "I understand you can build that Slingshot laser self-protection system into any aircraft?"

"Yes, sir, we can," Boomer said. "All it needs is a power source and a twelve-inch open access panel through the aircraft's pressure vessel for the infrared detection sensor and beam director. We can install and calibrate a unit in a matter of days."

"Does it form a protective cocoon around the entire plane, or just shoot the beam toward the missile?"

"We focus the beam on the enemy missile to save power and maximize the destructive effect of the laser beam," Jon explained. "As soon as the infrared seeker detects a missile launch, it sends a beam of concentrated high-power laser energy along the same axis within milliseconds. Then, if the system can compute the approximate launch point, it'll automatically hit the enemy launch area to try to knock out the bad guy."

"What did getting hit by a laser beam feel like, Jon?" Patrick asked.

"Like being dunked in boiling cooking oil," Jon replied with a weak smile. "And that was at the *lowest* power setting."

"What else can that laser do, Jon?" Martindale asked. "I know HAWC has deployed offensive laser systems in the past. Is Slingshot like that?"

"Well, sir, the laser is *only* for self-defense, of *course*," Jon replied sarcastically.

"Just like the XC-57 is no longer a bomber, right, Jon?"

"Yes, sir. The U.S. government doesn't approve of its defense contractors building *offensive* weapons and using the technology in a manner that might harm relations with other countries or violate any laws. So the laser system is fairly limited in range and capabilities—mostly for use against tactical antiaircraft systems and their operators."

"That leaves a lot left open for interpretation," Patrick noted. "But you *could* turn the knob and pump up the power a skosh, right?"

"As far as *you* know, Muck, the answer is no," Jon said.

The former president motioned toward the sky in the direction of the departing aircraft, which was just now entering the downwind pattern to set up for a landing. "Pretty risky using one of your new big test-bed planes to test the system, wasn't it, Doc?" Martindale asked. "That was a *real* Stinger missile you fired at your own aircraft, I take it? Your shareholders can't be too happy about risking a multi-million-dollar aircraft like that."

"I wanted to water your eyes, of course, Mr. President," Jon replied. "What the directors and shareholders don't know won't hurt them. Besides, this XC-57 'Loser' is unmanned."

"'Loser,' huh?" Patrick McLanahan commented. "Not the coolest name you've come up with, Jon."

"Why in the world do you call it that?" Martindale asked.

"Because it lost out in the Next Generation Bomber competition," Jon explained. "They didn't want an unmanned plane; they wanted it stealthier and faster. I was going for payload and range, and I knew I could arm it with hypersonic standoff weapons, so we didn't need stealth.

"Besides, I've been designing and building unmanned aircraft for years—just because they weren't comfortable with it doesn't mean it

couldn't be considered. Isn't the Next Generation Bomber *supposed* to be *next* generation? The
design wasn't even considered. Their loss. Then,
to add insult to injury, I was prohibited from
building the plane for ten years."

"But you built it anyway?"

"It's not a bomber, Mr. President—this is a
multirole transport," Jon said. "It's not designed
to drop anything; it's designed to put stuff *into* it."

Martindale shook his head woefully. "Tap-
dancing around the law . . . who else do I know
likes to do that?" Patrick said nothing. "So
you use an unmanned aircraft—that's *not* a
bomber—for the test of a laser that's *not* an offensive weapon, but then put *yourself* in the line
of fire to test its effects on a human? Makes perfect sense to me," Martindale said drily. "But you
certainly did water my eyes."

"Thank you, sir."

"You have how many of the Losers flying
now, Jon?" Patrick asked.

"There are just two others—we built three
for the NGB competition but stopped work on
the second and third when our design was re-
jected," Jon replied. "It's still a research-and-
development program, so it was low priority . . .
until you called, Mr. President. We're considering putting our system on commercial planes as
well as high-tech airframes."

"Let's have a closer look at it, Jon," Martindale said.

"Yes, sir. I'll have it fly over slowly so we
can take a look, then I'll bring it in for a landing. Watch this flyby—you won't believe it." He
picked up his walkie-talkie and tried to call his

control center, but the laser beam had fried it. "I forgot to take it out of my pocket before the test," he said sheepishly, smiling at the others' muffled chuckles. "I lose more phones that way. Boomer . . . ?"

"I got it, boss," Boomer said. "Low and slow?" Jon nodded, and Boomer winked and radioed the mobile control van.

Moments later the XC-57 appeared on final approach. It leveled off just fifty feet above ground, flying amazingly slow for such a large bird, as if it were a huge balsa-wood model drifting gently on a soft breeze.

"Like a pregnant stealth bomber with the engines on the outside," Martindale commented. "It looks like it's going to fall out of the sky at any moment. How do you do that?"

"It doesn't use any normal flight controls or lifting devices—it flies using mission-adaptive technology," Masters said. "Almost every square inch of the fuselage and wings can be either a lift or drag device. It can be flown manned or unmanned. About sixty-five thousand pounds of payload, and it can take up to four standard cargo pallets.

"But the Loser's unique system is a completely integral cargo handling capability, including the ability to move containers around inside while in flight," Masters went on. "That was Boomer's first idea when he came on board, and we've been scrambling to refit all of the production aircraft to include it. Boomer?"

"Well, the problem I've always seen with cargo planes is that once the cargo's inside you can't do anything with the plane, the space, or the cargo," Boomer said. "They're all wasted as soon as it's loaded on board."

"It's cargo on a cargo plane, Boomer. What else are you going to do with it?" Martindale asked.

"Maybe it's a cargo plane in one configuration, sir," Boomer replied, "but move the cargo around and slip a modular container through an opening in the belly, and now the cargo plane becomes a tanker or a surveillance platform. It's based on the same concept as the Navy's Littoral Combat Ship that's all the rage now—one ship that can do different missions depending on which hardware modules you put on board."

"Plug and play? That simple?"

"It wasn't easy to get the weight and balance, fuel system, and electrical systems to integrate," Boomer admitted, "but we think we have the bugs worked out. We pump fuel around between the various tanks to maintain balance. Without the mission-adaptive system, I don't think it would've been possible at all. The Loser can lift cargo or the mission modules inside through the cargo hatch or belly hatch—"

"Belly hatch?" Martindale interrupted him with a wink. "You mean the bomb bay?"

"It's not a bomb bay, sir, it's a *cargo access hatch*," Jon retorted. "It *used* to have a bomb bay, and I didn't think it was right to just seal it up—"

"So it became a 'cargo access hatch,'" the former president said. "Got it, Doc."

"Yes, sir," Jon said, feigning exasperation at having to continually remind people of his point. "Boomer's system automatically arranges the modules as necessary for the mission, plugs them in, and turns them on, all by remote control. It can do the same while in flight. When a module is needed or one is expended, the cargo handling system can replace it with another one."

"What modules do you have available, Jon?" Martindale asked.

"We're making up new ones every month, sir," Jon said proudly. "Right now we have boom aerial refueling modules along with hose-and-drogue wingtip pods, which are installed on the ground and can refuel probe-equipped planes. We also have laser radar modules for air and ground surveillance with satellite datalink; infrared and electro-optical surveillance modules; and the active self-defense module. We're pretty close on a netrusion module and a FlightHawk control system—launching, directing, and perhaps even refueling and rearming FlightHawks from the Loser."

"Of course, we would *want* to do attack modules, too, if we could get permission from the White House," Boomer interjected. "We're doing pretty well with the high-powered microwave and laser-directed energy technology, so that might happen sooner rather than later—if we can convince the White House to let us proceed."

"Boomer is highly motivated to say the least," Jon added. "He won't be happy until he gets a Loser into space."

Martindale and McLanahan looked at each other, each instantly reading the other's thoughts; they then looked at the otherworldly sight of the massive Loser aircraft gliding down the runway in that flying-saucer slow-motion pace.

"Dr. Masters, Mr. Noble . . ." President Martindale began. Just then, the XC-57 Loser suddenly accelerated with a powerful roar of its engines, climbing out at an impossibly steep angle and disappearing from sight within moments. Martindale shook his head, amazed all over again. "Where can we go to talk, boys?"

CHAPTER 2

The road to Hades is easy to travel.
—*Bion, 325–255 B.C.*

OFFICE OF THE PRESIDENT, ÇANCAYA, ANKARA, TURKEY
The next morning

Close the damn door before I start bawling like a damned baby," Kurzat Hirsiz, president of the Republic of Turkey, said, wiping his eyes once again before putting away his handkerchief. He shook his head. "One of the dead was a two-year-old. Completely innocent. Probably couldn't even pronounce 'PKK.'"

Thin, oval-faced, and tall, Hirsiz was a lawyer, academic, and expert on macroeconomics as well as the chief executive of the Republic of Turkey. He'd served for many years as an executive director of the World Bank and lectured around the world on economic solutions for the developing world before being appointed prime minister. Popular throughout the world as well as in his homeland, he'd received the largest percentage of the vote of the members of the Grand National

Assembly in the country's history when he was elected president.

Hirsiz and his top advisers had just returned from a press conference in Çancaya, the presidential compound in Ankara. He had read the list of names of the dead that had been given to him a few moments before the televised briefing, and had then taken some questions. When he was told by a reporter that one of the dead was a toddler, he suddenly broke down, openly weeping, and abruptly ended the presser. "I want the names, phone numbers, and some details about all the victims. I will call them personally after this meeting," Hirsiz's aide picked up the phone to issue the orders. "I will attend each of the families' services as well."

"Don't feel embarrassed breaking down like that, Kurzat," Ayşe Akas, the prime minister, said. Her eyes were red as well, although she was known in Turkey for her personal and political toughness, something to which her two ex-husbands would certainly attest. "It shows you're human."

"I can just hear the PKK bastards laughing at the sight of me crying in front of a roomful of reporters," Hirsiz said. "They win twice. They take advantage of both a lapse in security procedures and a lapse in control."

"It just solidifies what we have been telling the entire world for almost three decades—the PKK is and always will be nothing but murderous slime," General Orhan Sahin, secretary-general of the Turkish National Security Council, interjected. Sahin, an army general, coordinated all military and intelligence activities between Çancaya, the military headquarters at Baskanligi, and Turkey's six major intelligence agencies. "It is the most devastating and dastardly PKK attack in many years, since the cross-border attacks of 2007, and by far the most daring. Fifteen dead, including six on the ground; fifty-one injured— including the commander of the Jandarma himself, General Ozek—and the tanker aircraft a complete loss."

The president returned to his desk, loosened his tie, and lit a cigarette, the signal for everyone else in the office to do so as well. "What is the status of the investigation, General?" Hirsiz asked.

"Well under way, Mr. President," Sahin said. "The initial reports are disturbing. One of the deputy heads of security for the airport has not responded to orders to return to his post and cannot be located. I'm hoping he's just on vacation and will check in soon after he hears the news, but I'm afraid we'll find it was an inside job."

"My God," Hirsiz muttered. "The PKK infiltrates into our units and offices higher and higher every day."

"I think it is a very good possibility that PKK agents have infiltrated into the very office of the Jandarma, the organization tasked with defending the country against those murderous bastards," Sahin said. "My guess is that Ozek's travel plans were leaked and the PKK targeted that plane specifically to kill him."

"But you told me Ozek was going to Diyarbakir on a surprise inspection!" Hirsiz exclaimed. "Is it possible they've infiltrated so deeply and are organized so well that they can dispatch a kill squad with a shoulder-fired antiaircraft missile so quickly?"

"It has to be an inside job, but not just one man—that base must be infested with insurgents in deep cover, in highly trusted positions, ready to be activated and deployed within hours with specific attack tasks."

"It's a level of sophistication we've dreaded but have been expecting, sir," General Abdullah Guzlev, chief of staff of the Turkish military forces, said. "It's time we reacted in kind. We can't be content to just play defense, sir. We need to go after the leadership of the PKK and wipe them out once and for all."

"In Iraq and Iran, I suppose, General?" Prime Minister Akas asked.

"That's where they hide, Madam Prime Minister, like the cowards they are," Guzlev snapped. "We'll get an update from our undercover operatives, find a few nests with as many of the murderous bastards as possible in them, and eliminate them."

"Exactly what will that accomplish, General," Foreign Minister Mustafa Hamarat asked, "except further angering our neighbors, the world community, and our supporters in the United States and Europe?"

"Excuse me, Minister," Guzlev said angrily, "but I'm not much concerned about what someone on another continent thinks while innocent men, women, and children are being murdered by—"

Guzlev was interrupted by a ringing telephone, which was answered immediately by the president's chief of staff. The aide looked dumb-struck as he put down the receiver. "Sir, General Ozek is in your outer office and wishes to speak to the national security staff!"

"*Ozek*! I thought he was in serious condition!" Hirsiz exclaimed. "Yes, yes, get him in here immediately, and bring a corpsman to monitor him at all times."

It was almost painful to look at the man when he stepped into the office. His right shoulder and the right side of his head were heavily bandaged, several fingers on both hands were taped together, he walked with a limp, his eyes were puffy, and the parts of his face and neck that were visible were covered in cuts, burns, and bruises—but he was upright, and he refused any assistance from the Çancaya corpsman who arrived for him. Ozek stood at wobbly attention at the doorway and saluted. "Permission to speak to the president, sir," he said, his voice hoarse from breathing burning jet fuel and aluminum.

"Of course, of course, General. Get off your feet and sit, man!" Hirsiz exclaimed.

The president led Ozek over to the sofa, but the Jandarma commander held up a hand. "I'm sorry, sir, but I must stand. I'm afraid I wouldn't be able to get up again," Ozek said.

"What are you doing here, General?" Prime Minister Akas asked.

"I felt it necessary to show the people of Turkey that I was alive and doing my duties," Ozek said, "and I wanted the national security staff to know that I have formulated a plan for a retaliatory strike at the PKK leadership. Now is the time to act. We must not delay."

"I am impressed by your dedication to our country and your mission, General," the prime minister said, "but first we must—"

"I have a full brigade of *ozel tim* loaded and ready to deploy immediately." *Ozel tim*, or Special Teams, was the unconventional warfare branch of the Jandarma's intelligence department, specially trained to operate close to or in many cases within Kurdish towns and villages to identify and neutralize insurgent leaders. They were some of the best-trained commandos in the world—and they had an equally notorious reputation for brutality.

"Very good, General," Hirsiz said, "but have you discovered who is behind the attack? Who is the leader? Who pulled the trigger? Who ordered this attack?"

"Sir, that hardly matters," Ozek said, his eyes widening in surprise that he had to answer such a question. His intense eyes and rather wild-looking features, along with his wounds, made him look anxious and excitable, almost savage, especially compared to the other politicians around him. "We have a long list of known PKK insurgents, bomb makers, smugglers, financiers, recruiters, and sympathizers. Internal security and the Border Defense Forces can pick up the usual suspects and conduct interrogations—let me and *ozel tim* go after the ringleaders."

President Hirsiz averted his eyes from the fiery general. "Another attack inside Iraq . . . I don't know, General," he said, shaking his head. "This is something that needs to be discussed with the American and Iraqi governments. They must—"

"Pardon me for saying so, sir, but both governments are ineffectual and care nothing for Turkish security," General Ozek said angrily. "Baghdad is perfectly willing to let the Kurds do whatever they please as long as the oil revenues flow south. The Americans are pulling out of Iraq as fast as they can. Besides, they have never lifted a finger to stop the PKK. Even though they rail on and on about the global war on terror and have labeled the PKK a terrorist outfit, except for occasionally tossing us a few photos or phone intercepts, they haven't done a damn thing to help us."

Hirsiz fell silent, worriedly puffing on his cigarette. "Besir is right, sir," Guzlev, the military chief of staff, said. "This is the time we have been waiting for. Baghdad is clinging by its fingernails to keep its government intact; they don't have the power to secure their own capital, much less the Kurdish frontier. America has stopped replacing combat brigades in Iraq. There are just three brigades in the north of Iraq, centered on Irbil and Mosul—almost no one on the border."

Guzlev paused, noting no opposition to his comments, then added, "But I suggest more than just Special Teams involvement, sir." He looked at the defense minister, Hasan Cizek, and National Security Council secretary-general Sahin. "I propose a full-scale invasion of northern Iraq."

"*What*?" President Hirsiz exclaimed. "Are you joking, General?"

"Out of the question, General," Prime Minister Akas immediately added. "We would be condemned by our friends and the entire world!"

"To what end, General?" Foreign Minister Hamarat asked. "We send in thousands of troops to root out a few thousand PKK rebels? Do you propose we occupy Iraqi territory?"

"I propose a buffer zone, sir," Guzlev said. "The Americans helped Israel set up a buffer zone in southern Lebanon that was effective in keeping Hezbollah fighters out of Israel. We should do the same."

Hirsiz looked at his defense minister, silently hoping for another voice of opposition. "Hasan?"

"It's possible, Mr. President," the defense minister said, "but it would not be a secret and it would be hugely expensive. The operation would take a fourth of our entire military force, perhaps up to a third, and it would certainly entail calling up the reserve forces. It would take months. Our actions would be seen by all—first of all by the Americans. Whether we are successful depends on how the Americans react."

"General Sahin?"

"The Americans are in the process of an extended drawdown of forces throughout Iraq," the secretary-general of the Turkish National Security Council said. "Because it is relatively quiet and the Kurdish autonomous government is better organized than the central government in Baghdad, northern Iraq has perhaps twenty thousand American troops still in the region, assisting in guarding oil pipelines and facilities. They are scheduled to go down to just two combat brigades within a year."

"*Two combat brigades*—for *all* of northern Iraq? That doesn't seem realistic."

"The Stryker brigades are very potent weapon systems, sir, very fast and agile—they should not be underestimated," Sahin warned. "However, sir, we expect the Americans to employ private contractors to supply most of the surveillance, security, and support services. This falls in line with President Joseph Gardner's new policy of resting and restoring ground forces while he increases the size and power of their Navy."

"Then it *is* possible, sir," Defense Minister Cizek said. "The Iraqi Kurds' *peshmerga* forces have the equivalent of two infantry divisions and one mechanized division, centered on Mosul, Irbil, and the Kirkuk oil fields—a third of the size of our forces that are within marching distance of the border. Even if the PKK has the equivalent of a full infantry division, and the United States throws their entire ground forces against us, we are still at parity—and, as Sun-tzu wrote, if your forces are of equal strength: attack. We can do this, Mr. President."

"We can mobilize our forces within three months, with *ozel tim* scouting enemy positions and preparing to disrupt the private contractors performing surveillance on the border region," General Ozek added. "The mercenaries hired by the Americans are there only to earn money. If a fight is brewing, they will run for cover and hide behind regular military forces."

"And what if the Americans stand and fight to help the Kurds?"

"We push south and crush the rebel camps and Kurdish opposition forces until the Americans threaten action, then pull back in contact and set up our buffer zone," Ozek said. "We have no desire to fight the Americans, but we will not allow them to dictate the terms of our sovereignty and security." He turned to Foreign Minister Hamarat. "We convince them a no-fly, no-drive buffer zone, patrolled by the United Nations, will enhance security for all parties. Gardner doesn't want a ground war, and he certainly doesn't care about the Kurds. He'll agree to anything as long as it stops the fighting."

"That may be true, but Gardner will never admit that publicly," Hamarat said. "He will openly condemn us and demand a full withdrawal from Iraq."

"Then we stall for time while we root out all the PKK rat's nests and wire the border region for sound," Ozek said. "With six divisions in northern Iraq, we can scour the place clean in just a few months while we promise to leave. We can decimate the PKK enough so they'll be ineffectual for a generation."

"And we look like butchers."

"I don't care what others may call me as long as I don't have to worry about my innocent sons or daughters being killed in a damned playground by an aircraft downed by the PKK," Defense Minister Cizak said bitterly. "It is time to *act*."

"It is not just the PKK we need to address, sir, but the security situation with the Kirkuk-Ceyhan pipeline," military chief of staff Guzlev added. "The Iraqi *peshmerga* are still not trained or equipped well enough to protect the pipeline on their side of the border. We invested billions of lira on that pipeline, and the Iraqis still can't adequately protect their portion, and won't allow any outside forces except the Americans to assist. We can earn three times the amount we receive in flowage fees if we can convince the oil producers in northern Iraq—including our own companies—to increase production, but they won't do it because the pipeline is too vulnerable to attack."

President Hirsiz stabbed out his cigarette in the ornate ashtray on his desk, then returned to his seat. He was quiet for a few long moments, lost in thought. It was rare that the national security staff was so divided, especially when it came to the PKK and their brutal insurgent attacks. The unexpected appearance of Besir Ozek in his office just hours after surviving the crash should have united their determination to stamp out the PKK once and for all.

But the national security staff—and he himself, Hirsiz had to admit—were conflicted and divided, with the civilian military leadership desiring a peaceful, diplomatic solution as opposed to a call for direct action by the uniformed commanders. Opposing the Americans and world public opinion with a divided council was not a smart move.

Kurzat Hirsiz got to his feet again and stood straight, almost at attention. "General Ozek, thank you for coming here and addressing me and the national security staff," he said formally. "We will discuss these options very carefully."

"Sir . . ." Ozek lurched forward from shock, forgetting his injuries and wincing in pain as he struggled for balance. "Sir, respectfully, you must act swiftly and decisively. The PKK—no, the *world*—must know that this government takes these attacks seriously. Every moment we delay only shows that we are not committed to our internal security."

"I agree, General," Hirsiz said, "but we must act deliberately and carefully, and in close consultation with our international allies. I will instruct General Sahin to put together a plan for the Special Teams to hunt down and capture or kill the PKK operatives who might have planned and led this attack, and to aggressively investigate the possibility of spies in the Jandarma.

"I will further instruct Foreign Minister Hamarat to consult with his American, NATO, and European counterparts and inform them of this council's outrage at this attack and a demand for cooperation and assistance in tracking down the perpetrators." He inwardly winced at General Ozek's incredulous expression, which only served to accentuate his weak, shaky stance. "We will act, General," Hirsiz quickly added, "but we will do it wisely and as a member of the world community. This will further isolate and marginalize the PKK. If we act rashly, we will be seen as no better than the terrorists."

"The . . . world . . . community?" Ozek murmured bitterly.

"What did you say, General?" Hirsiz snapped. "Do you have something you would like to tell me?"

The wounded Jandarma officer briefly yet openly scowled at the president of the Republic of Turkey, but quickly straightened himself as best he could, assumed a stern but neutral expression, and said, "No, *sir.*"

"Then you are dismissed, General, with the national security council's and the Turkish people's sincere thanks and relief that you are alive following this treacherous and dastardly attack," Hirsiz said, his acidic tone definitely not matching his words.

"Permission to accompany the general to transient quarters, sir," armed-forces chief of staff Guzlev said.

Hirsiz looked at his military chief of staff questioningly, finding no answers. He glanced at Ozek, inwardly wincing again at his horrific wounds but finding himself wondering when the best time would be to dismiss the wild raging bull before him. The sooner the better, but not before he had taken every propaganda advantage of his incredible survival.

"We shall reconvene the national security staff in twenty minutes in the Council of Ministers' conference center to map out a response, General Guzlev," the president said warily. "Please be back by then. Dismissed."

"Yes, sir," Guzlev said. He and Ozek stood at attention momentarily, then headed for the door, with Guzlev carefully holding Ozek's less-wounded arm for support.

"What in the world possessed Ozek to come all the way to Ankara after barely surviving a plane crash?" Foreign Minister Hamarat asked incredulously. "My God, the pain must be *excruiating!* I was once in a minor fender bender and I hurt for *weeks* afterward! That man was pulled from the burning wreckage of a downed aircraft just a few hours ago!"

"He's angry and he's out for blood, Mustafa," Prime Minister Akas said. She stepped over to Hirsiz, who still appeared to be standing at attention as if placed in a brace by Ozek. "Don't pay attention to Guzlev and Ozek," she added in a whisper. "They're out for blood. We've spoken about an invasion many times before and dismissed it every time."

"Maybe this is the right time, Ayşe," Hirsiz whispered back. "Guzlev, Cizek, Ozek, and even Sahin are for it."

"You're not *seriously* considering it, are you, Mr. President?" Akas whispered back with an incredulous hiss. "The United States would never agree. We'd be pariahs in the world's eyes . . ."

"I'm beginning to not care what the world thinks of us, Ayşe," Hirsiz said. "How many more funerals do we have to attend before the world lets us do something about the rebel Kurds out there?"

ALLIED AIR BASE NAHLA, TALL KAYF, NEAR MOSUL, IRAQ
Two days later

"Nahla Tower, Scion One-Seven, nine miles out, requesting visual approach to runway two-niner."

"Scion One-Seven, Nahla Tower, you are number one, cleared to land," the supervising Iraqi army controller responded in very good but heavily accented English. "Recommend Nahla enhanced arrival procedure three, the base is at Force Protection Condition Bravo, cleared for enhanced arrival procedure three, acknowledge."

"Negative, Nahla, Scion One-Seven wants clearance for the visual to two-niner."

The supervisor was unaccustomed to anyone not following his instructions to the letter, and he stabbed at his mike button and shot back: "Scion One-Seven, Nahla Tower, a visual approach is not authorized in FPCON Bravo conditions." FPCON, or Force Protection Condition (formerly called "Threat Condition" or THREATCON), Bravo was the third highest level, indicating that actionable intelligence had been received that an attack was possible. "You *will* execute procedure three. Do you understand? Acknowledge."

A phone rang in the background, and the deputy tower controller picked it up. A moment later he handed the receiver to the supervisor: "Sir? The deputy base commander for you."

The supervisor, further annoyed by being interrupted while he was working an inbound flight, snatched the receiver away from his deputy. "Captain Saad. I've got an arriving flight, sir, can I call you back?"

"Captain, let that inbound flight do the visual pattern," he heard the familiar voice of the American colonel say. The deputy base commander was obviously listening in on the tower frequency awaiting this flight. "It's his funeral."

"Yes, Colonel." Why an American special mission aircraft would risk getting shot at by not performing the high-performance arrival procedure was unclear, but orders were orders. He gave his deputy the receiver, sighed, and touched the mike button again: "Scion One-Seven, Nahla Tower, you are cleared for the visual approach and overhead pattern to runway two-niner, winds two-seven zero at twenty-five knots gust-ing to forty, RVR four thousand, FPCON Bravo in effect, cleared to land."

"Scion One-Seven, cleared for the visual and overhead to two-niner, cleared to land."

The supervisor picked up the crash phone: "Station One, this is the tower," he said in Arabic. "I have a flight on final approach to land, and I've cleared him for a visual approach and pattern."

"Say again?" the dispatcher at the airport fire station queried. "But we're at FPCON Bravo."

"The American colonel's orders. I wanted to put you guys on notice."

"Thanks for the call. The captain will probably move us out to our 'hot spots' on taxiway Delta."

"You're cleared to preposition on Delta." The supervisor hung up the phone. He then made a similar call to base security and to the hospital. If there was going to be an attack—and this was the perfect opportunity for one—the more alerts he could issue, the better.

Through his binoculars, the tower supervisor searched for the aircraft. He could see it on his tower radar display, but not yet visually. It was about six miles out, coming straight in but offset to the west, appearing to line up for the down-wind leg for Runway 29—and he was ridiculously *slow*, as if configured for landing while still several minutes from touchdown. Did this guy have some sort of death wish? He relayed the aircraft position to security and crash responders so they could move to a better position . . .

. . . or get out of the way of the wreckage, in case the worst happened.

Finally, at three miles he saw it—or rather, saw *part* of it. It had a broad, bulbous fuselage, but he could not make out the wings or tail. It had no visible passenger windows and a weird paint color—sort of a medium bluish gray, but the shading seemed to change depending on background clouds and lighting levels. It was unusually hard to maintain a visual on it.

He checked the BRITE tower radar display, a repeater of Mosul Approach Control's local radar, and sure enough the plane was flying only ninety-eight knots—about fifty knots *slower* than normal approach speed! Not only was the pilot making himself an easy target for snipers, but he was going to stall the plane and crash. In these winds, a sudden errant gust could flip that guy upside down fast.

"Scion One-Seven, Nahla Tower, are you experiencing difficulty?"

"Tower, One-Seven, negative," the pilot replied.

"Copy. You are cleared to land. We are in FPCON Bravo. Acknowledge."

"Scion One-Seven copies FPCON Bravo and cleared to land."

Stupid, just plain stupid. The supervisor watched in amazement as the strange plane executed a standard left downwind pattern on the west side of the runway. It resembled an American stealth bomber, except its engines were *atop* the rear fuselage and it appeared much larger. He expected to see RPG or Stinger missiles flying through the sky any second. The aircraft rocked a few times in the gusty winds, but mostly maintained a very stable flight path despite its unbelievably slow flight speed—it was like watching a tiny Cessna in the pattern instead of a two-hundred-thousand-pound airplane.

Somehow, the plane managed to make it all the way around the rectangular traffic pattern without falling or being shot from the sky. The tower supervisor could not see any wing flaps deployed. It maintained that ridiculously slow airspeed all the way around the pattern until short final, when it slowed to precisely *ninety knots*, then dropped as lightly as a feather on the numbers. It easily turned off at the first taxiway; he had never seen a fixed-wing plane land in such a short distance.

"Tower, Scion One-Seven is clear of the active," the pilot reported.

The supervisor had to shake himself from his shock. "Roger, One-Seven, stay on this frequency, report security vehicles in sight straight ahead, they will lead you to parking. Use caution for fire trucks and security vehicles on the taxiways. Welcome to Nahla."

"Roger, Tower, One-Seven has the security vehicles in sight," the pilot responded. Several armed Humvees with gunners in turrets manning .50 caliber machine guns or forty-millimeter rapid-fire grenade launchers had surrounded the aircraft, and a blue Suburban with flashing blue lights and a large yellow "Follow Me" sign pulled out ahead. "Have a nice day."

The convoy escorted the plane to a large aircraft shelter north of the control tower. The Humvees deployed around the shelter as the Suburban pulled inside, and an aircraft marshaler brought the plane to a stop. A set of air stairs was towed

out to the plane, but before it was put into position a hatch opened under the cockpit behind the
nose gear, and personnel began climbing down a
ladder.

At the same time, several men exited the
Humvee and stood at the plane's left wingtip,
one of them visibly upset. "Man, they weren't
kidding—it's *hot* out here!" Jon Masters exclaimed. He looked around at the aircraft shelter.
"Hey, this hangar has air conditioning—let's
crank it up!"

"Let's check in with the base commander
first, Jon," the second man out, Patrick McLanahan, suggested. He nodded to the Humvee below
them. "I think that's Colonel Jaffar and our contact right there."

"Jaffar looks pissed. What did we do now?"

"Let's go find out," Patrick said. He stepped
over to the Iraqi colonel, bowed slightly, and
extended a hand. "Colonel Jaffar? I'm Patrick
McLanahan."

Jaffar was just a bit taller than Patrick, but he
raised his chin, puffed out his chest, and flexed
himself on his toes to make himself look taller
and more important. When he was satisfied the
newcomers took notice, he slowly raised his right
hand to his right eyebrow in a salute. "General
McLanahan. Welcome to Nahla Air Base," he
said in very good but heavily accented English.
Patrick returned the salute, then reextended his
hand. Jaffar slowly took it, smiled faintly, then
tried to crush Patrick's hand in his. When he realized it wouldn't work, the smile disappeared.

"Colonel, may I present Dr. Jonathan Colin
Masters. Dr. Masters, Colonel Yusuf Jaffar, Iraqi

Air Forces, commander of Allied Air Base Nahla."
Jaffar nodded but did not shake hands with Jon.
Patrick gave a slight exasperated shake of his
head, then read the name tag of the young man
standing beside and behind Jaffar. "Mr. Thompson? I'm Patrick—"

"General Patrick McLanahan. I know who
you are, sir—we *all* know who you are." The tall,
impossibly young-looking officer behind Jaffar
stepped forward, grinning from ear to ear. "Nice
to meet you, sir. Kris Thompson, president of
Thompson International, security consultants."
He shook Patrick's hand with both of his, pumping it excitedly and shaking his head in disbelief.
"I can't believe it . . . General Patrick McLanahan. I'm actually shaking hands with *the* Patrick
McLanahan."

"Thanks, Kris. This is Dr. Jon Masters. He's—"

"Hiya, Doc," Thompson said, not taking his
eyes off or releasing the hand of Patrick McLanahan. "Welcome, sir. It's a real honor and privilege
to meet you and welcome you to Iraq. I will—"

"You will please stop your chattering, Thompson, and let us get to business," Jaffar said impa-
tiently. "Your reputation assuredly precedes you,
General, but I must remind you that you are a
civilian contractor and bound to obey my rules
and regulations and those of the Republic of Iraq.
I have been asked by your government to extend
you all possible courtesies and assistance, and as
a fellow officer, I am honor-bound to do so, but
you must understand that Iraqi law—which is to
say, in this place, *my* law—must be followed at
all times. Is that clear, sir?"

"Yes, Colonel, it's clear," Patrick said.

"Then why did you disobey my regulations concerning arrivals and approaches to Nahla?"

"We thought it was necessary to assess the threat condition ourselves, Colonel," Patrick replied. "Doing a max-performance arrival wouldn't have told us anything. We decided to assume the risk and do a visual approach and pattern."

"My staff and I assess the threat condition on this base every hour of every day, General," Jaffar said angrily. "I issue orders that govern all personnel and operations at this base to ensure the safety and security of everyone. They are not to be disregarded for any reason. You cannot assume the risk at any time for any reason, sir: the responsibility is *mine*, at all times, and that is inviolate. Disregard my law again, and you shall be asked to perform your tasks at another base. Is that clear, sir?"

"Yes, Colonel, it's clear."

"Very well." Jaffar put his hands behind his back, puffing out his chest again. "I think you are very fortunate you were not hit by enemy fire. My security forces and I swept the entire area in a ten-kilometer radius outside the base for threats. I assure you, you were in little danger. But that does not mean you can—"

"Excuse me, but we *did* come under fire, Colonel," Jon Masters cut in.

Jaffar's eyes blazed at the interruption, then his mouth opened and closed in confusion, then turned rigid in indignation. "What did you say, young man?" he growled.

"We were hit by ground fire a total of one hundred and seventy-nine times while within ten miles of the base, Colonel," Jon said. "And forty-one of the shots came from *inside* the base."

"That is impossible! That is *preposterous*! How could you know this?"

"That's our job here, Colonel: assess the threat condition at this and other allied air bases in northern Iraq," Patrick said. "Our aircraft is instrumented and allows us to detect, track, identify, and pinpoint the origin of attacks. We can locate, identify, and track weapon fire down to nine-millimeter caliber." He held out his hand, and Jon put a folder in it. "Here's a map of the origin of all the shots we detected. As you can see, Colonel, one of the heaviest volleys of gunfire—a six-round burst of 12.7-millimeter cannon fire— came from *this base*. From the security-forces training range, to be exact." He took a step toward Jaffar, his blue eyes boring into the Iraqi's. "Tell me, Colonel: Who's out on that range right now? What caliber of antiaircraft weapons do you have here at Nahla?" Jaffar's mouth bobbled again in confusion. "Whoever did this, I expect them to be placed under arrest and charged with deliberately firing upon allied aircraft."

"I . . . I will look into it . . . personally, sir," Jaffar said, sweat popping out on his forehead. He made a slight bow, backing away. "I will look into this immediately, sir." He almost ran headlong into Thompson in his haste to get away.

"What a butthead," Jon said. "I hope we don't have to put up with his shit every day out here."

"He's actually one of the *more* competent commanders in northern Iraq, Doc," Thompson said. "He expects a lot of ass kissing and genuflecting. But he's not the one that gets things done—he just cracks heads whenever one of his underlings doesn't do the job. So, is that true about you detecting and tracking attacks against your aircraft?"

"Absolutely," Jon replied. "And we can do a lot more, too."

"We'll give you details once we get your security clearance, Kris," Patrick said. "It'll water your eyes, believe me."

"Cool," Thompson said. "The colonel may act like a preening peacock, but when he finds the jokers who shot at you, he'll bring the hammer down on them for sure."

"Unfortunately it wasn't just some bozos out on the range—we detected several other locations both inside the base and just outside the perimeter," Jon said. "The colonel may be the best around, but it's not good enough. He's got sappers inside the wire."

"As I texted you when you told me you were coming, sir," Thompson said, "I believe the FPCON here should be Delta—active and ongoing terrorist contact. It makes Jaffar look bad to Baghdad to be any higher than Bravo. But my guys and the Army security forces are behaving as if it's Delta. So if you'll follow me, sir, I'll show you to your quarters and offices and show you around the base a bit."

"If you don't mind, Kris, we'd like to get our area of responsibility set up and our first series of flights scheduled," Patrick said. "I'd like to fly the first mission tonight. The support staff will get our quarters set up."

"Tonight? But you just got here, sir. You must be beat."

"One hundred and seventy hits on our plane with one-fourth of them from *inside* this base—we need to get busy," Patrick said.

"Then we need to go to operations and see Colonel Jack Wilhelm," Thompson said. "Officially he's the second in command under Jaffar, but everyone knows who's really in charge, and it's him. He's usually in the Triple-C—Command and Control Center."

They all piled into another up-armored white Suburban, with Thompson driving. "*Nahla*, which means 'bumblebee' in Arabic, used to be a U.S. Air Force supply base," he said as he drove down the flight line. They saw rows and rows of cargo planes of every size, from C-5 Galaxys down to bizjets. "In Saddam's time it was set up to quell the ethnic Kurdish population, and it became one of the biggest Iraqi military bases in the country. They say this was the base where the chemical weapons that Saddam used on the Kurds were stored, and so this is a major target for Kurdish insurgents that we deal with from time to time, along with AQI—al-Qaeda in Iraq—Shiite insurgents, and foreign jihadists.

"Early this year Nahla was formally transferred from U.S. control to the Iraqi military. The Iraqis still don't have much of an air force, however, so they designated it an 'allied' air base. The United States, NATO, and the United Nations lease facilities and ramp space from the Iraqis."

"We build it and then get charged to use it," Jon commented. "Swell."

"If we didn't pay to use it, we'd still be considered an 'occupying force' in Iraq," Thompson explained. "It's the politics of withdrawal from Iraq.

"The main fighting unit here at Nahla is Second Brigade, nicknamed 'Warhammer,'" Thompson went on. "Second Brigade is a Stryker Combat Brigade Team, part of I Corps, Second Division, out of Fort Lewis, Washington. They're one of the last units to do a fifteen-month rotation—all of the other units do twelve months. They support the Iraqi army with reconnaissance, intelligence, and training. They're scheduled to rotate out within three months when the Iraqis will take full control of security in northern Iraq."

"Do we really have half of all American transports somewhere in the Middle East, Kris?" Patrick asked.

"I'd say easily half of the Air Force's transports are either on the ground in the theater or flying in or out of it, and the real number is probably closer to three-quarters," Thompson said. "And that doesn't include the civil reserve charters and contractors."

"But it'll still take a *year* to draw down our forces?" Jon asked. "That doesn't seem right. It didn't take that long to get our stuff out of Iraq after the first Gulf War, did it?"

"Different plan, Doc," Thompson said. "The plan is to take everything out of Iraq except for the stuff at the two air bases and the embassy complex in Baghdad. After the first Gulf War, we left a lot of stuff in Kuwait, Saudi Arabia, Bahrain, Qatar, and the United Arab Emirates, and we had security locked up tight so we could roll with ease. It took over a year to get all our stuff out of Saudi when the U.S. was asked to leave there, and we just drove it up the highway to Kuwait. Here, we're shipping all our stuff either home or to new bare bases in Romania, Poland, the Czech Republic, and Djibouti."

"Still, it can't take *that* long to get out, can it?"

"We've been at it nonstop day and night for almost a year, and another year is being *really* optimistic," Thompson admitted. "It depends mostly on the security situation. The coup in Iran shut down the Persian Gulf completely for a year, and the few rail lines and highways in and out of the country weren't secure, so we had to wait for more favorable conditions. Stuff urgently needed elsewhere could be flown out, but taking up an entire C-5 Galaxy or C-17 Globemaster just to fly one or two M1A2 battle tanks out didn't make sense. And we're not about to leave over two thousand armored vehicles behind." He looked at Patrick. "That's why you're here, isn't it, sir? Improve the security situation?"

"We'll give it a shot," Patrick said. "Obviously the Iraqis can't get a handle on the security situation, and it wouldn't be politically correct for American troops—who aren't wanted in the country anyway—to be providing security, so they offer contracts to private companies to do the work."

"Well, you're certainly not alone, sir," Thompson said. "Contractors do just about everything out here these days. We still have a Marine air unit here at Nahla who fly in support of Iraqi missions, and every now and then a Special Forces unit or SEAL team will buzz in and out, but otherwise the troops here don't do much of anything except pack up the gear and wait for their ride home. Most training and security, intelligence, food service, transportation, communications, construction, demolition, recreation—all run by us contractors."

"After the American holocaust, it was easier and faster to hire and retrain veterans than train new recruits," Patrick said. "If you want to do more with less, you have to outsource the support functions and let the active duty soldiers do the specialized missions."

"I hadn't heard of Scion Aviation until the Army announced you were coming here," Thompson remarked. "Where are you guys based out of?"

"Las Vegas," Patrick replied. "It's basically a bunch of investors who acquired a few high-tech but surplus aircraft from various companies and offered their services to the Pentagon. I was offered a job after I retired."

"Sounds like the same deal with my company," Kris said. "We're a bunch of former and retired military physical, communications, and data security technicians and engineers. We still wanted to serve after getting out, so we formed the company."

"Like it so far?"

"Frankly, I started the business because I thought the money would be good—all those stories of companies like Blackwater Worldwide getting these fat contracts were really attractive," Kris admitted. "But it's a business. The contracts may look juicy, but we spend the money getting the best personnel and equipment we can find and offering an effective solution for the lowest price. I can tell you that I haven't seen a penny out of the business except what it costs me to survive. If there's a profit, it goes right back into the business, which allows us to do more services, or do a service for a lower cost."

"Just the *opposite* of the military," Jon Masters said. "The military *spends* every penny of its budget so the budget doesn't get cut the following year. Private companies *save* or *invest* every penny."

"So you don't have any trouble with these other companies, do you?" Patrick asked.

"I see some of these snake-eating ex–Special Forces guys wandering around the base," Thompson said, "and they're all decked out in top-of-the-line outdoor clothing, brand-new weapons, the latest gear, and tattoos up the wazoo. A lot of those guys just want to look cool, so they spend a lot of their own money on the latest and greatest. My company is mostly made up of computer geeks, ex–law enforcement officers, private investigators, and security guards. They pretty much ignore us. We get into scrapes every now and then when my guys deny them access, but we get it straightened out eventually."

"Doesn't sound like a good way to go to war, Kris."

Thompson chuckled. "Hopefully, it's *not* war," he said. "War should be left to the professionals. I'd be just as happy *supporting* the professionals."

The base was immense and very much resembled a small Army post back in the United States. "This place doesn't look half bad," Jon

Masters commented. "I used to be sorry for you guys being sent all the way out here, but I've seen worse Army posts back in the States."

"We never had a regular Burger King or Mc-Donald's, like some of the superbases," Thompson said, "and if we did, the Iraqis probably would've shut it down anyway after they took over. Most of the troops here are still sleeping in CHUs because we never got around to building regular housing units. Of course there are no families here, so it'll never compare to any regular overseas base like Germany or England. But the weather is a bit nicer and the locals are less hostile . . . at least a *little* less."

"CHUs?"

"Containerized Housing Units. They're a little bit bigger than a commercial truck trailer. We can stack them if we need the room, but as the Army draws down we have more room, so they're all on ground level now. That's where we'll bunk your guys. They're nicer than they sound, believe me—linoleum floors, fully insulated, air conditioning, Wi-Fi, flat-screen TVs. Two CHUs share a 'wet CHU'—the latrine. Much nicer than latrine tents."

A few minutes later they came to a twelve-foot-tall fence composed of concrete Jersey walls and reinforced corrugated metal sheeting topped by coils of razor wire. A few feet behind this wall was another twelve-foot chain-link fence topped with razor wire, with heavily armed civilian K-9 security officers roving between the fences. Behind the chain-link fence was a fifty-foot clear area. It was all surrounding a plain boxy-looking

three-story building with a sloped roof, several
satellite dishes and antennae atop it, and absolutely no windows. There were thirty-foot-high
security towers near the corners of the building. "Is this the headquarters building . . . or the
prison?" Jon asked.

"Command and Control Center, or the Triple-C,"
Thompson said. "Some call it Fobbitville—home
of the 'fobbits,' the guys who never leave the
FOB, or the Forward Operating Base—but we
do fewer and fewer missions outside the wire
these days so most of us could be considered
fobbits. Right about in the geographic center
of the base—the bad guys would need a pretty
big mortar to reach it from outside the base,
although they'll get lucky and lob a homemade
pickup-launched rocket in here every couple
weeks or so."

"Every *couple weeks*?"

"'Fraid so, Doc," Thompson said. He then
gave Jon a mischievous smile and added, "But
that's what *you're* here to resolve . . . right?"

Security was tight entering the Triple-C, but
it was still far less than what McLanahan and
Masters had to put up with at Dreamland for so
many years. There were no military security officers at all; it was all run by Thompson's civilian
contractors. They were a bit more respectful of
Patrick after checking his identification—most
of them were former or retired military; and
three-star generals, even retired ones, earned
their respect—but still seemed to perform brisk,
sometimes rough pat-down searches with enthu-
siasm bordering on sadism. "Jeez, I think I need

to use the bathroom to see if those guys pulled off any important parts," Jon said as they passed through the last inspection station.

"Everyone gets the same treatment, which is why a lot of guys just end up bunking in here rather than going back to their CHUs," Thompson said. "I think they laid it on a bit thicker because the boss was here. Sorry about that." They emerged into a wide entryway, and Thompson pointed to the hallway to the left. "The west hallway is the way to the various departments that make up the Triple-C—operations, air traffic control, communications, data, transportation, security, intelligence, interservice and foreign liaisons, and so forth. Upstairs above them are the commanders' offices and briefing rooms. The east hallway is the DFAC, break rooms, and admin offices; above them are crash pads, bunk rooms, bathrooms, showers, et cetera. The north hallways have the computers, communications stuff, backup power generators, and physical plant. In the middle of it all is the command center itself, which we call the 'Tank.' Follow me." Their IDs were checked and they were searched one more time at the entrance to the Tank—by an Army sergeant this time, their first encounter with a military security officer—and they were admitted inside.

The Tank actually resembled the Battle Management Center at Elliott Air Force Base in Nevada. It was a large auditorium-like room with twelve large high-definition flat-panel screens surrounding an even larger screen in the back of the room, with a narrow stage for human briefers. On either side of the stage were rows of consoles for the various departments that fed data to the display screens and the commanders. Above them was an enclosed observation area for VIPs and specialists. In the middle of the room was a semicircular row of consoles for the department chiefs, and in the center of the semicircle were the seats and displays for the Iraqi brigade commander, which was empty, and his deputy, Colonel Jack Wilhelm.

Wilhelm was a large bearlike man resembling a much younger, dark-haired version of retired Army general Norman Schwarzkopf. He appeared to be chomping on a cigar, but it was actually the boom microphone from his headset set very close to his lips. Wilhelm was leaning forward on his console, snapping out orders and directions for what he wanted displayed on the screens.

Thompson maneuvered himself to get within Wilhelm's field of vision, and when Wilhelm noticed the security contractor, he gave him a querying scowl and slid a headset earcup away from his ear. "What?"

"The guys from Scion Aviation are here, Colonel," Thompson said.

"Bunk 'em down in CHUville and tell them I'll see them in the morning," Wilhelm said, rolling his eyes and setting the earcup back in place.

"They want to start tonight, sir."

Wilhelm moved the earcup again in exasperation. "What?"

"They want to start tonight, sir," Thompson repeated.

"Start what?"

"Start doing surveillance. They say they're

ready to go right now and want to brief you on their proposed flight plan."

"They do, do they?" Wilhelm spat. "Tell them we're scheduled to brief at oh-seven-hundred tomorrow morning, Thompson. Bunk 'em down and—"

"If you have a few minutes to spare, Colonel," Patrick said, stepping up beside Thompson, "we'd like to brief you now and get under way."

Wilhelm turned in his seat and scowled at the newcomers and their interruption . . . and then blanched slightly when he recognized Patrick McLanahan. He got to his feet slowly, his eyes locked on Patrick's as if sizing him up for a fight. He turned slightly to the technician seated beside him, but his eyes never left Patrick's. "Get Weatherly in here," he said, "and have him supervise the log air departures and take the scout patrol briefing. I'll be back in a few." He slipped the headset off, then extended his hand. "General McLanahan, Jack Wilhelm. Pleasure to meet you."

Patrick shook his hand. "Same, Colonel."

"I didn't know you'd be on board that flight, General, or I never would have allowed a VFR pattern."

"It was important we did it, Colonel—it told us a lot. Can we brief you and your staff on our first mission?"

"I assumed you'd want the rest of the afternoon and evening to rest up and get organized," Wilhelm said. "I wanted to show you around the base, show you the Triple-C and the ops center here, meet the staff, get a good meal—"

"We'll have plenty of time for that while

we're here, Colonel," Patrick said, "but we ran into some hostile fire on the way in, and I think the sooner we get started, the better."

"Hostile fire?" Wilhelm looked at Thompson. "What's he talking about, Thompson? I wasn't briefed."

"We're ready to brief you on it right now, Colonel," Patrick said. "And then I'd like to plan an orientation and calibration flight for tonight to get started on finding the origins of that ground fire."

"Excuse me, General," Wilhelm said, "but your operations have to be carefully studied by the staff and then deconflicted with every department here in the Triple-C. That's going to take a lot longer than a few hours."

"We sent you our ops plan and a copy of the contract from the Air Force Civil Augmentation Agency a week ago, Colonel. Your staff should have had plenty of time to study it."

"I'm confident they have, General, but my briefing with the staff is scheduled for oh-five-thirty hours tomorrow morning," Wilhelm said. "You and I were supposed to meet at oh-seven-hundred to discuss it. I thought that was the plan."

"It *was* the plan, Colonel, but now I'd like to launch our first mission tonight, before our other planes arrive."

"Other planes? I thought we were just getting the one."

"As soon as we took hostile fire coming in here, I requested and received authorization from my company to bring in a second operations aircraft with a few more specialized payloads and equipment," Patrick said. "It'll be another Loser-size aircraft—"

" 'Loser'?"

"Sorry. Nickname for our plane. I'll need a hangar for it and bunks for twenty-five additional personnel. They'll be here in about twenty hours. When it arrives I'll need—"

"Excuse me, sir," Wilhelm interrupted. "May I have a word with you?" He motioned to a front corner of the Tank, indicating Patrick should follow him; a young Air Force lieutenant wisely evacuated his nearby console when he saw the colonel's warning glare as they approached.

Just as they reached the console so they could have their private chat, Patrick held up a finger, then reached up to touch a tiny button on an all but invisible earset in his left ear canal. Wilhelm's eyes bugged in surprise. "Is that a wireless earpiece for a *cell phone*?" he asked.

Patrick nodded. "Are cell phones prohibited in here, Colonel? I can take it outside—"

"They're . . . they're supposed to be jammed so no one can receive or make calls on them—defense against remotely detonated IEDs. And the nearest cell tower is six miles away."

"It's a special unit—encrypted, secure, jam-resistant, pretty powerful for its size," Patrick said. "We'll look at upgrading your jammers, or replace them with directional finders that will pinpoint the location of both sides of a conversation." Wilhelm blinked in confusion. "So it's okay if I take this?" Wilhelm was too stunned to respond, so Patrick nodded in thanks and touched the "call" button. "Hi, Dave," he said. "Yeah . . . yeah, have him make the call. You were right. Thanks." He touched the earset again to terminate the call. "Sorry for the interruption, Colonel. Do you have a question for me?"

Wilhelm quickly cleared the confusion out of his head, then put his fists on his hips and leaned toward Patrick. "Yes, sir, I do: Who in *hell* do you think you are?" Wilhelm said in a low, muted, growling voice. He towered over McLanahan, jutting out his chin as if daring anyone to try to hit it and impaling him with a severe direct glare. "This is *my* command center. No one gives *me* orders in here, not even the hajji who supposedly commands this fucking base. And nothing comes within a hundred miles of here unless they get my approval and clearance first, even a retired three-star. Now that you're here you can stay, but I guarantee the next sonofabitch who doesn't get my permission to enter will get kicked off this base so fast and so hard he'll be looking for his ass in the Persian Gulf. Do you read me, General?"

"Yes, Colonel, I do," Patrick said. He did not look away, and the two men locked eyes. "Are you finished, Colonel?"

"Don't give me any attitude, McLanahan," Wilhelm said. "I've read your contract, and I've dealt with thousands of you civilian augmentees or contractors or whatever the hell you call yourselves now. You may be high-tech, but as far as I'm concerned, you're still just one of the cooks and bottle washers around here.

"With all due respect, General, this is a warning: while you're in my sector, you report to *me*; you get out of line, you get hell from *me*; you violate my orders, and I will *personally* stuff

your balls down your throat." He paused for a
moment, then asked, "You have something you
want to say to me now, sir?"

"Yes, Colonel." Patrick gave Wilhelm a smile
that nearly sent the Army colonel into a flying
rage, then went on: "You have a phone call from
division headquarters waiting for you. I suggest
you take it." Wilhelm turned and saw the communications shift duty officer trotting toward
him.

He looked at McLanahan's smile, gave him a
glare, then went over to the nearby console, put
on a headset, and logged himself in. "Wilhelm.
What?"

"Stand by for division, sir," the communications technician said. Wilhelm looked at
McLanahan in surprise. A moment later: "Jack?
Connolly here." Charles Connolly was the two-
star Army general based at Fort Lewis, Washington, who commanded the division assigned to
northern Iraq.

"Yes, sir?"

"Sorry, Jack, but I just heard about it myself a
few minutes ago and thought I'd better call you
myself," Connolly said. "That contractor assigned
to run aerial surveillance missions on the Iraq-
Turkish border in your sector? There's a VIP on
board: Patrick McLanahan."

"I'm speaking to him right now, sir," Wilhelm
said.

"He's there *already*? Shit. Sorry about that,
Jack, but that guy has a reputation for just showing up and doing whatever the hell he pleases."

"That's not going to happen around here, sir."

"Listen, Jack, treat this guy with kid gloves until we figure out exactly what kind of horse-power he's got behind him," Connolly said. "He's a civilian and a contractor, yes, but Corps tells me he works for some heavy hitters that could very quickly make some career-altering phone calls if you get my drift."

"He just informed me that he's bringing an-other plane out here. Twenty-five more person-nel! I'm trying to draw *down* this base, sir, not pack more civvies in here."

"Yeah, I was told that, too," Connolly said, his morose tone making it obvious that he wasn't in the loop any more than the regimental executive officer was. "Listen, Jack, if he seriously violates one of your directives, I'll back you one hundred percent if you want him off your base and out of your hair. But he *is* Patrick fucking McLana-han, and he *is* a retired three-banger. Corps says give him enough rope and he'll eventually hang himself—he's done it before, which is why he's not in uniform anymore."

"I still don't like it, sir."

"Well, handle it any way you want, Jack," the division commander said, "but my advice is: put up with the guy for now, be nice to him, and don't piss him off. If you don't, and it turns out the guy has major juice behind him, we'll both be out on our ears.

"Just keep focused on the job, Jack," Con-nolly went on. "Our job is to transition that theater from a military to a civilian peacekeep-ing operation. Contractors like McLanahan will be the ones hanging their asses on the line.

Your job is to bring your troops home safely and honorably—and to make me look good in the process, of course."

Judging by the tone of his voice, Wilhelm thought, he wasn't totally joking. "Roger that, sir."

"Anything else for me?"

"Negative, sir."

"Very good. Press on. Division out."

Wilhelm broke the connection, then looked at McLanahan talking on his cellular earset again. If he had the technology to defeat all of their cellular jammers—the ones set up to defeat remote-controlled Improvised Explosive Device detonators—he had to have some first-class engineers and money behind him.

On the console, Wilhelm spoke: "Duty Officer, get the operations staff together right now in the main briefing room to discuss the Scion surveillance plan."

"Yes, sir."

McLanahan ended his conversation when Wilhelm took off his headset and approached him. "How did you know I was going to get a call from division, McLanahan?"

"Lucky guess."

Wilhelm scowled at that response. "Sure," he said, shaking his head dismissively. "Whatever. The staff will brief us right away. Follow me." Wilhelm led Patrick and Jon out of the Tank and upstairs to the main briefing room, a glassed-in soundproof meeting room that overlooked the consoles and center computer screens in the Tank. One by one, staff officers filed in with briefing notes and thumb drives containing their

PowerPoint presentations. They did not waste time greeting the two officers already in the room.

Wilhelm took a bottle of water from a small refrigerator in the corner, then sat down in a chair in front of the windows overlooking the Tank. "So, General, tell me about this Scion Aviation International outfit you work for," he said as they waited for the others to arrive and get ready.

"Not much to tell," Patrick said. He got a bottle of water for Jon and himself but did not sit down. "Formed a little over a year ago by—"

"About the same time you retired because of the bum ticker?" Wilhelm asked. Patrick did not respond. "How are you doing with that?"

"Fine."

"There was some scuttlebutt about President Gardner wanting to prosecute you for some of the things that happened in Iran."

"I don't know anything about that."

"Right. You knew I was going to get a secure satellite call from my headquarters ten thousand miles away, but you don't know if you're the target of a White House and Justice Department investigation." Patrick said nothing. "And you wouldn't know anything about the rumors that *you* were involved in the death of Leonid Zevitin, that it wasn't a skiing accident?"

"I'm not here to respond to crazy rumors."

"Of course not," Wilhelm said wryly. "So. The money must be pretty good to keep you in the game traveling all over the world with a friggin' heart condition. Most guys would be sitting by the pool in Florida collecting their pension money and hitting on divorcées."

"The heart is fine as long as I'm not traveling in space."

"Right. So, how is the money in this business of yours? I understand the mercenary business is booming." Wilhelm put on a feigned panicked expression as if he was afraid he had insulted the retired three-star general. "Oh my, I'm sorry, General. Do you prefer to call it 'private military company' or 'security consultant' or what?"

"I don't give a rat's ass what you want to call it, Colonel," Patrick said. A few of the field-grade officers getting ready for their briefing glanced over at their boss—some with humor in their expressions, others with fear.

Wilhelm gave a slight smile, pleased that he'd gotten a rise out of his VIP visitor. "Or is it just another name for the 'Night Stalkers'? That's the name of the outfit you're rumored to have been part of a few years back, right? I remember something about those Libyan raids, am I right? The first time you got tossed out of the Air Force?" Patrick didn't respond, which elicited another smile from Wilhelm. "Well, I think 'Scion' sounds a lot better than 'Night Stalkers' myself. More like a *real* security consultant outfit rather than a goofy, kids' TV cartoon superhero show." No response. "So how *is* the money, General?"

"I believe you know exactly how much the contract is for, Colonel," Patrick said. "It's not classified."

"Yeah, yeah"—Wilhelm mugged—"now I remember: one year, with an option for three more years, for a whopping ninety-four million dollars a year! I believe it's the largest single contract in the theater unless your name is Kellogg, Brand and Root, Halliburton, or Blackwater. But what I meant was, General, what's *your* slice? If I don't get a star in the next couple years, I might pull the plug, and if the money's right, maybe you can use a grunt like me in Scion Aviation International. How about it, General, sir?"

"I don't know, Colonel," Patrick said expressionlessly. "I mean, what is it you *do* around here other than act like a big fucking blowhard?"

Wilhelm's face turned into a mask of rage, and he shot to his feet, nearly popping the water bottle in his fist apart in anger. He stepped within inches of Patrick, face-to-face once again. When Patrick neither tried to push him nor backed away, Wilhelm's expression changed from fury to a crocodile's smile.

"Good one, General," he said, nodding. He lowered his voice. "What I'll be doing from here on out, General, is making sure you're doing what you're contracted to do—nothing more, nothing less. You slip up, just a red cunt hair's worth, and I'll see to it that your sweet rich-bitch contract is canceled. I have a feeling you won't be around very long. And if you put any of my men in any danger, I'll solve your little heart problem by ripping it out of your chest and stuffing it down your throat." He half turned to the others in the room. "Is my damned briefing ready yet, Weatherly?"

"We're ready, sir," one of the officers responded immediately. Wilhelm gave Patrick another sneer, then stormed off to his seat in the front row. Several field and company-grade officers were lined up to one side, ready to speak.

"Good afternoon, sirs. My name is Lieutenant-Colonel Mark Weatherly, and I'm the regimental executive officer. This briefing is classified Secret, NOFORN, sensitive sources and methods involved, and the room is secure. This briefing will cover the findings of the regimental staff's study of the surveillance plan presented by Scion Aviation International for—"

"Yeah, yeah, Weatherly, we're not getting any younger here," Wilhelm interrupted. "The good general here doesn't need the whole Air War College dog and pony routine. Let's cut to the chase."

"Yes, sir," the operations officer said. He quickly called up the proper PowerPoint slide. "The finding, sir, is that we're just not that familiar with the technology being employed by Scion to know how effective it'll be."

"They spelled it out clearly enough, didn't they, Weatherly?"

"Yes, sir, but . . . frankly, sir, we don't believe it," Weatherly said, nervously glancing at McLanahan. "*One aircraft* to patrol over twelve thousand square miles of ground and over one hundred thousand cubic miles of airspace? It would take two Global Hawks to do it—and Global Hawks can't scan the sky, at least not yet. And that's at the widest-scale MTI surveillance mode. Scion is proposing to have *half-meter* image resolution available *at all times* over the *entire* patrol area . . . with *one aircraft*? It can't be done."

"General?" Wilhelm asked with a slight smirk on his face. "Care to respond?" Turning to his staff officers, he interrupted himself by saying, "Oh, sorry, ladies and gents, this is retired Lieutenant-General Patrick McLanahan, the veep of Scion Aviation. Maybe you've heard of him?" The dumbfounded expressions and dropping jaws of the others in the room showed that they certainly had. "He decided to surprise us with his august presence today. General, my operations staff. The floor is yours."

"Thank you, Colonel," Patrick said, getting to his feet and giving Wilhelm an exasperated look. "I look forward to working with you on this project, guys. I could explain the technology that Dr. Jonathan Masters here has developed to improve the resolution and range of ground and air target surveillance sensors, but I think it would be better to show you. Clear the airspace for us tonight and we'll show you what we can do."

"I don't think that's possible, General, because of an op we just found out about for tonight." Wilhelm turned to a very young, very nervous-looking captain. "Cotter?"

The captain took a furtive step forward. "Captain Kelvin Cotter, sir, director of air traffic management. We just learned about a planned Iraqi operation that they requested backup for, sir. They're going to a village north of Zahuk to do a raid on a suspected Kurdish bomb-making and underground smuggling operation—supposedly a pretty big tunnel complex connecting several villages and running under the border. They've requested persistent surveillance support: a dedicated Global Hawk, Reapers, Predators, Strykers, the works, plus Air Force, Marine, and Army close air and artillery support. The spectrum is saturated. We . . . excuse me, sir, but we just don't know how your sensors will interact with everyone else."

"Then pull all the other UAVs out and let us do all the support," Jon Masters said.

"*What*?" Wilhelm thundered.

"I said, don't waste all that gas and flying time on all those UAVs and let us do all the surveillance support," Jon said. "We've got three times the image resolution of Global Hawk, five times the electro-optical sensor resolution, and we can give you better and faster aerial command and control for the ground support guys. We can do communications relay, act as a local area network router for a thousand terminals—"

"*A thousand terminals*?" someone exclaimed.

"At over three times the speed of Link sixteen—which isn't that hard to beat anyway," Jon said. "Listen, guys, I hate to break it to you, but you've been using last-generation stuff out here almost from day one. Block Ten Global Hawks? Some of you probably weren't even *in* the military when they started using those dinosaurs! Predator? You're still using low-light TV? Who uses LLTV anymore . . . Fred Flintstone?"

"How do you propose to tie in all those different aircraft into your communications network *and* the Tank . . . by *tonight*?" Wilhelm asked. "It takes days to link and verify an asset."

"I said, Colonel, you're using outdated technology—of *course* it takes that long for stuff made ten years ago or more," Jon responded. "It's all plug-and-play nowadays in the rest of civilized society. You just power up your planes, get 'em within range of our plane, turn on the equipment, and it's done. We can do it on the ground, or if the planes aren't colocated we can do it in-flight."

"Sorry, kids, but I have to see that before I'll believe it," Wilhelm said. He turned to another officer. "Harrison? Know anything about what they're talking about?"

An attractive red-haired woman stepped forward, dodging around Cotter in his hasty retreat. "Yes, Colonel, I've read about instant high-speed broadband networking for remotely piloted aircraft and their sensors, but I've never seen it done." She looked over at Patrick, then quickly stepped off the dais and extended a hand. Patrick stood and allowed his hand to be pumped enthusiastically. "Margaret Harrison, sir, formerly Air Force Third Special Operations Squadron ops officer. I'm a contractor directing UAV operations here in Nahla. It's a real pleasure to meet you, sir, a *real* pleasure. You are the reason I joined the Air Force, sir. You are a genuine—"

"Let the man go and let's finish this damned briefing, Harrison," Wilhelm interrupted. The woman's smile disappeared, and she scooted back to her place on the dais. "General, I am not going to risk sacrificing the mission by using unknown and unproven technology."

"Colonel—"

"General, my AOR is all of Dahuk province plus half of Ninawa and Irbil provinces," Wilhelm argued. "I'm also tasked to support operations in all of northern Iraq. The Zahuk operation is just one of about eight offensives that I've got to keep track of weekly, plus another six minor operations and dozens of incidents that occur daily. You want to put the lives of a thousand Iraqi and

American soldiers and dozens of aircraft and ground vehicles in jeopardy just to satisfy your rich contract, and I'm not going to allow that. Cotter, when's the next open window?"

"The Zahuk raid's air support window termi-nates in twelve hours, so three P.M. local time."

"Then that's when you can do your test, Gen-eral," Wilhelm said. "You can get a full night's sleep. Harrison, what UAVs can you let the gen-eral play with?"

"The Zahuk operation is using our division's dedicated Global Hawk and all but one of the regiment's Reapers and Predators, sir, and they won't be serviced and ready to fly for at least twelve hours after they land. I might be able to make a Global Hawk available from down south."

"See to it. Cotter, reserve the airspace for how-ever long they need for their setup." Wilhelm turned to the security contractor. "Thompson, take the general and his party to support services and get them bedded down."

"Yes, Colonel."

Wilhelm got to his feet and turned to McLan-ahan. "General, you can quiz the staff here on anything else you need. Put in your requests for aircraft service to the flight line guys ASAP. I'll see you for chow tonight." He started for the door.

"Sorry, Colonel, but I'm afraid we'll be busy," Patrick said. "But thanks for the invite."

Wilhelm stopped and turned. "How very in-dustrious you 'consultants' are, General," he said flatly. "You will be missed, I'm sure." Weatherly called the room to attention as Wilhelm strode out the door.

As if released from invisible chains, all of the staff members hurried over to Patrick to introduce or reintroduce themselves. "We can't believe you're *here*, of all godforsaken places, sir," Weatherly said after shaking hands.

"We all assumed you'd died or had a stroke or something when you suddenly disappeared off Armstrong Space Station," Cotter said.

"Not me—I thought President Gardner secretly sent an FBI hit squad up on the Space Shuttle to off you," Harrison said.

"Real nice, Mugs."

"It's Margaret, you dillweed," Harrison snapped with a smile. To McLanahan again: "Is it true, sir—did you really disregard orders from the president of the United States to bomb that Russian base in Iran?"

"I can't talk about it," Patrick said.

"But you *did* capture that Russian base in Siberia after the American holocaust and use it to attack those Russian missile sites, right, sir?" Reese Flippin, an impossibly thin, impossibly young-looking private contractor with a heavy southern accent and protruding teeth asked. "And the Russians shot nuke missiles at that base, and you *survived* it? Hot *damn* . . . !" And as the others laughed, the accent completely disappeared, even the teeth seemed to recede to normal positions, and Flippin added, "I mean, *outstanding*, sir, quite outstanding." The laughter grew even louder.

Patrick noticed a young woman in a desert

gray flight suit and gray flying boots gathering up her laptop computer and notes, staying separate from the others but watching with amusement. She had short dark hair, dark magnetic brown eyes, and a mischievous dimple that appeared and disappeared. She looked somewhat familiar, as many Air Force officers and aviators did to Patrick. Wilhelm hadn't introduced her. "I'm sorry," he said, talking around the others crowded around him but suddenly not caring. "We haven't met. I'm—"

"Everyone knows General Patrick McLanahan," the woman said. Patrick noticed with surprise that she was a lieutenant colonel and wore command pilot's wings, but there were no other patches or unit designations on her flight suit, just vacant squares of Velcro. She extended a hand. "Gia Cazzotto. And actually, we have met."

"We have?" Jerk, he admonished himself, how could you forget *her*? "I'm sorry, I don't remember."

"I was with the One-Eleventh Bomb Squadron."

"Oh," was all Patrick could say. The One-Eleventh Bomb Squadron was the Nevada Air National Guard B-1B Lancer heavy bomber unit that Patrick had deactivated, then reconstituted as the First Air Battle Wing at Battle Mountain Air Reserve Base in Nevada—and since Patrick didn't remember her, and he had handpicked each and every member of the Air Battle Force, it was quickly obvious to him that she hadn't made the cut. "Where did you go after . . . after . . ."

"After you closed down the guard unit? It's

okay to say it, sir," Cazzotto said. "I actually did okay—maybe closing the unit was a blessing in disguise. I went back to school, got my master's degree in engineering, then got a position at Plant Forty-two, flying the Vampires headed for Battle Mountain."

"Well, thank you for that," Patrick said. "We couldn't have done it without you." Air Force Plant 42 was one of several federally owned but contractor-occupied manufacturing facilities. Located in Palmdale, California, Plant 42 was famous for building aircraft such as Lockheed's B-1 bomber, Northrop's B-2 Spirit stealth bomber, Lockheed's SR-71 Blackbird and F-117 Nighthawk stealth fighter, and the Space Shuttle.

After the manufacturing lines shut down, the plants often did modification work to existing airframes as well as research and design work on new projects. The Air Battle Force's B-1 bomber, renamed the EB-1C "Vampire," was one of the most complex redesign projects ever done at Plant 42, adding mission-adaptive technology, more powerful engines, laser radar, advanced computers and targeting systems, and the capability of employing a wide array of weapons, including air-launched antiballistic missiles and antisatellite missiles. It eventually became a pilotless aircraft with even better performance.

"And you're still flying B-1s, Colonel?" Patrick asked.

"Yes, sir," Gia replied. "After the American holocaust, they brought a dozen Bones out of AMARC, and we refurbished them." AMARC, or the Aircraft Maintenance and Regeneration

Center—known to all as the "Boneyard"—was the vast complex at Davis-Monthan Air Force Base near Tucson, Arizona, where thousands of aircraft were taken to be stored and cannibalized for spare parts. "They're not quite Vampires, but they can do a lot of the stuff you guys did."

"Are you flying out of Nahla, Colonel?" Patrick asked. "I didn't know they had B-1s here."

"Boxer is commander of the Seventh Air Expeditionary Squadron," Kris Thompson explained. "They're based in various places—Bahrain, United Arab Emirates, Kuwait, Diego Garcia—and stand by for missions as coalition forces in theater need them. She's here because of the Iraqi operation tonight—we'll have her B-1s standing by just in case."

Patrick nodded, then smiled. "'Boxer'? Your call sign?"

"My great-grandfather came into the U.S. at Ellis Island," Gia explained. "Cazzotto was not his real last name—it was Inturrigardia—what's so hard about that?—but the immigration people couldn't pronounce it. But they heard the other kids calling him *cazzotto*—which means 'a hard punch'—and they gave him that name. We don't know if he was getting beat up all the time or if he was the one doing the punching."

"I've seen her on the punching bag at the gym; she deserves that call sign," Kris said.

"I see," Patrick said, smiling at Gia. She smiled back, their eyes locking . . .

. . . which gave the others around them an opening. "When can we see this plane of yours, sir?" Harrison asked.

"Can it really do everything you said . . . ?"

"Are you taking over for all the military units in Iraq . . . ?"

"All right, boys and girls, all right, we have work to do," Kris Thompson interjected, holding up his hands to stop the fast-moving questions being fired at Patrick. "You'll have time to pester the general later." They all jostled to shake Patrick's hand again, then gathered up their thumb drives and papers and exited the briefing room.

Gia was the last to depart. She shook Patrick's hand, keeping it an extra moment in her own. "Very nice to meet you, sir," she said.

"Same here, Colonel."

"I prefer Gia."

"Okay, Gia." He was still clasping her hand when she said that, and he felt an instantaneous rush of warmth in it—or was his own hand suddenly sweating? "Not Boxer?"

"You don't get to pick your own call signs, do you, sir?"

"Call me Patrick. And bomber guys didn't have call signs when I was in."

"I remember my old ops officer at the One-Eleventh had some choice names for you," she said, and then smiled and headed off.

Kris Thompson was grinning at Patrick. "She's cute, in a Murphy Brown kind of way, eh?"

"Yes. And wipe that grin off your face."

"If it makes you uncomfortable, sure." He kept on grinning. "We don't know that much about her. We hear her on the radios once in a while, so she still flies. She comes in to run missions occasionally, like tonight, and then she's off again to another command center. She rarely stays for longer than a day."

Patrick felt an unexpected pang of disappointment, then quickly shook the uncomfortable feeling aside. Where did *that* come from . . . ? "The B-1s are great planes," he said. "I hope they resurrect more of them from AMARC."

"The grunts love the Bones. They can get to the fight as fast as a fighter; loiter for long periods of time like a Predator or Global Hawk, even without air refueling; they have improved sensors and optics and can pass a lot of data to us and other planes; and they have as much precision-guided payload as a flight of F/A-18s." Thompson noted the quiet, slightly wistful expression on Patrick's face and decided to change the subject. "You're a real inspiration to those kids, General," he said. "That's the most excited I've *ever* seen them since I've been here."

"Thanks. It's infectious—I feel energized, too. And call me Patrick, okay?"

"Can't guarantee I will all the time, Patrick, but I'll try. And I'm Kris. Let's get you settled."

"Can't. Jon and I have a lot of work to do before tomorrow afternoon's test flight. The staff will set up quarters for us, but I'll probably take naps in the plane."

"Same here," Jon added. "Certainly wouldn't be the first time."

"We'll have support services bring meals out to the plane, then."

"Good. Kris, I'd like clearance to be in the Tank when the operation at Zahuk begins."

"The colonel doesn't usually allow off-duty personnel to be in the Tank during an operation, especially one this big," Kris said, "but I'm sure he'll let you listen in from up here."

"That'll be fine."

"I'm not sure if I want to get any closer than that to Wilhelm anyway," Jon said. "I thought for sure he was going to punch your lights out, Muck . . . *twice*."

"But he didn't, which means he *does* have some common sense," Patrick said. "Maybe I can work with him. We'll see."

CHAPTER 3

*In the one hand he is carrying a stone, while he shows
the bread in the other.*
—*Titus Maccius Plautus, 254–184 B.C.*

ALLIED AIR BASE NAHLA, IRAQ

Thompson took Patrick and Jon back out to
the hangar, where the crew chiefs and support crew were unloading bags and servicing the
Loser. This gave Thompson a chance to look the
plane over carefully. "This thing is beautiful," he
remarked. "Looks like a stealth bomber. I thought
you were just going to do reconnaissance."

"That's what we were hired to do," Patrick
said.

"But this *is* a bomber?"

"*Was* a bomber."

Thompson noticed technicians working under
the aircraft's belly and saw a large opening. "Is
that a bomb bay? This thing still has a *bomb bay*?"

"That's a module access hatch," Jon Masters
said. "We don't drop anything from it—we load
and unload modules through them."

"The Loser had two bomb bays, similar to the B-2 stealth bomber except much bigger," Patrick explained. "We combined the two bays into one big bay but retained both lower doors. We then split the bay into two decks. We're able to move mission modules around and between decks and maneuver each module either up or down through the module hatches, all by remote control."

"A flying-wing reconnaissance plane?"

"The flying-wing design works well as a long-range multimission plane," Jon Masters said. "Airliners in the future will be flying wings."

"Scion's planes are designed to be multifunction platforms; we plug in different mission modules to perform different tasks," Patrick said. "This plane can be a tanker, cargo plane, do electronic warfare, photoreconnaissance, communications relay, command-and-control—even several of these functions at the same time.

"Right now we're configured for ground moving-target indication, ground target identification and tracking, air surveillance, datalink, and command-and-control," Patrick went on. "But if we brought different modules, we can load them up and perform different missions. Tomorrow we'll have the air surveillance emitters up top."

He then stepped underneath the plane and showed Thompson a large opening in the belly. "Through here, we'll suspend the ground target emitter module for ground target identification and tracking. All of the modules are 'plug-and-play' through the ship's digital communications suite, which uploads the data via satellite to the end users. Other modules we've installed are for the very-wide-area networking, threat detection and response, and self-protection."

" 'Threat *response*'? You mean, *attack*?"

"I can't really get into that system because it's not part of the contract and it's still experimental," Patrick said, "but we'd like to do a little more to the bad guys than just decoy or jam their weapons."

Patrick took Kris up the ladder and into the Loser. The cockpit looked roomy and comfortable. The instrument panel was composed of five wide monitors with a few normal "steam" gauges tucked away almost out of sight. "Pretty nice flight deck."

"Aircraft commander and mission commander up front as usual," Patrick said. He put a hand on the side-facing seat behind the copilot's seat. "We have a flight engineer here who monitors all of the ship's systems and the mission modules."

Kris motioned to a counter behind the boarding ladder. "You even have a galley in here!"

"Flushing head, too; that comes in handy on these long flights," Jon said.

They ducked through a small hatch in the rear of the cockpit, walked down a short narrow passageway, and emerged into an area fairly stuffed with cargo containers of all sizes, leaving only narrow aisles to walk around. "I thought you contractors rode around in planes with bedrooms and gold-plated faucets," Kris quipped.

"I've never even *seen* a gold faucet, let alone ride in a plane with them," Patrick said. "No, every square foot and every pound has to count." He pointed to a half cargo module, the thinnest of all the ones installed in the plane that Kris could see. "That's our baggage and personal items container. Each of the twenty-five persons we brought on this flight was limited to twenty pounds of luggage, and that included their laptops. Needless to say we'll be visiting your commissary a lot on this deployment."

They had to maneuver around a large gray-colored torpedo-shaped object that took up a great deal of the middle of the plane. "This must be the antenna that'll stick out the top, I presume?" Kris asked.

"That's it," Patrick said. "It's a laser radar module. Range is classified, but we can see well into space and it's powerful enough to even look underwater. The electronically scanned laser emitters 'draw' pictures of everything they see millions of times a second with resolution three times better than Global Hawk. There's another one down below that's set up to scan for ground targets."

"Kind of looks like a missile," Kris observed. "And that opening down below still looks to me like a bomb bay." He looked at Patrick with a curious expression. " 'Threat response,' eh? Maybe you're not out of the strategic bomber business after all, General?"

"Our contract calls for observing and reporting. Like the colonel said: no more, no less."

"Yeah, right, General—and when I open a potato chip bag, I *can* eat only one," Kris quipped. He looked around. "I don't see any passenger seats on this thing. Did you take them out already?"

"If you're going to report us to the FAA for

not having approved seats and seat belts for each occupant—yes, Kris, we already took them out," Patrick said.

"Jeez, you're really blowing the image of you aviation contractors all to hell, sir," Kris said, shaking his head. "I always thought you guys lived large."

"Sorry to burst your bubble. There are two extra seats in the cockpit and some engineer seats at some of the modules topside and below-decks that we share depending on who needs some *real* rest, but everyone brings sleeping bags and foam mats and stretches out wherever. I prefer the luggage cargo container myself—quiet and very well padded."

"I think our containerized quarters will seem luxurious compared to this, sir," Kris said. "You don't have any radar operators on board?"

"The only way we can fit all this stuff inside the plane is to leave the radar operators, weapons controllers, and battle staff officers on the ground and datalink the info to them," Patrick said. "But that's the easy part. We can tie into anyone's network pretty quickly, and we can send the data to just about anyone in the world—from the White House all the way down to a commando in a spider hole—via a multitude of methods. I'll show you tonight in the briefing room."

With technicians swarming all around the plane like ants, Thompson soon felt he was in the way. "I'm headed back to the Tank, Patrick," he said. "Holler if you need anything."

He didn't see Patrick again until nine P.M. that evening. Thompson found him and Jon Masters in the conference room overlooking the Tank sitting in front of two large wide-screen laptop computers. The screens were divided into many different windows, most dark but some displaying video images. He took a closer look and was surprised to see what appeared to be a video feed from an aerial platform. "Where's that image coming from, sir?" he asked.

"That's Kelly Two-Two, a Reaper on its way to Zahuk," Patrick replied.

Thompson looked at the laptops and realized that they didn't have any data connections attached—the only cords coming into them were from AC adapters. "How did you get the feed? You're not hooked up to our data stream, are you?"

"We've got the Loser fired up and scanning for datalinks," Jon said. "When it picks up a datalink, it splices itself into the feed."

"Your 'Wi-Fi hot spot' thingy, right?"

"Exactly."

"And you got a wireless connection into here?"

"Yep."

"How? We prohibit wireless networking inside the Triple-C, and the Tank is supposed to be shielded."

Jon looked over at Patrick, who nodded his permission to explain. "Turned one way and a shield can be used to block things," Jon said. "Turn it the other way and a shield can be used to *collect* things."

"Huh?"

"It's complicated and not always reliable, but we can usually penetrate most metallic shields," Jon said. "Sometimes we can even get the shield-

ing to act as an antenna for us. Active electromagnetic shields are tougher to penetrate, but
you rely on the metal walls of the Tank and reinforced concrete and physical distance to shield
the Triple-C. All that works in our favor."

"You'll have to explain to my physical security guys how you did this."

"Of course. We can help you fix it, too."

"Hack into our system and then charge us to
plug the leak, General?" Thompson asked, only
partially sarcastically. "Hell of a way to make a
living."

"My son grows out of his shoes every six
months, Kris," Patrick said with a wink.

"I'll submit it," Thompson said. He didn't feel
comfortable knowing it was apparently so easy
to tap into their datalinks. "Who else are you
plugged into?"

Jon looked over at Patrick again, who nodded
assent. "Just about the whole operation," Jon
said. "We've channelized the entire command
VHF and UHF radio net and the intercom here in
the Triple-C, locked into the wide-area network
created by the Stryker Combat Team, and we're
receiving the IMs between the tactical, brigade,
and theater controllers."

"IMs?"

"Instant messages," Patrick said. "The easi-
est way for controllers to pass information like
target coordinates or imagery analysis to others
who are on the same network but can't exchange
datalinks is by plain old instant messages."

"Like my daughter texting messages to her
friends on her computer or cell phone?"

"Exactly," Patrick said. He expanded a window,

and Thompson saw a stream of chat messages—
combat controllers describing a target area, sending geographic coordinates, and even passing
along jokes and commenting on a ball game.
"Sometimes the simplest routines are the best."

"Cool." When the IM window was moved so
Kris could see it, it uncovered another window
underneath it, and he was surprised . . . to see
himself looking over Patrick's shoulder! "Hey!" he
exclaimed. "You tapped into my video security
system?"

"We weren't *trying* to do that—it just happened," Jon said, grinning. Thompson didn't
look amused. "No joke, Kris. Our system searches
for all the remote networks to plug into, and it
found this one as well. It's just the video system,
although we did happen across some other
security-related networks and declined access."

"I'd appreciate it if you'd decline access on all
of them, General," Thompson said stonily. Patrick nodded to Jon, who entered some instructions. The video feed disappeared. "That was not
wise, General. If there's a security problem after
this, I'll have to look at you as a probable source
of the breach."

"Understood," Patrick said. He turned to look
at the security chief. "But there obviously *is*
some sort of breach, because there is someone
on Nahla Air Base shooting at friendly aircraft.
Since we've been hired to enhance security
around this whole sector, I can argue that I can
legally access something like video feeds."

Thompson peered concernedly at McLanahan, his mouth rigid. After a few rather chilly
moments he said, "The colonel said you were the

kind of guy who'd rather ask forgiveness than ask permission."

"I get more done that way, Kris," Patrick said matter-of-factly. But a moment later, he got to his feet and faced Thompson directly. "I apologize for that, Kris," he said. "I didn't mean to sound so flippant about security matters. It's your job and your responsibility. I'll notify you the next time we stray across something like that again, and I'll get your permission before I access it."

Thompson realized that if Patrick had hacked into the security system once, he could just as easily do it again, with or without his permission. "Thank you, sir, but frankly I don't believe that."

"I'm serious, Kris. You tell me to shut it down, and it's done . . . period."

What if he didn't shut it down? Thompson asked himself. What recourse did he have against a private contractor? He vowed to research the answer to that question right away. "I'm not going to argue about it, sir," Kris said. "But you *are* here to assist me in securing this sector, so you can tie back in if you think it's essential to your job. Just tell me when you're back in, why, and what you've found."

"Done. Thank you."

"What other security-related areas were you able to access?"

"Colonel Jaffar's internal security network."

A cold sweat popped out under Kris's collar. "Internal security? He doesn't have an internal security staff. You mean his personal bodyguards?"

"That may be what you think it is, Kris, but it

looks to me like he's got an entire shadow J-staff—operations, intelligence, logistics, personnel, training, *and* security," Jon said. "They do everything in Arabic, and there's no foreigners on it that we can see."

"That means that he has his men in charge of the entire regiment's departments and command structure," Patrick summarized, "so he's kept abreast of everything *you* do, *plus* he's got an entire J-staff operating in the background, paralleling the regimental staff functions." He turned to Kris and added, "So if, for example, something were to happen to the Triple-C . . ."

"He'd be able to take over right away and continue operations himself," Kris said. "Pretty fucking scary."

"It could be suspicious, or it could be smart on his part," Jon said. "He could even argue that your Status of Forces agreement allows him to have his own separate command staff."

"Besides," Patrick added, "you guys *are* trying to wind down military operations in Iraq and turn it over to the locals; this could just help facilitate that. No reason to automatically think something nefarious is going on."

"I've been in security long enough to know that if the 'oh shit' meter starts twitching, something bad is happening," Kris said. "Can you plug back into Jaffar's network and advise me if you see something unusual, sir?"

"I'm sure we can link it up again, Kris," Patrick said. "We'll let you know."

"I feel bad about giving you the hairy eyeball about hacking our security systems and then asking you to spy for me, sir."

"Not a problem. We're going to be working together for a while, and I do tend to jump first and ask questions later."

A few minutes later the mission briefing commenced. It was very much like the mission briefings Patrick had conducted in the Air Force: time hacks, overview, weather, current intelligence, status of all the units involved, and then briefings by each unit and department on what they were going to be doing. All of the participants sat at their stations and briefed one another over the intercom system, while putting PowerPoint or computerized slides up on the screens in the back of the Tank and on individual displays. Patrick saw Gia Cazzotto at one of the consoles farthest from the dais, taking notes and looking very serious.

"Here's the rundown on the Iraqi army's operation, sir," the "Battle Major," Kenneth Bruno, began. "The Iraqi Seventh Brigade is sending the entire Maqbara Company of heavy infantry, about three hundred shooters, along with Major Jaafar Othman himself in the headquarters element. Maqbara Company is probably Seventh Brigade's only pure infantry unit—all the rest are focused on security, police, and civil affairs—so we know this is a big deal.

"The target, what we are calling Reconnaissance Objective Parrot, is a suspected hidden tunnel complex north of the small village of Zahuk. Contact time is oh-three-hundred hours local. Othman will deploy two platoons of Iraqi troops to establish security around the town east and west, while two platoons will drive in for the tunnel network from the south and sweep it clean."

"What about the north, Bruno?" Wilhelm asked.

"I think they're hoping they'll escape to the north so the Turks will take care of them."

"Are the Turks involved in this thing at all?"

"Negative, sir."

"Anyone advise them that the IA is going to be operating close to the border?"

"That's the Iraqis' job, sir."

"Not when *we* have guys in the field."

"Sir, we're prohibited from contacting the Turks about an Iraqi operation without permission from Baghdad," Thompson said. "It's considered a security breach."

"We'll see about that shit," Wilhelm spat. "Comm, get division on the line—I want to talk with the general directly. Thompson, if you have any back-channel contacts in Turkey, call them and unofficially suggest that something might be going on at Zahuk tonight."

"I'll get on it, Colonel."

"Make it happen," Wilhelm snapped. "The Turks are bound to be jumpy as hell after what just happened to them. Okay, what about Warhammer?"

"Warhammer's mission is to back up the Iraqi army," Bruno went on. "In the air, Third Special Ops Squadron will launch two MQ-9 Reapers, each carrying an imaging infrared sensor ball, laser designator, two 160-gallon external fuel tanks, and six AGM-114 Hellfire laser-guided missiles. On the ground, Warhammer will send Second Platoon, Bravo Company, to recon behind the Iraqis. They'll be positioned south, east, and west of Maqbara Company and observe. The

Strykers' main task is to fill in the picture of the battle space and assist if necessary. Division is sending their Global Hawk to keep an eye on the entire battle space."

"The operative word here is *observe*, kiddies," Wilhelm cut in. "Weapons will be tight on this op, understand? If you come under fire, take cover, identify, report, and await orders. I don't want to be accused of shooting friendlies, even if the IA gets turned around and takes a shot at us. Continue."

"Back at Nahla, Warhammer has two Apache helicopters from Fourth Aviation Regiment armed and fueled and ready to fly, loaded with rockets and Hellfires," Bruno said. "We also have the Seventh Air Expeditionary Squadron, one B-1B Lancer bomber in patrol orbit Foxtrot. Colonel Cazzotto is acting as air combat controller."

"A real cluster fuck all right," Wilhelm growled. "That's all we need is for the Air Farce to scream in and start dropping JDAMs on the IAs—they're liable to trample our Strykers as they turn tail and run." Patrick looked for a reaction from Gia, but she kept her head down and continued to take notes. "Okay: security. What's the FPCON on the base, Thompson?"

"Currently Bravo, Colonel," Kris replied, a telephone to his ear, "but an hour before we open the gates and deploy, we automatically go to Delta."

"Not good enough. Go to Delta right now."

"Colonel Jaffar wants to be notified before any change in THREATCON level."

Wilhelm glared over at Thompson's station and his mouth tightened when he saw he was not there. He turned to his deputy. "Send Jaffar a message telling him that I'm recommending bumping up the THREATCON now," he said, "then do it, Thompson. Don't wait for his approval." Weatherly got right to it. They saw Wilhelm look around the Tank. "Where the hell are you, Thompson?"

"Up in the observation deck making sure the general is situated."

"Get your ass down here where you belong, put us at THREATCON Delta, then assign someone to babysit the contractors. I need you at your damned post."

"Yes, Colonel."

"General, where is your plane and your guys?" Wilhelm asked, glaring up at the observation deck. "They better be put away."

"The plane and all my technicians are in the hangar," Patrick responded. He was happy to see Gia had looked up at him, too. "The plane is on external power and with full connectivity."

"Whatever the hell *that* means," Wilhelm shot back, glaring up at McLanahan. "I just want to make sure you and your stuff are not in my way when we break out."

"We're all in the hangar as requested, Colonel."

"I don't request *anything* around here, General: I order it, and it gets done," Wilhelm said. "They stay put until oh-three-hundred unless I say otherwise."

"Got it."

"Intel. Who is the biggest worry out there—other than our *hajji* allies, Bexar?"

"The biggest threat in our sector continues to be the group that calls itself the Islamic State of

Iraq, based in Mosul, led by Abu al-Abadi, a Jordanian," the regiment's privately contracted intelligence officer, Frank Bexar, responded. "The Iraqis think the tunnel network near Zahuk is his stronghold, which is why they are sending such a large force. However, we have no actionable intelligence ourselves that al-Abadi is there."

"The *hajjis* must have some pretty solid intel, Bexar," Wilhelm growled. "Why don't you?"

"The Iraqis say he's there and they want him, dead or alive, sir," Bexar responded. "But Zahuk and the countryside are controlled by the Kurds, and al-Qaeda is strongest in the cities, like Mosul. It's not credible to me that al-Abadi would be allowed to have a 'stronghold' in that area."

"Well, apparently he *does*, Bexar," Wilhelm snapped. "You need to firm up your contacts and interface with the *hajjis* so we're not sucking hind tit all the time intelwise. Anything else?"

"Yes, sir," Bexar replied nervously. "The other biggest threat to coalition troops is the ongoing conflict between Turkey and Kurdish guerrillas operating in our AOR. They continue to cross the border to attack targets in Turkey then retreat back into Iraq. Although the Kurdish rebels are not a direct threat to us, Turkey's occasional cross-border retaliatory attacks against PKK rebel hideouts in Iraq have sometimes put our forces in danger.

"The Turks have told us that they have approximately five thousand troops deployed along the Turkey-Iraq border adjacent to our AOR. This agrees with our own observations. The

Jandarma has conducted a few retaliatory raids in the past eighteen hours, but nothing too massive—a few of their commando strike units slipping their leashes, out looking for vengeance. Their latest intel shows a rebel leader they call Baz, or the Hawk—an Iraqi Kurd, possibly a woman—engineering daring raids on Turkish military targets, possibly including the downing of that Turkish tanker in Diyarbakir."

"A woman, huh? I knew the women around here were ugly, but tough, too?" Wilhelm remarked with a laugh. "Are we getting current info from the Turks about their troop movements and antiterrorist operations?"

"The Turkish defense and interior ministries are pretty good about giving us the straight dope on their activities," Bexar said. "We've even linked up via telephone on some of their air raids to deconflict the airspace."

"At least you got your shit together with the Turks, Bexar," Wilhelm said. The intelligence contractor swallowed hard and wrapped up his briefing as fast as he could.

After the last briefer finished, Wilhelm stood up, pulled off his headset, and turned to face his battle staff. "Okay, kiddies, listen up," he began brusquely. The staff members made shows of pulling off their headsets to listen. "This is the IA's show, not ours, so I don't want any heroics and I sure as shit don't want any slipups. This is a big op for the Iraqis but a routine one for us, so do it nice and smooth and by the book. Keep your eyes and ears open and your mouths shut. Restrict voice reports for operations to urgent ones only. When I ask to see something you'd

better have it up on my screen a nanosecond
later or I'll come by and feed you your breakfast
through your nostrils. Stay on your toes and let's
give the IA a good show. Get to it."

"A regular Omar Bradley," Jon Masters
quipped. "A real soldier's soldier."

"He's very highly regarded at division and
Corps and will probably be pinning a star on
soon," Patrick said. "He's tough but it looks like
he runs a tight ship and gets the job done."

"I just hope he lets us do *ours*."

"We'll do it *with* him or *despite* him," Patrick
said. "Okay, Dr. Jonathan Colin Masters, build
me a picture of this gaggle and knock my socks
off."

The young engineer raised his hands like a
neurosurgeon examining a brain he was about
to operate on, accepted an imaginary scalpel,
then began typing on his computer's keyboard.
"Prepare to be amazed, my friend. Prepare to be
amazed."

NEAR RECONNAISSANCE OBJECTIVE PARROT, OUTSIDE ZAKHU, IRAQ
A few hours later

"I was expecting Grand Central Station or Tora
Bora, not a Hobbit house," groused Army First
Lieutenant Ted Oakland, leader of a platoon of
four Stryker Infantry Combat Vehicles. He was
studying the objective area about a mile ahead of
him through his night thermal imaging system,
which was a repeater of the gunner's sights.
The southern entrance to the so-called al-Qaeda

tunnel stronghold was a tiny mud hut that the twenty-ton Stryker could plow through with ease. It didn't quite jibe with the intel they had received from locals and their Iraqi counterparts, who variously described it as a "fortress" and "citidel."

Oakland switched from the thermal image to an overhead shot provided by a battalion MQ-9 Reaper armed unmanned aerial vehicle flying eight thousand feet overhead. The image clearly showed the deployment of Iraqi troops around the hut. There was a cluster of huts in the area, along with outbuildings and small corrals for livestock. At least eight platoons of Iraqi regulars were slowly moving in on the area.

"Pretty quiet out there, sir," the gunner remarked.

"For a major bad guy stronghold, I'd agree," Oakland said. "But the way the Iraqis are clod-hopping their way out there, it's a wonder the whole province hasn't run off."

Actually, the presence of the Stryker reconnaissance platoon had probably alerted the bad guys even better than the Iraqis. The platoon consisted of four Stryker infantry carrier vehicles. The twenty-ton vehicles had eight wheels and a 350-horsepower turbo diesel engine. They were lightly armed with .50-caliber machine guns or forty-millimeter rapid-fire grenade launchers operated by remote control from inside the vehicles. Because they were designed for mobility and not hitting power, the Strykers were lightly armored and could barely withstand ordinary squad-level machine gun fire; however, these vehicles wore slat armor—cagelike tubes of steel around the outside meant to dissipate most of the explosive energy of a rocket-propelled grenade, which made them look top-heavy.

Despite their ungainly appearance and low-tech wheeled footprint, the Strykers brought a real twenty-first-century capability to a battlefield: networkability. The Strykers could set up a node of a wide-area wireless computer network for miles around, so everyone from an individual vehicle to the president of the United States could track their position and status, see everything the crew could see, and pass information on targets to everyone else on the net. They brought an unprecedented level of situational awareness to every mission.

Along with the commander, driver, and gunner, the Strykers carried six dismounts—a section leader or assistant leader, two security troops, and three reconnaissance infantrymen. Oakland had the dismounts out to check the area ahead on foot. While the security teams set up a perimeter around each vehicle and watched the area through night-vision goggles, the section leader and recon soldiers carefully walked ahead of their intended route of travel, checking for booby traps, hiding spots, or any signs of the enemy.

Although they were marching behind the Iraqis and weren't expected to come into contact, Oakland kept the dismounts out there because the Iraqi soldiers often did things that made absolutely no sense. They would find "lost" Iraqi soldiers—men heading the wrong way, mostly away from the direction of the enemy—or soldiers taking a break, eating, praying, or relieving themselves far from their units. Oakland often surmised that his platoon's main mission behind the main force was to keep the Iraqis headed in the right direction.

But tonight the Iraqis looked like they were pressing forward well. Oakland was sure this was because it was a relatively large-scale operation, because the Maqbara Company was leading the way, and because Major Othman was in the field instead of hiding under an *abayah* whenever an operation got under way.

"About fifteen mike to contact," Oakland said into the secure platoon net. "Stay sharp." Still no sign that they had been discovered. This, Oakland thought, will either go off relatively well— or they were blundering off into an ambush. The next few minutes would tell . . .

COMMAND AND CONTROL CENTER, ALLIED AIR BASE NAHLA, IRAQ
That same time

"I'm impressed, Jon, really impressed," Patrick McLanahan said. "The gear is working as advertised."

"You expected anything less?" Jon Masters retorted smugly. He shrugged, then added, "Actually, I'm surprised myself. Networking the regimental stuff was a bigger hurdle than networking our own sensors, and that went pretty smoothly."

"That could be a bad thing: it shouldn't be so easy to link the regiment's network," Patrick observed.

"Ours isn't nearly as easy to hack as the regiment's," Jon said confidently. "It'll take an army of Sandra Bullocks to crack our encryption." He pointed to one blank window on his laptop monitor. "Division's Global Hawk is the only player not hooked up yet."

"I may have been responsible for that," Patrick admitted. "I told Dave that we'd be ready to start surveillance tonight, and he probably passed that along to President Martindale, who probably passed it along to Corps headquarters. Division might have retasked the Global Hawk."

"That's not your fault—that's Wilhelm's," Jon said. "If he let us fly, we'd be on it like stink on shit. Well, they have lots of eyes up there without it."

Patrick nodded, but he still looked uneasy. "I'm concerned about the northern portion of those tunnels," he said. "If any AQI escapes we should get an eye on them so we can steer the Turks over to nab them, or use a Reaper to pick 'em off." He brought a window from Jon's laptop over to his display, studied it for a moment, entered some commands into his keyboard, and spoke. "Miss Harrison?"

"Harrison. Who is this?"

"General McLanahan."

He could see the unmanned aerial vehicle contractor look around herself in confusion. "Where are you, General?"

"Up in the observation deck."

She looked up and saw him through the large slanted windowpanes. "Oh, hello, sir. I didn't know you were on this net."

"Officially I'm not, but Kris said it was okay. I have a request."

"Yes, sir?"

"You have Kelly Two-Two on station in the southern part of the op, and Kelly Two-Six ready to go as a backup. Could you move Two-Two up north to cover the northern tunnel entrance and move Two-Six to cover the south?"

"Why, sir?"

"The Global Hawk isn't on station, so we don't have any coverage in the north."

"I'd have to fly the Reaper to within maximum missile range of the Turkish border, and that requires permission from Corps and probably from the State Department. We could download weapons from Two-Six and send it up."

"This thing will most likely be over by then, Lieutenant."

"True, sir."

"If we can get some eyes up there, I'd feel a little more relieved," Patrick said. "How about we send Two-Two right up to the distance limit until I coordinate with Corps?"

"I'll have to deconflict Two-Six so it can launch," Harrison said. "Stand by." Patrick flipped over to the approach radar picture of Nahla Air Base and found it relatively free of traffic, undoubtedly because the airspace had been closed down as a result of the operation to the north. A moment later: "Airspace says we can launch when ready, sir. Let me get permission from the battle major."

"It was my idea, Lieutenant, so I'd be happy to give him a call and explain what I had in mind."

"You're not supposed to be on this net, sir," Harrison said, glancing up at Patrick and giggling. "Besides, if you don't mind, I'd like to take credit for your idea."

"I'll take the blame if there's any snafu, Lieutenant."

"No problem, sir. Stand by." She clicked off the connection, but Patrick was able to eavesdrop on her conversation with Major Bruno and the conversation between Bruno and Lieutenant Colonel Weatherly about the launch. They all agreed it was a good idea to move the Reaper as long as it didn't violate any international agreements, and soon Kelly Two-Six was airborne and Two-Two was moving north to take up a patrol orbit near the Turkish border.

"Whoever's idea it was to move the Reaper up north . . . hoo-ah," Wilhelm said over the Tank network.

"Harrison's idea, sir," Weatherly said.

"I wasted a perfectly good 'hoo-ah' on a contractor?" Wilhelm said, feigning disgust at himself. "Oh, well, I know we gotta toss the mercs a bone every once in a while. Good heads-up, Harrison."

"Thank you, Colonel."

"Is that his way of giving out praise?" Jon asked. "What a sweet guy."

The picture of the operation looked considerably better once the Reaper had taken up a patrol orbit near the Turkish border, although it was still too far south to completely fill in the picture. "It was a good idea, sir," Harrison said to Patrick, "but the ROE restrictions still can't give us a look at where the tunnel supposedly exits. I'll check on the Global Hawk."

"We'd have that entire area covered seven ways to Sunday with the Loser," Jon said. "Wait'll these guys see us in action."

"I really wish you'd change that name, Jon."

"I will—but first I want to rub the Air Force's face in it for a while," Jon said happily. "I can't wait."

RECONNAISSANCE OBJECTIVE PARROT
A short time later

"There they go, sir," the gunner aboard Lieutenant Oakland's Stryker said, studying the image of the tunnel entrance through his imaging infrared sights. Several bright flashes of light erupted on the screen, and seconds later the sounds of the explosion rippled over them. "Looks like the lead platoons are on the move."

Oakland checked his watch. "Right on time, too. I'm impressed. We'd be hard-pressed to get an op this size going dead on time." He flipped a switch on his monitor, checking the areas around each of his Strykers deployed around the area, then keyed his mike. "Weapons tight and stay sharp, guys," he radioed to his platoon. "The IA is on the move." Each section leader clicked an affirmative in response.

When all of them had checked in, Oakland sent an instant message to the Tank in Nahla, reporting friendly force movement. He briefly switched over to Maqbara Company's command radio network and was met with an insane and completely incomprehensible cacophony of excited, shouted Arabic. He quickly switched it off. "Good radio discipline, guys," he said under his breath.

"They're going in, sir," the Stryker gunner said. He and Oakland watched as a squad of eight Iraqi soldiers approached the building. Two soldiers used grenade launchers to blow the door open, showering themselves with wood and stone fragments because they had moved in far too close.

"Oh, c'mon, guys, where's your entry team?" Oakland said aloud. "You should know that the guys who blew the door aren't going to be able to do a smooth entry. One squad blows the door while another squad who's shielded from the light and concussion do the entry. My seven-year-old knows this." But soon he could see a sergeant reorganizing his entry team and getting the breaching team out of the way, so after a brief stutter step the operation appeared to be progressing.

Back at the Tank, Patrick and Jon were watching the action via feeds from the Strykers and unmanned aircraft . . . except Patrick was not looking at the raid on the suspected tunnel entrance, but farther north along the Iraq-Turkey border. The view from the MQ-9 Reaper's imaging infrared scanner showed rolling hills punctuated by tall rocky crags and deep forested valleys.

"Sorry, sir, but you're not going to get too much contrast or detail at this looking angle," Margaret Harrison, the regiment's Reaper liaison officer, said to him over the intercom. "Reapers are meant to look down at a fairly steep angle, not across to the horizon."

"Copy," Patrick responded. "Just a few more seconds." He touched another key on his keyboard and spoke: "Mr. Bexar?"

"Bexar here," the privately contracted intelligence officer replied.

"This is McLanahan."

"How are you, General? Are you authorized to be on the net now?"

"Mr. Thompson said it was okay. I have a question."

"I don't personally know your security clearance, General," Bexar said. "I assume you have a 'top secret' or else you couldn't have sat in on the briefing, but until I verify, I'll have to refrain from answering any questions that might compromise operational security."

"Understood. You briefed that the Turks have five thousand troops in the area immediately adjacent to the regiment's area of responsibility?"

"Yes, sir. The equivalent of two mechanized infantry brigades, one each in Sirnak and Hakkari provinces, plus three Jandarma battalions."

"That's a lot, isn't it?"

"Considering recent events, I don't think so," Bexar said. "They've roughly tried to mirror American and Iraqi force levels over the past couple years. The Jandarma have maintained many more forces in southeast Turkey in the past depending on PKK activity levels. The problem is, we don't always get regular updates on Jandarma unit movements."

"Why is that?"

"The Turkish Ministry of the Interior is pretty

tight-lipped—they're not obligated by NATO treaty to share information like the Ministry of Defense is."

"But the mechanized infantry movement in the area is a relatively new development?"

"Yes."

"Interesting. But my question is, Mr. Bexar: Where *are* they?"

"Where are who?"

"Where are all these Turkish forces? A mechanized infantry brigade is pretty hard to hide."

"Well, I suppose . . ." The question had obviously taken the intelligence man by surprise. "They . . . could be anywhere, General. My guess is they're in garrisons in the provincial capitals. As for the Jandarma, they can evade our surveillance easily in this terrain."

"Kelly Two-Two has been looking at the frontier for the past few minutes and I haven't seen any indications of any vehicles whatsoever," Patrick said. "And according to my charts, Two-Two is looking right at the town of Uludere, correct?"

"Stand by." A moment later, after checking the telemetry readouts from the Reaper's imaging infrared sensor: "Yes, General, you're right."

"We're looking at the town, but I don't see any lights or even any evidence of life out there. Am I missing something?"

There was a slight pause; then: "General, why are you asking about Turkey? The Turks aren't involved in this operation."

Yeah, Patrick thought, why *am* I looking at Turkey? "Just curious, I guess," he finally responded. "I'll let you get back to work. Sorry for the—"

"Harrison, what is Two-Two looking at?" Wilhelm asked over the intercom. "It's looking fifteen miles in the wrong damned direction. Check your ground surveillance plan."

Patrick knew he had to step in himself—it wasn't Harrison's idea to look across the border into Turkey. "I just wanted to have a look across the border, Colonel."

"Who is this?"

"McLanahan."

"What are you doing on my net, General?" Wilhelm thundered. "I said you could observe and listen in, not talk, and I sure as hell didn't authorize you to direct my sensor operators!"

"I'm sorry, Colonel, but I had a funny feeling about something, and I had to check it out."

"Better to ask forgiveness than ask permission, eh, General?" Wilhelm sneered. "I heard that about you. I don't care about your 'funny feelings,' McLanahan. Harrison, move that Reaper to cover . . ."

"Aren't you even going to ask what I wanted to look at, Colonel?"

"I'm not, because nothing in Turkey interests me at the moment. In case you forgot, General, I have a reconnaissance platoon on the ground in action in *Iraq*, not Turkey. But as long as you bring it up, what in hell were you—"

"*Rocket launch!*" somebody cut in. On the monitor showing images broadcast from Kelly Two-Two, dozens of bright streaks of fire arced across the night sky—from across the border in Turkey!

"What the hell is that?" Wilhelm snapped. "Where is that coming from?"

. *"That's a multiple rocket barrage from Turkey!"* Patrick shouted. "Pull your men out of there, Colonel!"

"Shut the hell up, McLanahan!" Wilhelm shouted. But he rose out of his seat in horror, studied the image for a few heartbeats, then hit the button for the regimental network and cried, "All Warhammer players, all Warhammer players, this is Warhammer, you have incoming artillery from the north, reverse direction, get away from Parrot *now*!"

"Say again?" one of the recon sections responded. "Say again, Warhammer!"

"I say again, all Warhammer players, this is Warhammer, you have twenty seconds to reverse direction of movement away from Objective Parrot, and then five seconds to take cover!" Wilhelm shouted. "Artillery inbound from the north! *Move! Move!*" On the Tank's intercom he shouted, "Someone get the fucking Turkish army on the line and tell them to cease fire, we've got troops on the ground! Get medevac choppers in the air and get reinforcements out there immediately!"

"Send the B-1 across the border to those launch points, Colonel!" Patrick said. "If there are any more launchers, it'll be able to—"

"I said *shut up* and get off my net, McLanahan!" Wilhelm snapped.

The Stryker reconnaissance patrols moved quickly, but not as fast as the incoming rockets. It took only ten seconds for the two dozen rockets to fly thirty miles and shower the Zahuk tunnel complex area with thousands of high-explosive antipersonnel and antitruck mines. Some mines exploded a few yards overhead, spraying the area below them with white-hot tungsten pellets; other mines detonated on contact with the ground, buildings, or vehicles with a high-explosive fragmentary warhead; and still others sat on the ground, where they would explode when disturbed or automatically after a certain period of time.

The second barrage occurred just a few moments later, aimed a few hundred yards west, east, and south of the first target area, designed to catch any who might have escaped the first bombardment. This was the attack that caught most of the retreating members of the American recon platoon. The mines tore through the light top armor on the Strykers from above, ripping them apart and leaving them open for the other high-explosive munitions to follow. Many of the dismounts who escaped the carnage inside their vehicles were lost to submunitions exploding overhead or underfoot as they tried to run for their lives.

In thirty seconds it was over. The stunned staff members watched it all in absolute horror, broadcast live via the Reaper and Predator drones high above.

THE WHITE HOUSE, WASHINGTON, D.C.
A short time later

President Joseph Gardner was logging off his computer in the private study adjacent to the Oval Office and had just reached for his jacket to call it a night and head up to the residence when the phone rang. It was his national security adviser, longtime friend, and former assistant secretary of the Navy, Conrad Carlyle. He hit the speakerphone button: "I was just about to call it a day, Conrad. Can it wait?"

"I wish it could, sir," Carlyle said from a secure cell phone, probably in his car. His friend rarely called him "sir" when they spoke one-on-one unless it was an emergency, and this immediately got the president's attention. "I'm en route to the White House, sir. Reports of a cross-border attack into Iraq by Turkey."

Gardner's heart rate went down a few percentage points. Neither Turkey nor least of all Iraq was a strategic threat to him right now—even goings-on in Iraq rarely caused long sleepless nights anymore. "Any of our guys involved?"

"A bunch."

Heart rate back up again. What in hell happened? "Oh, shit." He could almost taste that glass of rum over ice that he had his mind set on back up in the residence. "Are they set up in the Situation Room for me yet?"

"No, sir."

"How much info do you have?"

"Very little."

Time for one glass before the action really started ramping up. "I'll be in the Oval Office. Come get me."

"Yes, sir."

Gardner put a few ice cubes in an old Navy coffee mug, splashed some Ron Caneca rum into it, and took it out to the Oval Office. There was a crisis brewing somewhere, and it was important for onlookers around the world to stare through the windows and see the president of the United States hard at work—but that didn't mean he had to deprive himself.

He turned the TV in the Oval Office to CNN, but there was nothing yet about any incident in Turkey. He could get the feeds from the Situation Room in his study, but he didn't want to leave the Oval Office until the emergency was broadcast on worldwide TV and he was seen already watching it.

It was all about image, and Joe Gardner was a master at presenting a certain, specific, carefully crafted image. He always wore a collared shirt and tie except right before bed, and if he wasn't wearing a jacket, his sleeves were rolled up and his tie was slightly loosened to make it look like he was hard at work. He used speakerphones often, but when others could see him he always used a telephone handset so everyone could see him busily talking. He never used the delicate china cups either, preferring heavy, thick Navy coffee mugs for all his beverages, because he thought they made him look manlier.

Besides, like Jackie Gleason on TV with his teacup filled with booze, everyone would assume he *was* drinking coffee.

The White House chief of staff, Walter Kordus, knocked on the Oval Office door, waited the requisite few seconds in case there was any sign of protest, then let himself in. "I got the call from Conrad, Joe," Kordus said. He was dressed in jeans, sweatshirt, and Topsiders. Another longtime Gardner friend and ally, he was always available in a heartbeat and was probably lurking around the West Wing somewhere instead of being home with his wife and sizable stable of children. He looked at the flat-screen TV hidden in a cabinet. "Anything yet?"

"No." Gardner raised his mug. "Have a drink. I'm almost one ahead of you." The chief of staff dutifully fixed himself a mug of rum, but as usual he did not drink any of it.

It wasn't until Carlyle blew through the Oval Office doors with a briefing folder in his hands that there was something on CNN, and it was only a mention on the scroll at the bottom of the screen of a "shooting incident" in northern Iraq. "It's looking like a friendly-fire incident, sir," Carlyle said. "An Army platoon was backing up an Iraqi infantry company on a sweep of a suspected al-Qaeda in Iraq tunnel entrance when the area was hit by Turkish medium-range unguided rockets."

"Crap," the president muttered. "Get Stacy Anne out here."

"She's on her way, and so is Miller," Carlyle said. Stacy Anne Barbeau, a former U.S. senator from Louisiana who was as ambitious as she was flamboyant, had recently been confirmed as the new secretary of state; Miller Turner, yet another longtime Gardner friend and confidant, was the secretary of defense.

"Casualties?"

"Eleven dead, sixteen wounded, ten critically."

"Je-sus."

Over the next ten minutes, the president's advisers or deputies filtered in to the Oval Office one by one. The last to arrive was Barbeau, looking as if she was ready for a night on the town.

"My staff is in contact with the Turkish embassy and with the Turkish foreign ministry," she said, heading right over to the coffee tray. "I'm expecting a call from each of them shortly."

"Casualty count is up to thirteen and is expected to go higher, sir," Turner said as he listened to a call from the Army corps commander. "They can't say that the platoon itself was targeted, but it appears that the Iraqis and Turks were going after the same target."

"Then if our guys were backing up the Iraqis, how did they get hit?"

"The contractors making the initial assessment say that the second round of rockets was meant to catch any survivors escaping from the target area."

"Contractors?"

"As you know, sir," National Security Adviser Carlyle said, "we've been able to greatly draw down our uniformed military forces in Iraq, Afghanistan, and many other forward areas around the world by replacing them with civilian contractors. Almost all military functions not involving direct action—security, reconnaissance, maintenance, communications, the list goes on—are done by contractors these days."

The president nodded, already moving on to other details. "I need the names of the casualties so I can call the families."

"Yes, sir."

"Any of these contractors get hurt?"

"No, sir."

"Figures," the president said idly.

The phone on the president's desk rang, and chief of staff Walter Kordus picked it up, listened, then held the receiver out to Barbeau. "Turkish prime minister Akas herself, Stacy, patched in from State."

"That's a good sign," Barbeau said. She activated the translator on the president's computer. "Good morning, Madam Prime Minister," she said. "This is Secretary of State Barbeau."

At the same moment another phone rang. "Turkish president Hirsiz on the line for you, sir."

"He better have some explanations," Gardner said, taking the receiver. "Mr. President, this is Joseph Gardner."

"President Gardner, good evening," Kurzat Hirsiz said in very good English, his voice fairly quivering with anxiety, "I am sorry to disturb you, but I just heard about the terrible tragedy that occurred on the Iraq border, and on behalf of all the people of Turkey, I wanted to immediately call and express my sadness, regret, and sorrow to the families of the men that died as a result of this horrible accident."

"Thank you, Mr. President," Gardner said. "Now what the hell happened?"

"An inexcusable error on the part of our interior security forces," Hirsiz said. "They received information that Kurdish PKK insurgents and terrorists were massing at a tunnel complex in Iraq and were planning another attack on a Turkish airport or military airfield, larger and more devastating than the recent attack in Diyarbakir. The information came from very reliable sources.

"They said that the numbers of PKK fighters were in the hundreds in the tunnel complex, which is very extensive and crisscrosses the Iraq border over a wide area. It was determined that we did not have enough time to gather a force sufficient to destroy such a large force in so dangerous an area, so it was decided to attack using a rocket barrage. I gave the order to attack personally, and so it is my error and my responsibility."

"For God's sake, Mr. President, why didn't you tell us first?" Gardner asked. "We're allies and friends, remember? You know we have forces in that area operating day and night to secure the border area and hunt down insurgents, including the PKK. One quick phone call alerting us and we could've pulled our forces out without alerting the terrorists."

"Yes, yes, I know that, Mr. President," Hirsiz said. "But our informant told us that the terrorists would be on the move shortly, and we had to act quickly. There was no time—"

"No time? *Thirteen dead Americans* who were in a support role only, Mr. President! And we don't even have the Iraqi casualty count yet! You should have *made* the time!"

"Yes, yes, I agree, Mr. President, and it was a horrible omission that I deeply regret and for which I personally apologize," Hirsiz said, this time with an obvious edge in his voice. There was a slight pause; then: "But may I remind you, sir, that we were not informed about the Iraqi operation, either from you or the Iraqi government. Such a notification would have also prevented this accident."

"Don't start passing around the blame now, Mr. President," Gardner snapped. "Thirteen

Americans are *dead* because of *your* artillery barrage, which was targeted *inside Iraq*, not on Turkish soil! That is inexcusable!"

"I agree, I agree, sir," Hirsiz said stonily. "I do not dispute that, and I do not seek to lay blame where it does not belong. But the tunnel complex was under the Iraq-Turkish border, the terrorists were massing in Iraq, and we know the insurgents live, plot, and gather weapons and supplies in Iraq and Iran. It was a legitimate target, no matter which side of the border. We know the Kurds in Iraq harbor and support the PKK, and the Iraqi government does little to stop them. We must act because the Iraqis will not."

"President Hirsiz, I'm not going to get into an argument with you on what the Iraqi government does or does not do with the PKK," Gardner said irritably. "I want a full and complete explanation of what happened, and I demand a pledge from you to do everything in your power to see to it that it doesn't happen again. We're *allies*, sir. Disasters like this can and must be avoided, and it appears that if you had done your duty as an ally and friendly neighbor of Iraq and communicated better with us, this could have . . ."

"*Bir saniye!* Excuse me, sir?" Hirsiz said. There was a lengthy pause on the other end of the line, and Gardner heard someone in the background say the word *sik*, which the computerized translator said meant "head of a penis." "Pardon me, Mr. President, but as I explained to you, we thought we were attacking PKK terrorists that have only recently killed almost two dozen innocent men, women, and children in a major Turkish city. The incident in Zahuk was a horrible mistake, for which I am fully responsible and sincerely apologize to you, the families of the dead, and the people of America. But this does not give you the right to demand anything from this government."

"There's no reason for obscenities, President Hirsiz," Gardner said, so flustered and angry that veins stood out on his forehead. He noticed Hirsiz did not deny or dispute the allegation, or was surprised that Gardner knew of it. "We will conduct a full investigation on this attack, and I expect your utmost cooperation. I want your complete assurance that you communicate with us and your NATO partners better in the future so attacks like this won't happen again."

"It was not an *attack* against your troops or the Iraqis, but against suspected PKK insurgents and terrorists, sir," Hirsiz said. "Please choose your words more carefully, Mr. President. It was an *accident*, a tragic mistake that occurred in the defense of the homeland of the Republic of Turkey. I take responsibility for a terrible *accident*, sir, not an *attack*."

"All right, Mr. President, all *right*," Gardner said. "We will be in contact shortly regarding the arrival of forensic, military, and criminal investigators. Good night, sir."

"*İyi akşamlar*. Good night, Mr. President."

Gardner slammed the phone down. "Damn, you'd think *he* lost thirteen men!" he said. "Stacy?"

"I caught a little of your conversation, Mr. President," Barbeau said. "The prime minister was apologetic, almost over-the-top so. I felt she was sincere, although she clearly sees it as an accident for which they only *share* responsibility."

"Yeah? And if it was an American rocket barrage and dead Turkish troops, we'd be crucified by not just Turkey but by the entire world—we'd get *all* the blame and then some," Gardner said. He sat back in his chair and ran an exasperated hand over his face. "All right, all right, screw the Turks for now. Someone messed up here, and I want to know who, and I want some butts— Turkish, Iraqi, PKK, or Americans, I don't care, I want some *butts*." He turned to the secretary of defense. "Miller, I'm going to appoint a chair to handle the investigation. I want this public— in-your-face, rough, tough, and direct. This is the greatest number of casualties in Iraq since I've been in office, and I'm not going to get this administration bogged down in Iraq." He glanced for a moment at Stacy Barbeau, who made a very slight gesture with her eyes. Gardner picked up on it immediately and turned to the vice president, Kenneth T. Phoenix. "Ken, how about it? You definitely have the background."

"Absolutely, sir," he replied without hesitation. Kenneth Phoenix, just forty-six years old, could have been one of America's fastest rising political stars—if only he didn't work so hard. Law degree from UCLA, four years as a judge advocate in the U.S. Marine Corps, four years in the U.S. attorney's office in the District of Columbia, then various offices in the Department of Justice before being nominated as attorney general.

In the years after the horror of the American holocaust, Phoenix worked tirelessly to assure the American public and the world that the United States of America would not slip into martial law. He was relentless with lawbreakers and pursued anyone, regardless of political affiliation or wealth, who sought to prey on victims of the Russian attacks. He was equally relentless with Congress and even the White House to make sure that individual rights were not violated as the government got to work rebuilding the nation and resecuring its borders.

He was so popular with the American people that there was talk of him being nominated for president of the United States to oppose another very popular man, then secretary of defense Joseph Gardner. Gardner had switched party affiliations because of his disagreements with the Martindale administration, and the move hurt his chances of winning. But in a flash of political genius, Joseph Gardner asked Phoenix to be his running mate, even though they were not in the same party. The strategy worked. The voters saw the move as a strong sign of unity and wisdom, and they won in a landslide.

"Do you think it's a good idea sending the vice president to Iraq and Turkey, Mr. President?" the chief of staff asked. "It's still pretty dangerous out there."

"I've been monitoring the security status of Iraq, and I believe it's plenty safe for me," Phoenix said.

"He's got a point, Ken," the president said. "I thought about your qualifications and expertise, not about your safety. I'm sorry."

"Don't be, sir," Phoenix said. "I'll do it. It's important to show how serious we are about this attack—to all the players in the Middle East, not just the Turks."

"I don't know . . ."

"I'll keep my head down, sir, don't worry," Phoenix said. "I'll put a team together from the Pentagon, Justice, and National Intelligence and leave tonight."

"*Tonight*?" Gardner nodded and smiled. "I knew I picked the right guy. Okay, Ken, thank you, you're on. Stacy will get all the clearances you'll need from Baghdad, Ankara, and anywhere else the investigation takes you. If we need you back in the Senate to break a tie, maybe I'll send a Black Stallion spaceplane out to get you."

"I'd love to get a ride in one, sir. Send one for me, and I'll take it."

"Be careful what you wish for, Mr. Vice President." Gardner got to his feet and started to pace. "I know I've said I want to draw down our forces in Iraq over sixteen months, but it's taken longer than I thought. This incident highlights the dangers our troops face out there every day, even when we're not in direct contact with the enemy. It's time to talk about drawing down our forces quicker and removing more forces. Thoughts?"

"The American people will certainly agree, Mr. President," Secretary of State Barbeau said, "especially after news of this disaster gets out in the morning."

"We've spoken about the possibility many times, sir," National Security Adviser Carlyle said. "One mechanized infantry brigade in Baghdad on a twelve-month rotation; one training regiment on a six-month rotation; and we conduct frequent joint training exercises with units deployed from the States for no more than a month or two throughout the country. Day-today security and surveillance provided by private contractors, with infrequent special ops missions around the region as needed."

"Sounds good to me," the president said. "One soldier dies and it's front-page news, but it takes at least six contractors to die before anyone notices. Let's work up the details and get a plan drawn up pronto." To his other advisers, he said, "Okay, I want an update on the Iraq attack at the seven A.M. staff briefing. Thank you, everyone." Just as the group was departing the Oval Office, the president asked, "Secretary Barbeau, a word with you in the study?"

After the door was closed, the president fixed the former senator from Louisiana a bourbon and water. They toasted each other, then she lightly kissed him on the lips, being careful not to get too much lipstick on him—after all, the first lady was upstairs in the residence. "Thanks for recommending Phoenix, Stacy," Gardner said. "Good choice—it'll get him out of here for a change. He's always underfoot."

"I agree—he's much *too* curious sometimes," Barbeau said. She curled her lower lip in a pout. "But I wish you had consulted me first. I can think of a dozen better-qualified persons from *our* party that could've headed the team."

"Walter briefed me that there were rumblings in Washington about keeping Phoenix too deep in the background and squashing his political future," Gardner said.

"Well, that's what typically happens to vice presidents."

"I know, but I need to keep him on the ticket when I run for the second term, and I don't want pissed-off party bosses encouraging him to leave so he can run himself," Gardner said, fixing himself another coffee mug of Puerto Rican rum on ice. "This is a good high-profile assignment that'll please his supporters, but it's out of the country with not a lot of media around; it'll show I'm serious about investigating the incident, but nothing will come of it, so if anyone gets hurt, it'll be him; but more importantly, it's a subject that will fade from public attention quickly because it involves dead American soldiers. Send your experts' names to Phoenix and let's see if he takes any of them."

"Perhaps," Barbeau said, her eyes glittering with intrigue, "the vice president will forget to duck or put on his body armor, and just like *that* we'll need a new vice president."

"Je-sus, Stacy, don't even joke about shit like that," Gardner breathed. His eyes rose in surprise at her words; he waited to see if she would smile and laugh the dark thought away, but was not shocked to see that she did not.

"I would never wish any harm on the lovely and hunky Kenneth Timothy Phoenix," she said. "But he *is* going into harm's way, and you need to think about what we'll do if the worst happens."

"I would have to appoint his replacement, of course. I've got a list."

Barbeau put the bourbon on a table and slowly, tantalizingly, approached the president. "Am I on your list, Mr. President?" she asked in a low, sultry voice, running her fingers under the lapels of his jacket, caressing his chest.

"Oh, you're on many lists, darlin'. But then

I'd have to hire a food taster around here, wouldn't I?"

She didn't stop—and, he noticed, she didn't refute his joke, either. "I don't want the office by succession, Joe—I know I can earn it on my own," she said in a low, rather singsong voice. She looked up at him with her beautiful green eyes . . . and Gardner saw nothing but menace in them. She kissed him lightly on the lips again, her eyes open and staring directly into his, and after the kiss she added, "But I'll take it any way I can."

The president smiled and shook his head ruefully as she headed for the door. "I don't know who's in greater danger, Miss Secretary of State: the vice president in Iraq . . . or whoever gets in your way right here in Washington."

RESIDENCE OF THE PRESIDENT OF THE REPUBLIC OF TURKEY
That same time

"How *dare* he?" Turkish minister of national defense Hasan Cizek stormed as President Hirsiz replaced the receiver on the hook. "That is an *insult*! Gardner should apologize to you, and do it *immediately*!"

"Calm yourself, Minister," Prime Minister Ayşe Akas said. With her, Hirsiz, and Cizek was the entire national security staff: secretary-general of the Turkish National Security Council General Orhan Sahin, foreign minister Mustafa Hamarat, military chief of staff General Abdullah Guzlev, and Fevsi Guclu, the director of the National Intelligence Organization, which performed all domestic and foreign intelligence operations. "Gardner was upset and not thinking straight. And he heard that obscenity. Are you insane?"

"Don't apologize for that drunkard lech, Prime Minister," Foreign Minister Mustafa Hamarat said. "The president of the United States shouldn't pop off at a head of state and an ally—I don't care how tired or upset he is. He lost his head in a time of crisis, and that was wrong."

"Everyone, quiet down," President Kurzat Hirsiz said, holding up his hands almost as if in surrender. "I took no offense. We made the requisite call and apologized—"

"Groveled is more like it!" Cizek spat.

"Our rockets killed a dozen Americans and probably several dozen Iraqis, Hasan; maybe a little groveling is warranted here." Hirsiz scowled at the minister of national defense. "It's what he says or does next that will tell." He turned to the secretary-general of the National Security Council. "General, are you absolutely positive that your information was accurate, actionable, and an immediate response was required?"

"*I* am positive, sir," he heard a voice say. He turned and saw General Besir Ozek, commander of the Jandarma, standing in the doorway to his office, with a frightened aide behind him. Ozek had taken off all the bandages on his face, neck, and hands, and the sight was truly repulsive.

"General Ozek!" Hirsiz blurted out, momentarily shocked by the general's presence, then nauseated by his appearance. He swallowed hard, squinting against the revulsion he felt, then ashamed for letting the others see it. "I didn't summon you, sir. You are not well. You should be in hospital."

"There was no time to notify the Americans either—and if we did, the information would have been leaked to PKK sympathizers, and the opportunity would have been lost," Ozek went on, as if the president had not said a word.

Hirsiz nodded, turning away from Ozek's awful wounds. "Thank you, General. You are dismissed."

"If I may speak freely, sir: my heart is sickened by what I just heard," Ozek said.

"General?"

"Sickened by the number of times I heard the president of the Republic of Turkey apologize like a young boy caught feeding the goldfish to the cat. With all due respect, Mr. President, it was repulsive."

"That's enough, General," Prime Minister Akas said. "Show some respect."

"We were doing nothing more than defending our nation," Ozek said angrily. "We have nothing to apologize for, sir."

"Innocent Americans died, General . . ."

"They thought they were chasing al-Qaeda in Iraq terrorists, not PKK," Ozek retorted. "If the Iraqis had any brains, they would know as well as we that the tunnel complex was a PKK hide-out, not al-Qaeda."

"Are you sure of this, General?"

"Positive, sir," Ozek insisted. "Al-Qaeda in-surgents hide and operate in the cities, not the countryside like the PKK. If the Americans bothered to learn this—or if the Iraqis cared— this incident would not have happened."

President Hirsiz fell silent and turned away— to think, as well as not to have to look at Ozek's terrible wounds. "Nevertheless, General, the incident has sparked anger and outrage in Washington, and we must appear conciliatory, apologetic, and utterly cooperative," he said after a few moments. "They will send investigators, and we must assist their inquiry."

"Sir, we can't let that happen," Ozek cried. "We can't let the Americans or the international community keep us from defending this nation. You know as well as I that the focus of any investigation will be about *our* faults and *our* policies, not about the PKK or their attacks. We must act, *now*. Do *something*, sir!"

The prime minister's eyes blazed in anger. "As you were, General Ozek!" she shouted. The veteran Jandarma officer's eyes blazed, which made his visage even more frightful. The prime minister raised a finger at him to silence his expected retort. "Not another word, General, or I will order Minister Cizek to relieve you of your post, and I will strip the rank off your uniform *myself*."

"If all we had hit were PKK terrorists, few outside our country would have cared about the strike," Ozek said. "Our people would have seen this as what it truly was: a major victory against the PKK, not an example of military incompetence or racism."

"Minister Cizek, you will relieve General Ozek of command," Akas said.

"I recommend calm here, Madam Prime Minister . . ." Cizek sputtered. "There has been a terrible accident, yes, but we were only doing our duty to protect our country . . ."

"I said, I want Ozek *dismissed*!" the prime minister shouted. "Do it *now*!"

"Shut up!" President Hirsiz shouted, almost pleading. "Everyone, please *shut up*!" The president looked as if his internal struggles were ready to tear him apart. He looked at his advisers and seemed to find no answers. Turning back to Ozek, he said in a quiet voice, "Many innocent Americans and Iraqis were killed tonight, General."

"I am sorry, sir," Ozek said. "I take full responsibility. But will we ever learn how many PKK terrorists we killed tonight? And if the Americans or Iraqis leading this so-called investigation ever told us how many terrorists were eliminated, will we ever get the chance to tell the world what they did to innocent Turks?" Hirsiz did not respond, only stared at a spot on the wall, so Ozek stiffened to attention and turned to leave.

"Wait, General," Hirsiz said.

"You're *not* going to consider that idea, Kurzat!" Prime Minister Akas said, her mouth dropping open in surprise.

"The general is right, Ayşe," Hirsiz said. "This is yet another incident for which Turkey will be vilified . . ." And at that, he reached down, grasped his chair with both hands, and toppled it over with a quick thrust: "and I am *sick* of it! I am not going to look into the eyes of Turkish men and women and make more promises and excuses! I want it to *end*. I want the PKK to fear this government . . . no, I want the Americans, the Iraqis, the whole *world* to fear us! I'm tired of being everyone's patsy! Minister Cizek!"

"Sir!"

"I want to see a plan of action on my desk as soon as possible, outlining an operation to destroy the PKK training camps and facilities in Iraq," Hirsiz said. "I want to minimize non-combatant casualties, and I want it quick, efficient, and thorough. We know we're going to get blasted by the entire world, and the pressure will be on to withdraw almost from day one, so it will have to be an operation that is fast, effective, and massive."

"Yes, sir," Cizek said. "With pleasure."

Hirsiz stepped over to Ozek and placed his hands on the general's shoulders, this time not afraid of looking him in his badly injured face. "I vow," he said, "never to have one of my generals take responsibility for an operation I authorized. I am the commander in chief. When this operation begins, General, if you're up to it, I want you to lead the forces that will strike at the heart of the PKK. If you're strong enough to get out of a crashed plane and then come here to Ankara to confront me, you're strong enough to crush the PKK."

"Thank you, sir," Ozek said.

Hirsiz turned to the other advisers in the room. "Ozek was the only one who spoke his mind to the president—that's the kind of person I want advising me from this day forward. Put a plan together to defeat the PKK once and for all."

CHAPTER 4

An argument needs no reason, nor a friendship.
—*Ibycus, c. 580 B.C.*

ALLIED AIR BASE NAHLA, IRAQ
Two days later

Voices in the Tank were much more muted than before; no one spoke except to make a report or observation. If they were not otherwise occupied, the department heads, operators, and specialists sat straight up in their seats and stared straight ahead—no chatting with comrades, no stretching, no sign of idleness.

Colonel Wilhelm entered the battle staff room, took his seat at the front console, and donned his headset. Without turning to face his staff, he spoke over the intercom: "We've been ordered to suspend all operations except logistics, reconnaissance, and intel. No IA combat support until further notice."

"But all that stuff is done by the contractors, sir," someone remarked on the intercom. "What are *we* going to do?"

"We are going to train in case the shit hits the fan with Turkey," Wilhelm replied.

"Are we at war with Turkey, sir?" the regimental executive officer, Mark Weatherby, asked.

"Negative," Wilhelm replied tonelessly.

"Then why are *we* standing down, sir?" the regimental ops officer, Kenneth Bruno, asked. "We didn't fuck up. We should be blasting hell out of the Turks for—"

"I asked the same questions and made the same comments," Wilhelm interrupted, "and I was told by the Pentagon to pipe down, too, so now I'm telling you: pipe down. Listen up and pass the word to your troops:

"We are permanently on Force Protection Condition Delta. If I see you in the sunshine without your full battle rattle, and you're not already dead, I will kill you myself. This base will be sealed up tighter than a flea's poop chute. Woe befalls anyone who is seen without ID visible and displayed in the proper location, and that includes the senior staff and especially the civilians.

"As of this moment, this base is on a wartime footing—if we're not allowed to defend the Iraqi army that is living and working with us, we'll sure as hell defend ourselves," Wilhelm went on. "We will not be sitting idly around with our thumbs up our asses—we'll continue training as much as we're allowed until we rotate out. Next, the Triple-C will be turned over to the IA as soon as—"

"*What*?" someone exclaimed.

"I said, pipe down," Wilhelm snapped. "Official word from the Pentagon: we're not going to be relieved. We're closing up shop and turning the Triple-C over to the IA. All combat forces are moving out of Iraq, ahead of schedule. The IA is taking over." It was the day many in that room had been praying for, the day they were going to leave Iraq for good, but strangely no one was celebrating. "Well?" Wilhelm asked, looking around the Tank. "Aren't you mokes happy?"

There was a long silence; then Mark Weatherly said, "It makes us look like we're running, sir."

"It makes us look like we can't take a hit," someone else chimed in.

"I know it does," Wilhelm said. "But we know differently." That didn't seem to convince anyone—the silence was palpable. "We'll uninstall all the classified stuff—which in the absence of detailed instructions will be most of our gear as far as I'm concerned—but the rest will be turned over to the Iraqi army. We'll still be here to train and assist the IA, but not with combat operations. It hasn't been worked out whether their idea of 'security operations' is the same as ours, so we may still see some action, but I wouldn't bet on it. Where's McLanahan?"

"I'm up, Colonel," Patrick replied over the command network. "I'm in the hangar."

"The regiment's main task now is to support the contractors," Wilhelm said, his voice dead-cold and emotionless, "because all surveillance and security will be done by them. The Army is now just a trip-wire force, like we were in Korea before unification, and we'll probably be reduced to an even lower size than we were before we left there completely. General McLanahan, get together with Captain Cotter and figure out airspace coordination with logistics flights, the UAVs, and your spook planes."

"Yes, Colonel."

"McLanahan, I'll meet you at the hangar in five. Everyone else, the exec will be meeting with you to discuss removing the classified gear and starting a training program. Oh, one more thing: the memorial service for Second Platoon will be tonight; they'll be flown out to Germany tomorrow morning. That is all." He threw his headset onto the desk and strode out without as much as a glance to anyone else.

The XC-57 had been moved to a large tent outdoors so the air-conditioned hangar could be used to prepare the fallen members of Second Platoon for their flight out of Iraq. A C-130 Hercules transport had flown aluminum transfer cases in from Kuwait, and they were being unstacked in preparation for loading. Tables with the remains of the troops in body bags were lined up, and medical personnel, mortuary and registration volunteers, and fellow soldiers moved up and down the rows to assist, pray for them, or to say good-bye. A refrigerated truck was set up nearby to hold the remains of the more seriously decimated soldiers.

Wilhelm found Patrick standing beside one of the body bags, with a volunteer waiting to zip the bag up. When Patrick noticed the regimental commander standing across from him, he said, "Specialist Gamaliel came in last night before the mission. He said he wanted to know what it was like to fly heavy bombers and spaceplanes. He told me he always wanted to fly and was thinking about crossing over to the Air Force so he could go into space. We talked for about fifteen minutes, and then he left to join his platoon."

Wilhelm looked at the badly scarred and bloodied body, said a silent *thank you, Trooper,* then said aloud, "We need to talk, General." He nodded at the waiting soldiers, who reverently finished zipping the body bag closed. He followed Patrick down the line of body bags, then to an isolated portion of the hangar. "We've got VIPs flying in later today on a CV-22 Osprey," he said.

"Vice President Phoenix. I know."

"How the hell do you know all these things so quickly, McLanahan?"

"He's flying in on our second XC-57 aircraft, not on the Osprey," Patrick said. "They're afraid the Osprey is too much of a target."

"You guys must be plugged into the White House pretty tightly to pull that off." Patrick said nothing. "Did you have anything to do with the decision to cease combat operations?"

"You knew you were winding down combat ops, Colonel," Patrick said. "The Zakhu incident just accelerated things. As for how I know certain things . . . it's my *job* to know or learn things. I use all the tools at my disposal to gather as much information as I can."

Wilhelm took a step toward Patrick . . . but this time it was not menacing or threatening. It was as if he had a serious, direct, and urgent question, one that he didn't want others to hear in case it might reveal his own fears or confusion. "Who *are* you guys?" he asked in a low voice, almost a whisper. "What in hell is going on around here?"

For the first time, Patrick softened his opinion of the regimental commander. He certainly knew what it was like to lose men in combat and lose control of a situation, and he understood what Wilhelm was feeling. But he didn't yet deserve an answer or explanation.

"I'm sorry about your loss, Colonel," Patrick said. "Now, if you'll excuse me, I've got a plane coming in."

The second XC-57 Loser aircraft touched down at Nahla Allied Air Base at eight P.M. local time. It had been preceded by a CV-22 Osprey tiltrotor transport plane that the press and local dignitaries had been told would be carrying the vice president. The CV-22 executed the standard "high-performance" arrival—a high-speed dash into the base from high altitude, followed by a steep circle over the base to lose speed and altitude—and encountered no difficulties. By the time security forces had escorted the Osprey into a hangar, the XC-57 had already landed and taxied safely to another part of the base.

Jack Wilhelm, Patrick McLanahan, Jon Masters, Kris Thompson, and Mark Weatherly, all wearing identical civilian clothes—blue jeans, boots, plain shirt, sunglasses, and a tan vest, very similar to what Kris Thompson's security forces typically wore—stood beside the XC-57 as the vice president climbed down the boarding ladder.

The only one in uniform was Colonel Yusuf Jaffar, the Iraqi commander of Allied Air Base Nahla. He was in his usual desert gray battle dress uniform, but this time was wearing a green beret with an array of medals pinned to the blouse, black ascot, spit-shined boots and pistol holster, and a .45 caliber automatic pistol. He did not say anything to anyone except his aide, but he seemed to be watching Patrick, as if he wanted to speak with him.

No one except Jaffar saluted as Vice President Kenneth Phoenix stepped to the ground. Phoenix was dressed almost exactly as the other Americans—it looked like a gaggle of civilian security guards. Several other men and women alighted, dressed similarly.

Phoenix looked around, grinning at the sight, until his eyes finally locked onto a familiar face. "Thank God I recognize someone. I was starting to feel like I was having a weird dream." He stepped over to Patrick and extended a hand. "Good to see you, General."

"Good to see you, too, Mr. Vice President. Welcome to Iraq."

"I wish it was under happier circumstances. So, you're working for the 'dark side' now: the evil defense contractors." Patrick made no response. "Introduce me around."

"Yes, sir. Colonel Yusuf Jaffar, commander of Allied Air Base Nahla."

Jaffar did not lower his salute until he was introduced, and then he stood at rigid attention until Phoenix extended his hand. "A pleasure to meet you, Colonel."

Jaffar shook his hand as stiffly as he stood. "I am honored to have you visit my base and my country, sir," he said in a booming voice, his words obviously well rehearsed. *"Es salaam alekum.* Welcome to the Republic of Iraq and to Allied Air Base Nahla."

"*Es salaam alekum*," Phoenix said with a surprisingly good Arabic accent. "I am sorry for your losses, sir."

"My men served with honor and died as martyrs in the service of their country," Jaffar said. "They sit at the right hand of God. As for the ones who did this, they shall pay dearly." He snapped to attention and looked away from Phoenix, terminating their conversation.

"Mr. Vice President, Colonel Jack Wilhelm, regimental commander."

Phoenix extended a hand, and Wilhelm took it. "I'm very sorry for your losses, Colonel," he said. "If there's anything you need, anything at all, you come directly to me."

"For now my only request is your presence at the departure ceremony for Second Platoon, sir. It'll be in a couple hours."

"Of course, Colonel. I'll be there." Wilhelm introduced the others from his command, and the vice president introduced the others who arrived with him. Kris Thompson then led them to waiting armored vehicles.

Before Patrick climbed into an armored Suburban, Jaffar's aide came up to him and saluted. "My apologies for the interruption, sir," the aide said in very good English. "The colonel wishes to speak with you."

Patrick looked over at Jaffar, who was partially turned away from him. "Can it wait until our briefing with the vice president is over?"

"The colonel will not be attending the briefing, sir. Please?" Patrick nodded and motioned for the driver to go.

The Iraqi snapped to attention and saluted

when Patrick stepped over to him. Patrick returned his salute. "General McLanahan. I apologize for the interruption."

"You won't be attending the briefing with the vice president, Colonel?"

"It would be an insult to my commander and the chief of staff of the Iraqi army for me to attend such a meeting before them," Jaffar explained. "These protocols must be observed." He glared at McLanahan, then added, "I should think that your commanding officers and diplomats in Baghdad would be similarly offended."

"It's the vice president's decision, not ours."

"The vice president cares little for such protocols?"

"He's here to find out what happened and how our government can help get things straightened out, not observe protocols."

Jaffar nodded. "I see."

"He might think that you not attending the briefing is a breach of protocol, Colonel. He is here to help Iraq and the Iraqi army, after all."

"Is that so, General?" Jaffar asked, a razor-sharp edge to his voice. "He comes unbidden to our country and expects me to attend a briefing that our *president* has not yet heard?" He made a show of thinking about his point, then nodded. "Please make my apologies to the vice president."

"Of course. I can brief you later if you'd prefer."

"That would be acceptable, General," Jaffar said. "Sir, may I have permission to inspect your reconnaissance aircraft at your earliest convenience?"

Patrick was a little surprised: Jaffar hadn't shown any interest in their activities whatsoever in the short time he'd been there. "There are some systems and devices that are classified and I can't—"

"I understand, sir. I believe you call it NO-FORN—no foreign nationals. I understand completely."

"Then I'd be happy to show it to you," Patrick said. "I can brief you on tonight's reconnaissance run, show you the aircraft before the preflight inspections, and go over the unclassified data as we receive it to show you our capabilities. I'll have to get Colonel Wilhelm's and my company's permission, but I don't think that'll be a problem. Nineteen hundred hours, in your office?"

"That is acceptable, General McLanahan," Jaffar said. Patrick nodded and extended a hand, but Jaffar snapped to attention, saluted, spun on a heel, and walked quickly away to his waiting car, followed by his aide. Patrick shook his head, confused, then jumped into a waiting Humvee, which took him to the Command and Control Center.

Wilhelm was waiting for him in the conference room overlooking the Tank. Mark Weatherly was introducing the vice president to some of the staff members and explaining the layout of the Triple-C and the Tank. "Where's Jaffar?" Wilhelm asked in a low voice.

"He's not coming to the briefing. Said it would insult his commanders if he spoke with the vice president first."

"Damn *hajjis*—this was supposed to be for *his* benefit," Wilhelm said. "Why the hell didn't he tell me himself?" Patrick didn't answer. "What were you two talking about?"

"He wants to tour the Loser, get a briefing on our capabilities, and watch the next recon mission."

"Since when is *he* interested in any of that stuff?" Wilhelm growled. "Today, of all days, just after us getting our asses chewed up and with Washington crawling up and down our backs."

"I told him I needed your permission first."

Wilhelm was about to say no, but he just shook his head and muttered something under his breath. "He's entitled to be in the Tank for all operations—we keep the commander's seat open for him, for God's sake, even though he's never been in it—so I guess I don't have any choice. But he doesn't get to see the NOFORN stuff."

"I told him the same thing, and he understands. He even knew that term."

"Probably saw it in a movie and likes to parrot it every chance he gets. I'll bet it sticks in his craw." Wilhelm shook his head again, as if erasing the entire conversation from his head. "Are you still going to tell the vice president your theory?"

"Yes."

"Only you can add two and two and come up with five. It's your funeral. Okay, let's get this over with." Wilhelm nodded to Weatherly, who cut his talk short and motioned the vice president to a waiting seat.

Wilhelm stood uncomfortably at the dais as everyone settled in. "Mr. Vice President, distinguished visitors, thank you for this visit," he began. "Your presence so quickly after the tragedy last night sends a clear and important signal to not just the regiment but to all of the players in this conflict. My staff and I stand ready to assist you in your investigation.

"I know there are a lot of VIPs—the Iraqi prime minister, the ambassador, the commander of coalition forces in Iraq—waiting to greet you who will be very angry to learn that you came here instead of going to base headquarters to meet them," Wilhelm went on, "but General McLanahan and I thought you needed to hear from us first. Unfortunately, the base commander, Colonel Jaffar, will not be here."

"Did he say why not, Colonel?" the vice president asked.

"He told me it would be a breach of protocol to talk with you before his superior officers did, sir," Patrick replied. "He sends his regrets."

"It was his men that were killed and his homeland that was attacked. Who cares who hears from us first?"

"Would you like me to get him back here, sir?"

"No, let's press on," Phoenix said. "I'm not really concerned about stepping on toes right now, except for the ones responsible for killing our soldiers, and then I'll make sure that bastard is taken down.

"Okay, gents, I wanted to get this briefing from you because I know the Iraqis, Kurds, and Turks want to brief me soon, and I know they're going to spin it their way; I wanted to get the first word from you. The word from the Turks is that they're not doing anything except defending their homeland against the PKK and that the bombardment was a tragic but simple mistake. Let's hear your take."

"Roger that, sir." The electronic display behind Wilhelm flared to life, showing a map of the border region between northern Iraq and southeast Turkey. "They've increased their Jandarma border forces over the past year or so, including special ops battalions, along with a few more aviation units, to help deal with the PKK cross-border incursions. They've sent a few regular army units to the southwest as well, perhaps one or two brigades."

"Much bigger than normal deployments, I assume?" the vice president asked.

"Substantially bigger, sir, even considering the recent PKK terror attacks at Diyarbakir," Wilhelm replied.

"And what do we have on this side?"

"Together with the Iraqis, sir—about a third of their force, and a fraction of the air forces," Wilhelm replied. "The biggest threat is their tactical air forces in the region. Diyarbakir is home to Second Tactical Air Forces Command, responsible for the defense of the Syria, Iraq, and Iran border regions. They have two wings of F-16 fighter-bombers and one wing of F-4E Phantom fighter-bombers, plus one new wing of A-10 Thunderbolt Two close air support aircraft and one wing of F-15E Strike Eagle fighter-bombers, recently acquired from the United States as surplus equipment."

"Surplus F-15s—that's the craziest thing I've ever heard," the vice president said, shaking his head. "Aren't they still undefeated in combat?"

"I believe so, sir," Wilhelm said. "But with the

recent drawdown of U.S. Air Force fighters in favor of Navy and Marines carrier-based tactical fighters, a lot of good American weapons came on the export market."

"I know, I know—I fought hard to stop the outflow of such high-tech stuff," Phoenix said. "But President Gardner is a real military expert as well as a big supporter of the Navy, and Congress was solidly behind his transformation and modernization plans. The Air Force got hosed, and countries like Turkey are reaping the benefits. If we can't convert F-22s for carrier ops, Turkey is likely to get Raptors, too. Okay, soapbox over. Please continue, Colonel. What other threats are you facing?"

"Their larger antiaircraft systems such as the Patriot missile, large-caliber radar-guided triple-A, and British Rapier surface-to-air missiles are arrayed against Iran and Syria," Wilhelm went on. "We can expect them to move some systems farther west, but of course Iraq is not a threat from the air, so I think they'll keep their SAMs deployed against Iran and Syria. Smaller guns and shoulder-fired Stinger missiles can be encountered anywhere and are widely deployed in armored battalions.

"The Turkish Jandarma paramilitary forces deploy several special operations battalions, mostly to hunt down and destroy PKK insurgent and terror units. They get a lot of good training, and we consider them to be equivalent to a Marine recon unit—light, fast, mobile, and deadly."

"Their commander, General Besir Ozek, was badly hurt in the last big PKK attack in Diyarbakir," Patrick added, "but he's apparently up and around and directing his forces in hunt-and-kill operations throughout the border regions. He's undoubtedly the one who executed the rocket attack on Zakhu."

"I definitely need to have a talk with him," the vice president said. "So, Colonel, what's your explanation for all this activity?"

"It's not my job to analyze, sir," Wilhelm said, "but they're gearing up for an offensive against the PKK. They're backing up the Jandarma with regular military forces in a show of force. The PKK will scatter and keep their heads down; the Turks will hit a few bases, and then everything will go back to relative normalcy. The PKK's been doing this for over thirty years—Turkey can't stop them."

"Sending in the regular military—that's something they haven't done before," Phoenix observed. He glanced at Patrick. "General, you are suddenly quiet." He looked back at Wilhelm. "There appears to be disagreement here. Colonel?"

"Sir, General McLanahan is of the opinion that this buildup of Turkish forces in this region is a prelude to a full-scale invasion of Iraq."

"*An invasion of Iraq?*" Phoenix exclaimed. "I know they've done a lot of cross-border raids over the years, but why a full invasion, General?"

"Sir, it's exactly because they *have* done a lot of raids, and they haven't succeeded in stopping or even slowing the number of PKK attacks, that will prompt them to stage an all-out assault on the PKK in Iraq—not just the strongholds, training bases, and supply dumps along the border, but on the Kurdish leadership themselves. I think they'll want to crush the PKK problem in one lightning thrust and kill as many as they can before American and international pressure forces them to withdraw."

"Colonel?"

"The Turks simply don't have the manpower, sir," Wilhelm said. "We're talking about an operation similar in scope to Desert Storm—two hundred and fifty thousand troops, minimum. The Turkish army is approximately four hundred thousand *total*, mostly conscripts. They would need to commit one-third of their regular armed forces plus another one-*half* of their reserves for this *one* operation. That would take months and billions of dollars. The Turkish army is simply not an expeditionary force—they're built for anti-insurgent operations and self-defense, not for invading other countries."

"General?"

"The Turks would be fighting from their own soil and fighting for self-preservation and national pride," Patrick said. "If they committed half of their regular and reserve forces, they'd have close to half a million troops available, and they have a very large pool of trained veterans to use. I see no reason why they wouldn't order a full mobilization of all forces for a chance to destroy the PKK once and for all.

"But the new game-changing factor in play here is the Turkish air force," Patrick went on. "In years past, the Turkish military was mostly an internal counterinsurgency force with a secondary role as a NATO trip wire against the Soviet Union. Its navy is good but it's tasked mostly for defending the Bosporus and Dardanelles and patrolling the Aegean Sea. The air force was relatively small because it relied on the U.S. Air Force for support.

"But in just the past two years that's changed, and now Turkey has the largest air force in Europe except for Russia. They've been buying a lot more than surplus F-15s, sir—they bought all sorts of surplus noncarrier qualified attack aircraft, including the A-10 Thunderbolt tactical bombers, AC-130 Spectre gunships, and Apache gunship helicopters, along with weapons such as Patriot surface-to-air missiles, AMRAAM air-to-air missiles, and Maverick and Hellfire precision-guided air-to-ground missiles. They license-build F-16 fighters right in Turkey; they have as many F-16 squadrons available for action as we did in Desert Storm, and they'll all be fighting right from home. And I wouldn't discount their air defenses so easily: they can move their Patriots and Rapiers to oppose any action from us very easily."

Vice President Phoenix thought for a moment, and then nodded to both men. "You both make convincing arguments," he said, "but I'm inclined to agree with Colonel Wilhelm." Phoenix eyed Patrick warily, as if waiting for an argument, but Patrick kept silent. "I find it very hard to believe that—"

At that moment a phone buzzed, and it was as if a Klaxon had gone off—everyone knew that no phone calls would have been allowed during this briefing unless it was extremely urgent. Weatherly picked up the phone . . . and moments later, his expression made everyone in the room take notice.

Weatherly went over to a computer monitor nearby, read a dispatch silently with a quivering lip, then said, "Top-priority message from division, sir. The State Department has notified us that the president of Turkey may announce a state of emergency."

"Crap, I was afraid something like that might happen," Phoenix said. "We may not get a chance to meet with the Turks to investigate the shelling. Colonel, I'll need to speak with the White House."

"I can set that up right away, sir." Wilhelm nodded to Weatherly, who immediately got on the phone to the communications officer.

"I'll get the briefings from the ambassador, the Iraqis, and the Turks, but my recommendation to the president will be to step up border monitoring." The vice president turned to Patrick. "I still can't believe Turkey would invade Iraq with three thousand U.S. troops in the way," he said, "but obviously things are changing fast, and we'll need to get some eyes up there. I assume that's what your pregnant stealth bomber is for, General?"

"Yes, sir."

"Then I'd get it ready to go," Phoenix said as Wilhelm motioned to him that his link to the White House was ready, "because I think we'll need it . . . soon. Very soon." Weatherly motioned for him that his communications setup was ready, and he and the vice president departed.

Patrick hung back with Wilhelm as everyone else filed out of the conference room. "So, what do you have in mind, General?" Wilhelm asked. "Plan on sending your pregnant stealth bomber up over Turkey this time instead of just over our sector? That'll really calm everyone's nerves around here."

"I'm not going to send the Loser over Turkey, Colonel, but I'm not going to let the Turks relax, either," Patrick said. "I want to see what the Turks have in mind if any aircraft strays too close to the border. We know they'll hit back hard against any PKK land incursions. What will they do if it starts to look like the United States is poking around on their side of the border too much with aircraft?"

"Think that's smart, McLanahan? That could ratchet up the tension around here even more."

"We've got a lot of dead troopers in your hangar out there, Colonel," Patrick reminded him. "I want to be sure the Turks know that we are very, *very* angry at them right now."

OVER SOUTHEASTERN TURKEY
The next evening

"*Contact*, designating target bravo!" the MIM-104 Patriot tactical control officer shouted in Turkish. "I think it's the same one that's been popping in and out on us." The Patriot AN/MPQ-53 radar system belonging to the Turkish army had identified an aircraft and displayed the target to the operators in the Patriot Engagement Control System. The tactical control officer quickly determined that the target was right on the border between Iraq and Turkey, but because it was not in contact with Turkish air traffic controllers and not transmitting any transponder beacon codes, it was considered in violation of the thirty-mile protected Turkish air defense buffer zone; it was too low to be on approach to any airfields in the region and was far off any established civil airways. "Sir, recommend designating target bravo as hostile."

The tactical director checked the radar display—no doubt about it. "I concur," he said. "Designate target bravo as hostile, broadcast warning messages on all civil and military emergency and air traffic control frequencies, and stand by to engage." The tactical director picked up a secure telephone, linked by microwave directly to the sector air defense commander, Fourth Border Defense Regiment, in Diyarbakir. "*Kamyan, Kamyan*, this is *Ustura*, I have designated target bravo as hostile, standing by."

"*Ustura*, is this the same pop-up target you've been watching for the past two hours?" the sector commander inquired.

"We think so, sir," the tactical director said. "It's almost certainly a UAV in a reconnaissance orbit, based on speed and flight path. We couldn't get a firm altitude readout before, but it appears he's climbed to a higher altitude to get a deeper look north."

"Civilian traffic?"

"We've been broadcasting warning messages every time the target has popped up, and we're broadcasting now on all civil and military emergency and air traffic control frequencies. No responses at all. Unless the pilot completely switched off his radios, it's a hostile."

"I concur," the air defense commander said. He knew that some air defense sectors in busier areas used multicolored lasers to visually warn pilots away from restricted airspace, but he didn't have that courtesy—nor did he really care to use it even if he had it. Any innocent pilot stupid enough to fly in this area during this breakout of hostilities *deserved* to get his ass shot down. "Stand by." To his communications officer he ordered, "Get me Second Regiment at Nahla, and Ankara."

"Second Regiment on the line, sir, Major Sabasti."

That was quick, the sector commander thought—normally direct calls to the American Command and Control Center were filtered and redirected several times before connecting, and it took a few minutes. "Sabasti, this is *Kamyan*. We don't show any American air missions in the buffer zone scheduled for tonight. Can you confirm an American flight along the border?"

"I'm looking at the sector map now, sir," the liaison officer responded, "and the only aircraft in the buffer zone has been precoordinated with you, authorization number Kilo-Juliet-two-three-two-one, operating inside area Peynir."

"We're looking at a low-altitude aircraft that pops up and down out of radar coverage. It's not an American or Iraqi aircraft?"

"I'm showing three American and one Iraqi reconnaissance plane airborne, sir, but only one is in the buffer zone."

"What is it?"

"Its call sign is Guppy Two-Two, an American reconnaissance aircraft operated by private security contractors." He read off the aircraft's coordinates and location of its orbit box—it was exactly as earlier coordinated, inside the Peynir buffer zone but forty miles from the pop-up target.

"What kind of plane is it, Major?"

"I'm sorry, sir, but you know I can't tell you that. I have verified it with my own eyes and I know it's an unarmed reconnaissance plane."

"Well, Major, maybe you can tell me what it's *not*," the sector commander said.

"Sir . . ."

"Who the hell do you work for, Major—the Americans, or Turkey?"

"Excuse me, sir," a voice interjected. "This is an American interpreter. I work for Mr. Kris Thompson, Thompson Security, Second Regiment, Allied Air Base Nahla, Iraq."

"I know who the hell you are and where you are located," the sector commander snapped. "Are you monitoring my radio messages?"

"Mr. Thompson says that the Status of Forces agreement between the United States, Iraq, and Turkey allows monitoring of routine and emergency radio traffic between military units party to the agreement," the interpreter said. "He says you may verify this with your foreign ministry if necessary."

"I am well aware of the agreement."

"Yes, sir. Mr. Thompson wants me to tell you that specific information regarding the systems involved in operations inside Iraq is not permitted to be revealed except in accordance with the Status of Forces agreement. The agreement allows an observer to view the aircraft that will be used and to monitor it throughout its mission, but he may not reveal any other details."

"Thompson, I am about to shoot down an unidentified aircraft violating the Turkish airspace buffer zone," the sector commander said. "I wanted to get more information to be sure I was not attacking an American or Iraqi aircraft. If you wish to play word games or shake the Status of Forces agreement in my face instead of assisting me in validating this target's identity, so be it. Major Sabasti."

"Sir!"

"Inform the Americans that we are tracking an unknown aircraft in the buffer zone and that we consider it hostile," the sector commander said in Turkish. "I recommend to them that all allied aircraft and ground patrols stay well clear and the reconnaissance aircraft may want to vacate the patrol box."

"I'll pass the word along immediately, sir."

"Very well." The sector commander terminated the connection with an angry stab. "Is Ankara on the line yet?" he thundered.

"Standing by, sir."

"This is *Mat*," a voice responded. The sector commander knew that *Mat*, Turkish for "checkmate," was the operations officer for the military chief of staff. "We are monitoring your radar contact, and the liaison officer at Nahla has messaged us saying that you contacted them for coordination and identification and they say it is not one of theirs. Recommendation?"

"Engage immediately, sir."

"Stand by." Those two damned dreaded words . . . but moments later: "We concur, *Kamyan*. Engage as directed. Out."

"*Kamyan* copies, engaged as directed. *Kamyan* out." The sector commander changed to his tactical channel: "*Ustura*, this is *Kamyan*, engage as directed."

"*Ustura* copies, engage as directed. *Ustura* out." The tactical director hung up the phone. "We've been ordered to engage as directed," he announced. "Any change in target path or altitude? Any response to our broadcasts?"

"No, sir."

"Very well. Engage."

"I copy 'engage.'" The tactical control officer reached up, lifted a red-colored cover, and pressed a large red button, which activated a Klaxon throughout the four Patriot line batteries spread throughout southeastern Turkey. Each line battery consisted of four Patriot platoons, each with one Patriot Advanced Capability-3 (PAC-3) launcher with sixteen missiles, plus another sixteen missiles ready to load. "Engage."

"I copy 'engage,'" the Tactical Control Assistant repeated. He checked the target's location with the battalion's deployed Patriot batteries, picked the closest one to the hostile, and punched the communications button to that battery. "*Ustura* Two, *Ustura* Two, this is *Ustura*, operate, operate, operate."

"Two copies 'operate.'" There was a brief pause, and then the second firing battery's status report changed from "standby" to "operate," meaning the battery's missiles were ready to fire. "Second Battery reports status is 'operate,' ready to engage."

"Acknowledged." The tactical control officer kept on mashing the warning horn as he watched his computer readouts. The attack was all controlled by computer from here on out—the humans could do nothing but shut it off if they desired. Moments later, the Engagement Control Computer reported that it had designated one of the platoons located west of the mountain town of Beytussebap to engage. "Fifth Platoon has been activated . . . missile one away." Four seconds later: "Missile two away. Radar is active."

Traveling at over three thousand miles per hour, the Patriot missiles needed less than six seconds to reach their prey. "Missile one direct hit, sir," the Tactical Control Assistant reported. Moments later: "Missile two engaging a second target, sir!"

"*A second target?*"

"Yes, sir. Same altitude, rapidly decreasing airspeed . . . direct hit on second hostile, sir!"

"There were *two* aircraft out there?" the tactical director mused aloud. "Could they have been flying in formation?"

"Possible, sir," the tactical control officer responded. "But why?"

The tactical director shook his head. "It doesn't make sense, but whatever they were, we got them. It could have been debris from the first hit."

"It looked very large, sir, like a second aircraft."

"Well, whatever it was, we got the *merde* nonetheless. Good work, everyone. Those two targets were south of the border but in the security buffer, yes?"

"Actually, sir, for a brief moment it was in Turkish airspace, no more than a few miles, but definitely north of the border."

"A good kill, then." The tactical director picked up another phone linked to the Jandarma headquarters in Diyarbakir, where someone would be responsible for organizing a search party for wreckage, casualties, and evidence. "*Curuk*, this is *Ustura*, we have engaged and destroyed a hostile aircraft. Transmitting target intercept coordinates now."

"That sure didn't take them long," Jon Masters said. He was in the Tank's observation room on the second floor, watching the engagement on his laptop. "Two minutes from when we changed the target altitude to shoot-down. That's fast."

"We might not have brought the false target down fast enough . . . they might have seen the target even after the first Patriot 'hit,'" Patrick McLanahan said.

"I was trying to simulate debris by keeping the image up for another few seconds," Jon said. "I slowed it way down."

"Let's hope they think they hit them both," Patrick said. "Okay, so we know that the Turks moved their Patriots closer to the Iraqi border, and we know they mean business—they won't hesitate to open fire, even on something as small as a Predator or FlightHawk."

"Or a netrusion false target," Jon Masters said happily. "We were easily able to hack into the Patriot system's engagement control system and plant a UAV-size target into their system. As soon as we adjusted the false target's altitude up high enough, they reacted as if it was a real hostile."

"When they go out there and don't find any debris, they'll be curious and on guard next time," Patrick said. "What else do we know from this engagement?"

"We also know that they can see and engage as close as one thousand feet aboveground," Jon said. "That's pretty good in fairly rough terrain. They may have modified the Patriot's radar to give it a better de-clutter and low-altitude detection ability."

"Let's hope that's *all* they've done," Patrick said. He touched an intercom button: "Did you see the engagement, Colonel?"

"Affirmative," Wilhelm replied. "So the Turks did move their Patriots west. I'll notify division. But I still don't think Turkey will invade Iraq. We should be passing them all the intel we have on PKK movements, reassure them that our troops and the Iraqis aren't going to hit back, and let the crisis level cool down."

NORTH OF THE TOWN OF BEYTUSSEBAP, REPUBLIC OF TURKEY
The next evening

The squad of eight Iraqi Kurd guerrilla fighters had used sniper team tactics—self-taught by reading books, using the Internet, and learning information passed down to them by veterans— to make their way to their target: crawling for dozens of miles sometimes inches at a time, never rising up past knee height for any reason; changing camouflage on their clothing every time the terrain changed; being careful to erase any signs of their presence as they dragged heavy packs and rocket-propelled grenade launcher tubes behind them.

One of the fighters, a former police officer from Irbil named Sadoon Salih, broke off a piece of a fig candy bar, tapped the boot of the person ahead of him, and held it out. "Last piece, Commander," he whispered. The person made a "quiet" motion back at him—not with her left hand, but with a rakelike appliance attached to her wrist where a hand would normally be. Then the rake averted, open-handed, and the fighter dropped the candy into it. She nodded her thanks and kept moving.

They had brought food and water for only five days on this reconnaissance patrol, but with all the activity in the area she had decided to stay out. The food they brought ran out three days ago. They had cut back their daily rations to absurdly low levels and had begun subsisting on food they found in the field—berries, roots, and insects, with an occasional handout from a sympathetic farmer or herdsman they dared approach—and sipping stream water filtered through dirty kerchiefs.

But now she had discovered what all the military activity was about, and it was a lot more than just the Jandarma goon squads attacking Kurdish villages looking for revenge for the attack in Diyarbakir: the Turkish army was building these little fire bases in the countryside. Was Turkey bringing in the regular military to reinforce the Jandarma?

They had changed their reconnaissance patrol

plan because of the spectacular double missile launches they had observed the night before. They were accustomed to seeing artillery and air bombardments from Turkey against Kurdish villages and PKK training camps, but these were no artillery rounds—they were guided high-performance missiles that were maneuvering while ascending, not in a ballistic flight path, and they exploded far up in the sky. The Turks had a new weapon in the field, and they obviously had something to do with all this base construction activity along the Turkey-Iraq border. It was up to her and her squads to check it out.

Along with water and concealment, the most important aid to the fighters was preservation of night vision. All of the fighters carried red-lensed goggles, and the closer they got to their objective the more they had to use them in order not to spoil their night vision, because the perimeter of their objective was illuminated by banks of outwardly aimed portable floodlights, which threw the encampment beyond into total darkness. It was an interesting tactic, thought the squad leader: the Turkish army certainly had night-vision technology, but they weren't using it out here.

It could be a trap, but it was definitely an opportunity they couldn't waste.

The squad leader, Zilar Azzawi, motioned for her shooters to move forward. As they spread out and began setting up, she scanned the perimeter with her binoculars. Set between each portable floodlight setup was a sandbag firing nest, separated from one another by about twenty yards. Seventy yards to her right was a truck entrance

built of sandbags and lumber, blocked by a troop
transport truck with the right side covered with
a solid wall of green plywood panels, forming a
simple movable gate. There was a single layer of
thin five-foot-high metal rolled fencing between
the sandbag emplacements, held up by lightweight stakes. This was definitely not a permanent camp, at least not yet.

If they were going to take advantage, now was
the time.

Azzawi waited until her team was ready, then
pulled out a simple Korean-made hiker's walkie-
talkie and clicked the microphone button once,
then clicked twice. A few moments later, she got
two clicks in reply, followed by three clicks. She
clicked her walkie-talkie three times, put it away,
then touched the arm of the two men on either
side of her with the silent "get ready" signal.

She lowered her head, closed her eyes, then
spoke "*Ma'lēsh*—nothing matters," in a low, quiet
voice. She paused for a few more heartbeats,
thinking of her dead husband and sons—and at
that, the fury within her pushed the energy of a
jet engine through her body, and she smoothly
and easily stood up, raised her RPG-7 launcher,
and fired at the sandbag gun mount across from
her. As soon as her round hit, her other squad
members opened up on other emplacements,
and in seconds the entire section was wide open.
At that moment the two other squads under Azzawi's command on different sides of the base
also opened fire with rocket-propelled grenades.

Now the lights that had prevented the attackers from seeing inside the base gave them

an advantage, because they could see survivors and other Turkish soldiers preparing to repel the attack. Azzawi's sniper teams started picking them off one by one, which forced the Turks to retreat farther back from the perimeter into the darkness of their camp. Azzawi threw her RPG launcher aside, retrieved her radio, and yelled, "*Ala tūl*! Move!" She picked up her AK-47 assault rifle, screamed, "*IlHa'ūnī*! Follow me!" and ran toward the base, firing from the hip.

There was no alternative but to dash across the illuminated no-man's-land to the base—they were easy targets for anyone inside. But without her pack and RPG launcher, and with the surge of adrenaline mixed with fear coursing through her body, the fifty-yard run felt easy. But to her surprise, there was little resistance.

There were a few bodies in the destroyed gun nests, but she saw no signs of things like mine detonators, antitank weapons, or heavy machine guns or grenade launchers, just light infantry weapons. Apparently they hadn't been expecting much trouble, or they hadn't had time to set up properly. This notion was reinforced a few moments later when she found construction equipment, concrete, lumber for forms, and tools in piles nearby.

In less than five minutes of sporadic fighting, Azzawi's three squads met up. All three had pushed forward with relative ease. She congratulated each of her fighters with handshakes and motherly touches, then said, "Casualty report."

"We have one dead, three wounded," the first squad leader said. "Seventeen prisoners, including an officer." The other squad leader reported similarly.

"We have four wounded and eight prisoners," Salih, Azzawi's assistant squad leader, said. "What is this place, Commander? That was too easy."

"First things first, Sadoon," Azzawi said. "Set up perimeter guards in case their patrols come back." Salih ran off. To the second squad leader, she said, "Bring the officer to me," as she wrapped a scarf over her face.

The captive was a captain in the Turkish army. He was holding his left hand over a gaping wound on his right biceps, and blood was freely flowing. "Get a medical kit over here," Azzawi ordered in Arabic. In Turkish, she asked, "Name, unit, and purpose here, Captain, and quickly."

"You bastards nearly shot my damned arm off!" he shouted.

Azzawi raised her left arm, letting her *hijab* sleeve roll down to reveal her makeshift prosthetic. "I know exactly how it feels, Captain," she said. "Look at what the Turkish air force did to *me*." Even in the semidarkness, she could see the soldier's eyes widen in surprise. "And this is far better than what you did to my husband and sons."

"You . . . you are Baz!" the officer breathed. "The rumors are true . . . !"

Azzawi removed the scarf from her face, revealing her dirty but proud and beautiful features. "I said name, unit, and mission, Captain," she said. She raised her rifle. "You must understand that I don't have the desire or the ability to take prisoners, Captain, so I promise you I will kill you right here and now if you don't answer me." The officer lowered his head and started to shiver. "Last chance: name, unit, and mission." She raised her weapon to her hip and clicked the safety switch off with a loud *snap*. "Very well. Peace be with you, Captain—"

"All right, all right!" the officer shouted. It was obvious he wasn't a trained or experienced field officer—probably a desk jockey or lab rat pressed into service at the last minute. "My name is Ahmet Yakis, Twenty-third Communications Company, Delta Platoon. My mission was to set up communications, that's all."

"Communications?" If this was just a communications relay site, it might explain the lax security and ill-preparedness. "For what?"

Just then, Azzawi's assistant squad leader, Sadoon Salih, ran up. "Commander, you have *got* to see this," he said breathlessly. She ordered the prisoner to be bandaged up and secured, then ran off. She had to hop over a lot of cables strung throughout the camp, and she saw a large truck carrying what appeared to be a large steel container to which most of the cables were attached. They followed a bundle of cables up a slight rise to a large enclosure covered with camouflage netting.

Inside the enclosure, Azzawi found a large transport truck with a squat, square steel enclosure on the flatbed, along with two antenna masts lowered onto the deck of the truck and folded up in road-march configuration. "Well, here is the communications antennae the captain said he was setting up," Azzawi said. "I guess he was telling the truth."

"Not entirely, Commander," Salih said. "I

recognize this equipment because back home I guarded an American convoy of these things being set up to guard against an Iranian attack into Iraq. This is called an antenna mast group, which relays microwave command signals from a radar site to missile launch sites. That truck back there is a power generator . . . for a Patriot antiaircraft missile battery."

"*A Patriot missile battery*?" Azzawi exclaimed.

"They must be the advance team setting up a base station for a Patriot missile battery," Salih said. "They'll bring in a huge flat-screen radar and a control station and be able to control several launchers spread out over miles. It's all very portable; they can operate anywhere."

"But why on God's great earth are the Turks setting up an antiaircraft missile site out here?" Azzawi asked. "Unless the Kurdish government in Iraq somehow built itself an air force, who are they guarding against?"

"I don't know," Salih said. "But whoever it is, they must be flying over Turkish territory, and the Turks shot at them last night. I wonder who it was?"

"I don't really care who they are—if they're fighting Turks, that's good enough for me," Azzawi said. "Let's take these vehicles back home. I don't know what value they have, but they look brand-new, and maybe we can use them. At the very least, we won't have to walk as far to get home. Good job tonight, Sadoon."

"Thank you, Commander. It's a pleasure to serve under such a strong leader. I'm sorry we didn't do that much damage to the Turks, though . . ."

"Every little cut weakens them just a little bit more," Zilar said. "We are few, but if we keep on inflicting these little cuts, eventually we'll succeed."

ÇANKAYA KÖŞKÜ, ANKARA, REPUBLIC OF TURKEY
Later that day

"The initial reports were true, sir," General Orhan Sahin, secretary-general of the Turkish national security council said, running a hand through his dark sandy hair. "The PKK terrorists stole several components of a Patriot surface-to-air missile battery, specifically the antenna mast group, power generator, and cables."

"Unbelievable, simply unbelievable," President Kurzat Hirsiz muttered. He had assembled his national security council for an update on planning for the Iraq operation, but things seemed to be getting worse by the day and threatening to spin out of control. "What happened?"

"Early last night a PKK platoon, reportedly led by the terrorist commando mastermind they call the Hawk, attacked a Patriot headquarters emplacement that was being set up near the town of Beytussebap," Sahin said. "The terrorists killed five, wounded twelve, and tied up the rest. All of our soldiers and technicians are accounted for—they took no prisoners, which means it was probably just a surveillance team or patrol, not a strike force. They made off with major Patriot missile battery components that were mounted on trucks for easy deployment, parts that allow the headquarters to communicate with remote launchers. Fortunately the headquarters vehicle itself and the missile transporter-launchers were not present."

"Am I supposed to feel relieved about this?" Hirsiz shouted. "Where was security? How could this happen?"

"The base was not yet fully set up, so there was no perimeter fencing or barriers," Sahin said. "There was only a token security force in place—the rest had been sent to help search for wreckage of the engagement that happened the previous night."

"My God," Hirsiz breathed. He turned to Prime Minister Akas. "We must do this, Ayşe, and do it *now*," he said to her. "We must accelerate the Iraq operation. I want to declare a state of national emergency. You must convince the Grand National Assembly to declare war on the Kurdistan Workers' Party and all its affiliated groups throughout Turkey's neighboring region and order a call-up of reserves."

"That is craziness, Kurzat," Akas said. "There is no reason for a state of emergency. Whoever leaked that rumor should be thrown in jail. And how can you declare war on an ethnic group? Is this Nazi Germany?"

"If you don't want to participate, Prime Minister, you should resign," Minister of National Defense Hasan Cizek said. "The rest of the cabinet is with the president. You stand in the way of getting this operation fully under way. We need the cooperation of the National Assembly and the Turkish people."

"And I disagree with this plan, as do the legislators I have spoken with behind closed doors," Akas said. "We are all disgusted and frustrated by the PKK attacks, but invading Iraq is not the way to solve the problem. And if anyone should resign, Minister, it is *you*. The PKK has infiltrated the Jandarma, stolen valuable weapons, and run roughshod over the entire country. I am not going to resign. I appear to be the only voice of reason here."

"Reason?" Cizek cried. "You stand there and call for meetings and negotiations while Turks are slaughtered. Where's the reason in that?" He turned to Hirsiz. "We're wasting time here, sir," he growled. "She will never comply. I told you, she's a brainless ideological idiot. She'd rather stonewall than do the right thing to save the republic."

"How dare you, Cizek?" Akas shouted, stunned by his words. "I am the prime minister of Turkey!"

"Listen to me, Ayşe," Hirsiz said. "I can't do this without you. We've been in Ankara together for too many years, in the National Assembly and in Çancaya. Our country is under siege. We can't just talk any longer."

"I promise you, Mr. President, I will do everything in my power to make the world realize that we need help to stop the PKK," Akas said. "Don't let your hatred and frustration lead you to bad decisions or rash actions." She stepped closer to Hirsiz. "The republic is counting on us, Kurzat."

Hirsiz looked like a man who had been beaten and tortured for days. He nodded. "You're right,

Ayşe," he said. "The republic *is* counting on us."
He turned to the military chief of staff, General
Abdullah Guzlev: "Do it, General."

"Yes, *sir*," Guzlev said, and he went to the
president's desk and picked up a phone.

"Do what, Kurzat?" Akas asked.

"I'm accelerating the deployment of the armed
forces," Hirsiz said. "We'll be ready to begin the
operation in a few days."

"You cannot begin a military offensive without a declaration of war by the National Assembly," Akas said. "I assure you, we don't have
the votes yet. Give me more time. I'm sure I can
convince—"

"We won't need the votes, Ayşe," Hirsiz said,
"because I'm instituting a state of emergency and
dissolving the National Assembly."

Akas's eyes bugged out in complete shock.
"You're *what* . . . ?"

"We have no choice, Ayşe."

"*We*? You mean, your military advisers? General Ozek? *They're* your advisers now?"

"The situation demands action, Ayşe, not
talk," Hirsiz said. "I was hoping you'd help us,
but I'm prepared to take action without you."

"Don't do it, Kurzat," Akas said. "I know the
situation is grave, but don't make any rash decisions. Let me gather support from the Americans
and the United Nations. They are sympathetic to
us. The American vice president will listen. But
if you do this, we'll lose all support from everyone."

"I'm sorry, Ayşe," Hirsiz said. "It's done. You
may inform the National Assembly and Supreme
Court if you wish, or I will."

"No, it's my responsibility," Akas said. "I will tell them of the agony you are experiencing at the loss of so many citizens of Turkey at the hands of the PKK."

"Thank you."

"I will also tell them that your anger and frustration has turned you insane and blood-drunk," Akas said. "I will tell them that your military advisers are telling you exactly what they want you to hear instead of what you *need* to hear. I will tell them that you're not yourself right now."

"Don't do that, Ayşe," Hirsiz said. "That would be disloyal, to me and to Turkey. I'm doing this because it needs to be done, and it is my responsibility."

"Isn't that what they say is the beginning of madness, Kurzat: to insist that you have responsibilities?" Akas asked. "Is that what all dictators and strongmen say? Is that what Evren said in 1980 or Tağmaç said before him, when they dissolved the National Assembly and took over the government in a military coup? Go to hell."

CHAPTER 5

*Don't wait for the light to appear at the end
of the tunnel—stride down there and
light the bloody thing yourself.*
—*Dara Henderson, writer*

ALLIED AIR BASE NAHLA, IRAQ
The next day

It's total chaos and confusion up there in Ankara, Mr. Vice President," Secretary of State Stacy Anne Barbeau said from her office in Washington via a secure satellite video teleconference link. Also attending was vice president Ken Phoenix, meeting with Iraqi leaders and the U.S. ambassador in Baghdad; and Colonel Jack Wilhelm, the commander of U.S. forces in northern Iraq, at Nahla Allied Air Base near the northern city of Mosul. "The Turkish prime minister herself called our ambassador on the carpet for an ass chewing because of an apparent airspace violation by an American aircraft, but now he's sitting waiting in the outer office under heavy guard because of some security ruckus."

"What is the embassy saying, Stacy?" Phoenix asked. "Are they in contact with the ambassador?"

"Cellular service is currently down, but outages have been the norm for a few days since the rumors of a state of emergency, Mr. Vice President," Barbeau said. "Government radio and TV have been describing numerous demonstrations both for and against Hirsiz's government, but they've mostly been peaceful and the police are handling it. The military has been quiet. There was some kind of gunfire incident at the Pink Palace, but the Presidential Guard says the president is safe and will address the nation later today."

"That's pretty much what the embassy here in Baghdad has been telling me," Phoenix said. "Baghdad is concerned about the confusing news but hasn't bumped up readiness levels."

"I need an explanation of what happened on the Iraq-Turkish border, Colonel Wilhelm," Barbeau said. "The Turks claim they shot down an American unmanned spy plane over their territory, and they're hopping mad."

"I can assure everyone that all American aircraft, unmanned or otherwise, are accounted for, ma'am," Wilhelm said, "and we're not missing any aircraft."

"Does that include your contractors, Colonel?" Barbeau asked pointedly.

"It does, ma'am."

"Who operates reconnaissance aircraft operating along the border? Is it that Scion Aviation International outfit?"

"Yes, ma'am. They operate two large and

pretty high-tech long-range recon planes, and they're bringing in smaller unmanned aircraft to supplement their activities."

"I want to talk with the rep right now."

"He's standing by, ma'am. General?"

" 'General'?"

"The guy from Scion is a retired Air Force general, ma'am." Barbeau's eyes blinked in confusion—obviously she didn't have that information. "Most of our contractors are retired or former military."

"Well, where is he? Isn't he working there with you, Colonel?"

"He doesn't usually operate out of the Command and Control Center," Wilhelm explained, "but out on the flight line. He's networked his aircraft in with the Triple-C and to our few remaining assets."

"I have no idea what you just said, Colonel," Barbeau complained, "and I hope the Scion guy can make some sense and give us some answers. Get him on the line *now*."

Just then a new window popped open on the videoconference screen, and Patrick McLanahan, wearing a lightweight gray vest over a white collared shirt, nodded at the camera. "Patrick McLanahan, Scion Aviation International, secure."

"*McLanahan*?" Stacy Barbeau exploded, partially rising out of her seat. "Patrick McLanahan *is a defense contractor in Iraq*?"

"Nice to see you, too, Miss Secretary of State," Patrick said. "I assumed Secretary Turner had briefed you on Scion's management."

He suppressed a smile as he saw Barbeau

struggling for control of her senses and voluntary muscles. The last time he had seen her was less than two years earlier when she was still the senior senator from Louisiana and the chairman of the Senate Armed Services Committee. Patrick, who had surreptitiously returned from Armstrong Space Station, where he was under virtual house arrest, supervised loading Barbeau aboard an XR-A9 Black Stallion spaceplane to fly her from Elliott Air Force Base in Nevada to Naval Air Station Patuxent River in Maryland— a flight that took less than two hours.

Of course, Barbeau remembered none of this, because Patrick had had Hunter "Boomer" Noble seduce and then sedate her in a luxury hotel-casino suite in Las Vegas to prepare for her brief flight into space.

Patrick's armored Tin Men and Cybernetic Infantry Device commandos then spirited her to the presidential retreat at Camp David, subdued the Secret Service and U.S. Navy security forces, and set up a confrontation between her and President Joseph Gardner over the future of the men and women who made up the U.S. Space Defense Force, which the president was ready to sacrifice in order to make peace with Russia. In exchange for not revealing Gardner's secret dealings with the Russians, the president had agreed to allow anyone under McLanahan's command who didn't want to serve under Gardner to honorably retire from military service . . .

. . . and Patrick ensured the president's continued cooperation by taking the entire remaining force of six Tin Men and two Cybernetic Infantry Device combat systems with him, along with spare parts, weapon packs, and the plans to make more of them. The advanced armored infantry performance enhancement systems had already proven they could defeat the Russian and Iranian armies as well as the U.S. Navy SEALs, and infiltrate the most highly guarded presidential retreats in the world—Patrick knew he had a lot of backup just in case the president tried to relieve himself of his McLanahan issue.

"Is there a problem here, Miss Secretary?" Vice President Phoenix asked. "I know you've met General McLanahan before."

"I assure you, we made all the proper notifications and filings—I did them myself through the Air Force Civil Augmentee Agency," Patrick said. "There's been no conflict of—"

"Can we please get on with this?" Stacy Anne Barbeau suddenly blurted perturbedly. Patrick smiled to himself: he knew that a seasoned political pro like Barbeau knew how to pull herself into the here and now, no matter how utterly shocked she became. "General, it's nice to see you hale and hearty. I should have known that retirement would never mean a rocking chair on the porch to someone like you."

"I think you know me too well, Miss Secretary."

"And I also know that you are not shy about stepping right on, and sometimes sneaking a foot or two across, the boundaries in your eagerness to get a job done," Barbeau went on directly. "We received complaints from the Turks about stealthy aircraft, perhaps unmanned, overflying Turkish airspace without permission. Pardon me for saying so, sir, but this has your fingerprints all over it. What exactly did you do?"

"Scion's contract is to provide integrated surveillance, intelligence gathering, reconnaissance, and data communications relay support services on the Iraq-Turkey border," Patrick said. "Our primary platform for this function is the XC-57 multipurpose airlift aircraft, which is a turbofan-powered manned or unmanned aircraft that can be fitted with a variety of mission modules to change its function. We also employ smaller unmanned aircraft that—"

"Get to the bottom line, General," Barbeau snapped. "Did you or did you not cross the Iraq-Turkey border?"

"No, ma'am, we did not—at least, not with any of our *aircraft*."

"What in hell does *that* mean?"

"The Turks fired at a false target we inserted into their Patriot acquisition and tracking computers via their phased-array radar," he said.

"I knew it! You *did* provoke the Turks into launching their missiles!"

"Part of our contracted reconnaissance mission is to analyze and categorize all threats in this area of responsibility," Patrick explained. "After the attack on Second Regiment in Zakhu, I consider the Turkish army and border guards a threat."

"I shouldn't have to remind you, General, that Turkey is an important ally, in NATO and the entire region—*they* are *not* the enemy," Barbeau said hotly. It was clear to everyone whom she believed the enemy *really* was. "Allies don't spoof each other's radars, cause them to waste two million dollars' worth of missiles on chasing ghosts, or incite fear and mistrust in an area that is already undergoing a critical level of fear. I'm not going to let you disrupt our diplomatic efforts just so you can test out some new gadget or make your investors a little money."

"Madam Secretary, the Turks moved their Patriot batteries farther west, opposing Iraq instead of just Iran," Patrick said. "Did the Turks advise us of this?"

"I'm not here to answer your questions, General. You're here to answer *mine* . . . !"

"Madam Secretary, we also know that the Turks have long-range artillery systems similar to the ones they used to attack Second Regiment in Zakhu," Patrick went on. "I want to see what the Turks are planning. The shake-up in their military high command, and now the loss of communications from the embassy, tell me that something is going on, possibly something serious. I recommend we—"

"Pardon me, General, but I am also not here to take *your* recommendations," Secretary of State Barbeau interjected. "You're a *contractor*, not a member of the cabinet or the staff. Now you listen to me, General: I want all of your tracking data, radar pictures, and whatever other stuff you've gathered since your company signed the contract. I want—"

"I'm sorry, ma'am, but I can't give it to you," Patrick said.

"What did you say to me?"

"I said, Madam Secretary, that I can't turn any of it over to you," Patrick repeated. "The data belongs to U.S. Central Command—you'll have to ask them for it."

"Don't play games with me, McLanahan. I'm going to have to explain what you did to Ankara. It looks like it'll be another case of contractors overstepping their boundaries and operating too independently. Any costs incurred by the Turks for your actions will come out of *your* pocket, not the U.S. Treasury's."

"That'll be for a court to decide," Patrick said. "In the meantime, the information we collect belongs to Central Command, or whoever they designate to receive it, such as Second Regiment. Only they can decide who gets it. Any other information or resources not covered by the contract with the government belong to Scion Aviation International, and I can't release it to anyone without a contract or a court order."

"You want to play hardball with me, mister, fine," Barbeau snapped. "I'll slap a lawsuit on you and your company so fast it'll make your head spin. In the meantime, I'm going to recommend to Secretary Turner to cancel your contract so we can prove to the Turkish government that this won't happen again." Patrick said nothing. "Colonel Wilhelm, I'm going to recommend to the Pentagon that you resume security operations along the border area until we can get another contractor in to take over. Await further orders to that effect."

"Yes, ma'am." Barbeau made a swiping motion across her camera with the back of a hand, and her image disappeared. "Thanks, General," Wilhelm said angrily. "I'm flat-footed here. It'll take me weeks to get replacements sent in, equipment returned and unpacked, and patrols set up again."

"We don't have weeks, Colonel, we have days," Patrick said. "Mr. Vice President, I'm sorry about the diplomatic row I've caused, but we learned a great deal. Turkey is gearing up for something. We have to be ready for it."

"Like what? Your Iraq invasion theory?"

"Yes, sir."

"What's happened to make you think this invasion is imminent?"

"Plenty has happened, sir," Patrick responded. "Scion's own analysis shows that the Turks now have twenty-five thousand Jandarma paramilitary troops within three days' march of Mosul and Irbil, and another three divisions—one hundred thousand regular infantry, armor, and artillery troops—within a week's march."

"*Three divisions*?"

"Yes, sir—that's nearly as many troops as the United States had in Iraq at the height of Operation Iraqi Freedom, except the Turks are concentrated in the north," Patrick said. "Those ground forces are backed up by the largest and most advanced air force between Russia and Germany. Scion believes they're poised to strike. The recent resignation of Turkey's military leadership, and this very recent confusion and loss of contact with the embassy in Ankara, confirm my fears."

There was a long pause on the line; Patrick saw the vice president lean back in his seat and rub his face and eyes—in confusion, fear, doubt, disbelief, or all four, he couldn't tell. Then: "General, I didn't know you that well when you worked in the White House," Phoenix said.

"Most of what I know is what I heard in the Oval Office and Cabinet Room, usually during someone's angry tirade aimed at you. You have a reputation for two things: pissing a lot of people off . . . and making timely, correct analyses.

"I'm going to talk to the president and recommend that Secretary Barbeau and I make a visit to Turkey, to meet with President Hirsiz and Prime Minister Akas," he went on. "Stacy can be in charge of making apologies. I'm going to ask President Hirsiz what's going on, what he thinks his situation is politically and security-wise, and what the United States can do to help. The situation is obviously getting out of hand, and simply declaring the PKK a terrorist outfit is not enough. We should be doing more to help the Republic of Turkey.

"I am also going to recommend, General, that you be allowed to continue your surveillance operations on the Iraq-Turkey border," Phoenix went on. "I don't think he'll buy it, but if Colonel Wilhelm says it'll take weeks to get back into position, we don't have much choice. Obviously, there will be no more of that netrusion stuff against the Turks without express permission from the Pentagon or the White House. Clear?"

"Yes, sir."

"All right. Colonel Wilhelm, Secretary Barbeau is not in your chain of command, and neither am I. You should follow your last set of orders. But I'd recommend being on the defensive and ready for anything, just in case the general's theory comes true. I don't know how much warning you'll get. Sorry about the confusion, but that's the way it goes sometimes."

· "That's the way it goes *most* of the time, sir,"
Wilhelm said. "Message understood."

"I'll be in touch. Thank you, gents." The vice
president nodded to someone off camera, and his
worried, conflicted visage disappeared.

THE OVAL OFFICE,
THE WHITE HOUSE, WASHINGTON, D.C.
A short time later

"Patrick McLanahan is in Iraq!" Secretary of State
Stacy Anne Barbeau shrieked as she strode into
the Oval Office. "I just spoke with him on the
conference call with Phoenix and the Army.
McLanahan is in charge of aerial reconnaissance
in all of northern Iraq! How in hell could that
guy surface in Iraq and we not know about it?"

"Relax, Stacy Anne, relax," President Joseph
Gardner said. He smiled as he loosened his tie
and sat back in his seat. "You look even more
beautiful when you're angry."

"What are you going to do about McLanahan,
Joe? I thought he'd disappear, move out to some
condo in Vegas, play with his kid, take up fly-
fishing or something. Not only has he *not* van-
ished, but now he's stirring up shit between Iraq
and Turkey."

"I know. I got the briefing from Conrad. That's
what the guy does, Stacy. Don't worry about
him. Sooner or later he'll go too far, *again*, and
then we can prosecute him. He doesn't have his
high-tech air force to fight for him anymore."

"Did you hear what he told me? He refuses to

turn over his mission data to the State Department! I want him thrown into prison, Joe!"

"I said, relax, Stacy," Gardner said. "I'm not going to do anything that'll bring McLanahan's name back into the press. Everyone's forgotten about him, and that's the way I prefer it. We try to haul him into a federal court for putting up a few fake radar images to fool the Turks, and we'll turn him into a media hero again. We'll wait until he does something *really* bad, and then we'll nail him."

"That guy is bad news, Joe," Barbeau said. "He humiliated both of us, shit on us and rubbed our noses in it. Now he's gotten himself some kind of big government contract and is flying around northern Iraq." She paused for a moment, then asked, "Does he still have those robot things, the ones he . . . ?"

"Yes, as far as I know, he still has them," the president said. "I haven't forgotten about them. I have a task force in the FBI that scours police reports all over the world for sightings. Now that we know he's working in Iraq, we'll expand the search there. We'll get them."

"I don't see how you can allow him to keep those things. They belong to the U.S. government, not to McLanahan."

"You know damned well why, Stacy," Gardner said irritably. "McLanahan has got enough dirt on both of us to end our careers in a hot second. The robots are a small price to pay for his silence. If the guy was tearing up cities or robbing banks with them, I'd make it a priority to find them, but the FBI task force hasn't reported any sightings or received any tips about them. McLanahan's being smart and keeping those things under wraps."

"I can't believe he has such a powerful weapon like those robots and suits of armor or whatever they are and hasn't used them."

"Like I said, he's smart. But the first time he breaks those things out, my task force will pounce on him."

"What's taking them so long? The robots were ten feet tall and as strong as tanks! He used them to kill the Russian president *in his private residence* and then used them to break into Camp David!"

"There's only a handful of them out there, and from what I've been briefed they fold up and are pretty easy to conceal," the president said. "But the main reason I think they haven't is because McLanahan has some powerful friends that are helping deflect investigators away."

"Like who?"

"I don't know . . . yet," Gardner said. "Someone with political clout, influential enough to attract investors to buy the high-tech gadgets like that recon plane, and savvy enough on Capitol Hill and the Pentagon to get the government contracts and skirt around the technology export laws."

"I think you should pull his contracts and send him packing. The man is dangerous."

"He's not bothering us, he's doing a job in Iraq which allows me to pull the troops out of there faster—and I don't want to wake up one morning to find one of those robots standing over me in my bedroom," Gardner said. "Forget about

McLanahan. Eventually he'll screw up, and then
we can take him down . . . *quietly.*"

JANDARMA PROVINCIAL HEADQUARTERS, VAN, REPUBLIC OF TURKEY
Early the next morning

The eastern regional headquarters of the internal security forces of Turkey, the Jandarma,
was near Van Airport, southeast of the city and
not far from Lake Van. The main headquarters
complex consisted of four three-story buildings
forming a square with a large courtyard, caf-
eteria, and seating area in the center. Across
the parking lot to the northeast was a single
square four-story building that housed the detention center. Southeast of headquarters were
the barracks, training academy, athletic fields,
and shooting ranges.

The headquarters building was situated right
on Ipek Golu Avenue, the main thorough-
fare connecting the city to the airport. Since
the headquarters experienced so many drive-
by attacks—usually just some rocks or garbage
thrown at the building, but occasionally a pistol
shot or Molotov cocktail aimed at a window—
the sides of the complex facing the avenue to the
northwest, Sumerbank Street to the southwest,
and Ayak Street to the northeast were shielded
by a ten-foot-high reinforced concrete wall, decorated with paintings and mosaics along with
some anti-Jandarma grafitti. All of the windows
on that side were made of bulletproof glass.

No such protective walls existed on the southeast side; the sounds of gunfire on the weapon ranges day and night, the constant presence of police and Jandarma trainees, and the long open distance between there and the main buildings meant that the perimeter was just a twelve-foot-tall illuminated reinforced chain-link fence topped with razor wire, patrolled by cameras and roving patrols in pickup trucks. The neighborhood around the complex was light industrial; the nearest residential area was an apartment complex four blocks away, occupied mostly by Jandarma officers, staff, and academy instructors.

The academy trained law enforcement officers from all over Turkey. Graduates were assigned to city or provincial police department assignments, or they stayed for further training to become Jandarma officers or took advanced classes in riot control, special weapons and tactics, bomb disposal, antiterrorist operations, intelligence, narcotics interdiction, and dozens of other specialties. The academy had a staff and faculty of one hundred and a resident student enrollment of about one thousand.

Along with gunfire from the weapon training ranges, another constant at the Jandarma complex in Van were protesters. The detention facility housed around five hundred prisoners, mostly suspected Kurdish insurgents, smugglers, and foreigners captured along the frontier regions. The facility was not a prison and was not designed for long-term incarceration, but at least one-fifth of the prisoners had been there for over a year, awaiting trial or deportation. Most of the

protests were small—mothers or wives holding
signs with the pictures of their loved ones, demanding justice—but some were larger, and a
few had turned violent.

The demonstration that began that morning
started out large and grew swiftly. A rumor had
circulated that the Jandarma had captured Zilar
Azzawi, the infamous Kurdish terrorist leader
nicknamed the Hawk, and was torturing her for
information.

The protesters closed off Ipek Golu Avenue
and blocked all of the main entrances to the Jandarma facility. The Jandarma responded quickly
and with force. The academy outfitted all of the
students in riot gear and surrounded the two
main buildings, concentrating forces on the detention center in case the mob tried to rush the
building and free Azzawi and other prisoners.
Traffic was diverted around the protest site down
Sumerbank and Ayak streets to other thorough-
fares to avoid completely closing traffic to Van
Airport.

The chaotic situation and the diversion of
students, faculty, staff, and most of the security
forces to the main avenue where the protesters
were, made it all too easy to breach the facility
from the southeast.

A dump truck drove through the outer and
inner chain link service entrance gates on Sumerbank Street with ease, then sped past the
weapons range and across the athletic fields.
The handful of security guards gave chase and
opened fire with automatic weapons, but nothing could stop it. The truck drove straight into
the academy barracks building . . .

. . . where three thousand pounds of high explosives packed into the dump section detonated, destroying the three-story student barracks and heavily damaging the main academic building nearby.

STATE COMMUNICATIONS FACILITY, ÇANCAYA, ANKARA, TURKEY
A short time later

"Today I am saddened to announce that I am instituting a state of emergency in the Republic of Turkey," President Kurzat Hirsiz said. He read his statement from the state communications facility in Çancaya emotionlessly, woodenly, not even looking up from his paper. "This morning's dastardly PKK attack on the regional Jandarma headquarters in Van, which resulted in at least twenty deaths and scores injured, forces me to respond with urgency.

"Effective immediately, local and provincial law enforcement departments will be augmented by regular and reserve military personnel," he went on, still not looking up from his prepared statement. "They are there to assist in security operations only. This will free local and provincial police to make arrests and investigate crime.

"I must report that several threats by the PKK have been received via radio messages, coded classified ads in newspapers, and postings on the Internet, urging followers and sympathizers all around the world to rise up and strike at the Republic of Turkey. Our analysts have concluded that the messages are meant to activate sleeper cells throughout the region to begin concentrated attacks on government facilities all around the country.

"After the incident at Van, I am forced to take these threats seriously and respond in force. Therefore I am ordering the temporary shutdown of all government offices in Turkey, the establishment of a strict dusk-to-dawn curfew in all cities and towns, and mandatory one hundred percent individual and vehicle searches by security personnel.

"The next actions that I have ordered require the assistance and cooperation of the public at large. Because of the danger of unknowingly spreading terrorist instructions, I am asking that all newspapers, magazines, radio, television, and all private media outlets voluntarily cease publication of any advertisements, articles, or notices submitted by anyone who is not a reporter or editor of the publication, or where the source of the information is not verified or personally known. My intention is to avoid completely shutting down the media. It is essential that the availability of coded messages to sleeper cells be cut off completely, and my government will be contacting all outlets to ensure they understand the importance of their swift and thorough cooperation.

"Finally, I am asking that all of the Internet providers in the Republic of Turkey and those who provide service to Turkey voluntarily install and update filters and redirectors to block access to known and suspected terrorist Web sites and servers. This should not result in a massive denial of Internet services in Turkey.

E-mail, commerce, and access to regular sites and services should continue normally—only those servers that are known to host terrorist or anti-government sites will be shut down. We will closely monitor all the Internet providers available to the people of Turkey to be sure access to legitimate sites is not affected."

Hirsiz took a nervous sip of water from an off-camera glass, his hand visibly trembling, his eyes never looking at the camera. "I sincerely apologize to the people of Turkey for being forced to take these actions," he went on after a long, uncomfortable pause, "but I feel I have no choice, and I beg for your prayers, patience, and cooperation. My government will work tirelessly to stop the terrorists, restore security and order, and return our nation to normalcy. I ask the citizens of Turkey to be vigilant, helpful to government officials and law enforcement, and to be strong and brave. Our nation has been through this before, and we have always emerged stronger and wiser. We shall do so again. Thank you."

Hirsiz threw his statement pages away as Prime Minister Ayşe Akas came up to him. "That's the hardest speech I've ever given," Hirsiz said.

"I hoped you would change your mind, Kurzat," she said. "It's not too late, even now."

"I have to do this, Ayşe," Hirsiz said. "It's far too late to change course now."

"No, it's not. Let me help you do it. Please." An aide passed a note to Akas. "Perhaps this will help: the American embassy is requesting a high-level meeting in Irbil. The vice president,

Phoenix, is in Baghdad and wants to attend, along with the secretary of state."

"Impossible," Hirsiz said. "We can't stop this now." He thought for a moment. "We can't meet with them: the country is under a state of emergency. We can't guarantee the safety of the president or of our ministers in Iraq."

"But if you did attend, I'm sure they'll offer substantial military, technical, and economic assistance if they meet with us—they rarely come empty-handed," Akas said. "The American ambassador has already sent a message to the foreign ministry about compensation for the Patriot missile launches."

"Compensation? For what? What did they say?"

"The ambassador, speaking on behalf of Secretary of State Barbeau, said an unarmed reconnaissance plane run by a private firm contracted to provide surveillance of the northern Iraq border area inadvertently emitted what they called 'accidental electronic interference' that caused us to fire those Patriot missiles. The ambassador was very apologetic and said he was authorized to offer substantial compensation or replacement of the missiles, and also offered assistance in providing information on any unknown vehicles or persons crossing the border into Turkey." Hirsiz nodded. "This is a great opportunity, Kurzat. You can have the meeting, then cancel the state of emergency after the American vice president makes an agreement. You save face, and there's no war."

"Saved by the Americans again, eh, Ayşe?"

Hirsiz said emotionlessly. "You're so sure they'll want to help?" He motioned to an aide, who handed him a secure cellular telephone. "The timetable's been moved up, General," he said after speed-dialing a number. "Get your forces moving and the planes in the air, *now*!"

COMMAND AND CONTROL CENTER, ALLIED AIR BASE NAHLA, IRAQ
That evening

"Looks like the wheels are getting ready to come off the wagon up in Turkey, doesn't it?" Kris Thompson said. He was sitting at the security director's console in the Tank, watching news reports of the security crackdowns taking place in the Republic of Turkey on one of the big screens at the front of the Tank that was always tuned to an American all-news channel. The reports showed police and military forces clashing with protesters in the streets of Istanbul and Ankara. "Hirsiz is crazy. A state of emergency? Sounds like a military coup to me. I wonder if he's still in charge."

"Keep the chatter down, Thompson," Jack Wilhelm said, sitting at his console nearby. "We can all see what's going on. Put Sensor Eight up front and zoom ten-X." He studied an image of three delivery trucks driving down a road, the cargo sections swaying noticeably in the turns. "They're moving pretty fast, wouldn't you say? Zoom fifteen-X, get a description, pass it along to the IA. Who do they have in the area, Major Jabburi?" The Turkish liaison officer spread out his charts and logbooks, then picked up his telephone. "C'mon, Major, we don't have all damned day."

"There is a border patrol unit heading in the opposite direction, about ten miles away, sir," Major Hamid Jabburi, the Turkish army deputy liaison officer, responded, after a long delay. "They have been notified to investigate the vehicles. They requested we continue monitoring and advise if they turn."

"Of course—what else do we have to do around here except cater to the IA?" Wilhelm grumbled. "A monkey can do this job." At that moment Patrick McLanahan walked up to the brigade commander. "Speak of the devil. I gotta admit, General, your pregnant stealth bomber is killer. We're getting the same amount of looks all over the sector with a fourth of the airframes; we're saving network bandwidth, fuel, and personnel; and the ramp and the airspace are less congested."

"Thanks, Colonel. I'll pass that along to Jon and his engineers."

"You do that." Wilhelm motioned to the television monitor. "So, have you spoken with the veep about the shit happening in Turkey?"

"He's on his way to Irbil for a meeting with Iraqi, Kurdish, and maybe Turkish leaders," Patrick said. "He said he'd get an update from us when he landed."

"Still think Turkey will invade?"

"Yes. More than ever now. If Hirsiz doesn't have support for war, the only legal way he can start one is by dissolving the National Assembly and ordering it himself."

"I think that's crazy, General," Wilhelm said. "The Zakhu attack was a big screwup, that's all. The military is in the field because the generals want to show who's boss and to force the Kurds, Iraqis, and Americans to the bargaining table."

"I hope you're right, Colonel," Patrick said. "But they've got a big force out there, and it's getting bigger every hour."

"It's a show of force, that's all," Wilhelm insisted.

"We'll see."

"Let's say they do invade. How far do you think they'll go?"

"Hopefully they might just take Dahuk province and then stop," Patrick said. "But with this force they're rushing to the border, they might take Irbil International, besiege the city and half of Irbil province, and force the Kurdish government to flee. After that, they might march all the way to Kirkuk. They could say it's to protect the KTC pipeline from Kurdish insurgents."

" 'Besiege'—listen to you, General," Wilhelm said, chuckling and shaking his head. "Have you ever *been* in a siege, General, or do you just bomb the crap out of places from beyond visual range?"

"Ever heard of a place called Jakutsk, Colonel?" Patrick asked.

Wilhelm's jaw dropped, first in shock—at himself—and then in shame. "Oh . . . oh, shit, General, I'm sorry," he said quietly. He had certainly heard of Jakutsk, the third largest city in Russian Siberia . . .

. . . and the location of a large air base that was used as a forward tanker base to refuel Russian long-range bombers involved in the American holocaust—the nuclear attack on the United States that killed thirty thousand persons, injured almost a hundred thousand, and destroyed almost all of America's long-range manned bombers and land-based intercontinental ballistic missiles, just six years earlier.

Patrick McLanahan had devised a plan to strike back at Russia's land-based nuclear missiles by landing a Tin Man and Cybernetic Infantry Device commando team into Jakutsk, capturing the base, then using it to stage American bombers on precision air raids throughout Russia. The Russian president Anatoliy Gryzlov retaliated by attacking his own air base . . . with nuclear-tipped cruise missiles. Although Patrick's defenses stopped most of the cruise missiles and allowed most of Patrick's bomber and tanker force to escape, thousands of Russians and all but a handful of the American ground team members were incinerated.

"When did you acquire this habit of talking first and thinking second, Colonel?" Patrick asked. "Is it just being in Iraq, or have you been working on the technique for a long time now?"

"I said I'm sorry, General," Wilhelm said irritably—again, aimed directly at himself. "I forget who I'm talking to. And I *could* blame it on being in this shithole for almost eighteen months—that could drive anyone to mouth off, or worse. This is my third tour in Iraq, and I never had a solid handle on the mission—*ever*. They change it every couple months anyway: we're here to stay, we're leaving, we're staying, we're leaving; we're fighting foreigners, we're fighting Sunnis, we're fighting Shia, we're fighting al-Qaeda; now we're maybe fighting Turks." He paused, looked at Patrick apologetically, then added, "But I won't blame it on anything but being an asshole. Again, sir, I'm sorry. Forget I said it."

"It's forgotten, Colonel." Patrick looked at the sector composite map, then at the news coverage of the rioting around Turkey. "And you made your point: if the Turks head to Irbil and Kirkuk, they won't 'besiege' them—they'll level them, and kill hundreds of thousands of people as they do."

"Roger that, sir," Wilhelm said. "The final solution to their Kurdish problem." The intercom beeped, and Wilhelm touched his mike button: "Go . . . copy that . . . roger, I'll tell him. Warhammer out. Listen up, ladies and gents. Division has notified us that the vice president will be on his way to Irbil in about an hour to meet with members of the Kurdistan Regional Government in the morning. He'll transit our sector before being handed off to Irbil Approach, but Baghdad will be controlling and monitoring the flight and they'll follow normal VIP and diplomatic flight procedures. General, I've been ordered to—"

"I can maintain a detailed watch over the vice president's flight path for any signs of movement," Patrick interjected. "Just pass the waypoints to me and I'll set it up."

"You can do that *and* maintain a watch on our sector?" Wilhelm asked.

"If I had two more Losers out here, Colonel, I could maintain a twenty-four/seven watch on *all* of Iraq, southeast Turkey, and northwest Persia, and still have a ground spare," Patrick said. He touched his secure earset. "Boomer, you copy that last?"

"Already setting it up, sir," Hunter Noble responded. "The Loser we have airborne right now can track his flight inside Irbil province, but I assume you want eyes on the veep all the way from Baghdad, yes?"

"A-firm."

"Thought so. We'll have Loser number two on station in . . . about forty minutes."

"Fast as you can, Boomer. Move the first Loser south to monitor the vice president's flight, then place the second one in the surveillance track up north when it gets airborne."

"Roger that."

"So we'll be able to watch his flight from Baghdad all the way to Irbīl?" Wilhelm asked.

"No—we'll be able to track and identify every aircraft and every *vehicle* that moves in seven Iraqi provinces, from Ramadi to Karbala and everywhere in between, in real time," Patrick said. "We'll be able to track and identify every vehicle that approaches the vice president's plane before departure; we'll be able to watch his plane taxi out and monitor every other aircraft and vehicle in his vicinity. If there's any suspicious activity prior to departure or his arrival in Irbil, we can warn him and his security detail."

"With *two* aircraft?"

"We can almost do it with one, but for the kind of precision we want, it's better to split the coverage and go for the highest resolution we can get," Patrick said.

"Pretty cool," Wilhelm said, shaking his head. "Wish you guys had been around months ago:

I missed my youngest daughter's high school graduation last year. That's the second time I've missed something big like that."

"I've got a son getting ready to go into middle school, and I can't remember the last time I saw him in a school play or soccer game," Patrick said. "I know how you feel."

"Excuse me, Colonel," the Turkish liaison officer, Major Jabburi, interjected on the intercom. "I have been notified that the Aviation Transport Group of the Turkish air force is sending a Gulfstream Five VIP transport aircraft from Ankara to Irbil to participate in joint talks between the United States, Iraq, and my country starting tomorrow. The aircraft is airborne and will be within our coverage range in approximately sixty minutes."

"Very well," Wilhelm said. "Captain Cotter, let me know when you get the flight plan."

"Got it now, sir," Cotter, the regiment's air traffic management officer, responded moments later. "Origin verified. I'll contact the Iraqi Foreign Minister and verify its itinerary."

"Put it up on the big board first, then make the call." A blue line arced across the main large-screen monitor, direct from Ankara to Irbil Northwest International Airport, about eighty miles to the east, flying just to the east of Allied Air Base Nahla. Although the flight's course was curved, not straight, the six-hundred-mile "great circle" routing was the most direct flight path from one point to another. "Looks good," Wilhelm said. "Major Jabburi, make sure the IA has the flight plan, too, and make sure Colonel Jaffar is aware."

"Yes, Colonel."

"Well, at least the parties are talking to each other. Maybe this whole thing will blow over after all."

Things quieted down considerably for the next twenty minutes, until: "Guppy Two-Four is airborne," Patrick reported. "He'll be on station in fifteen minutes."

"That was quick," Wilhelm remarked. "You guys don't mess around getting those things airborne, do you, General?"

"It's unmanned and already loaded and fueled; we just type in flight and sensor plans and let it go," Patrick said.

"No latrines to empty, box lunches to fix, parachutes to rig, right?"

"Exactly."

Wilhelm just shook his head in amazement.

They watched the progress of the Turkish VIP plane as it made its way toward the Iraqi border. Nothing at all unusual about the flight: flying at thirty-one thousand feet, normal airspeed, normal transponder codes. When the flight was about twelve minutes from crossing the border, Wilhelm ordered, "Major Jabburi, verify again that Iraqi air defenses are aware of the inbound flight from Turkey and are weapons tight."

"Jabburi is off the net, sir," Weatherly said.

"Find his ass and get him back here," Wilhelm snapped, then Wilhelm clicked open his command-wide channel: "All Warhammer units, this is Alpha, inbound Turkish VIP aircraft ten minutes out, all air defense stations report weapons tight directly to me."

Weatherly changed one of the monitors to

a position-and-status map of all of the air defense units along the border area. The units consisted of Avenger mobile air defense vehicles, which were Humvees fitted with a steerable turret that contained two reloadable pods of four Stinger heat-seeking antiaircraft missiles and a .50 caliber heavy machine gun, along with electro-optical sensors and a datalink allowing the turret to be slaved to Second Regiment's air defense radars. Accompanying the Avengers was a cargo-carrying Humvee with maintenance and security troops, spare parts and ammo, provisions, and two missile pod reloads.

"All Warhammer AD units reporting weapons tight, sir," Weatherly said.

Wilhelm checked the monitor, which showed all of the Avenger units with steady red icons, indicating they were operational but not ready to attack. "Where's your second Loser, General?" he asked.

"Three minutes from the patrol box." Patrick flashed the XC-57's icon on the tactical display so Wilhelm could see it amid all of the other markers. "Passing flight level three-five-zero climbing to four-one-zero, well clear of the inbound Turkish flight. We'll start scanning the area shortly."

"Show me the veep's flight."

Another icon began blinking, this one far to the south over Baghdad. "He's just taken off, sir, about thirty minutes early," Cotter reported. The flight data readouts showed a very rapid increase in altitude and a relatively slow ground speed, indicative of a max-performance climb-out from Baghdad International. "Looks like he's on board the CV-22 tilt rotor, so he'll be well behind the

Turkish Gulfstream for the arrival," he added. "ETA, forty-five minutes."

"Roger."

Things seemed to be going along routinely—which always worried Patrick McLanahan. He scanned all the monitors and readouts, looking for a clue as to why something might be amiss. So far, nothing. The second XC-57 reconnaissance plane reached its patrol box and began its standard oval patrol pattern. Everything looked . . .

Then he saw it, and mashed the intercom button: "The Turkish plane is slowing down," he spoke.

"What? Say again, General?"

"The Gulfstream. It's down to three hundred and fifty knots."

"Is he getting ready for descent?"

"That far away from Irbil?" Patrick asked. "If he did a normal approach it might make sense, but what Turkish aircraft would fly into the heart of Kurdish territory on a normal approach? He'd do a max performance approach—he wouldn't start a descent until thirty miles out, maybe less. He's about a hundred out now. He's drifting south of course, too. But his altitude is—"

"*Bandits! Bandits!*" That was Hunter Noble, monitoring the data from the second XC-57 aircraft. "Multiple high-speed aircraft inbound from Turkey, heading south at low altitude, fifty-seven miles, *Mach one-point-one-five!*" The tactical display showed multiple tracks of air targets streaming south from Turkey. "Also detecting multiple heavy vehicles on Highways A36 and—" His voice was suddenly cut off in a jarring blare of static . . .

. . . and so was the tactical display. The entire screen was suddenly awash with glittering colored pixels, garbage characters, and waves of interference. "Say again?" Wilhelm shouted. "Where are those vehicles? And what's happened to my board?"

"Lost contact with the Loser," Patrick said. He began to enter instructions into the keyboard. "Boomer . . . !"

"I'm switching now, boss, but the datalink is almost completely shut down, and I'm down to one-sixty-K uplink speed," Boomer said.

"Will it switch over automatically?"

"If it detects a datalink dropout it will, but if the jamming has locked up the signal processors, it might not."

"What in hell is going on, McLanahan?" Wilhelm shouted, shooting to his feet. "What happened to my picture?"

"We're being jammed on all frequencies—UHF, VHF, LF, X, Ku- and Ka-band, and microwave," Patrick said. "Extremely powerful, too. We're trying to—" He stopped, then looked at the regimental commander. "The Turkish Gulfstream. It's not a VIP aircraft—it's gotta be a *jamming aircraft*."

"*What?*"

"An electronic jammer—and he's taken down the entire network," Patrick said. "We let him fly right on top of us, and he's powerful, so we can't burn through the jamming. Frequency-hopping's not helping—he's burning through *all* frequencies."

"Je-sus—we're blind down here." Wilhelm switched to the regiment's command channel:

"All Warhammer units, all Warhammer units, this is . . . !" But his voice was drowned out by an impossibly loud squeal coming from everyone's headsets that couldn't be turned down. Wilhelm threw his headset off before the sound burst his eardrums, and everyone else in the Tank was forced to do the same. "Damn, I can't get through to the Avengers."

Patrick activated his secure cellular phone. "Boomer . . ." But he quickly had to take the ear-piece out of his ear because of the noise. "Stand by, Colonel," Patrick said. "Noble will be shutting down the reconnaissance system."

"Shutting it down? Why?"

"The jamming is powerful enough that the datalink between us and the XC-57s has completely crashed," Patrick said. "The only way we can get it going again is to shut down."

"What good will that do?"

"The fail-safe mode for all the Losers is to switch to secure laser communications mode, and as far as we know no one has the ability to jam our laser comms," Patrick said. "Once we power back up, the system will immediately default to a clear and more secure link. The laser is line of sight, not satellite-relayed, so we'll lose a lot of capability, but at least we'll get the picture back . . . at least, we *should*."

It only took less than ten minutes to reboot the system, but it was an agonizingly long wait. When the picture finally returned, they saw only a small slice of what they were accustomed to seeing—but it was horrific enough all the same: "I've got three clusters of aircraft inbound—one each heading in the direction of

Mosul, Irbil, and the third I'm assuming is heading for Kirkuk," Hunter Noble reported. "Many high-speed aircraft in the lead, followed by lots of slow movers."

"It's an air assault," Patrick said. "SEAD aircraft to take out the radars and communications, followed by tactical bombers to take out the airfields and command posts, close air support to stand watch, and then paratroopers and cargo planes for a ground assault."

"What about Nahla?" Weatherly asked.

"The westerly cluster is passing to the west of us—I'm guessing they'll target Mosul instead of us."

"Negative—assume we're *next*," Wilhelm said. "Weatherly, organize a team and have them get the word out for everyone to take shelter. Do it any way you can—bullhorns, car horns, or yell like crazy, but get the regiment into shelters. Radio the Avengers to—"

"Can't, sir. The Scion recon plane is back on the air, but our comms are still being jammed."

"Damn," Wilhelm swore. "All right, let's hope the Avengers find good spots to hide, because we can't warn them. Get moving." Weatherly hurried off. "McLanahan, what about the veep?"

"We have no way of contacting his aircraft while we're being jammed," Patrick said. "Hopefully, once he switches to our freq, he'll hear the jamming and decide to turn back to Baghdad."

"Is there any way you can knock down that Gulfstream or whatever it is up there?" Wilhelm asked.

Patrick thought for a moment, then headed for the exit. "I'm headed for the flight line," he said, adding, "I'll get your comms back." Patrick hurried outside, hopped into one of the Humvees assigned to his team, and sped off.

He found the flight line in utter chaos. Soldiers were standing on Humvees shouting warnings; some had loudspeakers; others just beeped the horn. Half of the Scion Aviation International technicians were standing around, unsure of whether or not to leave.

"*Get into shelters, now!*" Patrick shouted after screeching to a halt outside the hangar, leaping out, and running for the command center. He found Jon Masters and Hunter Noble still at their consoles, trying without hope to counter the fierce jamming. "Are you guys nuts?" Patrick said as he started grabbing laptops. "Get the hell out of here!"

"They're not going to bomb *us*, Muck," Jon said. "We're Americans, and this is an Iraqi air base, not a rebel stronghold. They're going after—"

At that moment he was interrupted by triple sonic booms that rolled directly overhead. It felt as if the hangar was a giant balloon that had been shot full of air in the blink of an eye. Computer monitors, lamps, and shelving flew from desks and walls, bulbs shattered, walls cracked, and the air suddenly fogged over because every speck of dust in the entire place was blasted free by the overpressure. "Hol-ee *jeez* . . . !"

"I'm hoping that was a warning. Don't try to launch any aircraft, or the next pass will be a bomb run," Patrick said. Under the desk with one of the laptops displaying the laser radar image from the XC-57, he studied it for a few moments, then said, "Jon, I want that Turkish plane knocked out."

"With what? Spitballs? We don't have any antiair weapons."

"The Loser does. Slingshot."

"Slingshot?" Jon's eyes narrowed in confusion, then understanding, followed by calculation, and finally by agreement. "We gotta get close, maybe within three miles."

"And if the Turks catch the Loser, they'll shoot it down for sure . . . and then they'll come after *us*."

"I'm hoping they don't want to tangle with us—they're after Kurdish rebels," Patrick said. "If they wanted to bomb us, they'd have done it by now." He didn't sound too convincing, even to himself; but after another moment's reconsideration, he nodded. "Do it."

Jon cracked his knuckles and began to issue instructions, changing the XC-57's programmed flight path to take it inside the Turkish aircraft's loiter area, then having it steer itself to fly behind and below it, using its laser radars for precise station keeping. "I don't see any escorts," Boomer said, studying the ultradetailed laser radar image of the area around the Turkish aircraft as the XC-57 closed in. "It's a single-ship. Pretty confident, aren't they?"

"What kind of aircraft is it?" Patrick asked.

"Can't see it yet—it's smaller than a Gulfstream, though."

"Smaller?" That feeling of impending doom was back, crawling up and down Patrick's spine. "It packs a lot of power for an aircraft smaller than a Gulfstream."

"Inside ten miles," Jon said. "I'll hit it at five miles. Still trying to make out the engine nacelles." The XC-57 closed the distance quickly.

"I don't see any nacelles—it's not a passenger aircraft," Patrick said. As it got closer he could make out more detail: a small twin-engine bizjet, but with three pods underneath each wing and a pod under the belly. "Definitely not civilian," he said. "Lock onto anything you can, Jon, and fire as soon as you're . . ."

Before he could finish, suddenly the Turkish aircraft turned hard left and started a fast climb—and its turn rate was not that of a large passenger-size aircraft like a Gulfstream. At this close range, with its full profile showing on the laser radar image, its identity was unmistakable: "Oh, crap, it's an *F-4 Phantom fighter!*" Boomer shouted. "An F-4 with jamming capability? No wonder they didn't bring escorts—he can probably escort himself."

"Hit it, Jon," Patrick shouted, "and get the Loser out of there! The Phantom's bound to have defensive armament!"

"Hit it, Boomer!" Jon said, typing commands furiously to recall the XC-57.

"Slingshot active!" Boomer said. "Full power. Range six miles . . . it won't be enough."

"Don't worry—he'll be closing that distance real quick," Patrick said ominously. "Start a fast descent, Jon—maybe the F-4 won't want to go low. Put him on the deck."

"Going down!" Jon Masters said. Using the XC-57's mission-adaptive wing technology, which allowed almost every surface of the aircraft to be made into a lift or drag device, the XC-57 descended at over ten thousand feet per minute, its composite construction the only thing keeping it from ripping itself apart.

"Comms are back," a technician reported. "All jamming and interference down."

"He's slowing down," Boomer said. "Three miles . . . he should be feelin' the heat right about—" And at that instant the laser radar image showed two missiles leave each wing of the Turkish F-4E. *"Sidewinders!"* he shouted. But seconds into their flight, the Sidewinder missiles exploded. "Slingshot got 'em both," Boomer said. "The laser is redirecting on the Phantom. He's still slowing down even though he's in a descent."

"I think we hit something vital," Jon said. The magnified laser radar image clearly showed smoke trailing from the fighter's right engine. "He's got to break it off. He's down to five thousand feet aboveground—fighter guys don't like flying near the mud."

"Two miles and still closing," Boomer said. "C'mon, *aptal*, game's over."

"Aptal?"

"Turkish for 'idiot,' " Boomer said. "I figured if we're going to be facing off against the Turks, I'd better learn some Turkish."

"Leave it to you to learn the bad words first," Jon said. He turned back to the chase unfolding on his laptop. "C'mon, buddy, it's over, it's—" Just then, numerous warning messages appeared on Jon's laptop. "Crap, number one and two engines shutting down . . . hydraulics and electrical system in emergency! What happened?"

"He closed in to gun range," Patrick said. In

daylight, with clear skies . . . the XC-57 was a goner, and everyone knew it.

"C'mon, baby," Jon urged his creation, "you'll be okay, just keep going . . ."

And as they watched, they saw a puff of smoke from the forward part of the Turkish F-4 Phantom, the canopy peeled away, and the rear ejection seat flew skyward. They waited for the front seat to go . . . but as they watched, the altitude numbers continued to decrease, finally reading zero seconds later. "Got him," Boomer said quietly, with no trace of joy or triumph—watching any aviator die, even an adversary, was never a cause for celebration. "He must've been really hurting, with Slingshot in his face at full power, but he wasn't going to let the Loser get away."

"Can you bring her back, Jon?" Patrick asked.

"I don't know," Jon said. "The lower laser radar array's not retracting—that's a lot of drag, and we're down to one engine. We're losing gas, too. Just thirty miles to go—it'll be close."

There were a lot of crossed fingers, but the XC-57 did make it back. "Good job, Jon," Patrick said from his Humvee, parked near the approach end of the runway, as he peered at the aircraft through binoculars. He and Jon watched as the Loser set up for a straight-in approach. The crippled bird was trailing a long, dark line of smoke, but its flight path was fairly steady. "Didn't think she would make it."

"Neither did I," Jon admitted. "This landing is not going to be pretty. Make sure everyone is clear—I don't know what kind of braking or directional control we have left, and it could . . ."

"Scion, this is Three!" Boomer shouted on the command channel radio. *"Incoming aircraft from the south, extreme low altitude!"* Patrick swung around and searched the sky . . .

. . . and at that instant Jon yelled, *"Holy shit!"* Two massive clouds of fire erupted on the front of the XC-57. The plane seemed to simply hang in midair for several moments; then another explosion, and the plane nosed over and dove straight into the ground. There was not enough fuel in the tanks to start a large blaze.

Jon Masters's eyes were practically bugging out of their sockets in confusion. "What happened to my—"

"Get down, Jon!" Patrick shouted, pulling him down to the ground. Two American-made F-15E Eagle fighter-bombers streaked overhead at low altitude, heading north toward Turkey.

Jon tried to struggle to his feet. "Did those bastards shoot down my—"

"I said, get down!" Patrick screamed. An instant later, a string of eight massive explosions rippled directly down the center of the runway, the closest just a few hundred yards away. Both men felt as if their Humvee had rolled over on top of them. They were showered with debris and smoke, and they screamed and pressed their hands to their ears as the tremendous concussions shoved the air out of their lungs. Pieces of concrete zinged past them like bullets, then began to rain down on them. "Get inside the Humvee, Jon! *Hurry!*" Both men scrambled inside just as bigger and bigger pieces of concrete peppered them from above. They could do nothing else but crawl as far as they could on the floor and hope the roof

held. Windows shattered, and the big Humvee rocked on its wheels before they, too, exploded.

Several minutes later, Jon was still writhing on the floor of the Humvee, covering his ears and swearing loudly. Patrick could see a small trickle of blood oozing from between the fingers covering Jon's left ear. Patrick got on his portable radio to ask for help, but he couldn't hear a thing and could only hope his message got out. He crawled up onto the roof of the Humvee to inspect the damage.

Pretty good bombing, he thought. He saw eight blast marks, probably thousand-pounders, each no more than five yards from the runway centerline. Fortunately they hadn't used runway-cratering penetrating bombs, just general-purpose high-explosive ones, and the damage wasn't too bad—the detonations made holes but didn't heave large pieces of the steel reinforcement up to the surface. This was relatively easy to repair.

"Muck?" Jon was struggling out of the Humvee. "What happened?" He was shouting because his head was ringing so badly he couldn't hear himself speak.

"A little payback," Patrick said. He climbed down from the Humvee and helped Jon to sit down while he inspected his head for any other injuries. "Looks like you burst an eardrum, and you got some pretty good cuts."

"What in hell did they hit us with?"

"F-15E Strike Eagles dropping high-explosive GPs—more war surplus stuff purchased from the good 'ol U.S. of A.," Patrick said. Even though it was one of the world's premier fighter-bombers, capable of both bombing and air superiority roles on the same mission, the F-15E couldn't land on an aircraft carrier, and so they had been mothballed or sold as surplus to American-allied countries. "They tagged the runway pretty good, but it's repairable. Doesn't look like they hit the Triple-C, the hangars, or any other buildings."

"What's Turkish for 'damned pricks'?" Jon Masters asked, slamming a hand against the Humvee in sheer anger. "I think I'll borrow Boomer's phrase book and learn me some choice Turkish swear words."

A few minutes later Hunter Noble drove up in a Humvee ambulance. "Are you guys okay?" he asked as the paramedics attended to Patrick and Jon. "I thought you were goners."

"Good thing those crews were good," Patrick said. "A quarter second longer and a quarter-degree heading error and we would've been right under that last one."

"I don't think it's over," Boomer said. "We're tracking several slow movers throughout the area; the closest one is twenty miles to the east, heading this way."

"Let's get back to the hangar and see what we have left," Patrick said morosely. "We'll have to get an update on the third Loser and what mission modules we can use." They all piled into their Humvees and sped off to the flight line.

By the time they stopped at the infirmary to drop off Jon and then reached the hangar, the ringing in Patrick's ears had subsided enough so he could function fairly normally. With the jamming stopped, they were again in full reconnaissance and communications relay mode with the

first XC-57, which had moved back up to a new
patrol orbit southeast of Allied Air Base Nahla,
within laser radar range of the three major
northern Iraqi cities of Mosul, Irbil, and Kirkuk
that were under attack.

Patrick ran a visibly shaking hand across his
face as he studied the reconnaissance display.
The adrenaline rushing through his veins was
starting to subside, leaving him weary and jit-
tery. "Are you okay, sir?" Hunter Noble asked.

"I'm a little worried about Jon. He looked
pretty bad."

"You look pretty beat up, too, sir."

"I'll be okay." He smiled at the concerned expression on Boomer's face. "I forgot what it's like
to be under a bombardment like that. It really
rattles you."

"Maybe you ought to get some rest."

"I'll be okay, Boomer," Patrick repeated. He
nodded at the young pilot and astronaut. "Thanks
for being so concerned."

"I know about your heart thing, sir," Boomer
said. "The only thing worse than reentry from
space might be almost being clobbered by a
string of thousand-pound bombs. Maybe you
shouldn't push your luck."

"Let's get the vice president down safely and
get a clear picture of what's going on, and then
I'll go take a little nap." This didn't ease Boomer's concern one bit, and it showed on his face,
but Patrick ignored it. "Any jets bothering the
Loser?"

No use arguing with the guy, Boomer
thought—he was going to work until he dropped,
plain and simple. "Nope," he replied. "Every

fighter within fifty miles has lit it up, but nobody has attacked. They're not bothering our UAVs either."

"They know most of the planes flying up here are unarmed reconnaissance planes, and they're not going to waste ammo," Patrick guessed. "Pretty damned disciplined. They know there's very little resistance to what they're doing right now."

"Lots of slow movers coming in, and several columns of vehicles headed our way," Boomer said. They were intently watching several dozen slower-moving planes, mostly buzzing near Kirkuk and Irbil. One plane, however, was heading westbound directly for Nahla. "Any modes and codes on that one?" Patrick asked.

"Nope," Boomer replied. "He's very low and fast. No communications yet. The laser radar image shows it as a C-130-size twin turboprop, but he changes speed every now and then, slower than a tactical airlift plane should go. He might be having mechanical problems."

"Do we have contact with the Avengers?"

"I think they're all talking to Colonel Wilhelm in the Tank again."

Patrick opened the command channel: "Scion One to Warhammer."

"Good to see you're still with us, Scion," Wilhelm said from his command console in the Tank. "You're still yelling into the mic. Get your bell rung out there?"

"Advise you get your Avengers to ensure positive visual ID before engaging, Warhammer."

"The Turks just bombed the crap out of my runway, Scion, and they've got vehicles heading this way. We've received reports of three separate columns of armored vehicles. I'm not going to let them just traipse onto this base without taking a few down first."

"That inbound to the east might not be a Turk."

"Then who do you think it is?"

"Not on an open channel, Warhammer."

Wilhelm fell silent for a few moments; then: "Roger, Scion." He didn't know who or what McLanahan was thinking of, but the guy was on a roll; better help him keep his streak alive. "Break. All Warhammer units, this is Alpha, be advised, we have no aircraft authorized to approach the base, and we couldn't land them here if there were, but I want positive visual IDs of all inbound aircraft. Repeat, I want positive EO or direct visual ID. IR and no modes, and codes are not, repeat, *not* good enough." He paused for a moment, rethinking his next order, then continued: "If you don't have positive ID, report direction, speed, altitude, and type, but let it go. If you are unclear, sing out, but keep weapons tight unless you have positive ID it's a bandit. Warhammer out."

It did not take long for the first report to come in: "Warhammer, this is Piney One-Two," the easternmost Avenger unit called. "I have visual contact on single-ship bogey, one-five-zero degrees bullseye, heading west, one hundred and eighty knots, altitude base minus one-eight, negative modes and codes." The "base" altitude was two thousand feet, meaning that the aircraft was two hundred feet aboveground. "Looks like a Victor Two-Two."

"Oh, thank you, Lord," Wilhelm muttered to himself. How the hell many drinks and dinners am I going to have to owe McLanahan after this is all over . . . ? "Roger, One-Two. Continue patrol, weapons tight. All Warhammer units, this is Alpha, inbound aircraft approaching, weapons tight until it touches down, then back to FPCON Delta. Weatherly, take charge here. I'm headed out to the flight line. Thompson, get your guys out there to recover this inbound, and I want security as tight as a gnat's bunghole. Air traffic, let this guy in, and make sure there are no tails. Thompson, park him in Alpha security." He threw off his headset and sprinted for the door.

He found McLanahan and Kris Thompson at the secure aircraft parking area, a section of the aircraft apron surrounded by exhaust blast fences in front of the large hangar. Thompson had deployed his security forces along the south taxiway and the ramp leading from the taxiway to the apron. Wilhelm's eyes narrowed as he saw McLanahan. The retired general's head and the backs of his hands were covered in wounds from flying debris. "You should be in the infirmary, General," he said.

McLanahan was wiping his face, head, and hands with a large white moistened towel, which was already dirty from his ministrations. "That can wait," he said.

"How long? Until you pass out?"

"I dropped Jon off at the medic and had them take a look at me."

Bullshit, Wilhelm thought, but he didn't say
it aloud. He shook his head ruefully, not wanting to argue with the guy, then nodded off to the
east. "Why is he coming here?"

"I don't know."

"Not too smart, if you ask me." Wilhelm
pulled out his radio. "Two, this is Alpha. Where's
that closest column of vehicles?"

"Twenty klicks north, still approaching."

"Roger. Continue to monitor, let me know
when they're within ten klicks." Not yet in
shoulder-fired missile range, but the inbound
aircraft was in deadly danger if it was spotted by
Turkish warplanes.

A few minutes later they heard the distinc-
tive heavy high-speed *whupwhupwhup* of a large
rotorcraft. A CV-22 Osprey tilt-rotor aircraft
zoomed in low and fast over the base, made
a tight left turn while transitioning to vertical flight, then hover-taxied along the line of
security vehicles up the ramp to the apron and
touched down. It was directed inside the secure
parking area, where it shut down.

Thompson's security forces redeployed all
around the entire aircraft parking area while
Wilhelm, McLanahan, and Thompson approached the Osprey. The rear cargo ramp
opened up, and three U.S. Secret Service agents,
wearing body armor and carrying submachine
guns, stepped out, followed by Vice President
Kenneth Phoenix.

The vice president wore a Kevlar helmet,
goggles, gloves, and body armor. Wilhelm approached him but did not salute him—he was
already highlighted enough. Phoenix started to

pull off his protective gear, but Wilhelm waved
for him to stop. "Keep that stuff on for now just
in case, sir," he shouted over the roar of the twin
rotors overhead. He escorted the vice president
to a waiting up-armored Humvee, and they all
piled in and sped off toward the upstairs conference room in the Tank.

Once they were safely inside and secured, the
Secret Service agents helped Phoenix remove
his protective gear. "What happened?" Phoenix
asked. He looked at Wilhelm's grim face, then
at McLanahan's. "Don't tell me, let me guess:
Turkey."

"We detected the air assault, but they sent in
a jamming aircraft that took out our eyes and
ears," Wilhelm said. "Damn good coordination;
they were obviously poised to strike and just
waited for the right opportunity."

"Which was me, wanting to meet with everyone in Irbil," Phoenix said. "Didn't think I'd be
their cover for their invasion."

"If not you, sir, it would've been someone
else—or they might have staged something, like
I believe they staged that attack in Van," Patrick
said.

"You think that was staged?" Kris Thompson
asked. "Why? It was classic PKK."

"It *was* classic PKK—*too* classic," Patrick said.
"What got me was the timing. Why a daytime
attack, in the morning no less, with the entire
staff and security detail awake and alerted? Why
not a nighttime attack? They would've had better
chances of success and higher casualty counts."

"I thought they were pretty successful."

"I believe it was staged so few students would

be in the barracks," Patrick said. "They made sure the actual casualty count was low, and just inflated the figure for the media—enough for the president to declare a state of emergency."

"If there *is* a president of Turkey," Phoenix said. "The word from our ambassador in Ankara said that the president was 'conferring with his political and military advisers.' The foreign ministry won't say any more, and the president's calls to the prime minister and president of Turkey haven't been returned. He looked like a robot on television; he could have been under duress, even drugged."

"Sir, before we waste any more time trying to figure out what the Turks are going to do next, our first priority is to get you out of here and back to Baghdad—preferably back to the States," Wilhelm said. "Your Secret Service detail may have better options, but I recommend—"

"I'm not ready to leave yet, Colonel," Phoenix said.

"Excuse me, sir?" Wilhelm asked incredulously. "We're in the middle of a shooting war, sir. They just *bombed this base*! I can't guarantee your safety—I don't believe *anyone* can right now."

"Colonel, I came here to meet with the Iraqis, Turks, Kurds, and Americans to try to resolve the PKK situation," Phoenix said, "and I'm not leaving unless I'm ordered to do so by my boss." Wilhelm was about to say something, but Phoenix stopped him with an upraised hand. "Enough, Colonel. I need access to a telephone or radio to contact Washington, and I'll need—"

At that moment a buzzer sounded, and Wilhelm leaped for the phone. "Go."

"Multiple high-altitude aircraft approaching from the north, sir," Mark Weatherly reported. "Lower speed, perhaps turboprops. We suspect they're transports, possibly inserting paratroopers. The Iraqi army is reporting more comm jamming, too. We haven't picked it up yet."

"Continue to monitor and advise," Wilhelm said. He thought for a moment, then added, "Advise all Warhammer units, weapons tight, self-defense only, and recall the Avengers back into the base."

"Sir? Say again—"

"We're not at war with the damned Turks, Weatherly," Wilhelm interrupted. "Our intel says we're already outnumbered by at least ten to one, so they can just roll right over us if they get pissed off enough. I'll make it plain to them that they can buzz Iraq all they like, but they're not going to take this base. Recall the Avengers and all other Warhammer units that are outside the wire. Once they're back inside the fence, we go on full defensive posture, ready to repel all attackers. Got that?"

"Roger, sir."

"Advise Jaffar and tell him that I want to meet with him and his company commanders about what to do if the Turks invade," Wilhelm said. "They might feel like fighting, but we're not here to get in the middle of a shooting war." He looked at the vice president. "Still want to stay here, sir? It could get hairy."

"Like I said, Colonel, I'm on a diplomatic mission," Phoenix said. "Maybe when the Turks figure out I'm here, they'll be less likely to start shooting. I might even be able to start cease-fire talks from here."

"I'd feel better if you were at least down in Baghdad, sir," Wilhelm said, "but you sound good and positive, and I could sure use some positive vibrations around here right now."

The phone buzzed again, and Wilhelm picked it up.

"Weatherly here, sir. We got a problem: I phoned Jaffar's office—he's not here. No one in the IA senior staff is answering the phone."

"Ask Mawloud or Jabburi where they went."

"They're not here either, sir. I tried Jabburi's radio: no answer. He's been away from the Tank since before the attacks started."

Wilhelm looked out the windows of the conference room down to the main floor of the Tank; sure enough, the Turkish liaison officer's console was vacant. "Find some *hajii* in charge and tell him to get up here on the double, Weatherly." He hung up the phone. "Thompson?"

"Checking, Colonel." Kris Thompson was already on his portable radio. "Security control says a convoy of troop buses and trucks left the base about an hour ago, Colonel," he said a moment later. "Had men and equipment, proper authorizations signed by Jaffar."

"No one thought to notify me of this?"

"The gate guards said it looked routine, and they had proper orders."

"Have any of your guys seen *any* Iraqi soldiers *anywhere*?" Wilhelm thundered.

"Checking, Colonel." But everyone could tell by watching Thompson's incredulous expression what the answer was: "Colonel, the IA head-quarters is vacant."

"*Vacant?*"

"Just a couple soldiers busy breaking up hard drives and memory chips out of computers," Thompson said. "Looks like they've bugged out. Want me to stop those guys and question them?"

Wilhelm ran a hand across his face, then shook his head. "Negative," he said wearily. "It's their base and their stuff. Take pictures and statements, then leave them be." He practically threw the receiver back on its hook. "Un-friggin'-believable," he muttered. "An entire Iraqi army brigade just up and *walks out*?"

"And right before an attack," Thompson added. "Could they have gotten wind of it?"

"Doesn't matter—they're gone," Wilhelm said. "But I can tell you one thing: they're not getting back *on* this base unless I know about it first, that's for damn sure. Tell your guys that."

"Will do, Colonel."

Wilhelm turned again to the vice president. "Sir, you need any more reasons to head on back to Baghdad?"

At that instant an alarm buzzer sounded. Wilhelm picked up the phone and turned toward the displays in the front of the Tank. "What is it now, Weatherly?"

"That nearest column of Turkish armored vehicles inbound from the north are ten klicks out," Weatherly said. "They've spotted Piney Two-Three and are holding position."

Wilhelm ran as fast as he could downstairs to his console, with the others following. The video feed from the Avenger antiaircraft unit showed

a dark green armored vehicle, flying a large red
flag with a white crescent. Its machine guns were
raised. The XC-57's laser radar image showed the
other vehicles in line behind it. "Two-Three, this
is Alpha, weapons tight, road-march position."

"Copy, Warhammer, we're in road march
already," the Avenger vehicle commander replied, verifying that his weapons were safe and
the barrels of his Stinger missiles and twenty-
millimeter Gatling gun were aimed skyward,
not at the Turks.

"Can you back up or turn around?"

"Affirm to both."

"Very slowly, back up, turn around, and then
head back to the base at normal speed," Wilhelm
ordered. "Keep your barrels aimed away from
them. I don't think they're going to bother you."

"Hope you're right, Alpha. Two-Three copies
all, on the move."

It was a tense few minutes. Since the camera
on board the Avenger only aimed forward they
lost the video feed, so they couldn't see if the
Turkish APC crews were readying any antitank
weapons. But the XC-57 image showed the Turkish vehicles holding position as the Avenger
turned around, and then following it from a distance of about a hundred yards as it headed back
to the base.

"Here they come," Wilhelm said, removing
his headset and throwing it on the desk in front
of him. "Mr. Vice President, at the risk of stat-
ing the obvious, you'll be our guest for the near
future, courtesy of the Republic of Turkey."

"Well handled, Colonel," Ken Phoenix said.
"The Turks know they can blast us up, but

they're holding back. If we struck back, they'd have attacked for sure."

"We're allies, right?" Wilhelm said sarcastically. "Somehow I almost forgot that. Besides, it's an easy call not to hit back if you have almost nothing to hit back with." He turned to Kris Thompson. "Thompson, cancel the repel-forces order, but shut down the base, get everyone up, and man the gates and perimeter. I want a strong presence, but minimal visible weapons. No one fires unless fired upon. Weatherly, monitor the other inbound Avengers, let them know we have visitors, weapons tight and raised. I think the Turks will let them through."

In less than an hour, every major entrance to Allied Air Base Nahla had a team of two Turkish armored vehicles parked outside. They presented a very nonhostile appearance, with weapons raised and infantry crews remaining near their vehicles with rifles shouldered . . . but they weren't allowing anyone to come near. The base was definitely closed down.

CHAPTER 6

Failure to recognize possibilities is the most dangerous and common mistake one can make.
—*Mae Jemison, astronaut*

**OFFICE OF THE PRESIDENT,
ÇANCAYA, ANKARA, TURKEY**
Early the next morning

That's the third call from Washington, sir," an aide said as he hung up the phone. "The secretary of state herself this time. She sounded angry."

President Kurzat Hirsiz waved at the aide to shut him up, then said into his telephone, "Go ahead with your report, General."

"Yes, sir," General Abdullah Guzlev said via secure satellite telephone. "First Division has pushed all the way to Tall Afar, northwest of Mosul. They've surrounded the military airbase and secured the pipeline and the pumping station at Avghani. The Iraqis can still disrupt flow from the Baba Gurgur fields to the east and transshipped oil from the southern fields, but the oil from the Qualeh field is secure."

Amazing, Hirsiz thought. The thrust into Iraq was going better than expected. "The Iraqi army did not secure the pipeline or the pumping station?" he asked.

"No, sir. Private security companies only, and they did not resist."

That was truly great news; he had expected the Iraqis to vigorously defend the pipeline and infrastructure. The oil flowing through the Kirkuk-Ceyhan pipeline represented 40 percent of Iraq's oil revenue. An interesting development indeed . . . "Very well, General. Your progress has been amazing. Well done. Continue."

"Thank you, sir," Guzlev went on. "Second Division has pushed all the way to Mosul and has captured Qayyarah South Airport. Our air forces bombed the runway at Nahla, the Iraqi military air base north of the city near Tall Kayf, and we have that airfield surrounded. We are presently landing transport and armed patrol aircraft at Qayyarah South Airport."

"Any resistance from the Iraqi or Americans at Nahla?"

"The Americans are not resisting; however, we are not in contact with any Iraqi forces based there."

"Not in contact?"

"They seem to have left the base and retreated to Mosul or Kirkuk," Guzlev said. "We are on guard in case they pop up suddenly, but we believe they simply took off their uniforms and are hiding in the population."

"That could be a problem later on, but hopefully they'll stay hidden for a while. And General Ozek's forces?"

"The two Jandarma divisions operating in the east have encountered heavier resistance than the other two divisions, mostly facing *peshmerga* guerrillas," Guzlev replied, "but they have surrounded Irbil Northwest Airport."

"We were expecting resistance from the *peshmerga*—that's why we decided to send two Jandarma divisions east, with the other three divisions ready to move in if they're needed," Hirsiz said. The *peshmerga*, Kurdish for "those who face death," began as Kurdish freedom fighters battling Saddam Hussein's army against his brutal attempts to displace the Kurdish minority from the oil-rich areas of northeastern Iraq, which the Kurds claim as part of a future state of Kurdistan. After the U.S. invasion of Iraq, the *peshmerga* fought Saddam's army side by side with U.S. forces. Thanks to years of American training and assistance, the *peshmerga* became an effective fighting force and the defenders of the Kurdish Regional Government.

"We are still outnumbered if what our intelligence says is the full strength of the *peshmerga*," Guzlev went on. "We should advance two Jandarma divisions south to reinforce the supply lines, and leave the last in reserve. If General Ozek's forces solidly hold and control Highways Three and Four in and out of Irbil, plus keep the airport approaches clear, we'll have a solid line of defense from Irbil to Tall Afar, and we can force the *peshmerga* up into the mountains east of Irbil."

"Then I will give the order," Hirsiz said. "Meanwhile, I'll be negotiating a cease-fire with the Iraqis, Kurds, and Americans. Eventually we'll come to some sort of agreement for a buffer zone, including multinational patrols and monitoring, and we will eventually withdraw . . ."

"And as we withdraw, we'll root out every last stinking PKK training base we find," Guzlev said.

"Absolutely," Hirsiz said. "Do you have a casualty report?"

"Casualties have been minimal, sir, except General Ozek reports about two percent losses so far as he moves through the heavily Kurdish areas," Guzlev said. With Jandarma divisions equaling about twenty thousand men each, losing four hundred men in one day was serious stuff; those three reserve Jandarma divisions were going to be sorely needed. "We are having no difficulties evacuating the dead and wounded back to Turkey. Aircraft losses have been minimal as well. The worst were the loss of a transport plane that was departing Irbil to bring back more supplies—it may have been downed by enemy fire, we're not sure yet. A heavy transport helicopter was lost due to mechanical problems, and an RF-4E electronic jamming aircraft was shot down by an American reconnaissance aircraft."

"American *reconnaissance* aircraft? How can a reconnaissance aircraft shoot down one of ours?"

"Unknown, sir. The reconnaissance systems officer reported that they were under attack by what he described as heavy levels of radiation."

"*Radiation*?"

"That's what he said, moments before he lost communications with the pilot. The pilot and the aircraft were lost."

"What in hell are the Americans firing *radiation weapons* at us for?" Hirsiz thundered.

"We have been careful to minimize casualties, military and civilian, on both sides, sir," Guzlev said. "The division commanders are under strict orders to tell their men that they may fire only when fired upon, except for known or suspected PKK terrorists they discover."

"What sort of forces are you encountering, General? What units are you engaging?"

"We are encountering light resistance throughout the entire region, sir," Guzlev reported. "The Americans have not engaged us. They have set up strong defensive positions inside their bases and continue unmanned aerial reconnaissance, but they are not attacking, and we do not expect them to do so."

"That is correct, General—be sure your divisions remember that," Hirsiz warned. "We have no indications whatsoever that the Americans will attack us as long as we don't attack *them*. Don't give them a reason to come out and fight."

"I brief my generals every hour, sir. They know," Guzlev acknowledged. "The Iraqi army seems to have disappeared, probably fled toward Baghdad or simply took off their uniforms, hid their weapons, and will wait it out, like they did when the Americans invaded in 2003."

"I don't expect them to fight either, General; they don't like the PKK any more than we do. Let them hide."

"The PKK terrorists are on the run, trying to make it to larger towns and cities," Guzlev went on. "It will take hard work to dig them out, but we'll do it. We're hoping to keep them in the countryside so they don't escape to Irbil or Kirkuk and blend in with the population. The *peshmerga* remain a significant threat, but they are not engaging us as of yet—they are fierce defenders of their towns, but they are not attacking us. That may change."

"A diplomatic solution will be necessary with the Kurdish Regional Government to find some way to allow us to look for the PKK terrorists without battling *peshmerga*," Hirsiz said. "Washington has been calling all night demanding an explanation. I think now is time to talk to them. Press on, General. Pass on to your men: Job well done. Good luck, and good hunting."

"Excellent news indeed, sir," General Orhan Zahin, secretary-general of the Turkish National Security Council, said. "Better than anticipated. No one is opposing us except for a few *peshmerga* fighters and PKK terrorists." Hirsiz nodded but said nothing—he appeared to be lost in thought. "Don't you agree, sir?"

"Of course," Hirsiz said. "We expected to get bogged down in the hills, but without organized opposition, northern Iraq is wide open . . . especially Irbil, the capital of the Kurdistan Regional Government, who refuse to crack down on the PKK."

"What are you saying, sir?"

"I'm saying that if we squeeze Irbil, we can force the KRG to help us hunt down the PKK terrorists," Hirsiz said. "Everyone knows companies owned by the KRG cabinet and senior leadership funnel money to the PKK. Maybe it's time to make them pay a price. Destroy those businesses, close down the KTC pipeline, close the border crossings and airspace to anything or anyone associated with the KRG, and they'll be begging to help us." He turned to Minister of Defense Cizek. "Get a list of targets in Irbil that will specifically target KRG resources, and work with General Guzlev to add them to his target list."

"We should be careful about mission creep, sir," Cizek said. "Our goal is to set up a buffer zone in northern Iraq and wipe it clean of PKK. Attacking Irbil is far outside that objective."

"It is another way to destroy the PKK—by having the Iraqis help us," Hirsiz said. "If they want to see an end to our attacks and our occupation, they'll help us eradicate the PKK, as they should have been doing years ago." Cizek still looked concerned, but he nodded and made notes to himself. "Very good. Now I'll go talk with Joseph Gardner and see if he has any desire to help us."

THE OVAL OFFICE, THE WHITE HOUSE, WASHINGTON, D.C.
A short time later, early afternoon

A phone right beside Chief of Staff Walter Kordus's elbow beeped, and he picked it up immediately. "Call from Ankara, sir," he said. "Signals says it's from the president himself."

"*Finally,*" President Joseph Gardner said. He was behind his desk, watching the cable news reports about the invasion of Iraq with his national security adviser, Conrad Carlyle, Secretary of Defense Miller Turner, and the chairman of the Joint Chiefs of Staff, U.S. Marine Corps general Taylor J. Bain. On a video teleconference feed were Vice President Kenneth Phoenix at Allied Air Base Nahla in Iraq, and Secretary of State Stacy Barbeau from Aviano Air Base in Italy, where she had diverted instead of continuing on to Iraq from Washington. "Put him on." He thought for a moment, then shook his hand. "No, wait, I'll make him wait and see how he likes it. Tell him to hold for me and I'll speak with him in a minute."

Gardner turned to the others in the Oval Office. "Okay, we've been watching the shit flying all day now. What do we know? What do we tell whoever's at the other end of that call?"

"It's plain that the Turks are going after the PKK hideouts and training camps and are being very careful not to cause any Iraqi or American casualties," National Security Adviser Conrad Carlyle said. "If that's truly the case, we tell our guys to hunker down and stay out of it. Then we tell the Turks to back off in case there *are* unintended consequences."

"Sounds reasonable to me," Gardner said. "They're driving pretty deep into Iraq, aren't they, a lot farther than their usual cross-border raids?" Nods all around the Oval Office and on the video teleconference monitors. "Then the question is: Are they going to stay?"

"They'll stay long enough to slaughter any PKK rebels they find, and then I'm sure they'll leave," Secretary of State Stacy Anne Barbeau said via her secure video teleconference link from Italy. "We should call for United Nations monitoring as soon as possible in case Kurzat

Hirsiz is no longer in charge and the Turkish army wants to go on a rampage."

"Not on my watch they won't, Stacy," Gardner said. "I won't tolerate a bloodbath while American soldiers are stationed there and the Iraqis aren't powerful enough to defend their own people. They can crack down on their own Kurdish rebels in their own country if they want, but they're not going to commit genocide with American GIs as spectators."

"I think they'll agree to international monitors, Mr. President," Secretary of State Stacy Anne Barbeau said, "but they'll want a buffer zone created in northern Iraq, with round-the-clock international surveillance, looking for PKK activity."

"I can live with that, too," Gardner said. "Okay, Walter, put Hirsiz on the line."

A few moments later: "Mr. President, good afternoon to you, this is President Hirsiz. Thank you for speaking with me, sir."

"I'm very glad to see that you're all right," Gardner said. "We haven't heard from you since the announcement of a national emergency. You didn't return any of our calls."

"I apologize, sir, but as you can see, things are very serious here and I've been engaged almost continuously. I assume this call is in regards to our current antiterrorist operations in Iraq?"

Gardner's eyes bulged in disbelief by what he just heard. "No, sir, I'm talking about your *invasion of Iraq*!" Gardner exploded. "Because if this was just an antiterrorist operation, I'm sure you would have told us when, where, and how you were going to initiate it, is that not correct?"

"Mr. President, with all due respect, that tone of voice is not necessary," Hirsiz said. "If I may remind you, sir, it was a lack of respect such as this that caused this ill will between our countries in the first place."

"And may I remind *you*, Mr. President," Gardner retorted, "that Turkish warplanes are bombing bases and facilities manned by Americans? May I also remind you that I sent Vice President Phoenix and Secretary of State Barbeau on a diplomatic mission to Iraq to meet with their counterparts, and Turkey used that meeting as a smoke screen to attack positions inside Iraq, placing the vice president in mortal danger? The vice president is an emissary of the United States of America and *my personal representative*. You have no right to initiate military action when at the same time you . . ."

"I need no reminding from you, sir!" Hirsiz interrupted. "I need no lectures on when Turkey may initiate military actions against terrorists threatening our people! The Republic of Turkey will do whatever is necessary to protect our land and our people! It is America and Iraq who must help us defeat the terrorists! If you do nothing, then we must act alone."

"I'm not trying to lecture anyone, sir," Gardner said, forcing his anger back down into his chest, "and I agree that Turkey or any nation may take whatever steps are necessary to protect its self-interests, even preemptive military action. All I'm asking, sir, is that you inform Washington first and ask for advice and assistance. That's what allies do, am I correct?"

"Mr. President, we had every intention of no-

tifying you before the commencement of hostilities, if time allowed," Hirsiz said. Gardner rolled
his eyes in disbelief but said nothing. "But it did
not."

"That's the same thing you said before the
attack on the border, which resulted in over a
dozen American casualties," the president interjected. "Apparently you don't feel the need to
consult with Washington on a timely basis."

"I'm sorry, Mr. President, but what I tell you
is true—we are under enormous pressure to act
before any more loss of life occurs," Hirsiz said.
"But we have taken extraordinary care this time
to minimize noncombatant casualties. I have ordered my minister of defense to inform and con-
stantly remind our division commanders that
only PKK terrorists are to be targeted. We have
taken extraordinary steps to minimize noncombatant casualties."

"And I acknowledge those efforts," Gardner
said. "To my knowledge, no Americans or Iraqis
have been killed. But there have been injuries
and substantial loss and damage to equipment
and facilities. If the hostilities continue, there
could be bloodshed."

"Yet to *my* knowledge, sir, there has already
been substantial, deliberate, and egregious Turkish loss of equipment—and at least one death,
caused by *American* forces."

"What? *Americans*?" Gardner stared at his national security adviser and secretary of defense
in surprise. "I've been assured that none of our
combat units engaged with anyone, let alone
Turkish forces. There must be a mistake."

"Then you deny that an American flying-wing reconnaissance aircraft was orbiting over northern Iraq, with orders to use its radiation weapons to shoot down a Turkish combat support aircraft?"

"Flying-wing . . . reconnaissance aircraft . . . *radiation weapons* . . . ?"

"We have observed this aircraft flying near the Turkish border for many days now, sir," Hirsiz said. "Although it resembles an American stealth bomber, our intelligence analysts have assured our government that it was an unarmed reconnaissance aircraft owned and operated by a private contractor for the United States Army. The air attaché at the American embassy in Ankara acknowledged this to be true.

"Apparently our analysts were wrong, and your ambassador lied to us, because the crew of a combat support aircraft reported being under attack by that very same aircraft," Hirsiz went on. "The surviving crewmember reported that the so-called reconnaissance aircraft was in fact firing what he described as a radiation weapon; he reported feeling intense heat severe enough that it killed the pilot and destroyed the aircraft. Do you deny such an aircraft was operating at the time of our actions over Iraq, Mr. President?"

The president shook his head in confusion. "Mr. President, I don't know anything about such an aircraft, and I certainly did not order any American aircraft to attack *anyone*, let alone an allied aircraft," he said. "I'll find out who it was and make sure that no such actions happen again."

"That is little consolation to the family of the pilot who died as a result from the attack, sir."

"I'll find the ones responsible, Mr. President, and if it was a deliberate attack they will be punished, that I promise," Gardner said. "What are Turkey's intentions in Iraq, sir? When are you going to begin withdrawing troops?"

"Withdrawing? Did you say 'withdrawing,' sir?" Hirsiz asked in a high-pitched, theatrically incredulous voice. "Turkey is not withdrawing, sir. We are not withdrawing until every last PKK terrorist is dead or captured. We did not begin this operation and risk thousands of lives and billions in valuable equipment simply to turn around before the job is done."

"Sir, Turkey has committed an act of armed aggression against a peaceful country," Gardner said. "You may be hunting down terrorists, sir, but you're doing it on foreign soil, terrorizing innocent civilians, and damaging a sovereign nation's property. That cannot be allowed."

"And how are our actions different from America attacking Iraq, Mr. President?" Hirsiz asked. "That is your doctrine, is it not—hunt down and destroy terrorists wherever they may be, at a time of your own choosing? We are doing the very same."

Joseph Gardner hesitated. The bastard was right, he thought. How could I argue against Turkey invading Iraq when that's exactly what the United States did in 2003? "Um . . . Mr. President, you know it's not the same . . ."

"It is the very same, sir. We have a right to protect ourselves, just as America does."

Fortunately for the president, Walter Kordus held up a Post-it note with the letters *U.N.* scribbled on it. Gardner nodded, relieved, then spoke,

"The difference, sir, is the United States received authorization to invade Iraq by the United Nations Security Council. You did not seek such approval."

"We have sought that approval for many years, sir," Hirsiz said, "but it was always denied. The best you or the United Nations could ever do was declare the PKK a terrorist organization. We were authorized to call them names, but *they* could kill Turks with impunity. We have decided to take matters into our own hands."

"America was also offered assistance by many other nations in the effort to hunt down al-Qaeda terrorists and jihadists," Gardner said. "This sudden attack looks more like an invasion than an antiterrorist operation."

"Are you offering assistance, Mr. President?" Hirsiz asked. "That would certainly speed up our progress and ensure a more rapid retraction."

"Mr. President, the United States has often offered assistance in hunting down PKK terrorists many times in the past," Gardner said. "We have provided intelligence, weapons, and financial resources for years. But the intent was to avoid open warfare and violations of sovereign borders—to prevent exactly what has occurred, and what other calamities might happen if hostilities do not end."

"We are grateful for the assistance you have provided, sir," Hirsiz said. "Turkey will always be thankful. But it was simply not enough to stop the terrorists from attacking. It is not America's fault. We have been forced to act by the ruthless PKK. Any assistance you can provide in the future would be most helpful and gratefully accepted, of course."

"We'd be happy to help you hunt down the terrorists, Mr. President," Gardner said, "but as a sign of good faith, we would ask if United Nations peacekeeping forces could substitute for Turkish ground troops, and if you could allow international monitors and law enforcement officers to patrol the Turkey-Iraq border."

"I am sorry, Mr. President, but that would not do at all," Hirsiz said. "It is our belief that the United Nations is an ineffectual force and has not made any progress in any area of the world where its peacekeepers are deployed. In fact, it is our opinion that such a force would be biased against Turkey and in favor of the Kurdish minority, and that the hunt for PKK terrorists would be shuffled into the background. No, sir, Turkey will not accept peacekeepers at this time."

"I trust you and Prime Minister Akas will be willing to negotiate this matter, sir? By the way, I expected to hear from the prime minister. Is she well? We haven't seen or heard of her."

"I think you will find the prime minister to be just as firm on this issue as I, Mr. President," Hirsiz said flatly, ignoring Gardner's questions. "International observers would only complicate the security, cultural, ethnic, and religious tensions in the region. I'm afraid there is no room for compromise at this time."

"I see. I also want to discuss Vice President Phoenix," Gardner went on. "He was forced to evade Turkish warplanes and ground forces as he flew into Irbil for our scheduled negotiations."

"That is an unfortunate occurrence, sir. I assure you, no efforts were made to attack any aircraft whatsoever. As far as we know, the PKK does not have an air force. Where is the vice president now, sir?"

"The vice president is a virtual prisoner of the Turkish army and air force at the Iraqi air base at Tall Kayf, north of Mosul," Gardner said, after carefully considering whether or not he should reveal this information. "He is surrounded by Turkish troops and buzzed repeatedly by Turkish warplanes. He definitely fears for his safety. I demand that all Turkish forces evacuate the area and allow the vice president to leave the base and proceed to his next destination."

"His next destination?"

"His original destination: Irbil," Gardner said. "The vice president still has a mission: to negotiate a settlement between Iraq, America, the Kurdish Regional Government, and Turkey, to suppress the PKK and restore peace, security, and order to the border region."

"Lofty goals, that," Hirsiz said dismissively. There was a considerable pause at the other end of the line; then: "Mr. President, I am sorry, but the security situation is completely unstable and uncertain throughout northern Iraq and southern Turkey. No one can guarantee the vice president's safety in the cities, especially ones controlled by the Kurds and infested with the PKK."

"So you will keep the vice president imprisoned in Iraq? Is that what you're telling me, sir?"

"Of course not, sir," Hirsiz replied. "I am only thinking of the vice president's safety, nothing else." There was another long pause; then: "I will pledge, upon my honor, that I will see to it that the vice president is safely escorted to the Turkish border under heavy guard, with full cooperation with your Secret Service protection detail, and from there he can be escorted to the American air base at Incirlik for a return to the United States. I will also pledge that Turkish forces will not interfere in the least if the vice president decides to travel to Baghdad. But since Turkish forces have not traveled farther south than Mosul, I cannot guarantee his safety. I am afraid traveling right now is simply not advised."

"Let me get this straight, Mr. Hirsiz—you're telling me that *you* are going to dictate conditions, routes, and procedures by which the vice president of the United States of America can move about in a sovereign country not your own?" Gardner asked incredulously. "Let me advise *you*, sir: I'm going to dispatch the vice president or anyone else when I want, any*where* I want in Iraq or any other friendly nation, and by God, if I see or have any indication whatsoever that *any*one does so much as *gesture* in his direction with the merest *thought* of harm, I will see to it that he is pounded ten feet into the *ground*. Do I make myself clear, sir?"

"Crude and boisterous as always, but I understand," Hirsiz said in a completely neutral tone of voice.

"See that you do, sir," President Gardner said. "And when can I expect to speak directly to the prime minister regarding the state of emergency and opening a dialogue to address the withdrawal of forces from Iraq?"

"Prime Minister Akas is understandably very busy, sir, but I will relay your request to her immediately. I thank you for speaking with me, sir. Please keep us in your prayers, and until we speak again—"

"Tell me, Mr. Hirsiz," Gardner interrupted, "is Prime Minister Akas still alive, and if so, is she still in power? Are the generals calling the shots in Turkey now, and are you the president in name only?"

Another long pause; then: "I am offended by your insinuations, sir," Hirsiz said. "I have nothing more to say to you. Good day." And the connection was terminated.

"Bastard," Gardner breathed as he hung up the phone. "Who does he think he's talking to?" He paused, fulminating with red-hot intensity, then nearly shouted, "And what the hell was that about a stealth bomber flying over Turkey with a damned radiation weapon? What was *that* about?"

"There's only one outfit that flies a reconnaissance aircraft like Hirsiz described: Scion Aviation International," Secretary of Defense Miller Turner said.

"You mean . . . *McLanahan's* outfit?" Gardner asked incredulously. "He *brought radiation weapons into Iraq*?"

"I don't know anything about radiation weapons. He certainly wasn't authorized to bring *any* offensive weapons into Iraq or anywhere else," Turner said. "But if anyone's got high-tech weapons like that, it's McLanahan."

"I've had it with him—pull him *out*, and do it *today*." Gardner jabbed a finger at his secretary of defense like a dagger. "Get his ass out of Iraq and bring him stateside *now*. I want his contracts canceled and all funds due him and his company frozen until I have Justice investigate him and his activities." Turner nodded and picked up a phone. "Maybe we'll get more cooperation from the Turks if we start investigating McLanahan."

"McLanahan briefed me on what happened, Mr. President," Vice President Phoenix said from Allied Air Base Nahla. "The Turks were jamming the hell out of the base—they shut down all communications and sensor datalinks. McLanahan used a defensive laser on board his unmanned reconnaissance plane to . . ."

"A *defensive laser*? What in hell is that? He shot the Turkish jet with a *laser* . . . ?"

"Only to get the Turkish jet to shut off the jamming," Phoenix said. "He didn't know he was going to kill the pilot. The Turks ended up shooting the recon plane down."

"Serves him right," the president said. "He *should've* known the laser would've hurt the pilot; he tested the thing, didn't he? He's still responsible for the pilot's death. I want him brought in and indicted."

"If he hadn't shut that jamming down, I could've flown right into the middle of the Turkish attack," Phoenix said. "He acted responsibly against an unknown attack in a theater of combat, doing exactly what he was contracted to do."

"He wasn't contracted to kill people, Ken," the president said. "*No* Americans have the responsibility to kill *anyone* in Iraq, let alone an ally. We're supposed to be there to assist and train, not shoot lasers at people. McLanahan did what he always does: he uses whatever forces he commands to solve the problem, no matter what happens or who he kills or injures doing it. If you want to testify on his behalf, Ken, be my guest, but he *will* answer for what he did." Phoenix had no response. "Miller, how soon can you get McLanahan stateside?"

"Depending on what the Turks do, I can send a plane up from Baghdad and get him tonight."

"Do it."

Turner nodded.

"Mr. President, Colonel Wilhelm here at Nahla is keeping all of his forces inside the base," Vice President Phoenix said. "There is a company-size force of Turks outside the base here, but everyone is keeping a low profile. We've even given the Turks food and water."

"That just shows me that the Turks don't want a fight, unless you're a card-carrying member of the PKK," the president said. "What is the Iraqi army doing? Keeping a low profile too, I hope?"

"Very low, Mr. President—in fact, they evacuated the base and are nowhere to be found."

"*What*?"

"They simply got up and walked off the base," Phoenix said. "Everyone is gone, and they destroyed whatever they couldn't carry."

"*Why*? Why in the world would they do that?" the president thundered. "Why in hell are we over there *helping* them when they cut and run at the first sign of trouble?"

"Mr. President, I'd like to go to Baghdad and speak with the Iraqi president and prime minister," Vice President Phoenix said. "I want to find out what's going on."

"Jesus, Ken, haven't you had enough action for a while?"

"I guess not, Mr. President," Phoenix said, smiling. "Besides, I like flying in that tilt-rotor contraption. The Marines don't fly slow and leisurely unless they really have to."

"If you're serious about going, Ken, get together with the Army commander out there and your Secret Service detail and figure out the safest way to get you to Baghdad," the president said. "I don't like having you in the middle of an invasion, but having you right there in-country might help things along. I don't trust the Turks as far as I can throw them, so we'll rely on our own guys to get you safely to the capital. I just hope the Iraqis aren't flaking out on us, too, or it could get ugly out there. Keep me posted, and be careful."

"Yes, Mr..President."

"Stacy, I'd like to send you to Ankara or Istanbul as soon as possible, but we may have to wait until things cool down," the president said. "How about meeting with the NATO alliance in Brussels—together we should be able to put enough pressure on Turkey to get them to pull out."

"Good idea, Mr. President," Barbeau said. "I'll get it set up right away."

"Good. Tell the Turkish prime minister that we'll have a suspect on the shoot-down of their reconnaissance plane in custody within hours; that should make them a little more pleasant."

"Yes, Mr. President," Barbeau said, and signed off.

"Miller, let me know when McLanahan's on his way back to the States so I can inform Ankara," the president said. "I'd like to offer them a few carrots before I have to start raising sticks, and McLanahan in custody should be a sizable carrot. Thanks, everyone."

COMMAND AND CONTROL CENTER, ALLIED AIR BASE NAHLA, IRAQ
A short time later

"I said, it's too dangerous, Masters," Jack Wilhelm said irritably. He was at his console in the Tank studying what little information was coming in to him. "The Turks have grounded all aerial reconnaissance and restricted troop movements in and around the base. Things are too tense right now. If we try to go outside to the crash site, they might get spooked. Besides, you still don't look a hundred percent."

"Colonel, there's a quarter of a *billion* dollars' worth of equipment sitting in a pile out there less than two miles outside the fence," Jon Masters argued. "You can't let the Turks and the locals just walk off with it. Some of that stuff is classified."

"It's a crash site, Masters. It's been destroyed—"

"Colonel, my planes are not flimsy aluminum—they're composites. They're a hundred times stronger than steel. The Loser was flying slow and was on approach to land. There's a good chance some of the systems and avionics survived the impact. I've got to get out there to recover what I can before—"

"Masters, my orders are no one goes outside the base, and that includes you," Wilhelm insisted. "The Turkish army is in control out there, and I'm not going to risk a confrontation with them. They let food, water, and supplies come in and out—that's good enough for me right now. We're trying to open negotiations with the Turks for access to the wreckage, but they're pissed because you used it to shoot down one of their planes. So stop bugging me until they cool down and start talking to us, okay?"

"Every box they take out of that crash site costs me money, Colonel."

"I'm sorry about your money, Doc, but I really don't give a shit right now," Wilhelm said. "I know you were helping me out by shooting down that recon plane, but we have no options right now."

"Then I'll go out there and take my chances with the Turks."

"Doc, I'm sure the Turks would love to have a little chat with you right now," Wilhelm said. "They'd have your lasers, all the supersecret black boxes, the guy who designed and built them all, *and* the one who used them to shoot down one of their planes and kill one of their soldiers. Unless you like the taste of truth serum or enjoy having your fingernails pulled out with pliers, I think you're safer inside the wire." That made Jon Masters gulp, turn whiter than he looked before, and fall silent. "I thought not. I think we're damned lucky they're not demanding we turn you over to them right now. I'm

sorry about your stuff, Doc, but you stay put."
He watched Jon turn away and couldn't help but
feel a little sorry for him.

"I think you scared him, Colonel," Patrick
McLanahan said. He was standing with security director Kris Thompson beside Wilhelm's
console. "Do you really think the Turks would
torture him?"

"How the hell do I know, General?" Wilhelm
growled. "I just wanted him to stop harping
on me until I get things sorted out and until
someone in Washington or Ankara calls a stop
to all this. But shooting down that Phantom is
not going to sit well with the Turks." He studied
one of the data screens with updated air traffic
information. "You still bringing in one of your
planes tonight? Haven't you lost enough planes
already?"

"It's not an XC-57, just a regular 767 freighter,"
Patrick said. "It's already been cleared and mani-
fested by the Turks."

"Why bother? You know your contract is
going to get canceled, don't you? Shooting down
that Phantom—with a *laser* no less—is going
to land you in hot water. You'll be lucky if the
Turks don't intercept it and force it to land in
Turkey."

"Then I'll still need a freighter to start taking
my stuff out of the country now that they shot
down the Loser."

"It's your decision, General," Wilhelm said,
shaking his head. "I think the Turks okayed the
flight just so they can intercept it, force it to land
in Turkey, seize whatever stuff you're bringing
into Iraq, and hold the cargo and your plane hos-

tage until you pay reparations for the Phantom and probably stand trial for murder. But it's your call." Mark Weatherly stepped over to Wilhelm and handed him a note. He read it, shook his head wearily, then handed it back. "Bad news, General. I've been ordered to detain you in your quarters until you can be flown back to the States. Your contract has been canceled by the Pentagon, effective immediately."

"The Phantom incident?"

"Doesn't say, but I'm sure that's why," Wilhelm said. "From what we've seen, the Turks are being ultracareful not to attack us or the non-PKK Iraqis. That restraint may slip now that they've lost a jet and a pilot, and Washington needs to do something to show we don't want to get into a shooting match with the Turks."

"And I'm the guy."

"High-profile retired bomber commander turned mercenary. Hate to say it, General, but you're the poster child for retribution."

"I'm sure President Gardner was all too happy to serve you up, too, Muck," Jon Masters added.

"Sorry, General." Wilhelm turned to Kris Thompson. "Thompson, mind taking the general to his CHU? I don't even know if you've ever slept in it before—I've always found you out in the hangar or in your plane—but that's where I've got to keep you for now."

"Mind if I go with him, Colonel?" Jon asked.

Wilhelm waved a hand at him and turned back to his console, and the group left for the housing area.

The housing area—CHUville—seemed almost deserted. No one said anything as they walked down the rows of steel containers until they located the one reserved for Patrick. "I'll have your stuff brought out here, sir," Kris said. He opened the door, turned on a light, and inspected the room. There was an inner room to keep out blowing sand and dust. Inside was a small galley, desk and chair, guest chairs, closet, storage shelves, and a sofa bed. "We have plenty of room, so you have both CHUs and the wet-CHU in the middle to yourself. We set up the second CHU as a conference room for you and your guys; this side is your private space. You have full Internet access, telephone, TV, the works. If there's anything else you need, or if you want a different CHU closer to the flight line, just call."

"Thanks, Kris. This'll be okay."

"Again, Patrick, I'm sorry this is going down like this," Kris said. "You were trying to get our comms and datalinks back, not kill the guy."

"It's the politics kicking in, Kris," Patrick said. "The Turks feel totally justified in what they're doing, and they don't know or care why we'd fire on their plane. The White House doesn't want this thing to blow out of control—"

"Not to mention the president would love to stick it to you, Muck," Jon Masters added.

"Nothing we can do about it here," Patrick said. "I'll do my fighting once I get stateside. Don't worry about me."

Thompson nodded. "No one has said thank you for what you did, but I will. Thank you, sir," he said, then departed.

"Great, just great," Jon Masters said after Thompson had left the CHU. "The Turks are going to rummage through the Loser's wreckage, and you're stuck in here under house arrest with the president of the United States ready to serve you up to the Turks as a berserker warmonger. Swell. What do we do now?"

"I have no idea," Patrick said. "I'll get in touch with the boss and let him know what's happening—if he doesn't already know."

"I'll bet Pres—" Patrick suddenly raised his hand, which startled Jon. "What?" Jon asked. "Why did you . . . ?" Patrick put a finger to his lips and pointed around the room. Jon knotted his eyebrows in confusion. Rolling his eyes in exasperation, Patrick found a pencil and paper in the desk and wrote, *I think the CHUs are bugged.*

"*What*?" Jon exclaimed.

Patrick rolled his eyes again, then wrote, *No mention of the pres. Casual talk only.*

"Okay," Jon said, not really sure if he believed it but willing to play along. He wrote, *Off the bug?*

Only video if they have it, Patrick replied in writing. Jon nodded. Patrick wrote, *Tell Whack and Charlie on the freighter and the rest of the team in Las Vegas what happened to the Loser . . . and to me.*

Jon nodded, gave Patrick a sorrowful expression, then said, "Okay, Muck, I'll head back to the hangar, send the messages, check on the first Loser, and then turn in. This has been a really suck day. Buzz me if you need anything."

"Thanks. See you later."

Jack Wilhelm punched the button on his console and slid off his headset after listening to the recording several minutes after Kris Thompson returned from CHUville. "I didn't hear much of anything, Thompson," he said.

"They started being very cautious about what they were saying, Colonel," Kris Thompson replied. "I think they suspect they're being bugged."

"The guy's smart, that's for sure," Wilhelm said. "Can we confiscate the paper they're writing messages on before they destroy them?"

"Sure—if we want them to find out they're being bugged."

"Wish you had set up a video bug in there instead of just audio. All this high-tech gear around here and you couldn't set up one simple baby-crib camera?" Thompson said nothing—he could've easily set up a video bug, but he was uncomfortable enough installing an audio bug in the general's CHU; a video bug was too much. "He mentioned the 'boss,' and then Masters sounded like he was going to say 'the president,'" Wilhelm commented. "President of what?"

"The company, I assume," Thompson said. He paused, then added uncomfortably, "I don't feel right bugging the general's CHU, Colonel."

"I got the order straight from the Army chief of staff, who got it through the attorney general and the secretary of defense—gather information on McLanahan's activities, including eavesdropping and wiretaps, until the FBI and State Department take over," Wilhelm said. "They're gunning for this guy, that's for sure. The president wants his head on a platter. They ordered his freighter searched and every piece of equipment on board cross-checked with the official manifest. If he's bringing in any unauthorized stuff, they want to know about it. I don't think the Turks will allow it to land here, but if it does, Washington wants it searched for unauthorized weapons."

"What kind of weapons?"

"How the hell should I know, Thompson? You have the manifest—if it's not on there, it's contraband. Confiscate it."

"Isn't anyone around here going to support McLanahan at all? The guy's just trying to do his job. He saved our bacon during the attack and probably saved the vice president's, too."

"McLanahan will be okay, Thompson, don't worry about him," Wilhelm said. "Besides, we have our orders, and they come from the very top. I'm not going to let guys like McLanahan ruin *my* career. Send the recordings to division as soon as possible."

"Hiya, big guy."

"Dad?" There was nothing like hearing your son's voice saying "Dad," Patrick thought; it always gave him a thrill. "Where are you?"

"Still in Iraq."

"Oh." Bradley James McLanahan, who had just turned thirteen, was still a kid of few words—like his old man, Patrick surmised. "When are you coming home?"

"I don't know for sure, but I think it'll be soon. Listen, I know you're getting ready for school, but I wanted to . . ."

"Can I try out for football this year?"

"Football?" That was a new one, Patrick thought. Bradley played soccer and tennis and

could water-ski, but he never showed any interest in contact sports before. "Sure, if you want to,
as long as your grades are good."

"Then you got to tell Aunt Mary. She says I'll
get hurt and turn my brain to mush."

"Not if you listen to the coach."

"Will you tell her? Here." Before Patrick could
say anything, his youngest sister, Mary, was on
the line. "Patrick?"

"Hi, Mare. How are—"

"You are *not* going to allow him to play football, are you?"

"Why not, if he wants to and his grades—"

"His grades are okay, but they could be better
if only he would stop daydreaming, journaling,
and doodling about spaceships and fighter jets,"
his sister said. Mary was a pharmacist, with
grades good enough for medical school if she had
the time between raising Bradley and two of her
own. "Have you ever seen a middle school football game?"

"No."

"Those players get bigger and bigger every
year, their hormones are raging, and they have
more physical strength than the skills to control
themselves. Bradley's more of a bookworm than
a jock. Besides, he just wants to do it because his
friends are going to try out and some girls in his
class are going to try out for cheerleading."

"That always motivated me. Listen, I need to
speak with—"

"Oh, I got an e-mail this morning saying that
the automatic deposit from your company from
last week was reversed. No explanation. I'm
overdrawn, Patrick. It'll cost me fifty dollars plus

any other penalties from whoever I wrote checks
to. Can you get that straightened out so I don't
get buried in bounced check fees?"

"It's a new company, Mary, and the payroll
might be screwed up." His entire paycheck from
Scion went to his sister to help with expenses;
his entire Air Force retirement went into a trust
for Bradley. His sister didn't like that, because
paychecks from Scion were irregular depending
on if the company had a contract and had any
money to pay upper management, but Patrick
had insisted. That made Bradley more of an out-
sider than he wanted, but it was the best arrange-
ment he could make right now. "Give it a week
or so, okay? I'll get all the charges reversed."

"Are you coming home soon? Steve wants to
go to a rodeo in Casper next month."

And the trailer they brought on such trips
didn't have room for a third kid, Patrick thought.
"Yes, I think I'll be home by then, and you guys
can take off. Let me speak with . . ."

"He's running to catch the bus. He's always
drawing or doodling or writing in his note-
book and I have to tell him a dozen times to get
moving or he'll miss the bus. Everything okay?"

"Yes, I'm okay, but there was a little incident
lately, and I wanted to tell Bradley and you about
it before—"

"Good. There's so much stuff on the news
about Iraq and Turkey lately, and we think of
you every night when we watch the news."

"I think of you guys all the time. But early
this morning—"

"That's nice. I gotta run, Patrick. I'm inter-
viewing some pharmacy techs this morning.

Steve and the kids send their love. Bye bye." And the connection was broken.

That's how most of their phone conversations went, he thought as he hung up his phone: a very brief conversation with his son, a complaint and request from his sister or brother-in-law—usually a request for family time that didn't involve Bradley—followed by a harried good-bye. Well, what did he expect? He had a young teenage son who had been either dragged around the country or left with relatives most of his life; he didn't get to see his dad too much, only read about him in newspapers or on TV, usually involving harsh criticism about some questionable involvement in some near-catastrophic global calamity. His relatives certainly cared about Bradley, but they had their own lives to live and they frequently saw Patrick's escapades as a means of running away from mundane family life back home.

He made some calls to Scion's headquarters back in Las Vegas about his paycheck; they assured him the "check was in the mail" even though it was always transferred electronically. Then he was patched through to Kevin Martindale, former president of the United States and silent owner of Scion Aviation International.

"Hello, Patrick. Heard you had a tough day."

"Rough as sandpaper, sir," Patrick said. One of the code words that employees of Scion Aviation International were taught to use was *sandpaper*—if used in any conversation or correspondence, it meant they were under duress or being bugged.

"Got it. Sorry about the contract being canceled. I'll try to work things from here, but it doesn't look good."

"Do you know if I'm going to be arrested?"

"Sometime tomorrow or the next day. I haven't seen the warrant, but I expect it'll be served soon."

"The Turks were jamming the hell out of us. We had to shut down the plane."

"Don't worry about it, just do what they tell you to do and keep silent. You should send your freighter aircraft elsewhere. It won't be safe in Iraq."

"We'll need it to start packing up."

"It's risky. The Turks will want it. They may try to grab it when it flies through their airspace."

"I know."

"It's your call. Anything else for me?"

"Some snafu with the paycheck. A deposit that was made days ago was yanked out."

"No snafu," Martindale said. "Our accounts have been frozen solid. I'm working that, too, but now we've got multiple departments and the White House in on this, so it'll take longer. Try not to worry about it."

"Yes, sir." And the call abruptly terminated. Well, sleep was going to be impossible now, Patrick thought, so he powered up his laptop. Just as he started to surf the Internet and read the news from the outside world, he picked up a call. "McLanahan here."

"*Patrick*? I just heard! Thank God you're okay."

It sounded like his sister Mary calling him back, but he wasn't sure. "Mary?"

"This is Gia Cazzotto, you ninny—I mean, ninny *sir*," the voice of Lieutenant Colonel Cazzotto, the commander of the Seventh Air Expeditionary Squadron, said, laughing. "Who's Mary? Some young engineer in a lab coat and big glasses who transforms herself into Marilyn Monroe when she pulls a pin out of her hair?"

Patrick's laugh was a lot more strained and high-pitched than he wanted. "No, no, no," he said, confused that his mouth had suddenly turned so dry. "Mary is my sister. Lives in Sacramento. I just spoke with her. Thought it was her calling back."

"Sure, sure, sure, I've heard that one before," Gia said. "Listen, Patrick, I just heard about the attack on Nahla, and I wanted to make sure you were okay."

"Jon and I got our bells rung, but we're okay, thanks."

"I'm in Dubai right now, but I got permission to come over as soon as they're letting personnel come up north," she said. "I want to see you and find out what happened."

"That would be great, Boxer, really great," Patrick said, "but I might be shipping out soon."

"Shipping out?"

"Back to Washington. Long story."

"I've got plenty of time, Patrick. Lay it on me."

"Not 'long' as in time, but 'long' as in . . . a lot of stuff I can't talk about."

"Gotcha." There was a bit of an uncomfortable pause; then: "Hey, our seventh airframe just showed up today here in the United Arab Emirates, and we received our eighth airframe today at Palmdale. This one has got all kinds of weird gizmos in the forward bomb bay, and I figured it had to be one of yours."

"Did you get it from the Boneyard?"

"No, it was in flyable storage at Tonopah." Tonopah Test Range was an air base in southern Nevada used for classified weapons tests before an aircraft was delivered to active duty. "It's got all kinds of fuel lines running here and there through the bomb bays, and something that looks like a car assembly robot with arms and claws everywhere."

"We had B-1 bombers that could recover, rearm, refuel, and relaunch FlightHawk cruise missiles in-flight. That must be one of them."

"No shit! That's cool. Maybe we can put that system together again."

"I'm sure I can get Jon Masters at Sky Masters Inc. to send you the schematics."

"Great. Any other cool stuff like that, send it along, too. I'm not getting Air Force acquisition officers and budget weenies hanging up on me anymore when I call to ask about getting money for stuff—they actually seem interested in building bombers nowadays."

"Probably because they're taking everything else away from the Air Force other than tankers and transports."

"I'm sure." There was another few moments of quiet; then Gia said, "I hope you don't mind me calling."

"I'm glad you did, Gia."

"I also hope you don't mind me calling you Patrick."

"I'm glad you did. Besides, it *is* my name."

"Don't tease me . . . unless you really *want* to."

A loud-pitched squeal erupted in Patrick's ears, and he felt his face flush as if he had said a swearword in front of his sainted grandmother. What in hell was *that*? Did he just *blush* . . . ? "No . . . no . . ."

"You don't want to tease me?"

"No . . . I mean, I do want—"

"You *do* want to tease me? Oh, goody."

"No . . . jeez, Boxer, you're making me goofy over here."

"I like a little goofy now and then, too, but I prefer teasing to goofy."

"All right, Colonel, all right, that's enough."

"Pulling rank on me now, General?"

"If I have to," Patrick said. The chuckle came out like a strangled donkey's bray.

"Hey, Patrick."

"Yeah?"

"I really want to see you. What about you? Do you want to see me?"

Patrick felt the flushing in his cheeks turn into a warm spot in his chest, and he breathed it in and let it fill his entire body. "I would really like that, Gia."

"Mary is really your sister and not Mrs. McLanahan?"

"Really my sister. My wife, Wendy, passed several years ago." That was only true if you thought being nearly beheaded by an insane female Russian terrorist in Libya could be considered a "passing," but he wasn't going to go into that with Gia now.

"Sorry to hear that. I can't come up there?"

"I . . . don't know how long I'll be here," Patrick said.

"But you can't talk about what or why?"

"Not over the phone." There was an uncomfortable pause on the line, and Patrick said hurriedly, "I'll know by tomorrow night, Gia, and we'll arrange to get together then." He paused, then asked, "Uh, there's no Mr. Cazzotto, is there?"

"I was wondering if you'd ask," Gia said with a pleased tone in her voice. "Most guys I run into ask about a spouse *afterward*."

"After what?"

She laughed. "If you want me to describe it to you in detail, cowboy, settle in and get comfortable."

"I get the picture."

"Anyway, before I get distracted: there was a husband, but not since I went back into the Air Force and was assigned to Plant Forty-two. He's still in the Bay area with our teenagers, a boy and a girl. You have any kids?"

"A boy, just turned thirteen."

"Then you know how tough it is to be away."

"Yes." There was another pause, as if they were silently acknowledging the new bond between them; then Patrick said, "I'll let you know what's happening and tell you all about it when we see each other."

"I'll be waiting to hear from you."

"One more question?"

"I've got all night for you."

"How did you get my cell number? It's not published."

"Oooh, a secret number? Well, I feel privileged, then. I called Scion Aviation and your friend David Luger gave it to me. Thought you wouldn't mind."

"I owe him one."

"In a good way, I hope."

"In a *very* good way."

"Perfect. Good night, Patrick." And she hung up.

Well, Patrick thought as he hung up, this was turning into a very bizarre day—plenty of surprises, good ones as well as bad. Time to hit the rack and see what tomorrow had rigged up for—

Just then, a knock on the door. "Patrick? It's me," he heard Jon Masters say. "I brought the report on the number one Loser you wanted to see."

"C'mon in, Jon," Patrick said. He hadn't asked to see any report . . . what was going on? He heard the outer door open and close, and then the inner door open. "It could've waited for tomorrow morning, Jon, but as long as you're—"

He looked at the doorway and saw none other than Iraqi Colonel Yusuf Jaffar, commander of Allied Air Base Nahla, standing there!

Patrick put a finger to his lips, and Jaffar nodded that he understood. "How about some coffee, Jon? It's instant, but it's okay." He pulled out a pad of paper and wrote, *????*

"Sure, Muck, I'll give it a try," Jon said. On the paper he wrote, *New client.* Patrick widened his eyes in surprise and stared at Jaffar, who simply stood at the doorway with his hands behind his back, looking impatient. "Here's the report," he said. "The number one Loser is code one. The freighter has a bunch of spare parts, which we don't need right now—what we'll need is the room to start hauling our gear out. The Loser can carry a lot of it, but we'll need more space."

"We'll worry about that when the freighter

arrives," Patrick said. He wrote: *Hire Scion?* Jon nodded. Patrick wrote: *When? Why?*

Jon wrote: *Tonight. Defend Iraq against Turkey.*

How? Patrick wrote.

Take Nahla, Jon wrote.

I don't see how, Patrick wrote.

Jaffar's eyes widened with impatience. He snatched the pencil out of Jon's hands and wrote, *My base, my country, my home. Help, or get out. Decide. Now.*

OVER SOUTHERN TURKEY
Hours later

"Ankara Center, Scion Seven-Seven, level, flight level three-three zero over reporting point Afsin, estimating reporting point Simak in twenty-six minutes."

"Scion Seven-Seven, Ankara Center copies, good evening. Expect handoff to Mosul Approach five minutes prior to Simak."

"Scion Seven-Seven copies."

The radios fell silent for several minutes until: "Scion Seven-Seven, change to Diyarbakir Approach frequency VHF one-three-five-point-zero-five."

It was a rather unusual request—they were transitioning well above the local approach control's airspace—but the pilot didn't argue: "Roger, Ankara, Scion Seven-Seven switching to Diyarbakir Approach." He made the frequency change, then: "Diyarbakir Approach, Scion Seven-Seven, level, flight level three-three zero."

A heavily Turkish-accented voice responded

in English: "Scion Seven-Seven, this is Diyarba-kir Approach, descend and maintain one-seven thousand feet, turn left heading three-four-five, vectors to Irgani intersection, altimeter setting two-niner niner eight."

"Here we go," the pilot said cross-cockpit, taking a deep cleansing breath to control his quickly rising excitement. He keyed his intercom button: "They just vectored us for the ILS approach into Diyarbakir, sir."

"Question it but take the vector," David Luger said via encrypted satellite link from Scion head-quarters in Las Vegas. "We're ready."

"Roger." On the radio, the pilot said, "Uh, Diyarbakir, Seven-Seven, why the vector? We're on a priority international flight plan, destination Tall Kayf."

"Your transition through Turkish airspace has been canceled by the Turkish Ministry of Defense and Frontier Security, Seven-Seven," the approach controller said. "You are instructed to follow my vectors for approach and landing at Diyarbakir. Once your plane, crew, and cargo have been inspected, you will be permitted to continue to your destination."

"This is not right, Approach," the pilot protested. "Our flight did not originate or terminate in Turkey, and we filed a flight plan. We are not subject to inspection as long as we are only over-flying your airspace. If you want, we can exit your airspace."

"You are instructed to follow my vectors for approach and landing at Diyarbakir, or you will be considered a hostile aircraft and we will respond accordingly," the controller said. "There are fighters standing by that will intercept you and escort you to Diyarbakir if you do not comply. Acknowledge."

"Approach, we're turning to your heading and descending," the pilot responded, "but I will be messaging my headquarters and advising them of your threat. We will comply under protest."

"I have been informed to notify you that the American consulate has been notified of our actions and will meet you at Diyarbakir for the inspection and interviews," the controller said after a lengthy pause. "They will remain with you at all times while you are on the ground and will observe all of our enforcement actions."

"This is still not right, Approach," the pilot went on. "You can't divert us like this. This is illegal." On the intercom, the pilot asked, "You want us to keep descending, sir?"

"One more minute," Dave Luger said. The Boeing 767 freighter had actually been a test-bed aircraft for the high-tech sensors and transmitters mounted on the XC-57. Most of them were still installed, including the ability to network-intrude, or "netrude"—send digital instructions to an enemy computer or network by inserting code into a digital receiver return signal. Once the proper digital frequency was discovered, Luger could remotely send computer instructions into an enemy network that, if not detected and firewalled, could propagate throughout the enemy's computer network worldwide like any other shared piece of data.

"Diyarbakir's radar isn't digital, so we're going to have to do this the old-fashioned way," Luger went on. Netrusion only worked on digital systems—if the enemy had older analog radar systems it wouldn't work. "You guys strap in tight—this might get hairy." Both the pilot and copilot pulled their seat belts and shoulder harnesses as tight as they could and still reach all the controls.

Suddenly the radio frequency exploded into a crashing waterfall of squeals, popping, and hissing. The Turkish controller's voice could be heard, but it was completely unintelligible. "Okay, guys, the radar is jammed," Luger said. "You're cleared direct Nahla, descend smartly to seventeen thousand feet, keep the speed up. We're keeping an eye on your threat warning receiver." The pilot swallowed hard, made the turn, pulled the power back, and pushed the nose over until the airspeed readout was right at the barber-pole limit. With the airspeed and descent rate pegged, they lost the sixteen thousand feet in less than six minutes.

"Okay, guys, here's the situation," Dave radioed after they had leveled off. "They just launched a couple F-16s from Diyarbakir—that's the bad news. I can jam the approach radar but I don't think I can jam or netrude into the fire control radars on the jets—that's the really bad news. We think the F-16s have infrared sensors to locate you—that's the really *really* bad news. They've also brought several Patriot missile batteries into the area you're about to fly through—that's the *really really*—well, you get the picture."

"Yes, sir. What's the plan?"

"We're going to try to do a little low-level terrain masking while I try to link into the Patriot surveillance system," Luger said. "Front-line Turkish F-16s have digital radars and datalinks, and I think I can break in, but I'll have to wait until the datalink goes active, and it may take a while until the Patriot gets a glimpse of you."

"Uh, sir? It's dark out and we can't see anything outside."

"That's probably best," Luger said. The copilot furiously pulled out his aviation enroute charts for the area they were flying in and spread them out on the glare shield. "I think the F-16s will try to get vectors to you from the Patriot fire control radars until they can get a lock either with their radar or their IR."

"Copy." Over the ship's intercom, the pilot said, "Mr. Macomber? Miss Turlock? Come up to the cockpit, please?"

A few moments later, retired U.S. Air Force special operations officer Wayne "Whack" Macomber and former U.S. Army National Guard engineer Charlie Turlock stepped through the door and found seats. Macomber, a former Air Force Academy football star and Air Force special operations meteorologist, found it a bit difficult to wedge his large muscular frame into the port-side jump seat. On the other hand, it was easy for Charlie—her real name, not a nickname, given to her by a father who thought he was getting a son—to nestle her lean, trim, athletic body into the folding jump seat between the pilots. Both newcomers put on headsets.

"What the hell is going on, Gus?" Wayne asked.

"That situation Mr. Luger briefed us on? It's

happening. The Turks want us to land in Diyar-bakir and are probably going to scramble fighters after us."

"Is Luger—"

"Trying to netrude into their air defense and datalink systems," the pilot said. "We've jammed the approach control radar and started to evade them, but Mr. Luger can't netrude their analog systems; he has to wait for a digitally processed signal to come up."

"I didn't understand it when Luger first said it, and I don't understand it now," Macomber grumbled. "Just keep us from crashing or getting shot down, will ya?"

"Yes, sir. Thought you'd want to know. Strap in tight—this will get hairy."

"Your passengers all buckled in?" David Luger asked.

"You just shut down those Turkish radars or I'll come back and haunt you for all eternity, sir," Whack radioed back.

"Hi, Whack. I'll do my best. Charlie strapped in, too?"

"I'm ready to fly, David," Charlie replied.

"Excellent, Charlie."

Even faced with a dangerous ride ahead, Charlie turned and saw the amused smirk on Macomber's face. "'Excellent, Charlie,'" he mimicked. "'Ready to fly, David.' The general wants to be sure his lady love is safely tucked in. How cute."

"Bite me, Whack," she said, but she couldn't help but smile.

"Ready, guys?"

"As ready as we'll ever be," the pilot said.

"Good. Descend right now to eleven thousand feet and fly heading one-five-zero."

The pilot pushed his control wheel forward to begin the descent, but the copilot held out his hand to stop him. "The minimum descent altitude in this area is thirteen-four."

"The high terrain in your sector is twelve o'clock, twenty-two miles. You'll be above everything else . . . well, *most* everything else. I'll steer you around the high stuff until your moving-map terrain readout starts showing you the terrain." The pilot gulped again but pushed the controls forward to start the descent. The moment they descended through fourteen thousand feet, the computerized female voice in the Terrain Advisory and Warning System blared, *"High terrain, pull up, pull up!"* and the GPS moving-map display in the cockpit started flashing yellow, first ahead of them and then to their left side, where the terrain was the highest.

"Good going, guys," Luger radioed. "On your moving map you should see a valley at your one o'clock position. The floor is nine-seven. Take that valley. Stay at eleven thousand for now." The pilots saw a very narrow strip of dark surrounded by flashing yellow and now red boxes, the red indicating terrain that was above their altitude.

"What's the width, sir?"

"It's plenty wide for you. Just watch the turbulence." At that exact moment the crew was bounced against their harnesses by wave after wave of turbulence. The pilot was struggling to maintain heading and altitude. "It's . . . getting

. . . worse," the pilot grunted. "I don't know if I can hold it."

"That valley should be good until you reach the border in about eighteen minutes," Luger radioed.

"Eighteen minutes! I can't hold it for—"

"Climb!" Luger interrupted. "Full power, hard climb to thirteen, heading two-three-zero, *now*!"

The pilot shoved the throttles to full power and hauled back on the controls with all his might. "I can't turn! The terrain—"

"Turn now! Hurry!" The pilots could do nothing else but turn, pull on the controls until the plane hung on the very edge of a stall . . . and pray. The flashing red blocks on the terrain warning display were touching the very tip of the plane's icon . . . they were seconds from a crash . . .

. . . and then at that moment the red turned to yellow, signifying that they were within five hundred feet of the ground. "Oh Jesus, oh God, we made it . . ."

And at that instant a flash of fire streaked past the cockpit windows, less than a hundred yards in front of them. The cockpit was filled with an eerie yellow burst of light like the world's largest flashbulb had just gone off right in front of them, and the pilots could even feel a burst of heat and pressure. *"What was that?"* the copilot screamed.

"Heading two-three-zero, eleven thousand feet," Luger said. "Everyone okay? Acknowledge."

"What was that?"

"Sorry, guys, but I had to do it," Luger said.

"Do what?"

"I flew you into the engagement envelope of a Patriot missile battery."

"*What?*"

"It's the only way I could get the datalink frequency for the Patriot and between the Patriot and the F-16s," Luger said.

"*Holy crap . . .* we almost got nailed by a *Patriot missile . . . ?*"

"Yeah, but only one—they must be trying to conserve missiles," Dave said. "They may have just launched it as a warning, or it might have been a decoy missile."

"How about a little warning next time you put us in the gun sights, sir?" Macomber snapped.

"No time for chitchat, Whack. I've got the Patriot's datalink frequency locked in, and I'm waiting for them to start talking to the F-16. As soon as they do, I can shut both of them down. But I need to keep you high, right on the edge of the Patriot's engagement envelope. If I keep you too low, the F-16 might switch to his infrared sensor and not use the Patriot radar. That means I'm going to have to give him another good look at you. Fly heading one-nine-zero and climb to twelve thousand. You're fifteen minutes to the Iraq border."

"This is loco," the 767 pilot murmured, flexing knots out of his hands and fingers. He began a shallow climb and a turn to—

"Okay, guys, the Patriot's back up, and he's got you, seven o'clock, twenty-nine miles," Dave said a few moments later. "Still in sector scan mode . . . now he's in target-tracking mode . . . c'mon, boys, what are you waiting for . . . ?"

"If he's verbally vectoring in the F-16, he can get him within range of his IR sensor without using the datalink, right?" the freighter pilot asked.

"I was hoping you wouldn't think about that," Luger said. "Fortunately most Patriot radar techs aren't air traffic controllers; their job is to get the *system* to do its job. Okay, descend to eleven thousand, and let's hope as you go down they'll . . ." An instant later: "*Got it!* Datalink is active. Couple more seconds . . . c'mon, baby, *c'mon* . . . got it. Quick turn to heading one-six-five, keep going to eleven thousand. The F-16 is at your six o'clock, fifteen miles and closing, but he should be turning off to your right. The Iraqi border is at your eleven o'clock, about thirteen minutes."

The picture was looking better and better. "Okay, guys, the F-16s closed to six miles but he's way off to your right," Luger said a few minutes later. "He's chasing a target being sent to him by the Patriot battery. Descend to ten thousand."

"What happens when he gets within his IR sensor range and we're not there?" the freighter pilot asked.

"Hopefully he'll think his sensor malfunctioned."

"Scion Seven-Seven, this is Yukari One-One-Three flight of two, Republic of Turkey Air Force air defense fighter interceptors," they heard on the UHF emergency GUARD frequency. "We are at your six o'clock position and have you in radar contact. You are ordered to climb to seventeen thousand feet, lower your landing gear, and turn

right to a heading of two-nine-zero, direct to Diyarbakir."

"Go ahead and answer him," Dave said.
"Maintain this heading. Your radar blip is going
to comply with his orders."

"Yukari, this is Scion Seven-Seven, we are
turning and in a climb," the freighter pilot radioed. "Safe your weapons. We're unarmed."

"Scion flight, Yukari One-One-Three leader
will join on your left side," the F-16 pilot radioed.
"My wingman will remain at your six o'clock position. You will see our inspection light. Do not be
alarmed. Continue your turn and your climb as
ordered."

"He's within six miles of the ghost target,"
Dave said. "Hang in there, guys. You're eight
minutes to the border."

Another sixty seconds passed without any radio
chatter until: "Scion flight, what is your altitude?"

"One-four thousand," Dave Luger said.

"Scion Seven-Seven is passing one-four thousand for one-seven thousand," the freighter pilot
responded.

"Activate all of your exterior lights immediately!" the Turkish fighter pilot ordered. "All
lights on!"

"Our lights are on, Yukari flight."

"He's within two miles of the false target,"
Dave Luger said. "He's probably got his inspection light on and is looking at nothing but . . ."

The freighter pilots waited, but heard nothing.
"Scion base, this is Seven-Seven, how copy?" No
response. "Scion base, Seven-Seven, how do you
hear?"

The copilot's mouth dropped open in shock. "Oh, shit, we lost the downlink with headquarters," he breathed. "We're dead meat."

"Great. Perfect time for all this high-tech gear to go tits-up," Whack complained. "Get us out of here, Gus!"

"We're going direct Nahla," the pilot said, shoving the throttles forward. "Hopefully those guys won't shoot us down if we're across the border."

"Let's try that terrain-masking stuff again," the copilot suggested. The terrain depicted on the moving map display in the cockpit still showed some hills, but it was quickly smoothing out the farther south they went. "We can go down to nine-seven in a few miles, and in twenty miles we can go all the way to—"

At that instant the cockpit was filled with an intense white light coming in from the left side as hot and bright as noon. They tried to look at whoever it was, but they couldn't look anywhere in that direction. "Holy shit!" the pilot screamed. "I'm flash-blinded, I can't see—"

"Straighten up, Gus!"

"I said I can't take the controls, I can't see, dammit," the pilot said. "Ben, take the wheel . . . !"

"Scion Seven-Seven, this is Yukari One-One-Three flight of two, we have you in sight," the Turkish fighter pilot radioed. "You will immediately lower your landing gear and turn right to heading two-nine-zero. You are being tracked by Turkish surface-to-air missile batteries. Comply immediately. The use of deadly force has been authorized."

"Your light has blinded the pilot!" the copilot radioed. "Don't shine it in the cockpit! Turn that thing off!"

A moment later the light was extinguished . . . followed seconds later by a second-long burst of cannon fire from the Turkish F-16's twenty-millimeter nose cannon. The muzzle flash was almost as brilliant as the inspection floodlight, and they could feel the fat supersonic shells beating the air around them, the shock waves reverberating off the Boeing 767's cockpit windows just a few dozen yards away. "That was the final warning shot, Scion Seven-Seven," the Turkish pilot said. "Follow my instructions or you will be shot down without further warning!"

"What the hell do we do now?" Whack asked. "We're sunk."

"We have no choice," the copilot said. "I'm turning . . ."

"No, keep heading toward Nahla," Charlie said. She reached over and switched her rotary transmit switch from "intercom" to "UHF-2." "Yukari One-One-Three flight, this is Charlie Turlock, one of the passengers on Scion Seven-Seven," she radioed.

"What the hell are you doing, Charlie?" Macomber asked.

"Playing the gender and sympathy cards, Whack—they're the only ones we have left," Charlie said cross-cockpit. On the radio, she went on, "Yukari flight, we are an American cargo aircraft on a peaceful and authorized flight to Iraq. We are not a warplane, we are not armed, and we have no hostile intent against our allies, the people of Turkey. There are nineteen souls on board this flight, including six women. Let us continue our flight in peace."

"You will comply immediately. This is our final order."

"We are not going to turn around," Charlie said. "We are almost at the Iraqi border, and our transmissions on the international emergency GUARD channel are certainly being monitored by listening posts from Syria to Persia. We are an unarmed American cargo plane on an authorized overflight of Turkey. There are nineteen souls on board. If you shoot us down now, the bodies and the wreckage will land in Iraq, and the world will know what you've done. You may think you have valid orders or a good reason to open fire, but you will be held responsible for your own judgment. If you believe your leaders and wish to follow their orders to kill all of us, fine, but *you* must pull the trigger. Our lives are in *your* hands now."

A moment later they saw, then felt a tongue of white-hot flame zip by their left cockpit windows—the single afterburner plume from an F-16 fighter. "He's going around, maneuvering behind us," the copilot said. "Shit; oh *shit* . . . !" They could sense the presence of the jets behind them, practically taste the adrenaline and sweat emanating from the Turkish pilots' bodies as they swung around for the kill. Seconds passed . . .

. . . then more seconds, then a minute. No one breathed for what seemed like an eternity. Then they heard: "Scion Seven-Seven, this is Mosul Approach Control on GUARD frequency, we show you at your scheduled border crossing point. If you hear Mosul Approach, squawk modes three and C normal and contact me on two-four-three-point-seven. Acknowledge immediately."

The copilot shakily responded, and everyone else let out a collective sigh of relief. "Man, I thought we were goners," Macomber said. He reached up and patted Charlie on the shoulder. "You did it, darlin'. You sweet-talked our way out of it. Good job."

Charlie turned to Macomber, smiled, nodded her thanks . . . and promptly vomited on the cockpit floor in front of him.

ALLIED AIR BASE NAHLA, IRAQ
A short time later

"Are you eggheads *insane*?" Colonel Jack Wilhelm exploded as Wayne Macomber and Charlie Turlock led the other passengers and crew off the Boeing 767 freighter once it was parked at the base. "Don't you realize what's going on out there?"

"You must be Colonel Wilhelm," Macomber said as he reached the bottom of the air stairs. "Thanks for the warm welcome to Iraq."

"Who are *you*?"

"Wayne Macomber, chief of security for Scion Aviation International," Wayne replied. He did not offer his hand to Wilhelm, a fact that made the regimental commander even angrier. The two men were about equal in height and weight, and they immediately started sizing each other up. "This is Charlie Turlock, my assistant." Char-

lie rolled her eyes but said nothing. "I'm going
to drain the dragon—and probably change my
undies after that flight—and then I need to
speak with the general and the head egghead,
Jon Masters."

"First of all, you're not going anywhere until
we inspect your papers and your cargo," Wilhelm said. "You're not even supposed to get off
the damn plane before customs does an inspection."

"Customs? This is an American flight sitting
on an American base. We don't do customs."

"You're a private aircraft sitting on an *Iraqi*
base, so you need to be processed by customs."

Macomber looked around Wilhelm. "I don't
see any Iraqis here, Colonel, just private security
. . . and *you*." He took a folder out of the pilot's
hands. "Here's our paperwork, and here's the
pilot. He'll do all the customs shit with you and
whatever Iraqis want to tag along. We don't have
time for customs. Let us do our thing. You stay
out of our way, and we'll stay out of yours."

"My orders are to inspect this plane, Macomber, and that's what we'll do," Wilhelm said.
"The crew stays on board until the inspection is
completed. Thompson here and his men will do
the inspection, and you'd better cooperate with
them or I'll put all of you in the brig. Clear?"

Macomber looked as if he was going to argue,
but he gave Wilhelm a slight nod and smile and
gave the paperwork packet back to the pilot.
"Ben, go with Gus." Wilhelm was going to
argue, but Macomber said, "The pilot was hurt
in the flight in. He needs help. Make it quick,
boys," and motioned for the others to follow him

back up the air stairs. They were followed by two of Thompson's security officers and a German shepherd on a leather leash. A group of Thompson's security men began opening cargo doors and baggage compartment hatches to begin their inspections.

Inside the plane, one security officer began inspecting the cockpit while the other herded Macomber and the other passengers to their seats and inspected the inside of the plane. The forward part of the Boeing 767 freighter's interior behind the cockpit had a removable galley and lavatory on one side, and two fiberglass containers marked LIFE RAFTS with reinforced tape seals marked DEPT OF DEFENSE wrapped around them on the other beside the entry door. Behind them was the removable forward-facing passenger seat pallet, with seating for eighteen passengers. Behind them were eight semicircular cargo containers, four on each side of the plane, with narrow aisles between them, and behind them was a pallet with luggage covered by nylon netting and secured with nylon webbing.

The second security officer raised a radio to his lips: "I count eighteen crew and passengers, two life raft containers, galley and lavatory, and eight A1N cargo containers. The life raft inspection seals are secure."

"Roger," came the reply. "Passenger count checks. But the manifest only says six A1Ns." The officer looked at the passengers suspiciously.

"No wonder it took so long to get here—we're overloaded," Macomber said. "Who brought the extra containers? Is that all your makeup back there, Charlie?"

"I thought it was your knitting, Whack," Turlock replied.

"I'm going to pass down the aisle with the K-9," the security officer said. "Don't make any sudden movements."

"Can I go pee first?" Macomber asked.

"After the lavatory has been inspected and the K-9 passes through the cabin," the officer replied.

"How long will that be?"

"Just cooperate." The guard began to walk the dog down the aisle, touching the seat pockets and motioning under and between the seats, indicating where he wanted the dog to sniff.

"Nice doggie," Wayne said when the dog came to him.

"No talking to the K-9," the officer said. Macomber smiled, then scowled in reply.

"Cockpit is clear," the first security officer said. He began inspecting the galley and lavatory, finishing a few minutes later.

"C'mon, guy, I'm going to explode over here."

"No talking," the second officer said. It took another three minutes for the K-9 to finish. "You may get up and exit the plane," the second officer announced. "You must proceed directly to the officer outside, who will match you up with your passports and identification papers. Leave all belongings on the plane."

"Can I use the can first?"

The second security guard looked like he was going to say no, but the first guard waved a hand. "I'll keep an eye on him," he said. Macomber rushed to the lavatory while the others filed out. The second officer continued his inspection in the rear of the cabin among the cargo containers.

It was controlled bedlam outside the plane. The security officers were using forklifts to unload containers from the cargo holds underneath the plane, which K-9s sniffed around. The crew could see K-9s sitting before some of the containers; these were marked and brought to a separate area of an adjacent hangar. Another officer checked each passport with its owner, then had each person wait with the others nearby, under the watchful eye of an armed security officer.

Kris Thompson came over a short time later and looked at the group of passengers. "Where's Macomber?"

"Still in the lavatory," Charlie Turlock replied. "He's not a strong flier."

Thompson looked over to the air stairs. "Chuck? What's going on up there?"

"A lot of grunting, groaning, and brown clouds," the first security officer waiting for Macomber replied.

"Hurry him up." Thompson turned back to Charlie. "Can you help me with the manifest, miss?" he asked. "There are a few discrepancies I'm hoping you can clear up for me."

"Sure. I'm familiar with all the stuff on board." She followed Thompson along to the various piles of containers.

Up in the cabin, the first security officer said, "Let's go, buddy."

"Almost done." The officer heard sounds of flushing, then running water, and the lavatory door was unlocked. Even before the door was fully open, the unbearable odors within made the officer gasp for breath. "Jeez, buddy, what in hell were you eating on this—"

Macomber hit him once on the left temple with his right fist, knocking him unconscious without another sound. He quickly dragged the officer forward, put him on the cockpit floor, closed the door, then went back to the cabin and stripped off the security tape around the first life raft container.

Outside the plane, Thompson motioned to different piles of containers. "These are clear and match with the manifest," he said to Charlie, "but these here don't match." He motioned to a large pile of containers across the taxiway in the hangar, now under armed guard. "The dogs alerted to either drugs or explosives in those, and they didn't match the manifest either. The manifest doesn't mention you bringing in explosives."

"Well, they're certainly not drugs," Charlie said. "There's a perfectly good explanation for all these undocumented containers."

"Good."

Charlie motioned to the squarish containers. "These are CID battery packs," she explained. "There are four pairs of battery packs in each case. Each pair attaches to recesses behind the thighs. Those other containers have battery packs, too, but they're for Tin Man units. They're worn in pairs on the belt."

"CID? Tin Man? What's that?"

"CID stands for Cybernetic Infantry Device," Charlie said matter-of-factly. "A CID is a piloted combat robot. Tin Man is a nickname for a commando who is enclosed in a suit of armor called

BERP, or Ballistic Electronically Reactive Process. The suit has an exoskeleton that gives the commando increased strength, and the BERP material makes him invulnerable to . . . well, any infantry- and squad-level weapon and even some light artillery. The stuff over there is the mission packs for the CID units, some of which contain grenade and UAV launchers." She smiled at the shocked expression on Thompson's face. "Are you getting all this?"

"Are . . . are you joking, miss?" Thompson stammered. "Is this some kind of joke?"

"No joke," Charlie said. "Watch. I'll show you." She turned to a large, irregularly shaped device about the size of a refrigerator and spoke, "CID One, activate." Before Thompson's disbelieving eyes, the device began to unfold piece by piece, until seconds later a ten-foot-tall robot stood before him. "That's a CID." She turned and motioned to the top of the air stairs. "And *that* is a Tin Man." Thompson looked and saw a man dressed head to foot in a smooth dark gray outfit, wearing a bullet-shaped multifaceted eyeless helmet, a belt with two circular devices attached, thick knee-high boots, and gloves with thick gauntlets that extended to the elbows.

"CID One, pilot up," she said. The robot crouched down, extended a leg and both arms backward, and a hatch popped open on its back. "Have a nice day," Charlie said, patting Thompson on the shoulder, then climbed up the extended leg and inside the robot. The hatch closed, and seconds later the robot came to life, moving just like a person with incredible smoothness and animation.

"Now, sir"—the robot spoke in a man's voice through a hidden speaker with a low electronically synthesized voice—"order your men not to interfere with me or the Tin Man. We're not going to hurt you. We're going to—"

At that moment someone inside the plane yelled, "Freeze or I'll send my dog!" The Tin Man turned inside the cargo compartment, and immediately shots could be heard. Thompson saw the Tin Man flinch, but he didn't go down.

"Oh, my, that wasn't a good idea," the woman inside the CID robot said. "Whack really hates getting shot at."

The Tin Man didn't raise any weapon, but Thompson saw a bright flash of light briefly illuminate the cargo compartment of the plane. No more shots were heard. The Tin Man jumped from the plane to the tarmac as easily as stepping off a curb. He motioned to one of the men being guarded and jabbed a finger at the plane. "Terry, suit up. José, climb aboard." He electronically searched his list of radio frequencies stored in onboard computer memory. "General? Whack here."

"Hi, Whack," Patrick replied. "Welcome to Iraq."

"We dropped trou and the shit's bound to hit the fan real soon. Do something to calm the grunts unless you want a fight on your hands."

"I'm on my way to the ramp. I'll get Masters, Noble, and the rest of the Scion guys to help you. I'm sure we'll meet Colonel Wilhelm out there shortly."

"No doubt. We're sorting out the—"

"*Freeze!*" the security officer guarding the passengers yelled, raising an MP5 submachine gun.

"Excuse me one sec, General," Macomber radioed. Again, the Tin Man did not move or even look at the officer, but Thompson saw a blue lightning bolt arc from the Tin Man's right shoulder and hit the security officer square in the chest, immediately knocking him unconscious.

The Tin Man stepped over to Thompson. The other security officers around them were all frozen in surprise; a few backed up and ran off to warn others. None of them even dared to reach for a weapon. The Tin Man grabbed Thompson by his jacket and lifted him off the ground, jamming his armored head right in Thompson's face. "Did Charlie here tell you to tell your men we're not going to hurt anyone here as long as you leave us alone?" Thompson was too stunned to reply. "I suggest you get your head out of your ass, get on the radio, and tell your men and the Army guys to stay in their barracks and leave us alone, or else we might hurt someone. And they better not have broken any of our stuff, the way they're driving those forklifts." He dropped Thompson and let him scurry clear.

Macomber electronically scanned the radio frequencies detected by his sensors built into the CID unit and compared them with a list downloaded from the Scion Aviation International team at Nahla, selected one, then spoke: "Colonel Wilhelm, this is Wayne Macomber. Do you read me?"

"Who is this?" Wilhelm replied a moment later.

"Are you deaf or just stupid?" Macomber

asked. "Just listen. My men and I are off-loading our equipment on the ramp and getting ready to fly. I don't want to see any of your men anywhere in sight, or we're going to tear you a new one. Do you copy me?"

"*What in hell did you say*?" Wilhelm thundered. "Who is this? How did you get on this frequency?"

"Colonel, this is Charlie Turlock," Charlie interjected on the same frequency. "Pardon Mr. Macomber's language, but he's had a long day. What he meant to say is we're out here on the ramp beginning our new contract operations, and we'd appreciate it if your men wouldn't come around here. Would that be okay?" There was no response. "Good going, Whack," Charlie radioed. "Now he's pissed, and he's going to bring the entire regiment."

"Not if he's smart," Wayne said. But he knew that's exactly what he'd do. "You and José, get backpacks on and stand by. Terry, let's put the rail guns together and get ready to rumble."

Charlie hurried off to the hangar where the weapon backpacks had been segregated, followed shortly by the other CID unit, and they selected and attached large backpacklike units on each other's back. The backpacks contained forty-millimeter grenade launchers, each with twin movable barrels that could fire rounds in almost any direction no matter which way they were turned and could fire a variety of munitions, including high explosive, antiarmor, and antipersonnel. Whack and another Tin Man located and assembled their weapons—massive

electromagnetic rail runs, each of which electri-
cally fired a thirty-millimeter depleted uranium
shell thousands of feet per second faster than a
bullet.

It didn't take long for Wilhelm to arrive in a
Humvee. He screeched to a halt just inside the
parking ramp area far enough in to get a good look
at the scene. As he studied the area in stunned
disbelief, three soldiers with M-16s raced out of the
Humvee, one hiding behind the Humvee and the
other two fanning out and taking cover behind
nearby buildings.

"Warhammer, this is Alpha, those Scion guys
are not in custody," Wilhelm radioed from the
Humvee. "They are off-loading their aircraft.
Security is not in sight. They've deployed unidentified robot-looking units with weapons visible. Get First Battalion out here on the double.
I want—"

"Hold on, Colonel, hold on," Macomber cut in
on the command frequency. "We don't want a
fight with you. Calling out the troops and starting a gunfight will just get the Turks outside
riled up."

"Warhammer switching to Delta."

But on the secondary channel, Macomber
went on: "You can flip channels all day long,
Colonel, but we'll still find it. Listen, Colonel, we
won't bother you, so don't bother us, okay?"

"*Sir, vehicle approaching, five o'clock!*" one of the
soldiers yelled. A Humvee was driving up to Macomber's position.

"Don't shoot, Colonel, that's probably McLanahan," Macomber radioed.

"Shut the hell up, whoever you are," Wilhelm radioed, drawing a .45 caliber pistol from his holster.

The newcomer came to a stop, and Patrick McLanahan stepped out, with his hands raised. "Easy, Colonel, we're all on the same side here," he said.

"Like hell," Wilhelm shouted. "Sergeant, take McLanahan into custody and put him in the Triple-C under guard."

"*Look out*!" one of the soldiers shouted. Wilhelm just caught a blur of motion out of the corner of an eye—and as if by magic, the gray-suited figure who had been near the hangar appeared *out of the sky* right beside the soldier closest to McLanahan. In an instant he snatched the M-16 rifle out of the soldier's startled hands, bent it in half, and handed it back to him.

"Now cut the shit, all of you," Macomber shouted, "or I break the next M-16 over someone's head."

The other armed soldiers raised their weapons and aimed them at Macomber, but Wilhelm raised his hands and shouted, "Weapons tight, weapons tight, put 'em down." It wasn't until then that he noticed that one of the large robots had appeared *right beside him*, covering the twenty or thirty yards between them with incredible speed and stealth. "*Jeez . . . !*" he breathed, startled.

"Hi, Colonel," Charlie said in her electronically synthesized voice. "Good call. Let's have a chat, okay?"

"*McLanahan*!" Wilhelm cried. "What in hell is going on here?"

"Change in mission, Colonel," Patrick replied.

"What mission? Whose mission? *Your* mission is over. Your contract's been canceled. You're under *my* jurisdiction until someone takes your ass back to Washington."

"I've got a new contract, Colonel, and we're going to get it set up and running right now."

"New contract? With whom?"

"With me, Colonel," a voice said, and to Wilhelm's surprise, Iraqi colonel Yusuf Jaffar emerged from the back of Patrick's Humvee, followed by Vice President Ken Phoenix and two Secret Service agents.

"*Jaffar* . . . I mean, Colonel Jaffar . . . what is this about? What's going on?"

"General McLanahan's company has been hired by the government of the Republic of Iraq to provide . . . shall we say, specialized services," Jaffar said. "They shall be based here, at Nahla, under my supervision."

"But this is *my* base . . . !"

"You are wrong, sir. This is an *Iraqi* air base, not an American one," Jaffar said. "You are guests here, not landlords."

"McLanahan can't work for you! He's an American."

"Scion Aviation International has State Department approval to operate in three dozen countries worldwide, including Iraq," Patrick said. "The original contract was a joint cooperation agreement with both U.S. Central Command and the Republic of Iraq—I just reported to you. Now I report to Colonel Jaffar."

"But you're under arrest, McLanahan," Wilhelm argued. "You're still in *my* custody."

"As long as the general is in my country and on my base, he is subject to my laws, not yours," Jaffar said. "You may deal with him as you wish when he leaves, but now he is mine."

Wilhelm opened his mouth, then closed it, and opened it again in blank confusion. "This is insane," he said finally. "What do you think you're going to do, McLanahan?"

"Baghdad wants help inducing the Turks to leave Iraq," Patrick said. "They think the Turks will start tearing up the country trying to eradicate the PKK, and then create a buffer zone along the border to make it harder for the PKK to come back."

"All that's going to accomplish is angering the Turks and widening the conflict," Wilhelm said. "You're crazy if you think President Gardner's going to let you do this."

"President Gardner is not my president, and he is not Iraq," Jaffar said. "President Rashid does this thing because the Americans will not help us."

"Help you? Help you do what, Colonel?" Wilhelm asked, almost pleading. "You want us to go to war with Turkey? You know how these Turkish incursions work, Colonel. They come in, they attack some isolated camps and hideouts, and they go home. They drove a little deeper this time. So what? They're not interested in taking any land."

"And General McLanahan will be here to make sure it does not happen," Jaffar said. "America will not interfere with this."

"You're going to replace my regiment with McLanahan and his robot planes and robot . . .

whatever *these* things are?" Wilhelm asked. "His little company up against at least four Turkish infantry divisions?"

"It is said that Americans have little faith—they believe only what is in front of their noses," Jaffar said. "I have seen it is true for you, Colonel Wilhelm. But I look at General McLanahan's amazing aircraft and weapons, and all I see are possibilities. Perhaps as you say the Turks will not take our land or slaughter any innocent Iraqis, and we will not need the general's weapons. But this is the largest force ever to enter Iraq, and I fear they will not stop at breaking apart a few camps."

Jaffar stepped over to Wilhem and stood right in front of him. "You are a fine soldier and commander, Colonel," he said, "and your unit is brave and has sacrificed much for my people and my country. But your president is abandoning Iraq."

"That's not true, Colonel," Wilhelm said.

"I am told by Vice President Phoenix that he was ordered to go to Baghdad and speak with my government about the Turkish invasion," Jaffar said, "including establishing a security buffer zone in Iraq. Gardner not only condones this invasion, but he is willing to give up Iraqi land to placate the Turks. That is not acceptable. I look at you and your forces here on my base, and I see only hardship for my people."

He stepped over to Patrick and looked at the Tin Man and CID unit there on the ramp. "But I look at General McLanahan and his weapons, and I see hope. He is willing to fight. It may be for money, but at least *he* is willing to lead his men into battle in Iraq."

The expression on Wilhelm's face was changing from anger to surprise to outright confusion. "I don't believe what I'm hearing," he said. "I have an entire brigade here . . . and I'm supposed to do *nothing*, in the middle of a Turkish invasion? I'm supposed to sit back and watch while you fly missions and send out these . . . these Tinker Toys? Baghdad is going to fight the Turks? Five years ago you didn't have an organized army! Two years ago your unit didn't even exist."

"Excuse me, Colonel, but I don't think you're helping yourself here," Vice President Phoenix said. He walked over to the Army colonel. "Let's go to your command center, let me inform Washington about what's going on, and ask for guidance."

"You're not buying into this nonsense, are you, sir?"

"I don't see we have much choice right now, Colonel," Phoenix said. He put a hand on Wilhelm's shoulders and led him back to his Humvee. "Kind of like watching your daughter go off to college, isn't it? They're ready for their new life, but you're not ready to see them off."

"So, General McLanahan," Yusuf Jaffar said after Wilhelm and his men departed, "as you Americans say, the ball is now in your court. You know Baghdad's desires. What will you do now?"

"I think it's time to test the Turks' real intentions," Patrick said. "Everyone has been very cooperative so far, and that's good, but they're still in your country with a lot of troops and aircraft. Let's see what they do when you start insisting."

CHAPTER 7

Courage is the price that life exacts for granting peace.
—*Amelia Earhart*

ALLIED AIR BASE NAHLA, IRAQ
The next morning

Movement at the front gate, sir!" the Turkish captain of the troops surrounding Nahla Air Base heard on his portable radio. "Combat vehicles lining up to exit!"

"*Bombok*!" the captain swore. "What's going on?" He threw his coffee out the window and exited his armored personnel carrier. A Humvee flying an American flag and pulling a trailer was entering the entrapment area, with another Humvee-trailer combo outside waiting its turn. The weapon cupolas on each vehicle had machine guns and grenade launchers mounted, but they still had canvas covers on them, they were locked in road-march position, and the gunner's stations were not manned.

"Where do they think they are going?" the Turkish infantry captain asked.

"Should we stop them?" his first sergeant asked.

"We have no orders to interfere with them unless they attack us," the captain said. "Otherwise we observe and report only."

The Turks watched as the first Humvee exited, then pulled out away from the front gate and stopped to wait for the second. The Turkish captain stepped over to the front passenger side of the lead vehicle. "Good morning, sir," he said. He saw it was a civilian. He knew the Americans employed a lot of civilians to work at their military bases, but to see one out here was rather bizarre.

"Good morning . . . er, I mean, *günaydin*," the man said in clumsy but understandable Turkish. "How's it going?"

"Very well, sir," the captain said in a low voice. The American just smiled and nodded. The Turk used the opportunity to peek inside the Humvee. There were two civilians in the rear seats and a lot of supplies under green tarps in the very back. One civilian passenger looked military, and he wore a strange outfit, like a scuba diver's wet suit, covered by a jacket. He looked straight ahead and did not return the Turk's gaze. The twenty-foot flatbed trailer was empty.

The American stuck out his right hand. "Jon Masters."

The Turkish captain frowned, but took his hand and shook it. "Captain Evren."

"Nice to met you," Jon said. He looked around. "You guys doing okay out here? Anything we can get you?"

"No, *efendim*," Evren said. He was waiting for

some kind of explanation, but apparently this man was not interested in offering anything but chitchat. "May I ask where you are going, sir?"

"Just driving around."

Evren looked at the gaggle of Humvees, then back at Jon with a stern expression. "At this hour, and with trailers?"

"Why not? I've been here in Iraq for a couple weeks and I haven't seen anything of the countryside. Thought I'd better do it while the doin' is good."

Evren didn't understand half of what the guy just said, and he was getting tired of his goofy smile. "May I ask please where you are going, sir, and what you intend to do with the trailers?" he repeated, much more forcefully.

"Just around." Jon drew a circle with his finger. "Around. Around here."

Evren was getting angry with the guy, but he had no authority to detain him. "Please be mindful of other military vehicles, sir," he said. "Some of our larger vehicles have limited visibility for the driver. An encounter with a main battle tank would be unfortunate for you."

The veiled threat didn't seem to have any effect on the American. "I'll tell the others," he said idly. "Thanks for the tip. Bye-bye now." And the convoy headed off.

"What should we do, sir?" the first sergeant asked.

"Have the checkpoints report their position to me as they pass," Evren said, "then get someone to follow them." The first sergeant hurried off.

The convoy of Humvees drove around to the north side of the base on public highways.

They passed a Turkish army checkpoint at one intersection, where they were stopped so soldiers could look inside the vehicles, but not detained or searched. They continued north for a couple more miles, then exited the highway and drove farther north through a muddy open field. Ahead they saw stakes pounded in the ground with yellow "Caution" and "Keep Out" tape strung between them, and a few hundred yards beyond that was the wreckage of Scion Aviation International's XC-57 Loser. The Turkish missiles apparently hadn't hit the plane directly, but proximity fuses exploded the warheads near the pod-mounted engines atop the fuselage, shearing two of them off and sending the plane hurtling to the ground. It had landed on its left front side, crumpling most of the left wing and left side of the nose, and there had been a fire, but the rest of the plane sustained what might be called moderate damage; most of the right side of the plane was relatively intact.

There was a lone Russian IMR engineer vehicle parked at the tape border, with two Turkish soldiers on guard duty with it. The IMR had a crane mounted on the back and a blade in front resembling a bulldozer. The soldiers discarded cigarettes and coffee and got on portable radios as they saw the convoy approach. *"Hayir, hayir!"* one of them shouted, waving his hands. *"Durun! Gidin!"*

Jon Masters got out of the Humvee and trudged through the mud toward the soldiers. "Good morning! *Günaydin!*" he shouted. "How's it going? Any of you guys speak English?"

"No come here! No stay!" the soldier shouted. "*Tehlikeli*! Dangerous here! *Yasaktir*! Prohibited!"

"No, it's not dangerous at all," Jon said. "You see, that's *my* plane." He patted his chest. "Mine. It belongs to me. I'm here to take a few parts back with me and check it out."

The first soldier waved his arms in front of his face in a crossing motion while the second picked up his rifle, not pointing it but making it visible to all. "No entry," the first said sternly. "Prohibited."

"You can't prohibit me from examining my own plane," Jon said. "I have permission from the Iraqi government. You guys aren't even Iraqi. What right do you have to stop me?"

"No entry," the first soldier said. "Go away. Go back." He pulled out his portable radio and began speaking while the second soldier raised his rifle to port arms in an obvious threatening gesture. When the first soldier finished radioing his report, he waved his hands as if trying to shoo away a youngster, shouting, "Go now. *Siktir git*! Go!"

"I'm not leaving without looking at my plane . . . what *you* guys did to my plane," Jon said. He quickly walked past both soldiers, then walked backward toward the plane. The soldiers followed him, shouting orders in Turkish, confused and getting angrier by the second. Jon held up his hands and walked backward quicker. "I won't be long, you guys, but I'm going to look at my plane. Leave me alone!" Jon started to run toward the plane.

"*Dur*! Stop!" The second soldier raised his rifle

into firing position but not aiming it at Jon, obviously to fire a warning shot. "Stop or I will—"

Suddenly the rifle was snatched out of his hands in the blink of an eye. The soldier turned . . . and saw a person wearing a head-to-toe suit of dark gray, an eyeless helmet right out of a science-fiction comic book, a framework of thin flexible tubules all across its skin, and thick gauntlets and boots. *"Aman allahim . . . !"*

"Don't be rude," the figure said in electronically synthesized Turkish. "No weapons"— he reached out with incredible quickness and snatched the portable transceiver away from the second soldier—"and no radios. I'll give them back only if you show me you can behave." The Turks backed away, then started to run when they realized they weren't going to be captured.

"C'mon, guys, let's go," Jon said, trotting toward the stricken XC-57. "See, I told you it wouldn't so bad."

"Rascal One, this is Genesis," Patrick McLanahan radioed to Wayne Macomber. "You've got a couple vehicles headed your way, about ten minutes out." Patrick had launched a small unmanned attack aircraft called an AGM-177 Wolverine, which had been brought in via the 767 freighter. It resembled a cross between a cruise missile and a surfboard. It was normally air-launched, but had the ability to be fired from a truck-mounted catapult. The Wolverine carried infrared and millimeter-wave imaging and targeting sensors so it could autonomously locate, attack, and reattack targets programmed for it. It had three internal weapons bays for attacks on different types of targets, and it could also attack a fourth target by flying into it kamikaze style. "Radar has a helicopter about ten minutes to the east," he added. "We don't know if it's headed this way or just on patrol, but it's close."

"Copy, Genesis," Macomber replied. He waved at the Humvees to move in. "C'mon, we've got company, get in there and help the egghead," he ordered. "I want to be out of here ASAP." The Humvees rolled in, and technicians began unloading power tools to start opening the plane up.

"I'll be here all day at least, probably for the next two days," Jon Masters radioed.

"Masters, I'm not here to cart the entire aircraft back to the base," Macomber radioed back. "Grab any classified stuff and only the most essential black boxes that are intact, and let's get out of here. We're out in the open with three hundred Turkish soldiers coming for us and another fifty thousand in the area." That reminder seemed to make everyone work a little quicker.

"That helicopter is definitely coming your way," Patrick radioed. "About seven minutes out. The ground forces have increased in size—looks like six vehicles now, four troop carriers and two armored vehicles. How's the plane look?"

"Masters says it doesn't look that bad," Whack said. "I think he'd say that if it was nothing but a smoking hole in the ground."

"You're right about that. Okay, they're setting up roadblocks north and south on the highway, and all six vehicles are headed your way."

"Copy."

"No fighting unless it's absolutely necessary, Rascal. We're all still friends, remember."

"I know. I've been extremely cordial and nice so far."

"They should be in sight on the highway now."

Wayne turned and saw the trucks unloading a total of about twenty troops with rifles, the armored vehicles on guard flanking the trucks and off-loading their own dismounts, and the same Captain Evren Jon spoke with at the front gate, scanning them with binoculars. "In sight. I see infantry weapons only so far. Rascal, this is One, we've got lookylous, stand by." A few minutes later, Whack saw several soldiers and Captain Evren board their armored personnel carriers and slowly drive toward them. "Here they come."

Evren's APC stopped about thirty yards in front of Whack, and five soldiers dismounted, fanned out about six yards apart from one another, and lay prone on the ground with rifles raised. Whack noticed that the gunner's cupola atop the APC was manned and the barrel of the 12.5-millimeter machine gun aimed right at him; there was also a Russian-made AT-3 "Sagger" antitank missile mounted on its launch rail, aimed at one of the Humvees. The second APC moved away, heading around Whack toward the XC-57.

"You!" Evren shouted in English. "Raise your hands and turn around!"

"*Hayir*," Whack replied in Turkish via his electronic translator. "No. Leave us alone."

"You are not permitted access to the plane."

"We have permission from the Iraqi government and the plane's owner," Whack said. "This is a legal salvage operation. Leave us alone."

"I repeat, raise your hands and turn around, or we will open fire."

"I am an American, I'm not armed, and I have permission from the Iraqi government. You're a Turkish soldier. I don't take orders from you."

Now Evren seemed to be confused. He pulled out his portable transceiver and spoke into it. "He's obviously reached the limit of his rules of engagement," Whack said over the command network. "Here's where it'll start getting interesting. Keep an eye on the second APC; it's flanking me and heading your way."

"Got it in sight, One," came the reply from Charlie Turlock.

"The helicopter is about five minutes out, Rascal," Patrick said.

"Copy. Let's hope it's just the TV news." Whack thought for a moment. "I'm starting to get nervous about that machine gun and Sagger missile on this APC, guys," he said. "Everyone, find some cover away from the Humvees." Through his translator, he said, "Point your weapons away right now!"

"You will surrender immediately or we will open fire!" Evren shouted in return.

"I'm warning you, point your weapons away and leave us alone, or I'm going to rough you up," Whack said. "I don't care about this NATO ally shit—lower your weapons and go away or you're all going to wake up in the hospital."

Through the sensitive microphones built into the Tin Man suit, Whack heard Evren say the word *ates*. A three-round burst of rifle fire rang out, and all three rounds hit Macomber's left thigh. *"God bless it,"* Macomber snarled. "The guy shot me in the damned leg."

"He was only trying to wound you," Charlie said. "Take it easy, Whack."

Evren was obviously startled to see the figure still standing, even though he'd clearly seen all rounds hit. "One more warning, bub," Whack shouted in Turkish. "If you don't drop your weapons, I'm going to play a little tune on your skull with my fists."

He heard Evren say, *"Ohn ekee, bebe, sicak!"* which meant, "The twelve and the baby, go hot," and Whack radioed, "Take cover, knock out the APCs, *now!*" just as the gunner on the 12.5-millimeter machine gun opened fire.

With a blast of supercompressed air, Whack launched himself through the air and landed atop the armored vehicle. The gunner tried to follow him as he sailed at him, nearly knocking himself out of the cupola. After Whack landed, he bent the barrel of the machine gun until the weapon exploded from the pressure of unexpelled gases. But he wasn't quick enough to stop the AT-3. The wire-guided missile flew off its launch rail and hit one of the Humvees, sending it flying through the air on a cloud of fire. "Everyone okay?" he radioed.

"Everyone was clear," Jon Masters said. "Thanks for the warning."

"Can I bust some heads now, General?" Macomber asked.

"I don't want anyone hurt, Rascal, unless they go for Jon and the techs," Patrick said. "Take their weapons only."

"When are we going to knock off the 'Kum-

baya' routine around here, sir?" Macomber
asked half aloud. "Rascal Two, can you take out
the twelve-point-five and the Sagger without
hurting—" But at that moment there was a small
explosion on top of the second APC, and the
gunner jumped out of the cupola, beating sparks
and small flames off his uniform. "Thank you."

"Don't mention it," Charlie said.

Whack was taking sustained rifle fire from the
Turks as he jumped off the APC and walked over
to Evren; they didn't stop firing until Whack
grasped Evren by his jacket and lifted him off
the ground. "I asked you nicely to leave us
alone," Whack said. "Now I'm going to be not so
nice, *arkadas*." As easily as tossing a tennis ball,
Whack threw Evren a hundred yards through
the air, almost all the way back to the highway.
He then raced over and did the same to the other
Turkish soldiers around him who hadn't run
away. "Is that okay, Genesis?"

"Thank you for showing restraint, Rascal,"
Patrick replied.

Macomber jumped over to the other APC, but
the Turkish troops had already run off . . . because they got a look at Charlie Turlock, aboard
a Cybernetic Infantry Device guarding the other
side of the crash site. She carried her own electromagnetic rail gun and wore a forty-millimeter
rocket launcher backpack containing eight verti-
cally launched rockets with high-explosive, antipersonnel bomblet, and smoke warheads, plus
a reload backpack in the Humvee. "Everything
okay, Two?"

"I'm clear," Charlie replied. She pointed to
the east. "That helicopter is in sight. Looks like a

standard-issue Huey. I see a door gunner but no other weapons."

"If he points that gun anywhere near our guys, take it out."

"I got him zeroed in already. Looks like a cameraman in the door with him. Smile—you're on *Candid Camera*."

"Just great. Masters . . . ?"

"I don't even have all the access doors open yet, Wayne," Jon said. "I'll need at least an hour just to find out what's what. It shouldn't take long to pull the major components and LRUs— maybe three hours, tops. But I'd like at least eight hours to—"

"I don't know if you have eight *minutes*, let alone eight hours, but get moving and we'll hold them off as long as we can," Whack said.

"Maybe if you'd help us, we'd be done quicker," Jon suggested.

Whack sighed inside his armor. "I was afraid you'd say that," he said. "Charlie, you got security. I'm going to be a mechanic for a while."

"Roger. That helicopter is starting to orbit us. Looks like they're taking pictures. The door gunner's not tracking anything on the ground."

"If it looks like he's going to engage, nail him."

"With pleasure."

"We're *engineers*, not mechanics," Jon corrected him. "But *you'll* be the demolition guy."

"Well, that sounds more like it," Whack said.

**THE OVAL OFFICE,
THE WHITE HOUSE, WASHINGTON, D.C.**
A short time later

The president picked up the phone. "Hello, President Hirsiz. This is President Gardner. What can I do for you today?"

"You can call off your attack dogs for one, sir," Kurzat Hirsiz said from Ankara, "unless you are looking for war."

"You refer to the incident at the crash site north of Mosul?" Gardner asked. "As I understand it, three of your soldiers were injured and two armored vehicles were damaged. Is that accurate?"

"Have you an explanation for this deliberate attack?"

"You'll have to talk with the Iraqi government. The United States government had nothing to do with it."

"That is not the truth. Those . . . those *things* are American weapon systems. The whole world knows this."

"The robot and the armored commando were experimental designs and they were never used directly by the U.S. government," Gardner said, using the story he and his staff had conjured up the minute they got the call from Vice President Ken Phoenix from Nahla. "They belong to a private company that had been contracted by the U.S. Army to provide security for its forces in Iraq."

"So they *do* work for the American government!"

"No, because after the incident with your reconnaissance plane, their contract with my government was immediately canceled," Gardner said. "The company was then contracted by the Iraqi government. They were working for the Iraqis when that incident occurred. Frankly I don't know why your troops were at that crash site to begin with. They weren't looting the plane, were they?"

"I resent that implication, sir," Hirsiz said. "Turkish soldiers are not criminals. The aircraft was involved in the downing of a Turkish jet and the killing of a Turkish pilot; the troops were merely guarding the plane until a formal inquiry could begin."

"I see. You should have communicated your intentions better to the Iraqis and to us. But that would have been difficult in the middle of an invasion, wouldn't it?"

"So is this your plan now, Mr. Gardner: let the Iraqis take the blame for American actions?"

"Mr. President, your forces are on Iraqi soil, bombing Iraqi villages and killing Iraqi civilians—"

"We target only PKK terrorists, sir, terrorists that kill innocent Turks!"

"I understand, sir, and I agree something needs to be done about the PKK, and the United States has pledged more assistance to Turkey for this. But we do not condone a full-scale ground invasion of Iraq. I warned you about unintended consequences.

"As for the contractors at Nahla: they are working for the Iraqis and not under our direct control, but we are still allies of Iraq and can intercede on your behalf. The United States would be happy to sit down with Turkey, the Kurdish Regional Government, and Iraq to facilitate an immediate cease-fire by all parties, including contractors; a withdrawal timetable; and more comprehensive security arrangements on the Iraq-Turkey border, including international monitors, to eliminate PKK terrorists from crossing the border. But nothing will happen while Turkish troops are engaged in combat operations inside Iraq, sir."

"So, this *is* a conspiracy: America uses these robots against Turkish troops, pretends they are not involved, but then offers to be an intermediary in negotiations as long as there is a cease-fire," Hirsiz said angrily. "Again, Turkey is the victim, forced to concede everything, pushed aside and ignored. Then no one notices when another Turkish plane is brought down or another police station blown apart."

"Believe me, Mr. President, we want to help Turkey," Gardner said. "Turkey is one of America's most important friends and allies. I understand your anger. We can send in monitors, technology, even personnel to patrol the border. But nothing will happen while combat operations are ongoing. They must stop immediately, and Turkish troops must leave Iraq. There's no other way."

"There is only one way we will agree to international monitors along our border, Mr. Gardner: the Kurdistan Regional Government must disavow the PKK and all plans to form an independent state of Kurdistan," Hirsiz said. "The KRG must remove its flag from all public places, arrest the PKK leaders and turn them over to us for trial, dismantle all PKK training bases, and shut down all companies that support the PKK."

"Mr. President, what you're asking for is impossible," President Gardner said after a moment's confusion. "The KRG administers the constitutionally authorized Kurdish region of northern Iraq. To my knowledge, they've never supported the PKK."

"As long as the KRG exists and tries to separate its territory from the rest of Iraq, the PKK will use terrorism to try to force that into effect," Hirsiz said. "You know as well as I that some members of the KRG leadership have businesses that secretly launder money and transport weapons and supplies from Iraq and overseas into Turkey. Many, not just Turkey, consider the Iraqi PKK a secret military wing of the KRG."

"That's nonsense, Mr. President," Gardner insisted. "There is no relationship between the KRG and PKK."

"They both want an independent Kurdistan carved out of provinces of Turkey, Iraq, Persia, and Syria," Hirsiz said angrily. "The Kurdistan regional government obviously does not want to openly recognize a terrorist group like the PKK, so they support them in secret, and they oppose any efforts to shut them down. That will stop immediately! The KRG can administer the three Iraqi provinces of Dohuk, Irbil, and Sulaymaniyah, but they must do so without advocating an independent Kurdistan or trying to expand to the western provinces that have a Turkmen majority. Otherwise, our offensive continues."

Joseph Gardner ran a hand over his face in frustration. "Then you'll agree to negotiations, Mr. President?"

"No negotiations until the KRG agrees to stop supporting an independent Kurdistan state and agrees to denounce the PKK and bring its leaders to trial for crimes against humanity," Hirsiz said. "If Baghdad and Irbil cannot get the PKK under control in Iraq and force them to stop killing innocent Turks, we will do the job. Good day, sir." And he hung up.

The president slammed the phone down. "Humans shouldn't be allowed to have this much fun," he murmured. He turned to his advisers in the Oval Office. "Tell the KRG to stop all plans for independence?" He snapped his fingers. "Sure, we can do that. The only part of Iraq that has its shit together, and Hirsiz wants it shut down. Great."

"But he opened the door to negotiations, sir," chief of staff Walter Kordus said. "Always come in high and hope everyone meets somewhere in the middle." The president gave him a sideways glance. "At least it's a *start* at negotiations."

"I guess you could call it that," the president said. "Did you hear all that, Ken? Stacy?"

"Yes, Mr. President," Ken Phoenix said from Allied Air Base Nahla. "The Turkish air force is pounding the Iraqi northeastern provinces, especially Irbil and Dohuk provinces. I doubt if either the KRG or Baghdad will negotiate while the Turks are attacking their towns and villages."

"NATO is meeting later today to discuss a resolution ordering Turkey to cease fire," Secretary of State Stacy Anne Barbeau said from Brussels, Belgium, the headquarters of the North Atlantic Treaty Organization. "But the resolution has already been watered down to a *request* to cease fire. The Turks have a fair amount of support in the council here—they're sympathetic about the continuous PKK attacks despite Turkey's attempts to give the Kurds in Turkey more aid, a stronger voice in government, and fewer cultural and religious restrictions. I don't think Turkey is going to get much pressure from NATO or the European Union."

"They're not getting much from Congress either," the president said. "Most don't understand the whole Kurdistan question, but they do understand terrorism, and right now they see the PKK as the problem. Turkey will eventually overstay in Iraq and public opinion will turn, especially if they try to widen the conflict."

"And the last thing they need is a reason to widen the conflict . . . which brings me back to McLanahan," Barbeau said acidly. "What in hell is he doing out there, Mr. Vice President?"

"He is apparently going to help the Iraqis defend themselves against the Turks," Phoenix replied. "This mission out to his crashed plane was a test to see what the Turkish army would do. They seemed to do nothing until they went out to the crash site. The Turks were getting ready to move or dismantle the plane, and they tried to chase them away."

"And McLanahan attacked."

"I watched the images coming from a UAV over the scene," Phoenix said, "and I listened to the audio as it was happening. McLanahan's forces didn't attack until the Turks did, and they even gave them a second warning after a soldier shot at the Tin Man commando. After it was obvious the Turks were going to attack the workers, the Tin Man and the CID unit went to work."

"And now what's happening?"

"Some of the Turks surrounding Nahla Air Base here deployed near the crash site," Phoenix said. "Dr. Masters and his workers are still at the crash site recovering black boxes and classified equipment. McLanahan's UAVs have detected some Turkish ground units en route, but they're afraid the Turkish air force will attack. The Turks have flown helicopters near the site and shot a few mortars at them, trying to scare them into retreating."

"You know, I don't have much sympathy for McLanahan right now," Gardner said. "He decided to twist the tiger's tail, and now he might get his ass chewed off. We're trying to find ways to de-escalate the conflict, and he just goes and finds new ways to *escalate* it."

"We'll find out what will happen next as soon as Masters starts to head back here to Nahla," Phoenix said. "There's about a hundred soldiers and six armored vehicles waiting for him on the highway, and I'll bet they're pissed."

"I want our guys to stay out of it," the president ordered. "No Americans get involved. This is McLanahan's fight. If he gets his guys hurt or killed, it's *his* fault."

"We should contact the Turkish prime minister and urge restraint, sir," Phoenix said. "McLanahan's guys are outnumbered. Even with the Tin Man and CID out there, there's no way they can fight through the Turkish army. The Turks are going to want some payback."

"I hope McLanahan is smart enough not to try to take on the Turks," the president said. "Stacy, contact Akas's office again, explain the situation, and ask her to communicate to the Ministry of Defense for the army to hold back."

"Yes, Mr. President."

"McLanahan stepped in it big-time," the president said as he turned to other business. "Unfortunately, it's his guys that are going to suffer for it."

NEAR ALLIED AIR BASE NAHLA, IRAQ
A short time later

"*Incoming!*" Charlie Turlock shouted. "Whack . . . ?"

"I got it," Wayne Macomber responded. He had had his electromagnetic rail gun out and ready ever since the first mortar shell had been fired toward them about an hour or so ago. Charlie Turlock's millimeter wave radar system built into her CID robot scanned the skies around them for miles, allowing her to detect the projectiles and instantaneously transmit tracking and targeting information to Wayne's targeting computers.

Charlie Turlock also carried her electromagnetic rail gun, but all of her projectiles had already been expended shooting down mortars and her reloads had been blown up when the Sagger destroyed the first Humvee. The forty-millimeter rockets in her backpack might not be fast enough to intercept the mortar shells, but Macomber's rail gun was more than capable. He simply raised his rifle, using his suit's powered exoskeleton like a precision aiming platform, and followed the tracking information relayed from the CID unit. He didn't have to lead the mortar round very much—the electromagnetic rail gun projectiles flew a dozen times faster than a sniper rifle bullet and destroyed the round easily.

"Salvo!" Charlie shouted. "Four more inbound!"

"Bastards," Whack muttered. That was the first time they'd fired more than one at a time. He hit all four easily, but now problems were developing. "I'm getting low on ammo—I'm on the last magazine, six more left," he said. "I'm also going to need fresh batteries for the rifle and for me."

One of the technicians ran over to the remaining Humvee, searched for a few moments, then ran over to Macomber. "No more fresh batteries left," he said. "We'll have to plug you in."

"Swell," Whack said. The tech unreeled a power cord from a storage hatch on the back of Macomber's suit, ran it back to the Humvee, and plugged it into a power receptacle. "Charlie, you're going to have to try intercepting any more rounds. I'm going to boost my power levels before we have to start moving out. I've got just enough juice in the gun to fire the last remaining projectiles."

"Roger," Charlie responded. "I haven't seen any of those rounds explode, and the projected track shows them missing us. Maybe they're not live rounds. They're lobbing them in just to see what we'd do."

"Glad we're providing them with some entertainment," Whack said. "Can you compute the firing location?"

"Already have. They haven't moved it. I can take it out if you want, or drop a gas rocket on them."

"I don't want those guys riled up just yet, and we have to save ammo," Whack said.

"Another helicopter inbound, guys," Patrick McLanahan radioed. "Coming from Turkey this time, higher speed. Might be a gunship. About ten minutes out."

"Copy," Wayne Macomber replied. "Okay, Doc, time to pack it up."

"Patrick said ten minutes? I'll take that."

"No, because in ten minutes we'll be in range of whatever missiles or rockets that chopper might be carrying, and then it'll be too late," Whack said.

"All right," Jon said dejectedly. "We got the laser radar and satellite comm boxes. I guess that'll have to do. Too much stuff for one Humvee; we'll have to put it all on the trailer."

It didn't take long for the group to pack up their equipment. Whack led the way, carrying his rail gun high so the Turkish soldiers could all see it. Charlie carried her spare backpack in her left armored hand and her empty electromagnetic rail gun in her right, hoping just the sight of it might scare some of the Turks. All the engineers squashed together in the surviving Humvee, and all their tools, equipment, and retrieved boxes were in the trailer.

"How long until our help arrives, General?" Whack asked on his secure command channel.

"They look like they're changing formations, Whack," Patrick asked. "Try to stall as long as you can."

"What about that chopper?"

"Couple minutes more."

"Those numbers aren't matching, General," Whack said grimly. On the Turkish command channel he had detected, he said, "Listen up, Captain Evren. We're coming out. We don't want a fight with you guys. We're going to bring our stuff back into the base. Make way."

"No, Americans," Evren responded a moment later, the surprise that his radio channel was being used by the robots obvious in his voice. "You will be detained and that equipment confiscated. You assaulted members of my unit and myself. For this you must be punished."

Whack stopped the convoy. "Captain, listen to me very carefully," he said. "You know what *we* can do. What you might not know is that we have an unmanned aircraft circling overhead. If you don't believe me, look up." At that instant Patrick shut down and restarted the engine on the AGM-177 Wolverine he had orbiting over the area, which caused a streak of brown smoke to become visible for a few seconds. "That is an attack drone, and it can take out all of your armor and your men with guided bomblets. I'll order it flown over your positions before we move in, and when it's done we'll take care of anyone that's still standing. Now move aside."

"I have my orders, American," Evren said. "You will lay down your weapons and power off the robot and the drone and surrender. If you do not, we will attack."

"Got an ID on that inbound chopper, Whack," Charlie said. "Cobra gunship. More U.S. surplus. Can't see his weapons but I'll bet he's loaded for bear."

"Last chance, Captain," Whack said. "Otherwise we start shooting. Move aside."

"I will not. Surrender or be killed. In case you have not noticed, we have our own air support. It is not as advanced as your unmanned aircraft, but I assure you it is deadly. After it attacks, there will be nothing left of you for us to, as you say, take care of."

"I'm going to have to take out that Cobra first, Charlie," Whack said. "Watch my back—they're bound to open fire when—"

Suddenly Charlie shouted, "Missile launch!"

"From where, Charlie?"

"Behind us!" Just then they heard a loud BANG! Whack and Charlie turned just in time to see a spiral of white smoke arc skyward and hit the Cobra. The helicopter started a hard right bank, seemed to wobble, then started a downward autorotational spin until it hit the ground in a hard but survivable crash.

"*Hold your fire! Hold your fire!*" Whack shouted on the Turkish command channel. On their discrete channel, he radioed, "I hope that was you, Jaffar."

"Yes, Macomber," Colonel Yusuf Jaffar responded on the discrete command channel. His northern battalion had hit the Cobra gunship with a Stinger shoulder-fired missile. "Sorry we are late, but I believe you are early. No matter. We are all here and ready to take on the Turks."

"Hopefully no one will take on anyone here," Whack said. He gave Jaffar the Turkish company's frequency, then said on that channel, "The Cobra gunship was hit by an Iraqi antiaircraft missile, Captain Evren," he said. "The Iraqi Nahla brigade is advancing on this position." At that moment he could see the Turkish troops on the right start to fidget and rustle about; they had apparently gotten a visual on the northernmost battalion. "Captain Evren?"

After a somewhat long and uncomfortable pause: "Yes, American."

"I don't command the Iraqi army, and you did invade their country," Whack said, "but my forces are not going to attack unless we are attacked first. I ask Colonel Jaffar not to attack as well. He is listening in. He is going to escort my team back to Nahla Air Base. I urge everyone to remain calm and keep your fingers off the trigger. Captain, if you would like to send a team out to inspect the downed Cobra, you may do so. Colonel Jaffar, would that be acceptable?"

"That would be acceptable," Jaffar replied.

"Good. Captain, we're on the move. Make way, and everyone be calm."

It was quite an impressive sight. Off the main highway north of Nahla, the Tin Man and the CID robot, with their rail gun rifles now slung over their shoulders, led the Humvee towing the trailer full of parts and tools across the open field. The Turkish platoons were arrayed on either side of the highway in front of them. Coming in from the northwest was a full battalion of Iraqi infantry, and coming in on the highway northeast of the base was another Iraqi battalion. They all converged on the intersection of the two highways.

Wayne found Captain Evren at the side of the highway, stopped, and gave him a salute. The captain returned the salute, but kept his eyes on the spectacle of the ten-foot-tall CID unit striding up to him and rendering a salute as well. "My God . . . !"

"Charlie Turlock, Captain Evren," Charlie said, holding out a large armored hand after lowering her salute. "How are you? Thanks for not shooting."

Evren was stunned by the robot's flexibility and lifelike movements. It took him several long amusing moments to take the robot's hand and shake it. "It . . . it is a machine, but it moves like a man . . . !"

"A woman, if you don't mind," Charlie said.

Colonel Jaffar approached a few minutes later. Evren rendered a salute, but Jaffar didn't return it. "So, you command this company, Turk?"

"Yes, sir. Captain Evren, Siyah Company, Forty-first Security—"

"I do not care who you are or what unit you are with, Turk," Jaffar said. "All I care about is when you will return home and leave my country in peace."

"That depends on when Iraq stops protecting murderous Kurds that drive bomb trucks into police buildings and kill innocent Turks, sir!"

"I am not here to listen to your political tirades, Turk! I need to know when you will move your goons out of my country!"

Whack glanced at Charlie. She didn't have to

move much, but a ten-foot-tall robot just raising its armored hands in surrender was plenty to get everyone's attention. "Can't we all just get along?" she said. She clasped her hands to her cheek. "Pretty please?" The sight of the big combat robot acting like a shy schoolgirl made even the gruff Colonel Jaffar chuckle, and hundreds of soldiers, Turks and Iraqis alike, joined in the laughter.

"This is not the time or place for an argument, guys," Whack said. "Why don't we take this back to the base? It's almost dinnertime, if I'm not mistaken. Why don't we all sit down, have a meal, and take a load off?"

IRBIL, IRAQ
That same time

"Where's my damned air?" General Besir Ozek shouted. "They're ten minutes late!" He grabbed the microphone out of the communications officer's hand. "*Resim*, this is *Sican* One. Your squadron had better get their shit together or I'm coming back up there to kick your ass!"

Ozek was in the cab of an ACV-300 command post vehicle, part of headquarters company of Third Division, which was smashing through eastern Iraq. Ozek's forces were ordered to proceed only as far as Irbil Northwest Airport, seize it for resupply and to cut off trade and commerce to the Kurdistan capital, and hold, but he had ordered a mechanized infantry battalion to proceed to the outskirts of the city itself.

The battalion had established a security perimeter in a large area that had been cleared of older buildings to make room for newer high-rise housing, northwest of the city itself. He had good visibility all around him for any signs of counterattack from *peshmerga*, PKK, regular Iraqi forces, or the Americans; so far none of those fighting organizations had meaningfully threatened his army, but it was better to be safe than sorry. The *peshmerga* was the biggest threat. Reports differed as to the size of the *peshmerga*, but even the most optimistic estimate made them twice as large as the four divisions Ozek had at his command, and they had some armor as well.

And there had been reports of growing resistance in Iraq. Like good rats, the PKK was deep in hiding, of course, but the Americans were starting to become restless, and the Iraqi units that had mysteriously disappeared right before the invasion were starting to pop up. Ozek had heard some reports of contact with American and Iraqi forces near Mosul, but no word on any casualties so far.

Ozek picked the area for other reasons as well: he was just north of Sami Abdul Rahman Park, a memorial park for a slain Kurdistan Regional Government official and PKK sympathizer; he was also well within mortar range of the parliament building of the Kurdistan Regional Government, so the Kurdish politicians should be able to get a good look at his army advancing on their city.

Ozek exited the command post vehicle and shouted, "Major!" A very young-looking infantry major stepped quickly over to him. "Our air is late, so you'll have to continue for a few more minutes."

"We've dropped on every target in the list, sir," the battalion commander said. "We've re-attacked the top ten on the list."

Ozek pulled a slip of paper out of his jacket. "I made up a new list. The defense ministry was talking about targeting businesses in Irbil that support the PKK . . . well, until they give me the official go-ahead, I found a bunch of them myself. Those are their addresses. Find them on the map and drop."

The major studied the list, and his eyes wid-ened in surprise. "Uh, sir, this address is inside the Citadel."

"I know that," Ozek said. "It's a bazaar that has shops owned by some of the same guys we've already been bombarding. Why should they be left out?"

"But it's inside the Citadel, sir," the major repeated. The Citadel of Irbil was an ancient stone wall in the center of the city encircling the archaeological ruins of the original city, which dated back to 2300 B.C. Although the city had been occupied by many nations over the cen-turies, the Citadel had been considered sacred ground to all of them, and some sections of it were a thousand years old. "What if we hit the archaeological sites?"

"I'm not worried about a few mud huts and cart paths," Ozek said. "I can look out there and see a Kurdistan flag flying from inside that place, so I know the PKK hides out there. I want those shops brought down. Do it."

"With respect, sir," the major said, "our job is to root out the PKK. They may run and hide in the cities, but they don't live in Irbil. Our scouts and counterintelligence units tell us the *peshmerga* have been shadowing us, but they haven't dared make contact. We shouldn't give them a reason to do so. We've already shelled targets in the city; bombing the Citadel might be the last straw."

"I understand you are afraid of the *peshmerga*, Major," Ozek said. "I've encountered them more than once in my career in the border areas. They are good in the mountains and the outback, but they are nothing but glorified guerrilla fighters. They're not going to come after a regular army unit in a frontal assault. They have never fought as anything other than tribal enforcers. They're just as likely to fight each other as us. In fact, I would welcome the chance to get a few of their battalions to engage us—destroy a few of their braver units, and the whole Kurdistan conglomeration might fold once and for all."

"Yes, sir," the major said, "but may I recommend we fire only smoke into the Citadel? You know how some revere that place, especially in the Kurdish region. They—"

"I don't need a history lesson from you, Major," Ozek snapped. "Get going on that list immediately. Same procedures as before: smoke to disperse the residents and mark for accuracy, high explosive to bring down the roofs, and white phosphorus to burn the place down. Get on it."

Just as he dismissed the artillery commander with a wave of his hand, a soldier ran up to him and saluted. "Gunship is moving into position, sir."

"About damned time." He went back to the

command post vehicle and grabbed the radio microphone. "*Resim* One-Eight, this is *Sican* One, how do you read?"

"Loud and clear, *Sican*," the pilot of the AC-130H Spectre gunship reported. "One minute to on station."

"Show me Tango One," Ozek said. A television monitor flared to life, showing the sensor image being transmitted from the gunship. It showed a wide-angle image of the southern part of Irbil, about eight hundred yards south of the Citadel. The sensor operator switched to narrow field of view and zoomed into an overhead view of the Irbil bazaar. He followed the main highway south along the edge of the bazaar until crossing a major avenue, then started counting buildings as he continued south. "Just south of the bakery, north of the apartment building . . . that's the one," Ozek radioed. The sensor operator had locked onto the headquarters of the Masari Bank of Kurdistan, one of the largest banks in northern Iraq . . . and widely known to support the PKK through money laundering, international money exchange, and collecting donations around the world.

"*Resim* is locked and ready, *Sican*," the pilot reported. The AC-130 began a left orbit around the target, with a side-mounted heads-up display and Instrument Landing System–like director needles showing the pilot exactly where to position the plane.

"Proceed, " Ozek said, then stepped out of the command vehicle and looked to the southeast. This was his first time seeing an AC-130 attack in person . . .

. . . and he felt a little disappointed. Most AC-130 attacks take place in darkness, where the muzzle flashes of the aircraft's 40-millimeter cannon and 105-millimeter howitzer lit up the night like nothing else. He saw the howitzer round hit and a column of smoke arc into the sky before he heard the BOOM! of the gun and the explosion on the ground, and he wished he had stayed to watch the hit on the screen—he was going to have to wait for the video replay.

He went back to the command vehicle and looked at the sensor image. Smoke still mostly obscured the view, but the bank building looked obliterated, as did parts of the bakery and apartment building facing the bank. The precision of that gunship was amazing—that shot was from over twenty thousand feet overhead!

"Looks like a good shot, *Resim*," Ozek radioed. "No signs of antiaircraft response. If you're good to go, we've got quite a few targets on our list. We'll be firing some mortar rounds from our position into the north part of the city; they should be no factor for you. Let's have a look at Tango Two."

OFFICE OF THE PRESIDENT, THE PINK PALACE, ANKARA, REPUBLIC OF TURKEY
Later that evening

"It's the first encounter with an Iraqi military unit," Minister of National Defense Hasan Cizek said as he entered President Kurzat Hirsiz's office. "Report from Tall Kayf, north of Mosul.

The brigade based at Nahla has reappeared and reoccupied their base."

"Any contact with our forces?" Hirsiz asked.

"Yes, sir. A helicopter pilot and a crewmember were injured when his aircraft was shot down by an Iraqi man-portable air defense missile."

Hirsiz waited, but that was all Cizek had to report. "That's it? No other casualties? What about the Iraqis?"

"No casualties, sir."

"What did they do, throw water balloons at each other? What do you mean, no casualties?"

"They didn't fight, sir," Cizek said. "Our unit let the Iraqis and the American engineers who were out at their reconnaissance plane back into Nahla Air Base."

"They let them back in? The Americans, too? I ordered that plane dismantled and brought back to Turkey! The Americans were allowed back onto the base with parts from the plane?"

"The unit commander was going to stop them, but the armored commando and the robot threatened retaliation with their weapons and from an orbiting unmanned aircraft. Then the Iraqi brigade arrived. The unit commander saw he was outnumbered and decided not to engage. The Iraqis and Americans did not engage as well. They went into the base, and the security unit went back to their posts."

The anger Hirsiz felt at having his orders ignored quickly subsided, and he nodded. "That was probably a good decision on the commander's part," he said. "Send a 'well done' to his parent unit."

"Our unit there reports the Americans launched an unmanned combat aircraft to support their detail examining the plane," Cizek said. "The American private security chief, McLanahan, explained it was a long-range loitering aircraft capable of releasing multiple types of precision and area munitions. It was apparently brought in on that Boeing 767 freighter that evaded our interceptors."

"McLanahan. Yes," Hirsiz said. "He is the wild card in all of this. Remember he commanded a very advanced bomber unit in the United States Air Force, and he was known for quite daring and successful operations—many of which were apparently done without official sanction, if we can believe the American media pundits. Now apparently he works for the Iraqis. I would guess if he says he has a cruise missile, he does, and probably more than one. The question is: As a tool of the Iraqis now, would he use it against us?"

"Hopefully we'll never find out," Cizek said. "I would have liked to get a look at that reconnaissance aircraft, though. The American secretary of state said our plane was disabled by a laser self-defense system, not a radiation weapon. That had to be a powerful laser. If we could get a peek at that system and cross-engineer it, we'd be decades ahead of most European and all of the Middle Eastern armies."

"I agree," Hirsiz said. "Have another try at bringing that plane back to Turkey. Fly as many troops as you can in tonight by helicopter. Send the entire First Division in if you have to. They don't seem to be having any trouble in their area of responsibility; it's the Kurdish regions that have me concerned, not the Arab ones."

"But what about the Iraqi Nahla brigade?"

"Let's see if they want to risk a fight over the American plane," Hirsiz said. "I think they might think twice. We may have to deal with the American robot and armored commando, but how many of those things could they have? Let's find out. I think the plane and its technology will be worth it."

"We have more information about the robot and the armored commando; we won't be as surprised as our smaller unit was, and we'll be on the lookout for their supposed unmanned attack plane," Cizek said. An aide hurried in with a message and handed it to him. "I was able to get some details about the plane, the XC-57," he said as he read. "It was in a next-generation bomber competition but was not selected, so it was converted into a . . . *lanet olsun*!" he swore.

"What?"

"Third Brigade shelled Irbil," Cizek said, dumbfounded. Hirsiz did not react. "General Ozek, in personal charge of a mortar battalion, moved to the outskirts of Irbil less than a mile from the Kurdistan parliamentary building and started firing mortars into the city," he went on. "He even fired shells into the Citadel, the ancient city center. For the targets he couldn't reach with mortars, he called in an AC-130 gunship and destroyed numerous targets in the south of the city with heavy cannon fire from above!"

Instead of anger or surprise, Hirsiz smiled and sat back in his seat. "Well, well, it seems our

skeleton-faced berserker has made the decision
to strike at Irbil for us," he said.

"But how—" Cizek stopped, the concern
spreading across his face. "The proposed target
list the intelligence directorate drew up . . . ?"

"I gave it to Ozek," Hirsiz said. "He did exactly what I was hoping he'd do." The look of
concern on Cizek's face turned into one of sheer
disbelief. "The Security Council was undecided if
we should escalate the conflict by attacking the
capital of the Kurdistan Regional Government;
Ozek has done it for us."

"This is a serious matter, sir," Cizek said. "Irbil
is a city of a million people. Even with precision
firepower—which mortars are definitely *not*—
innocent civilians will get hurt. And the big
howitzer on those AC-130 can destroy an entire
building with one shot!"

"A few civilian casualties will only help us,"
Hirsiz said. "This battle has been too easy, too
sterile. The PKK and the Iraqi army run and
hide, the *peshmerga* stay out of reach, the Americans lock the gates to their bases, and the Iraqi
people turn on their televisions and watch us roll
down their streets. It's not a war, it's a parade
. . . until now." He then wore a worried expression. "Ozek didn't hit any schools or hospitals,
did he?"

Cizek called for a more precise list of targets
struck and received them a few minutes later.
"A Kurdish bank . . . a small shopping center . . .
some shops inside the Citadel . . . a memorial
park . . . one mortar even landed near the parliament building in a parking lot, close enough to
break some windows—"

"That was on the list—the parking space of a pro-PKK politician," Hirsiz said. "He followed the list to the letter. The Citadel hit . . . that was his idea, but he got the idea from that list. I'm sure the shop was owned by the same business-man that owned the other shops in the city on the list. Ozek is scary and a little crazy, but he's a fast learner."

"The Security Council was undecided on at-tacking Irbil because we wanted to see the reaction of the world first as the operation pro-gressed," Cizek said. "Up until now, the reaction has been very quiet . . . *remarkably* quiet. A few cries of outrage, mostly from militant Muslim groups and human rights organizations. It was tacit approval of what we are doing. But now we've attacked the Iraqi people, the Kurds, di-rectly. You should have sought the approval of the Security Council before ordering this, Kurzat!"

"I didn't order anything, Hasan," Hirsiz said. The minister of national defense looked uncon-vinced. "Don't believe me if you wish, but I did not order Ozek to shell Irbil. I gave him the list, that's all. But I knew he would not disappoint." He looked at his watch. "I suppose I should call Washington and explain things to them."

"You're going to tell them a rogue general did those attacks?"

"I'm going to tell them exactly what hap-pened: we had discussed attacking businesses and organizations known to be friendly to the PKK, and one of our division commanders took it upon himself to do just that." Hirsiz waved a hand at Cizek's disbelieving expression and lit a cigarette. "Besides, you and the rest of the council have deniability now as well. If it doesn't bring the Americans and the Iraqis around to helping us, you can blame it all on Ozek and me." He turned serious once more. "Make sure Ozek pulls back to the airport. If we give him too much encouragement, he's likely to try to take the entire city."

"Yes, sir," Cizek said. "And we will get Second Division moving on that American aircraft."

"Very good." Hirsiz picked up a telephone. "I'll call Gardner and set the stage with him, and let him vent about the attack on Irbil."

COMMAND AND CONTROL CENTER, ALLIED AIR BASE NAHLA, IRAQ
Later that evening

"Just got off the phone with the president," Vice President Ken Phoenix said as he entered the Tank. Colonel Jack Wilhelm was at his console in the front of the senior staff area, but beside him—in the real commander's chair—was Colonel Yusuf Jaffar. The Tank was very crowded, because both an American and an Iraqi now manned every combat staff console in the room. Also in the room were Patrick McLanahan, Wayne Macomber, and Jon Masters. "He spoke with President Hirsiz of Turkey and President Rashid of Iraq.

"First of all, he wanted me to give you a 'job well done' for your actions today. He said that although he didn't feel the risk was worth it, he commends all of you for exercising restraint and courage. It was an explosive situation and you handled it well."

"I spoke with President Rashid as well," Jaffar said, "and he wished me to pass along similar thoughts to all."

"Thank you, Colonel. However, we still have a situation. Turkey wants access to the wreckage of the XC-57 to gather evidence for a criminal trial against Scion Aviation International. They are asking permission for experts to examine the aircraft, including the stuff you removed from the plane, Dr. Masters."

"That stuff is classified and proprietary, Mr. Vice President," Jon said. "Letting the Turks examine it gives them a chance to reverse-engineer it. That's the reason we risked our lives yanking that stuff out of there! They don't care about a trial—they just want my technology. No way I'm letting the Turks get their grubby paws on it!"

"You might not have any choice, Dr. Masters," Phoenix said. "Scion was a U.S. government contractor at the time of the attack. The government may be entitled to direct you to turn the equipment over."

"I'm not a lawyer, sir, and I don't particularly like them, but I know armies of them," Jon said. "I'll let them handle it."

"I'm more concerned about what the Turks will do, Mr. Vice President," Patrick said.

"I'm sure they'll go to the World Court or to NATO, possibly to the International Admiralty Court, file the criminal charges, and try to compel you to—"

"No, sir, I don't mean a legal proceeding. I mean, what will the Turkish army do?"

"What do you mean?"

"Sir, do you expect the Turkish army to just forget everything that's happened here today?" Patrick replied. "They have twenty thousand troops spread out between the border and Mosul, and fifty thousand troops within a day's march of here. This is the first defeat they've suffered in their Iraqi operation. I think Jon's right: they want the systems on that plane, and I think they're going to come back and take it."

"They would not dare!" Jaffar exclaimed. "This is not their country, it is *mine*. They will not do whatever they please!"

"We're trying to prevent this conflict from escalating, Colonel," Vice President Phoenix said. "Frankly, I think we got lucky out there today. We caught the Turks flat-footed with the Tin Man and CID units. But if Jaffar's brigade hadn't shown up when it did, or if the Turks decided to attack right away instead of waiting for instructions, the results could've been a lot worse."

"We would've handled them just fine, sir," Wayne Macomber said.

"I'm glad you think so, Mr. Macomber, but I disagree," Phoenix said. "You told me yourself you were low on ammo and power. I appreciate the fear factor involved in the Tin Man and CID, but those Turkish troops had marched almost two hundred miles inside Iraq. They weren't going to run." Whack lowered his eyes and said nothing in response; he knew the vice president was right.

"Mr. Vice President, I think General McLanahan may be correct," Jaffar said. "I do not know about these classified things that Dr. Masters speaks of, but I do know generals in the field, and they do not take defeat well. We pushed around a small security unit today and made them back off, but they outnumber us here.

"The Turks have two brigades surrounding Mosul and deployed to the south of us," Jaffar went on. "The Iraqi army has sufficient units in hiding to contain them, if that becomes necessary. But my brigade is the only significant force facing the two Turkish brigades to our north. That is where I will concentrate my forces and prepare for any action by the Turks." He stood and put on his helmet. "General McLanahan, you will deploy your reconnaissance aircraft and ground teams to the northern approach sectors, as far north as you can go without making contact, and warn of any advances by the Turks."

"Yes, Colonel," Patrick said. "I'm also concerned about the Turkish air forces, particularly the Second Tactical Air Force's F-15Es, A-10s, and AC-130 gunships based in Diyarbakir. If they decide to bring them in, they could decimate our forces."

"What do you propose, Patrick?" Vice President Phoenix asked.

"Sir, you have to convince President Gardner that we need surveillance of Diyarbakir and a plan to respond should the Turks launch a massive attack against us." Patrick produced a Secure Digital memory card in a plastic case. "This is my proposed reconnaissance schedule and attack plan. Our primary reconnaissance platform is a constellation of microsatellites that Sky Masters Incorporated can place in orbit to provide continuous coverage of Turkey. They can be launched within hours. The attack plan centers around using specialized modules in our XC-57 aircraft that can disrupt and destroy the command and control facilities at Diyarbakir."

"I thought the XC-57 was just a transport and reconnaissance plane, Patrick," Phoenix said with a knowing smile.

"Until we attack Diyarbakir, sir, that's all it is," Patrick said. "The attack will be with a combination of netrusion—network intrusion—to confuse and overload their networks, followed by high-power microwave weapons to destroy the electronics aboard any operating aircraft or facility. We can follow up with bomber attacks if necessary."

"Bomber attacks?"

"The Seventh Air Expeditionary Squadron," Patrick said. "It's a small B-1B Lancer bomber unit formed by an engineering group in Palmdale, California, that takes planes in flyable storage and makes them operational again. They currently have seven bombers deployed to the United Arab Emirates. They've been used to fly contingency support missions for Second Regiment and other Army units in Iraq."

"Are they an Air Force unit, Patrick?"

"They have an Air Force designation, I believe they're organized under Air Force Matériel Command, and they're commanded by an Air Force lieutenant colonel," Patrick replied, "but most of the members are civilians."

"Is the entire military being taken over by contractors, Patrick?" Phoenix asked wryly. He nodded somberly. "I don't like the idea of bombing Turkey, even if they strike at us directly, but if that's the final option, it sounds sufficiently small and powerful to do the job without causing a world war to break out between NATO allies."

"My thoughts exactly, sir."

"I'll present your plan to Washington, Patrick," Phoenix said, "but let's hope we don't go anywhere near that level of escalation." He turned to the Iraqi commander. "Colonel Jaffar, I know this is your country and your army, but I urge you to practice the same restraint you showed today. We don't want to get into a shooting war with the Turks. This business with the classified boxes from that wreckage is of no consequence if lives are at stake."

"With respect, sir, you are wrong two ways," Jaffar said. "As I said, I do not know or care about black boxes. But this is not about black boxes—this is about a foreign army invading my home. And I did not practice restraint with the Turks today. We had them outnumbered; there was no reason to fight unless *they* chose to do so. They were the ones who showed restraint, not I. But if the Turks do return, they will come in large numbers, and then we will fight. General McLanahan, I expect a briefing on your deployment plan within the hour."

"I'll be ready, Colonel," Patrick said.

"Excuse me, sir, but I must prepare my troops for battle," Jaffar said, bowing to Vice President Phoenix. "Colonel Wilhelm, I must thank you for keeping Nahla secure in my absence. May I rely on you and your men to keep Nahla secure as we deploy, as you already have?"

"Of course," Wilhelm said. "And I'd like to attend your deployment briefings, if I could."

"You are always welcome, Colonel. You will
be notified. Good night." And Jaffar departed,
with Patrick, Wayne, and Jon behind him.

"You still think this is a good idea, General?"
Wilhelm asked before they left. "Jaffar's fighting
for *his* country. What are *you* fighting for now?
The money?"

Jaffar froze, and they could see him clench
and unclench his fists and straighten his back in
indignation, but he did not do or say anything.
But Patrick stopped and turned to Wilhelm.
"You know what, Colonel?" Patrick said with a
slight smile. "The Iraqis haven't paid me a dime.
Not one dime." And he departed.

CHAPTER 8

There are no great people in this world, only great challenges which ordinary people rise to meet.
—*Admiral William Frederick Halsey, Jr. (1882–1959)*

NEAR ALLIED AIR BASE NAHLA, IRAQ
Early the next morning

The two eight-man teams of Turkish *bordo bereliler*, or Maroon Beret, special operations Rangers arrived on station at about three A.M. They had executed a picture-perfect HALO, or high-altitude low-opening parachute jump, into the area about five miles north of Tall Kayf. After landing and stowing their parachutes, they verified their position, checked personnel, weapons, and gear, and headed south. Once near the checkpoint about two miles from the XC-57 crash site, they split up into two-man recon teams and proceeded to their individual objective points.

It took less than thirty minutes for the Maroon Berets to determine that all of the intel passed to

them from Captain Evren's unit stationed outside Allied Air Base Nahla was true: the Iraqis
had deployed four infantry platoons around the
XC-57 crash site and were setting up sandbag
machine gun nests to guard it. The rest of the
brigade was nowhere to be seen. Evren had also
reported that the Americans were still inside the
base, training and conditioning but remaining
very low profile as well.

The Iraqis were obviously expecting something to happen, the Ranger platoon leader
thought, but they weren't putting up more than
a token defense. They obviously weren't looking
for a fight over the reconnaissance plane. The
Rangers could stop their operation if the Iraqis
had deployed any more forces in the area, but
they hadn't. The operation was still on.

The timetable was razor-thin, but everyone
was executing it perfectly. Aviation elements of
First and Second Divisions had sent squadrons of
light infantry in low-flying UH-60 Black Hawk
and CH-47F Chinook helicopters from six different directions, all converging in the area around
Nahla, under the protection of AH-1 Cobra helicopter gunships. The helicopters came in under
a blanket of jamming across the entire electromagnetic spectrum that cut off all radar and
communications other than bands they wished
to use. At the same time ground forces were
rushing in to reinforce them. In less than thirty
minutes—the blink of an eye, even on a modern
battlefield—the four Iraqi platoons surrounding
the XC-57 crash site were surrounded themselves
. and outnumbered.

 Iraqi defenders, using night-vision goggles, could see the red lines of Turkish laser designators crisscrossing the field ahead of them, and they hunkered down behind sandbag machine gun nests and the XC-57 wreckage. The assault could begin at any moment.

"Attention, Iraqi soldiers," they heard in Arabic from a loudspeaker aboard a Turkish armored infantry vehicle, "this is Brigadier General Ozek, commander of this task force. You have been surrounded, and I am bringing in more reinforcements as I speak. I order you to—"

And at that moment one of the Chinook helicopters that had just touched down to off-load soldiers disappeared in a tremendous fireball, followed by a Cobra gunship that was hovering a few hundred yards away on patrol and a Black Hawk helicopter that had just lifted off. The entire horizon to the north and northeast of the XC-57 crash site suddenly seemed as if it was on fire.

"*Carsi, Carsi*, this is *Kuvvet*, we are taking heavy fire, direction unknown!" the Second Division task force commander radioed. "Say ETE. Over!" No response. The general looked over his left shoulder toward Highway Three, which his eastern battalion should have been racing up to flank the Iraqis . . .

. . . and through his night-vision goggles he saw an eerie glow on the horizon about three miles behind him—and the flickering of some very large objects burning and exploding. "*Carsi*, this is *Kuvvet*, say your pos!"

"Good strike, Boomer," Patrick McLanahan said. The first AGM-177 Wolverine strike mis-

sile released a CBU-97 Sensor-Fuzed Weapon
over the lead vehicles in the easternmost battalion driving southbound as part of the Nahla
operation. Dropped from fifteen thousand feet,
the CBU-97's dispenser released ten submunitions, each of which deployed four skeets and
laser and infrared seekers. As the submunitions
fell toward the column of vehicles, they started
to spin, and as they did they detected and classified all the vehicles below. At the proper altitude
each skeet detonated over a vehicle, sending a
molten blob of copper down onto its prey. The
blob of superheated copper easily penetrated the
usually thinner top armor of the Turkish vehicles, destroying every vehicle on the road for a
quarter of a mile.

"Roger that, General," Hunter Noble said.
"The Wolverine is maneuvering for the western
column for the second CBU-97 pass, and then it'll
attack the troops closest to Nahla with the eighty-
seven." The CBU-87 Combined Effects Munition
was a mine-laying weapon that dispensed over
two hundred bomblets over a three-thousand-
square-foot rectangular area, effective against
soldiers and light vehicles. "The second Wolverine is in a parking orbit to the south in case the
Iraqis have trouble with the Mosul brigades."

"Hopefully we won't need it," Patrick said.
"Let me know if—"

"Problem, Patrick—I think we lost the first
Wolverine," Boomer interjected. "Lost contact. It
might have been shot down if it was detected on
radar when it made its attack."

"Send in the second Wolverine on the western
battalion," Patrick ordered.

"Moving. But Jaffar's guys might make contact before it arrives."

The eastern column of Turkish infantry vehicles was initially stopped cold by the first Wolverine attack, but the survivors were soon on the move. As they raced forward to meet up with the center battalion, several Iraqi antitank teams in spider holes along the highway opened fire, destroying five Humvees and an M113 armored personnel carrier. But the Iraqis were soon coming under intense fire from other Turkish troops, and they were trapped in their spider holes. A line of three Humvees had discovered three spider holes and quickly destroyed the first one with forty-millimeter automatic grenade fire.

"*Wa'if hena! Wa'if hena*! Stop!" the Turks shouted in Arabic. They exited their Humvees, weapons raised. "Get out now, hands on your . . . !"

Suddenly they heard a loud CCRRACK! and one of the Humvees exploded in the blink of an eye. Before the explosion subsided they heard another CCRRACK! and the second Humvee detonated, followed by the third. The Turks flattened on their stomachs, searching for the enemy who had just blown up their vehicles . . .

. . . and a few moments later, they saw who it was: the ten-foot-tall American robot, carrying the impossibly large sniper rifle and a large backpack. "Time to run along," the robot said in electronically synthesized Turkish. It leveled the big rifle and ordered, "Drop your weapons." The Turks did as they were told, turned, and ran after their comrades. The Iraqis leaped out of their spider holes, scooped up the Turks' weapons and their remaining antitank missiles, and went looking for more targets.

"Jaffar's guys are doing pretty good on the eastern side," Charlie Turlock said. "I think we have the rest of this battalion broken up, thanks to the Wolverine. How's it going on the west, Whack?"

"Not so good," Wayne Macomber said. He was "tank plinking" on every large armored vehicle that came within range, but the column of Turkish vehicles coming toward them seemed endless.

"Need some help?"

"General?"

"The second Wolverine is five minutes out," Patrick said. "The first one went Tango-Uniform. But we still have two companies on the east that I want to get turned around first. We have to hope the Iraqis hold."

"Colonel Jaffar?"

"I am sorry I left such a small force at the reconnaissance plane," Jaffar radioed amid loud engine noises and a lot of out-of-breath gasping. "Some of our vehicles broke down as well."

Patrick could see where Jaffar's battalion was relative to the four platoons guarding the XC-57, and like the second Wolverine he was not going to make it before the Turks started their attack. "General, I'm closer," Charlie Turlock radioed. "Whack and I together might be enough to at least slow the Turks down long enough."

"No, you have the eastern flank, Charlie; we don't want anyone stunting around from that direction," Patrick said. "Martinez, I need you to sprint ahead of Jaffar's guys and engage."

"With pleasure, General," replied Angel Martinez, piloting a CID unit accompanying Yusuf
Jaffar's battalion. Martinez was a jack-of-all-
trades in Scion Aviation International: he had
police training; he fixed and drove trucks and
construction equipment; he could even cook.
When they were looking for volunteers to go to
Iraq, his was the first hand up. On the long flight
over, Wayne and Charlie gave him ground school
lessons on how to pilot a Cybernetic Infantry
Device; when Wayne Macomber ordered him to
mount up after they had arrived at Nahla and
were going to take down the local security force,
it was his first time actually piloting a CID.

Now this was only his second time—and he
was going to face an entire Turkish army battalion.

"Listen up, Angel," Charlie radioed. "The
armor and the rail gun are great, but your main
weapons aboard a CID are speed, mobility, and
situational awareness. Your main weaknesses
are massed platoon- or company-level weapons
because they can drain your power quickly. You
have to move to avoid heavy weapons being able
to concentrate fire on you. Shoot, move, scan,
move, shoot, move."

"Charlie, you drilled me on that mantra so
much I say it in my sleep," Martinez said. He was
racing ahead of Jaffar's battalion with breathtak-
ing speed, well over fifty miles an hour across
the open field. "Target's in sight."

"The Turks are concentrating on the platoons
ahead of them," Whack said, "but the minute
you open fire they'll—"

"Projectile away," Martinez said. He dove to

the ground in a prone position, selected a Turkish armored personnel carrier in his sights, and fired. The APC didn't explode or even stop when the tungsten-steel alloy projectile hit, because the sausage-size slug passed right through it as if it never existed—but every man inside the vehicle was shredded to bits by shards of the APC's thin steel fuselage flying uncontrollably inside the vehicle. "Damn, I must've missed," Martinez said.

"No, but you gotta remember to go for the engine compartment, transmission, magazine, or the tracks, not just the crew compartment," Whack said. "The projectiles will pass through the thin steel or aluminum easily. Every infantryman aboard may be dead, but the vehicle can still fight if the driver or commander made it."

"Roger that, Whack," Martinez said. As soon as he stood up, he started taking fire, including automatic forty-millimeter grenade rounds. He dashed sideways for a hundred yards, searching for the origin of those rounds. He soon found it—not one, but two APCs.

"Angel, keep moving!" Charlie shouted. "Those two APCs have you lined up!"

"Not for long," Martinez shouted back. He took aim and fired directly through the front of one APC. It immediately shuddered to a stop, and soon a fire broke out in the engine compartment. But Martinez couldn't enjoy the view, because two more APCs had zeroed in on him. He immediately loaded their locations in his target computer's memory, aimed, and fired. But they moved quickly, and he was only able to get one before having to run because he was being bombarded by the other. "Guys, I have a feeling they anticipated finding us out here," he said. "I'm getting clobbered."

"Target on the run and shoot at as many as you can when you stop," Whack said. "Don't target while you're stopped."

"It looks like they're gunning for us for sure," Charlie said. She fired four ballistic rockets from her backpack, which had infrared and millimeter-wave radars that guided them to a group of four Turkish armored personnel carriers that had appeared out of nowhere from the east. "At least it gives Jaffar's troops a chance to—"

"*Helicopters inbound, bearing northwest, five miles*!" Patrick shouted. "They look like gun-ships accompanied by a scout! Too low to spot them farther out!" Before Martinez could search for the newcomers, the Turkish Cobra gunship launched a Hellfire laser-guided missile.

"Evasive moves, Angel!" Whack shouted. Now that the scout helicopter, a U.S.-licensed but Turkish-built Kiowa, had to keep its laser on Martinez, it was an easy target for Macomber's rail gun, and he blew the sensor ball atop the helicopter's rotor mast apart seconds later . . . but not before the Hellfire missile hit Martinez on the left part of his chest.

"Angel's down! Angel's down!" Whack shouted. He tried to run over to him, but sustained fire from the battalion in front of Jaffar's security platoons kept him pinned down. "I can't get to him," he said as he fired at more oncoming APCs, then reloaded his rail gun. "I'm not sure how much longer we can hold these guys off. I'm down to fifty percent power and ammo."

"The Wolverine will be overhead in one minute," Patrick said. "More helicopters inbound!"

"I'm going to try to get to Martinez," Whack said.

"The Turks are too close, Wayne," Patrick said.

"We might have to retreat, but I'm not leaving without Martinez." Whack fired several more times, waited for the return fire to subside, then said, "Here I—"

At that moment several dozen flashes of light erupted from the west, and moments after that Turkish armored vehicles started exploding like firecrackers. "Sorry I am late once again, gentlemen," Yusuf Jaffar radioed, "but I am still not accustomed to your speed. I think you may get your comrade, Macomber."

"On the way!" Whack fired the thrusters on the boots of his Tin Man armor, and in three jumps he was with Martinez. At that moment the earth in front of him began to sizzle and pop like water sprayed on a hot pan as the Wolverine began sowing bomblets and antipersonnel mines on the Turkish troops. The air was getting thick with smoke and the screams of trapped Turks. "You okay in there, Angel?" Whack knew from his biometric datalink that Martinez was alive, but most of the left side of the robot was shattered, and he couldn't move or communicate. Whack picked up the robot. "Hold on, Martinez. This might hurt a bit on the landing."

Just as he hit his thrusters, a Hellfire missile fired from the Turkish Cobra gunship exploded at the spot he had just left, and Whack and

Martinez were swatted out of the sky like clay
pigeons hit by birdshot.

The BERP armor protected Whack from the
blast, but after he landed he found all of his
helmet systems dark and silent. He had no
choice but to take his helmet off. Illuminated
by the nearby fires of burning vehicles, he could
see Martinez lying about fifty yards away, and
sprinted over to him. But just as he got within
twenty yards, the ground erupted with heavy-
caliber shells peppering the area around the
robot. The Cobra gunship had moved into cannon
range and was spraying twenty millimeter shells
on him. Whack knew he was next. Without
power, his BERP armor wouldn't protect him.

He looked around for someplace to hide. The
nearest Iraqi machine-gun nest surrounding the
XC-57 was about a hundred yards away. He
hated to leave Martinez, but there was no way
he could carry him, so he started running. Hell,
he thought grimly, maybe running made it a *little*
harder for the Cobra pilot to kill him. He heard
a machine gun open fire, and he tried doing a
little dodging and weaving like he'd done as a
football player at the Air Force Academy. Who
knows how good those Turkish gunners are, he
thought as he waited for the shells to rip into
him. Maybe—

And then he heard a tremendous explosion,
big enough and near enough to knock him off
his feet. He turned and looked up just in time to
see the Cobra gunship crash into the field just a
couple dozen yards away. As the sound and feel
of burning metal wafted over him, he got to his
feet and ran. The heat and choking smoke made

him crouch down as he ran, and he could hear and feel the missiles and ammo on the burning chopper cooking off behind him. Wouldn't it be a bitch, he thought, to avoid getting turned into Swiss cheese by a Cobra gunship only to have the chopper's unexpended ammo get him? Of course, that's my luck, he thought, that's the way I'm supposed to—

Suddenly it felt as if he had run headlong into a steel barricade. "Whoa, whoa, slow down there, Mr. Jackrabbit," he heard the electronic voice of a CID unit say. It was Charlie, who had run over from her position to the east. "You're clear. Take a minute. You lose your headgear?"

"I lost everything . . . the suit's dead," Whack said. "Go get Martinez." Charlie waited a few moments, shielding Whack with her armor, until the explosions stopped on the downed Cobra, then ran off around the burning wreckage. She returned a few minutes later carrying the other CID unit. She then dragged Martinez with one hand and carried Macomber under her other arm back to the security post near the XC-57.

"Those other gunships are coming in," Charlie said, picking up her rail gun and scanning the skies with the CID unit's sensors. "Most are going after Jaffar's brigade, but there's a couple after us." She paused for a moment, studying the electronic images of the battlefield. "I'll draw them away," she said, then bolted off to the east.

Whack peeked out over the sandbag bunker . . . and when he looked in the sky he saw the unmistakable flare of a missile motor igniting, and he jumped to his feet and ran away from the bunker as fast as he—

He was instantly thrown off his feet, blinded, deafened, half-broiled, and pelted with supersonic pieces of debris when the missile hit just a few yards behind him. Unfortunately for him, he wasn't knocked unconscious, so all he could do was lie on the ground in pain, with his entire head feeling like a charcoal briquette. But a few seconds later, he was scooped up off the ground. "Ch-Charlie . . . ?"

"My rail gun's DOA," Charlie said as she ran. "I'm getting you out of—" She suddenly stopped, turned, and crouched down, shielding Whack from a thunderous burst of cannon fire from the Cobra. "I'm going to put you down and get that thing," she said. "He doesn't want you, he wants—" The Cobra pilot fired again. Whack could feel the heavy-caliber shells shoving him and Charlie as if they had their backs to a hurricane. "I . . . I'm losing power," she said after the last fusillade ended. "That last blast got something . . . a battery, I think. I don't think I can move." The Cobra opened fire again . . .

At that moment they heard an explosion behind them, the cannon fire ceased, and they heard the sounds of another helicopter crash. Neither of them moved until they heard vehicles approaching. "Charlie?"

"I can move, but it's real slow," she said. "You okay?"

"I'm okay." Whack painfully wriggled out from the CID unit's mechanical arms and looked around for the Turks. "Stay put. We've got company." The vehicles were almost on them. He had no weapons, nothing he could fight with. There was nothing he could—

"Raise your hands and don't move," he heard a voice say . . . an *American* voice. Whack did as he was told. He saw the vehicle was an Avenger mobile air defense unit. An Army sergeant came up to him, wearing night-vision goggles, which he raised. "You gotta be a couple of the Scion guys, because I ain't seen *nothin'* like you two before."

"Macomber, and that's Turlock," Whack said. "I've got another guy back there." The sergeant whistled and waved, and a few moments later an open-back Humvee came up. Whack helped load Charlie up on the Humvee. As she was taken back to Nahla, he got another Humvee, went back and found Martinez, had some soldiers load him up, and took him back to base as well.

Martinez was unconscious and had several broken bones and some internal bleeding and was taken to the infirmary for emergency surgery; Charlie and Whack were checked out and were fine, with Whack suffering a number of cuts, burns, and bruises. She and Whack were taken to a guard post near the departure end of the runway, where two Humvees, a Stryker wheeled armored command post vehicle, and an Avenger unit were partially hidden by runway end light structures and the Instrument Landing System transmitter building. Standing outside the Stryker watching the battle through image-intensified binoculars were Patrick McLanahan, Hunter Noble, Jon Masters, Captain Kelvin Cotter, the air traffic management officer, and Vice President Kenneth Phoenix with his Secret Service detail.

"Glad you guys are all right," Patrick said. He

handed out water and energy bars. "That was close."

"Why are you guys out here?" Macomber asked.

"The jamming has knocked out all our radars and most of our communications," Cotter said. "The Triple-C is pretty much dark. I can get line-of-sight laser comms out here."

"What's the word, General?" Wayne asked. "How bad did we get hit?"

"The word is, it's just about over," Patrick said. Wayne lowered his head dejectedly . . . until Patrick added, "It's almost over, and it looks like we won it."

"No shit?"

"Between the CIDs, you, and the Wolverines, we pretty much stopped the Turks completely," Patrick said. "The Turks weren't expecting the Iraqis to fight so hard, and Jaffar's guys went berserker on them. Then, when Wilhelm joined it, the Turks turned and headed north."

"I had a feeling Wilhelm wasn't going to just sit around while Jaffar went out there," Whack said.

"It was four brigades against two, plus you guys and the cruise missiles, but that was enough for the Turks," Vice President Phoenix said. "I have a feeling their hearts really weren't in it. They came to Iraq to hunt down PKK, not fight Iraqis and Americans. Then they started fighting robots and armored soldiers firing Buzz Light-year rail guns, and they split."

"I hope so, sir," Patrick said. "But I don't trust Hirsiz one bit. He's already been pushed over the brink by the PKK, and now we handed him a defeat. He's likely to lash out. I don't think it's likely he'll stop at bombing some suspected PKK-friendly businesses in Irbil."

"Looks like Jaffar will be reinforcing his forward battalions and start taking his casualties back to base," Cotter said, stepping out of the Stryker and scanning the area to the north of their position with binoculars. "Colonel Wilhelm and Major Weatherly will keep their battalions on the line in case . . . *yaaah*!" Cotter screamed as an impossibly bright flash of white light pierced the night sky, exactly where he was looking.

The first flash was followed by hundreds more, each one brighter than the last, and then the thunder of massive explosions and the roar of superheated air reached them. Clouds of fire rose hundreds of feet into the sky, and soon they could feel the heat wash over them like ocean waves rolling onto the beach.

"*What in hell was that*?" Phoenix cried. He and Jon Masters helped Cotter, who was flash-blinded, to the ground and poured water on his face.

"Smells like napalm, or thermobaric bombs," Macomber said. He took Cotter's binoculars, reset the optronic circuits so any more flashes wouldn't blind him, too, and scanned the area. "Je . . . *sus* . . ."

"Who got hit, Wayne?" Patrick asked.

"Looks like Jaffar's two forward battalions," Whack said in a quiet voice. "God, that must be what hell looks like down there." He scanned the area around the blast zone. "I don't see our guys. I'll try to get in contact with Wilhelm and—"

Just then there were two huge bright flashes,

followed moments later by two massive explosions . . . this time, *behind* them, inside the base. The chest-crushing concussions threw everyone to the ground, and they crawled for any bit of safety they could find. Two massive fiery mushroom clouds rose into the sky. *"Get under cover!"* Patrick screamed over the hurricane-like chaos as clouds of smoke rolled over them. *"Get under the Stryker!"* The Secret Service agents pulled Phoenix into his Humvee, and everyone else crawled under the Stryker just as they were pelted by massive chunks of falling debris.

It took a long time for the deadly debris to stop falling, longer before anyone could breathe well enough through the choking clouds of dust and smoke, and longer still before anyone found the courage to get up and survey the area. There was a massive fire somewhere in the center of the base.

"That's *twice* I've been too close to a bomb attack!" Jon Masters shouted. "Don't tell me—Turkish bombers again, right?"

"That would be my guess," Patrick said. "What got hit over there?"

One of the Stryker crewmembers got out of his vehicle, and when everyone else saw his eyes widen and his jaw drop, a chill of dread ran up their spines. "Holy shit," he breathed, "I think they just nailed the Triple-C."

THE PINK PALACE, ÇANCAYA, ANKARA, REPUBLIC OF TURKEY
A short time later

"What do you mean, they *retreated*?" President Kurzat Hirsiz asked. "Why did they retreat? They outnumbered the Iraqis five to one!"

"I know that, Mr. President, I know," Minister of Defense Hasan Cizek said. "But they weren't just fighting Iraqis. The American army helped them."

"God . . . so we were fighting Americans, too," Hirsiz said. He shook his head. "It was bad enough we decided to draw the Iraqis into a fight; I never expected the Americans to respond, too."

"As well as two of those American robots and one of those armored commandos . . . the Tin Man soldiers," Cizek added. "They also had two cruise missiles that attacked with bomblets and antipersonnel mines."

"*What*?" Hirsiz exploded. "How badly did we get hit?"

"Very badly, sir," Cizek said. "Possibly twenty percent or more."

"Twenty percent . . . *in one battle*?" a voice shouted. It was Prime Minister Ayşe Akas. She had not been seen in public since the declaration of a state of emergency and the disbanding of the National Assembly, but had been meeting with lawmakers most of the time. "Mr. President, what do you think you're doing?"

"I did not summon you here, Prime Minister," Hirsiz said. "Besides, we did much worse to the

Iraqis. What do you want? To turn in your resignation, I hope."

"Kurzat, please, stop this insanity now before this turns into full-scale war with Iraq and the United States," Akas pleaded. "End it. Declare victory and bring the troops home."

"Not before the PKK is wiped out, Ayşe," Hirsiz said.

"Then what are you doing attacking Tall Kayf?" Akas asked. "There are few PKK in that area."

"There is a situation at that air base that needed to be resolved," Hirsiz said.

"I know about the American spy plane—you still allow me to watch television, although you've taken away my telephone and passport and keep me under twenty-four/seven guard," Akas said. "But why would you waste Turkish lives for a hunk of burned metal?" She looked at Cizek. "Or are the generals in charge now?"

"I am still in charge here, Prime Minister, you can be assured of this," Hirsiz said.

"So you gave the order to bomb Irbil?"

"What is it you want, Prime Minister?" Hirsiz asked irritably, finding a cigarette.

"I think you should allow me to meet with Vice President Phoenix, in Irbil or Baghdad."

"I told you, no," Hirsiz said. "In a state of emergency the president must decide all actions, and I don't have time to meet with Phoenix or anyone else until the crisis is resolved. Besides, Phoenix is still at Nahla, and it's far too dangerous for him to travel."

"I won't go as an opponent of the war, but as the prime minister of Turkey, who, as you said, has little power in time of war, with the National Assembly disbanded and a council of war replacing the cabinet," Akas said. She stopped and blinked in disbelief. "You said Phoenix is still at Nahla? He's at Nahla Air Base? Isn't that where the fighting is, where all those men perished?" She saw Hirsiz and Cizek exchange glances. "Is there something else? What?"

Hirsiz hesitated to tell her, then shrugged and nodded to Cizek. "It's going to be in the news soon anyway."

"We bombed Nahla Air Base," Cizek said. Akas's jaw dropped in disbelief. "We targeted the headquarters building of the Iraqi and American forces."

"*You what*? *Bombed their headquarters*?" Akas shouted. "You *are* insane, both of you. Is Phoenix dead?"

"No, he was not in the building at the time," Hirsiz said.

"Lucky for *you*!"

"I did not start shooting at Iraqis and Americans until *they* started shooting at Turks!" Hirsiz shouted. "I did not start this war! The PKK murders innocent men, women, and children, and no one says a word to us. Well, they will talk to us now, won't they? They will scream and complain and threaten me! *I don't care*! I am not going to stop until Iraq stops harboring the PKK and promises to help eradicate them. Maybe with a few dead Americans in Iraq by our hands, they will talk to us about destroying the PKK."

Akas looked at Hirsiz as if studying an oil painting or an animal in the zoo, trying to find some hidden understanding or meaning in what she saw. All she could discern was hatred. He didn't even look back at her. "How many Americans were killed in the base, Minister?"

"Twenty or twenty-five, I don't remember; about a hundred injured," Cizek replied.

"My God . . ."

"Ayşe, maybe it is a good idea for you to meet with Phoenix and talk with Gardner," Cizek said. Hirsiz turned, his eyes wide with surprise and his jaw set in anger. Cizek held up a hand. "Kurzat, I'm afraid the Americans will retaliate—maybe not militarily, not right away, but with every other means at their disposal. If we don't start negotiating with them, they're more likely to hit back. Call a cease-fire, have our forces hold in position, and let Ayşe go to Baghdad. Meanwhile we'll resupply our forces, bring back our wounded and dead, and start collecting intelligence on the whereabouts of the PKK and their supporters. We have to be sure we don't lose support from our allies, but we don't have to give up everything we've gained."

Hirsiz's expression was a mixture of rage and confusion, and his head snapped back at his two advisers as if it were out of control. "End? End now? Are we any closer to destroying the PKK than we were five thousand lives ago? If we don't follow through with this, the five thousand soldiers who have lost their lives will have died for nothing."

"I think we have shown the world our crisis, Kurzat," Akas said. "You have also shown the world, and especially the PKK and their Kurdish supporters, that Turkey can and will lash out to protect its people and interests. But if you let the situation spin out of control, the world will simply think you're insane. You don't want that to happen."

Hirsiz studied both of his advisers. Akas could see the president looking more and more alone by the second. He returned to his desk and sat down heavily, staring through the large picture window. The sun was just coming up, and it looked like it was going to be a cold, drizzly day, Akas thought, which certainly must make Hirsiz feel even more alone.

"All I tried to do was protect the Turkish people," he said softly. "All I wanted to do was stop the murdering."

"We will, Kurzat," Akas said. "We'll do it together—your cabinet, the military, the Americans, and the Iraqis. We'll get everyone involved. You don't have to do it alone."

Hirsiz closed his eyes, then nodded. "Call an immediate cease-fire, Hasan," he said. "We have the phased withdrawal plan already drawn up: execute phases one and two."

The minister of national defense's mouth dropped open in surprise. "Phase two?" he asked. "But, sir, that pulls troops all the way back to the border. Are you sure you want to pull back that much? I recommend we—"

"Ayşe, you may notify the foreign minister that we wish to meet with the Americans and Iraqis right away to negotiate international inspectors and peacekeepers to monitor the border," Hirsiz went on. "You may also notify the speaker of the National Assembly that, pending a peaceful and successful withdrawal from Iraq, I will cancel the state of emergency and reseat the parliament."

Ayşe Akas walked over to Hirsiz and hugged him. "You've made the right choice, Kurzat," she said. "I'll get to work right away." She gave Cizek a smile and hurried out of the president's office.

Hirsiz stood by his desk and looked out the window for a long moment; then he turned and was surprised to see his minister of national defense still in his office. "Hasan?"

"What are you doing, Kurzat?" Cizek asked. "A cease-fire: fine. That will give us time to rearm, reinforce, and regroup. But a pullback all the way to the border, before we've had a chance to set up a buffer zone and eradicate the PKK?"

"I'm tired, Hasan," Hirsiz said wearily. "We've lost too many men . . ."

"The soldiers died defending their country, Mr. President!" Cizek said. "If you pull back before the operation is finished, they will have died for nothing! You said so yourself!"

"We will have other opportunities, Hasan. We have the world's attention now. They'll know we're serious when it comes to dealing with the PKK. Now give the orders."

Cizek appeared as if he was going to continue to argue, but instead gave a curt nod and walked out.

ALLIED AIR BASE NAHLA, IRAQ
A short time later

"I suppose it could've been a *lot* worse for us," Colonel Jack Wilhelm said. He was once again standing in their makeshift morgue in the large aircraft hangar, overseeing the preparation of the remains of the soldiers killed in action the night before. "Twenty-one soldiers killed in the Triple-C, including my ops officer, plus another thirty-two in action against the Turks, along with over two hundred injured, two dozen critical." He turned to Patrick McLanahan. "Sorry about Martinez, General. I heard he died a little while ago."

"Yes. Thank you."

"Your guys and your gadgets did great, General. You really came through."

"Not for our client, unfortunately," Patrick said. "The Iraqis lost over two hundred and fifty."

"But Jaffar and his men fought like wildcats," Wilhelm said. "I always thought the guy was all bluff and bluster. He turned out to be a good field commander and a hard charger." His radio beeped, and he listened in his earpiece, responded, and signed off. "The Turkish prime minister has announced a cease-fire and said that Turkish troops are pulling back to the border," he said. "It looks like it's over. What in hell were the Turks thinking? Why did they start this?"

"Frustration, anger, vengeance: dozens of reasons," Patrick said. "Turkey is one of those countries that just doesn't get any respect. They're not European, not Asian, not the Caucasus, not Middle Eastern; they're Muslim but secular. They control major land and sea routes, have one of the largest economies and armies in the world, powerful enough to have a seat on the United Nations Security Council, but they still aren't allowed into the European Union and they're treated like the red-haired stepchild in NATO. I think I'd be frustrated, too."

"They may deserve respect, but they also deserve to get their butts kicked," Wilhelm said. "So, I assume your contract is over . . . or is it? Maybe the Iraqis need you more than ever now?"

"We'll stay for now," Patrick said. "I'll recommend we monitor the Turkish cease-fire and pullback, and we'll probably be around awhile longer until the Iraqis get their own surveillance force built up. They have a small fleet of Cessna Caravans that have been modified for ground surveillance and communications relay, and there's talk of them leasing some UAVs."

"So you may be out of a job soon?"

"I think so." Patrick took a deep breath, one so deep that Wilhelm noticed. "This is a good job and a good bunch of guys and girls, but I've been away from home too long."

"To tell you the truth, it felt good to get out of the Tank and lead a bunch of troops into battle again," Wilhelm said. "I've been watching my guys do it on video screens and computer monitors for far too long." He gave McLanahan a slight smile. "But it *is* a young man's game, right, General?"

"I didn't say that." Patrick nodded to the tables of body bags once again lined up in the hangar. "But I've been around this too long."

"You flyboys see war completely different from the soldiers on the ground," Wilhelm said. "To you, combat is computers and satellites and UAVs."

"No, it's not."

"I know you've done a lot and seen a lot, General, but this is different," Wilhelm went on. "You manage systems and sensors and machines. We manage fighting men. I don't see dead men and women here, General—I see soldiers that put on a uniform, picked up a rifle, followed me, and who fell in battle. I'm not sad for them. I'm sad for their families and loved ones, but I'm proud of *them*."

THE PINK PALACE, ÇANCAYA, ANKARA, REPUBLIC OF TURKEY
That evening

The phone on the president's desk rang. "Uh . . . Mr. President, Minister Cizek and General Guzlev to see you," the president's aide stammered.

President Kurzat Hirsiz looked at his watch, then at the calendar on his computer. "Did we have a meeting scheduled, Nazim?"

"No, sir. They . . . they say it's urgent. Very urgent."

Hirsiz sighed. "Very well. Tell my wife I'll be a little late." He started to straighten up the papers on his desk, prioritizing the next day's activities, when he heard the door to his office open. "Come on in, gentlemen," he said distractedly as he worked, "but can we make this quick? I promised my wife I'd—"

When he looked up, he saw Minister of National Defense Hasan Cizek and military chief of staff General Abdullah Guzlev standing in the middle of the office, waiting patiently for him—

and both men were dressed in green camouflage battle-dress uniforms and glossy paratrooper boots, and both wore American-made M1911 .45-caliber sidearms in polished black leather holsters.

"What in hell is going on here?" Hirsiz asked incredulously. "Why are you in a military uniform, Hasan, and why are you carrying weapons in the Pink Palace?"

"Good evening, Kurzat," Cizek said. He motioned over his right shoulder, and several members of the Presidential Guard rushed in, with Hirsiz's outer office secretary bound in plastic handcuffs. The guards grabbed Hirsiz and bound his wrists in plastic handcuffs as well.

"*What in hell is this*?" Hirsiz shouted. "What are you doing? I am the president of the Republic of Turkey!"

"You are no longer president of Turkey, Kurzat," Cizek said. "I met with General Guzlev, the chiefs of staff, and the Ministry of the Interior, and we have decided that you are not competent to give orders anymore. You said so yourself, Kurzat: you're tired. Well, your weariness is a danger to the brave men and women in the field who are risking their lives on the president's word. We feel you cannot be trusted to give any more orders under a state of emergency. Prime Minister Akas, of course, is in no better shape. So we have decided to take over for you."

"*What*? What are you saying? What in *hell* are you doing?"

"You know what's happening here, Hirsiz," Cizek said. "The only question is, what will *you* do? Will you play the befuddled and embattled president, or will you take responsibility for your failures and do the responsible thing?"

"What on earth are you talking about? You . . . you are going to stage a coup d'état?"

"That won't be necessary," Cizek said. "Under a state of emergency, you can appoint anyone to be commander in chief of the armed forces. You appoint me and get some well-deserved rest for a few years until you are well enough to resume your duties; I rescind the order for the stage two pullback, and we consolidate our gains in Iraq."

"This is insanity! I will not comply! I will *never* relinquish my office! I am the president of Turkey! I was elected by the Grand National Assembly . . . !"

"You swore an oath to protect the people of Turkey, but instead you stand by and do nothing but moan and drool while thousands of soldiers are killed by the Iraqis and Americans," Cizek shouted. "I will stand for it no longer. The only proper response is a military one, not a political one, and so the army must be free to end this crisis. You are afraid to unleash the army and the Jandarma: I am not. Which will it be, Mr. President? Take your orders from me, and you and your family will be allowed to stay in a very comfortable residence in Tarsus or maybe even Dipkarpaz, under very careful security and seclusion—"

"As your puppet?"

"As president of the republic, Hirsiz, taking sound and urgent advice from your military advisers to end the attacks against our country," Cizek said. "If you do not agree to this, you will suffer a terrible heart attack, and we will remove you and your family from Ankara forever."

"You cannot do this!" Hirsiz protested. "I have done nothing wrong! You have no authority . . . !"

"I swore an oath to protect this country, Hirsiz," Cizek shouted, "and I will not sit idly by while you erase all the gains our brave soldiers have made for this country. You leave me absolutely no choice!"

Hirsiz hesitated again, and Guzlev pulled out his .45 and pointed it at the president. "I told you he wouldn't do it, Hasan . . . !" he said.

Hirsiz's eyes bulged, his arms and shoulders went limp, and his knees wobbled—it was as if all of the fluids in his body left him. "No, please," he whimpered. "I don't want to die. Tell me what to do."

"Good call, Hirsiz," Cizek threw some papers on the desk. "Sign these papers." Hirsiz signed them without reading them or even raising his head except to find the signature line. "We will escort you to the national communications center, where you will personally address the people of the republic." A sheaf of papers was placed in his hands. "Here is what you will say. It is important for you to address the people of Turkey as soon as possible."

"When can I see my wife, my family . . . ?"

"Business first, Hirsiz," Cizek said. He nodded to an officer of the Presidential Guard. "Take him away." Hirsiz mumbled something as he and his aide were led out of the office under heavy military guard.

Guzlev holstered his .45 with an exasperated

shove. "Balls, I thought I was going to have to shoot the fucking bastard after all, Cizek," he cursed. "He's going to look like shit on television."

"All the better," Cizek said. "If he can't or won't do it, I'll read it myself." He stepped toward Guzlev. "Rescind that phase one and two withdrawal order and be prepared to march on Irbil. If one *peshmerga* fighter, Iraqi soldier, or American—especially those robots and Tin Man creations—pops his head out just a centimeter, I want a squadron of jets to blow them all straight to Hell." He thought for a moment, then said, "No, I'm not going to wait for those robots and the Tin Men to come after us. I want Nahla Air Base shut down. They think they can kill a thousand Turks and just march away? I want the place leveled, do you understand me? Leveled!"

"With pleasure, Hasan . . . I mean, Mr. President," Guzlev said. "With pleasure."

ALLIED AIR BASE NAHLA, IRAQ
The next morning

Following the memorial service for the fallen soldiers from Second Regiment, Patrick McLanahan, Jack Wilhelm, Jon Masters, and chief of security Kris Thompson escorted Vice President Ken Phoenix to the flight line, where a newly arrived CV-22 Osprey tilt-rotor aircraft was waiting to fly him to Bahrain.

The vice president shook hands with Wilhelm. "You did an outstanding job out there last night, Colonel," Phoenix said. "I'm sorry for your losses."

"Thank you, sir," Wilhelm said. "I wish we hadn't gotten sucker-punched like that, but I'm glad the Turks decided to call the cease-fire, pull back, and start negotiations. It'll give us a chance to fly our boys home."

"I'll feel better when you're all home, safe and secure," Phoenix said. "Thank you for leading these men and women so well."

"Thank you, sir," Wilhelm said, saluting.

Phoenix returned the salute. "I'm not in your chain of command, Colonel," Phoenix said. "I don't rate a salute."

"You stood with my troops, you took enemy fire, and you didn't start crying, whining, ordering us around, or getting in the way," Wilhelm said. "You earned it, sir. If I may say so, you looked very . . . presidential."

"Why, thank you, Colonel," Phoenix said. "Coming from you, that's high praise. Lousy politics, but high praise."

"Good thing I don't do politics, sir," Wilhelm said. "Have a good trip."

"Thank you, Colonel." Phoenix turned to Patrick and shook his hand. "I don't know when I'll see you again, Patrick," he said, "but I think you and your team did an extraordinary job out there last night."

"Thank you, sir," Patrick said. "Unfortunately I still don't think it's over, but a cease-fire and a pullback is definitely good news."

"I read your plan for action against Diyarbakir," Phoenix said. "I don't think there's any chance the president will approve it, especially when he learns it comes from you. But I'll talk to him about it."

"We can put it into action in less than a day, and at the very least it would send a message that we're serious."

"That it does," Phoenix agreed. "I'd also like to talk to you about this company of yours and your incredible weapon systems like the CID, the Tin Man, and those electromagnetic rail guns. I don't know why we're not fielding thousands of them." He looked at Patrick with a puzzled expression, then added, "And I'd like to know why *you* have them, and not the U.S. Army."

"I'll explain everything, sir," Patrick said.

"I doubt it," Phoenix said with a wry smile, "but I still want to talk to you about them. Goodbye, General."

"Have a safe trip, sir." The vice president nodded, loaded aboard the CV-22, and the big twin rotors were turning moments later.

It was hard for Patrick to hear at first over the roar of the Osprey's twin rotors in full vertical takeoff power, but he did, and he opened his radio. Wilhelm was doing the same at that very moment. "Go ahead, Boomer," he said.

"*Bandits*!" Hunter Noble shouted. At that moment the air raid sirens sounded. "Two formations of ten bombers, supersonic, just crossed the Turkey-Iraq border, headed this way, *five minutes out*!"

"*Get the Osprey out of here*!" Patrick shouted. He waved at Jon Masters and Kris Thompson to follow him. "Get him the hell away from the base!"

Wilhelm was shouting into his radio as well:

"*Shelters, shelters, shelters!*" he cried. "Everyone into air raid shelters, *now!*"

As they ran for open ground, they could still see the CV-22 as it took off and headed south. At first its flight path looked totally normal—standard climb-out, gradual acceleration, smooth transition from vertical to turboprop flight. But moments later the Osprey banked hard left and dove for the ground, and they could hear the engines whine in protest as the big transport changed from turboprop to helicopter mode. It dodged left and right and made a low approach to a group of buildings in Tall Kayf, hoping to hide in the radar ground clutter.

But it was too late—the Turkish missiles were already in the air. The Turkish F-15Es had already locked up the CV-22 over a hundred miles away and had launched two Turkish-modified AIM-54 missiles—ironically nicknamed "Phoenix"—at the Osprey. Formerly serving with the U.S. Navy to provide long-range defense of an aircraft carrier battle group, the AIM-54 had been the mainstay of the U.S. Navy's carrier-based air wings, capable of destroying massive formations of Russian bombers before they could get within range to launch antiship cruise missiles. After it was retired in 2004, the U.S. military's inventory of its longest-range, hardest-hitting air-to-air missiles was put up for auction, and the Turkish air force snapped them up.

After launch, the Phoenix missiles climbed to an altitude of eighty thousand feet at a speed of almost five times the speed of sound and then began a dive toward the target area, guided by the Turkish F-15E's powerful radar. Within a

few seconds of impact, the AIM-54 activated
its own terminal guidance radar to close in for
the kill. One missile malfunctioned and self-
destructed, but the second missile hit the CV-22
Osprey's right rotor disk as the aircraft was
maneuvering to land in a parking lot. The right
engine exploded, sending the aircraft into a violent left spin for a few seconds before crashing to
the ground, then flipping upside down from the
force of the explosion.

Back at Nahla, the scene was complete
mayhem. With the Command and Control
Center already destroyed, the main targets for
the Turkish bombers were the flight line and
barracks. Every hangar, including the XC-57
Loser's storage hangar and the makeshift morgue
containing the remains of the fallen American
and Iraqi soldiers, was hit by at least one two-
thousand-pound Joint Direct Attack Munitions
bomb, a satellite-guided upgrade to a conventional radar-delivered gravity bomb. The parking
ramps and taxiways that had not been hit before
by the Turks in their initial invasion were hit
this time.

The soldiers at Nahla were on edge and ready
for anything following their battle the night
before, so when the air-raid siren went off, the
men were out the barracks doors immediately
and headed to shelters. A few soldiers stayed
behind too long to collect weapons or personal
items and were killed by the bombs, and a few
other soldiers helping the wounded evacuate the
building were caught in the open. Overall, casualties were light.

But the devastation was complete. Within minutes, most of Allied Air Base Nahla was destroyed.

THE SITUATION ROOM,
THE WHITE HOUSE, WASHINGTON, D.C.
A short time later

President Gardner hurried into the Situation Room, a high-tech conference room in the West Wing used for high-level national security meetings, and he took his place. "Take seats," he said. "Someone talk to me, right *now*. What happened?"

"Turkey declared martial law and executed a number of air strikes throughout northern Iraq," National Security Adviser Conrad Carlyle said. "The Turkish minister of defense, Cizek, says he was placed in charge of the military and ordered to launch a full-scale attack against the PKK and their supporters in Iraq and Turkey." An electronic map of northern Iraq was displayed on the large wall-size computer monitor in the front of the room. "Twenty cities and towns were hit by fighter-bombers, including Kirkuk, Irbil, Dahuk, and Mosul. Three joint Iraqi-American military bases were struck in Irbil, Kirkuk, and near Mosul. Casualty reports are coming in now. The bases had just minutes of warning time." He paused just long enough to draw the president's attention to him fully, then added, "And the vice president's aircraft is missing."

"*Missing*?" the president shouted.

"The vice president took off for Baghdad just minutes before the attack took place," Carlyle said. "The pilot was executing evasive maneuvers and looking for a place to make an emergency landing when they lost contact. The commander of Allied Air Base Nahla has organized a search and rescue team, but that base was hit hard and almost destroyed. It had already been hit last night by a Turkish air raid. An Air Force search and rescue team is being dispatched from Samarra but it'll take a few hours to get there."

"Good God," the president breathed. "Get Hirsiz or Cizek or whoever's really in charge in Ankara on the phone. I don't want any more Turkish planes flying over Iraq—*none*! Where are the carriers? What can we get up there?"

"We have the Abraham Lincoln carrier battle group in the Persian Gulf," chairman of the Joint Chiefs of Staff General Taylor Bain responded. "It'll be a stretch because of the distance involved, but we can start setting up air patrols over Iraq with E-2 Hawkeye radar planes doing C4I and pairs of F/A-18 Hornet fighters in patrol orbits."

"Do it," the president ordered. "Keep them over Iraq unless they are attacked." Secretary of Defense Miller Turner picked up his phone to issue the orders.

"Turkey has a very large air force, with a lot of surplus American warplanes and weapons," Carlyle pointed out. "Some of them, like the F-15 Eagles, can be a match for the Hornet."

"If Turkey wants to get into a shooting war with the United States, I'm ready to play," Gardner said angrily. "What about land attack assets? Tomahawks?"

"The conventional sea-launched cruise missiles in the Persian Gulf are out of range," Bain said. "We would have to move the ships and subs in the Mediterranean closer to get within range of the eastern Turkish air bases."

"Any ships or subs in the Black Sea?"

"No submarines, per treaty," Bain said. "We have a single Surface Action Group on patrol in the Black Sea, also per treaty, and they do have T-LAMs, but they're also the most vulnerable ships out there right now. We would have to assume that if the Turks want to fight, they'd attack that group first."

"What else do we have?"

"We have some tactical air based in various places in Europe—Greece, Romania, Italy, Germany, and the U.K.—but those wouldn't be quick-strike options," Bain said. "Our only other option is conventionally armed B-2 Spirit stealth bombers launched from Diego Garcia. We have six surviving planes ready to go."

"Get them armed and ready," the president said. "That's all we have? Six?"

"Afraid so, Mr. President," Bain said. "We have two XR-A9 Black Stallion space planes that can launch precision-guided weapons, and they can be armed and hitting targets within hours, and we also have a few conventionally armed intercontinental ballistic missiles that can hit targets in Turkey quickly."

"Get them briefed and ready, too," Gardner said. "I don't know what Ankara has in mind, or if they even *have* a mind, but if they want to take us on, I want everything ready to go."

The phone beside White House chief of staff

Walter Kordus blinked, and he picked it up. "Turkish prime minister Ayşe Akas for you, sir."

The president picked up the phone immediately. "Prime Minister Akas, this is President Gardner. What in hell is going on out there? Twelve hours ago you announced a cease-fire. Now you've attacked three American military bases! Are you out of your minds?"

"I'm afraid Minister of National Defense Cizek and General Abdullah Guzlev may be, Mr. President," she said. "Last night they arrested President Hirsiz, engineered a military coup d'état, and took over the Presidential Palace. They were unhappy about the president's decision to pull back to the border before the PKK and their supporters were eliminated."

"So why attack American bases?"

"Retaliation for the defeat near Tall Kayf," Akas said. "Two thousand Turks were killed or wounded in that battle. Cizek and the generals thought it was cowardly to retreat to the border after such a loss."

"Are you still prime minister, Mrs. Akas?"

"No, I am not," Akas said. "I was allowed use of my cellular telephone, which I am sure is being monitored, but I am not free to travel or go to my office. Under the state of emergency, the National Assembly has been dismissed. Cizek and the generals are in charge."

"I want to speak with them immediately," Gardner said. "If you can get Cizek a message, tell him that the United States is going to set up a no-fly zone in northern Iraq, and I warn them not to violate it or try to attack any of our planes, or we will consider it an act of war and retaliate immediately. We are readying all of our military resources and will respond with everything we have. Is that clear?"

"It is clear to me, Mr. President," Akas said, "but I do not know if it will be seen by Cizek as anything more than a clear threat of imminent attack. Are you sure you wish me to deliver this message, sir?"

"I don't have any intention of attacking Turkey unless they violate Iraqi airspace again," Gardner said. "All of our other responses will be by other means. But if Turkey intends to fight, we'll give them a fight." And he hung up.

OUTSIDE TALL KAYF, IRAQ
A short time later

The two Humvees rushed to the scene of the CV-22 crash and immediately surrounded the area with security forces while Kris Thompson and a medic rushed to the tilt-rotor aircraft. Fortunately the Osprey's fire suppression system had stopped a major fire, and Iraqi citizens put out the others. They found the vice president, the flight crew, and a Secret Service agent being treated by a local doctor, with another Secret Service agent covered by a rug. "Thank God you're alive, sir," Kris said.

"Thanks to these people," Ken Phoenix said. "If they hadn't helped, we probably would've all been killed in the fire. What's happened?"

"The Turks bombed the base—again," Kris said. "Pretty much destroyed it this time. A few casualties; we got just enough warning. The

Turks are carrying out bombing raids all over northern Iraq."

"So much for the cease-fire—if there ever was one," Phoenix said.

"We're setting up an evacuation center here in town," Kris said. "The colonel plans to join up with friendly forces in Mosul. I'll get you out of here and then we'll figure out a way to get you to Baghdad."

Ten minutes later, they met up with some of the survivors from Nahla, including Patrick McLanahan, Hunter Noble, Jon Masters, and a handful of contractors and soldiers, most of them injured. "Glad you made it, Mr. Vice President," Patrick said.

"Where's the colonel?"

"Supervising the evacuation," Patrick said. "He's going to send us down to Mosul and await a convoy out. Just about every building that was still standing after last night isn't standing any longer."

"Your plane, the XC-57?"

"They got all the hangars, even the one we were using as the morgue."

Ken Phoenix motioned Patrick to walk with him, and they stepped away from the others. Phoenix reached into his pocket and pulled out the plastic carrying case containing the Secure Digital card Patrick had given him. "What about this?" he asked. "Can we still do this?"

Patrick's eyes widened. He thought quickly, and his head began to nod. "We won't have the netrusion systems running," he said, "and I'll have to check the status of the Lancers in the UAE—"

"Find a phone and do it," Phoenix said. "I'm going to talk with the president."

THE PRESIDENTIAL PALACE, ÇANCAYA, ANKARA, TURKEY
A short time later

"*He* said *what*?" Hasan Cizek shouted. "Is Gardner threatening war with Turkey?"

"What did you expect him to say, Hasan?" Turkish Prime Minister Ayşe Akas asked. With them was former Turkish chief of the general staff General Abdullah Guzlev. "You killed a lot of Americans today, after Turkey declared a cease-fire! Did you expect him to say, 'I understand' or 'It's no worry'?"

"What I did was retaliation for what *he, his* robots, and *his* Iraqi goons did to my troops!" Cizek cried. "They killed thousands!"

"Calm yourself, Hasan," Akas said. "The president said he's going to set up a no-fly zone in northern Iraq, and he doesn't want you to cross it. If you try, he'll consider it an act of war."

"He's threatening war with Turkey? Is he crazy, or just suffering from delusions of grandeur? He doesn't have enough forces in this part of the world to take on Turkey!"

"Does he plan to use nuclear weapons against us?" Guzlev asked.

"Hasan, be quiet and think," Akas said. "We're talking about the United States of America. They may be less strong because of the wars in Iraq and Afghanistan, but they are still the most powerful military machine in the world.

You may be able to get away with attacking two or three bases in Iraq, but you can't withstand the full force of their military power. They can flatten this building a hundred different ways in the blink of an eye. You know this. Why are you denying it?"

"I'm not denying it, but I'm not backing away from my mission until it's completed," Cizek said. "The United States will have to use their vaunted military power to stop me." He paused to think for a moment, then said to Guzlev: "The quickest way he can set up a no-fly zone in northern Iraq is with carrier-based aircraft flying out of the Persian Gulf."

"Yes," Guzlev said. "The Mediterranean and bases in Europe are too far."

"How long?"

"Fighters, tankers, radar planes—it'll take a few hours to get them briefed and ready to deploy, maybe longer, then at least an hour or two to fly to northern Iraq," Guzlev said.

"That means we have only a few hours, maybe five or six, to act. Can we do it?"

"About half the force is just recovering at Diyarbakir and Malatya," Guzlev said, checking his watch. "The other half is being armed. If there are no delays or accidents . . . yes, I think we can have them airborne again in five or six hours."

"What do you intend to do?" Akas asked.

"I'm not going to violate the American no-fly zone; I'll just be sure to have my tasks completed before they set it up," Cizek said. To Guzlev: "I want every available plane loaded and launched to attack the final target sets in Irbil, Kirkuk, and Mosul. Every known or suspected PKK and *peshmerga* base, every known PKK supporter, and every Iraqi and American military base that might threaten Turkish occupation of Iraq gets destroyed as soon as possible."

OVER THE PACIFIC OCEAN, THREE HUNDRED MILES WEST OF LOS ANGELES, CALIFORNIA
A short time later

"Stand by for release," the mission commander said. He was aboard a Sky Masters Inc. Boeing DC-10 carrier aircraft, high above the Pacific Ocean. "Let's make this a good one, and I'll buy the first round."

The aircraft, initially built by McDonnell Douglas Aircraft before that company was purchased by Boeing, was highly modified for many purposes, including aerial refueling and instrument tests, but its major modification gave it the ability to launch satellite boosters into space. The booster, called ALARM or Air Launched Alert Response Missile, resembled a large cruise missile. It had three solid rocket motors and folding wings to give it lift while in the atmosphere. ALARM, in effect, used the DC-10 as its first stage engine.

The ALARM boosters carried four satellites internally. The satellites, called NIRTSats, or Need It Right This Second Satellites, were washing-machine-size multipurpose reconnaissance satellites designed to stay in orbit for less than a month; they carried very little maneuvering fuel and were meant to stay in one set orbit, with only a few minor orbit changes or realignments allowed. These satellites were being placed into orbit to serve field commanders in Afghanistan.

"Pretty friggin' amazing," the mission commander, a U.S. Air Force major from the Thirtieth Space Wing at Vandenberg Air Force Base in California, said. "Less than twelve hours ago I got the call to launch this constellation. Now, we're about to do it. Normally it takes the Air Force a week to do something like this."

"That's why you should just call on us from now on," the aircraft commander, a civilian working for Sky Masters Inc., said proudly.

"Yeah, but you guys are too expensive."

"You want the job done fast and right, you gotta pay for the best," the pilot said. "Besides, it's not your money, it's the Air Force's."

"Well, however you guys do it and however much we're paying you, it's worth it," the mission commander said.

"We aim to please," the pilot said. He flipped a page on his multifunction display when he received a blinking message annunciation, read the incoming satellite message, cleared it back to the main navigation page, switched his intercom to "private," and spoke.

"What was that?" the mission commander asked.

"Nothing, just a fast request to the release crews," the pilot said. The Air Force major didn't notice him, but the flight engineer sitting behind him was suddenly pulling out charts and typing on his mission planning computer. "How much longer to release?" the pilot asked.

"Sixty seconds . . . now," the mission commander said. He checked his own multifunction display, where he had the mission data displayed. They were flying to a precise location and a particular heading that would put the ALARM booster on the perfect trajectory for a successful insertion. Because the NIRTSats carried so little fuel, the closer they could shoot the booster into the perfect orbit, the better.

"Stand by, flight crew," the pilot said. "Report checklists complete to the MC."

"Flight deck configured and ready to go, MC," the flight engineer said.

"Cabin deck ready, MC," the civilian in charge of the cabin reported after getting a thumbs-up from his Air Force counterpart observing the release. The cabin of the modified DC-10 was split into pressurized and unpressurized compartments. In the pressurized compartment was a second ALARM booster, suspended on loading cables; the compartment could hold two ALARMs, plus one in the unpressurized compartment.

The first ALARM booster was already loaded into the unpressurized launch compartment, where it would be ejected into the slipstream underneath the DC-10. After release, its first solid rocket motor would fire, and it would fly under, then ahead of the DC-10, then start a sharp climb. Its second and third stage motors would fire in turn until the booster had accelerated to orbital speed and was at the proper altitude in space—in this case, eighty-eight miles above Earth—and then it would begin releasing the NIRTSats.

"Stand by," the MC said. "Five . . . four . . . three . . . two . . . one . . . drop." He waited for

the brief pitch-down caused by the ALARM
booster dropping free of the DC-10 before the
fuel and trim systems could rebalance the plane.
That was always the trickiest part of these releases; if the aircraft didn't rebalance itself and
the plane started rapid pitch motions, and if the
ALARM booster was caught up in the disrupted
slipstream, it could fly off course or out of control. That was a rare occurrence, but . . .

Then the MC realized he didn't feel the pitch
movement. He looked at his multifunction display . . . and saw that the ALARM booster hadn't
released! "Hey, what happened?" He checked
his indicators . . . and saw that the pilot's launch
override was engaged. "Hey, you stopped the
launch! You overrode the release! What's going
on?"

"We got orders," the pilot said. "We're going
to get refueled, and then we're going to change
to a different launch axis."

"Orders? Different launch? You can't do this!
This is an Air Force mission! Who told you to do
this?"

"The boss."

"What boss? Who? *Masters*? *He* can't change
this mission! I'm going to advise my command
post."

"You can tell them what we did after we
launch this booster."

"This booster, this mission belongs to the U.S.
Air Force! I'm not going to let you hijack an Air
Force missile."

"I'm sorry to hear you say that, Major," the
pilot said kindly . . . just as the flight engineer

reached up behind the MC, stuck a stun gun on the Air Force officer's neck, and pressed the switch, instantly knocking him unconscious.

"How long will he stay out, Jim?" the pilot asked.

"Couple hours, I think."

"Long enough," the pilot said. He clicked the intercom: "Okay, John, send him up." A few moments later the Air Force technician assigned to monitor the launch entered the flight deck, and he, too, was stunned unconscious by the flight engineer. "Okay, while the NIRTSats are reprogrammed by the front office in Vegas by satellite, I need a potty break before we rendezvous with the tanker. Double-check the new launch plan. Good job, everyone. Thanks for thinking on your feet. We'll all deserve a raise after this . . . if we're not in prison, that is."

"Where's the new tasking?" the launch deck technician asked.

"Turkey," the pilot said. "Looks like the shit is hitting the fan out there."

MARDIN PROVINCE, SOUTHEAST TURKEY
Early that evening

"*Radar contact! Radar contact!*" the tactical control officer, or TAO, of the area Turkish Patriot surface-to-air missile regiment shouted. "Multiple inbound contacts, medium altitude, medium subsonic, heading straight for us. It's going to enter Syrian airspace in three minutes."

The tactical director, or TD, studied the Patriot

radar display. "Medium speed, not maneuvering; medium altitude—probably reconnaissance drones," he said. "How many?"

"Eight. They're heading right for our radar sites."

"I don't want to waste missiles on drones," he said, "but we're supposed to seal this sector." He thought for a moment, then said, "If they change altitude, engage. Otherwise we'll try to get them with antiaircraft artillery."

"What if they dive onto our radar sites, sir?" the TAO asked.

"I don't know of any cruise missiles that start at a vulnerable altitude, then dive onto their targets," the tactical director said. "Attack missiles will fly very low or very high. This one is right in the envelope for antiaircraft artillery. Heck, even the lousy Syrian gunners might have a chance to nail them. Watch them for now. If they start to accelerate or descend, we'll—"

"Sir, Sector Four reports multiple inbound bogeys as well!" the communications officer shouted. That sector was the one adjacent to them in the east. "Another eight bogeys, medium altitude, medium subsonic, also headed for our radar sites!"

"Sixteen reconnaissance drones, all flying into Turkey at the exact same time . . . and from where?" the tactical director said aloud. "Turkey attacked all of the American bases this morning. There is no way they could launch so many drones so soon. They have to be air-launched."

"Or they could be false targets, like the last time we launched," the TAO said.

Sixteen targets . . . that meant thirty-two Patriots, since Patriot always launched two missiles at every target to ensure a kill. Thirty-two Patriots represented *every launcher* in the regiment. If they launched every missile at drones or false targets, it would represent a massive waste of missiles, and would leave them vulnerable until they were reloaded, which would take about thirty minutes.

The tactical director picked up the phone and passed all the information to the Sector Air Defense Coordinator in Diyarbakir. "Shoot them down," the sector coordinator said. "They're on an attack profile. Check your systems for any sign of spoofing."

"Acknowledged," the tactical director said. "TAO, prepare for—"

"Sir, they are starting to orbit," the TAO shouted. "They're right along the border, some in Syria. It looks like they're orbiting."

"Reconnaissance drones," the TD said, relieved. "Continue to monitor. What about Sector Four's bogeys?"

"Starting to orbit as well, sir," the TAO said.

"Very well." The TD needed a cigarette, but he knew that would not be possible until these things were out of his area. "Keep an eye on those things and . . ."

"*Bandits*!" the TAO shouted suddenly. "Four targets inbound, high subsonic, extreme low altitude, range forty miles!"

"*Engage*!" the TAO said immediately. "Batteries released! All batteries . . . !"

"The drones are leaving their orbits, accelerating, and descending!"

Damn, the tactical director thought, they just

went from on alert to under attack in the blink of an eye. "Prioritize the high-speed bandits," he said.

"But the drones are closing in!" the TAO said. "Patriot is prioritizing the drones!"

"I'm not going to waste missiles on drones," the TD said. "The fast movers are the real threat. Change priorities and engage!"

But that decision obviously wasn't going to stand, because it was soon obvious that the drones were going straight for the Patriot phased-array radars. "Should I switch priorities, sir—"

"*Do it! Do it*!" the TD said.

The TAO furiously typed commands into his targeting computer, ordering Patriot to engage the closer, slower targets. "Patriot engaging!" he reported. "The fast movers are accelerating to supersonic . . . sir. Sector Four reports the drones have left their orbits, descending, accelerating, and are heading into *our* sector!"

"Can they engage?" But he already knew the answer: one Patriot radar couldn't sweep into another's because of interference, which created false targets that the engagement computer might launch against. Only one radar could handle an engagement. Their battery would have to take on all twenty-two targets . . .

. . . which meant they would run out of missiles by the time the fast movers arrived! "Reprogram the engagement computer to fire only one missile!" the tactical director ordered.

"But there's not enough time!" the tactical action officer said. "I'd have to terminate this engagement and . . ."

"Don't argue, just do it!" The TAO had never

typed as fast as he did then. He managed to reprogram the engagement computer and reengage
the batteries . . .

. . . but he couldn't do it fast enough, and one
radar was hit by the cruise missiles. The missiles,
which were AGM-158A JASSMs, or Joint Air to
Surface Standoff Missiles, were turbojet-powered
air-launched cruise missiles with thousand-
pound blast fragmentation warheads and a range
of over two hundred miles.

Now one radar had to handle the entire
engagement. Patriot radars didn't sweep like
conventional mechanically scanning radars, and
didn't have to be steered, but they had a specific
section of sky that was assigned to them to avoid
interference problems. The remaining radar, located at Batman Air Base sixty miles east of
Diyarbakir, had been assigned to look south,
into Iraq, and not westerly toward Diyarbakir. On their current heading—actually tracking
through Syria—they were on the extreme edge
of the radar's airspace.

"Order the Batman radar to turn west-
southwest to cover that flight path," the tactical
director ordered. The TAO relayed the order. The
AN/MPQ-53 radar array was normally trailer-
mounted, and although it was fairly easy to move
to cover a new section of sky, it was generally
never done, especially when under attack. The
Batman emplacement was different, however:
even though Patriot is designed to be mobile, the
Batman site was set up semipermanently, which
meant its radar array could be easily moved as
necessary.

"Radar reset, good track on the fast movers,"

the TAO reported a few minutes later. "Patriot engaging—"

But at that moment, all radar indications went out. "*What happened*?" the tactical director shouted.

"The Batman radar is off the air," the TAO reported. "Hit by a cruise missile." A few moments later: "Ground observers reporting two fast-moving low-altitude jets flew overhead from the east." Now it was obvious what had happened: turning the radar to look farther to the west had reduced coverage to the east. Two jets had simply slipped in through the gap in radar coverage between Batman and Van and attacked the radar.

Diyarbakir was now wide open.

ABOARD FRACTURE ONE-NINE
That same time

"Fracture flight, this is One-Niner, your tail is clear," Lieutenant Colonel Gia "Boxer" Cazzotto radioed to the rest of her little squadron of B-1B Lancer bombers. "Let's go get them, what do you say?"

"Fracture One-Nine, this is Genesis," Patrick McLanahan radioed via their secure transceiver. "Are you getting the latest downloads?"

"Buckeye?"

"Roger, I got 'em," the offensive systems officer, or OSO, replied. "The images are great—even better than the radar." He was looking at ultra-high-resolution radar images of Diyarbakir Air Base in Turkey, taken by NIRTSat reconnaissance satellites only moments earlier. The images downloaded from the satellites could be manipulated by the B-1's AN/APQ-164 bombing system as if the bomber's own radar had taken the shot. They were over forty miles to the target, well outside low-altitude radar range, but the OSO could see and compute target coordinates well before flying over the target.

The OSO got busy grabbing target coordinates and loading them into their eight remaining JASSM attack missiles, and once all the missiles had targets loaded, they coordinated launches by time and azimuth and let them fly. This time the turbojet-powered cruise missiles flew low, avoiding known obstacles using inertial navigation with Global Positioning System updates. The six B-1 bombers each released eight JASSMs, filling the sky with forty-eight of the stealthy cruise missiles.

There was no time to pick and choose different warheads for the missiles, so they all sported the same one-thousand-pound blast fragmentation warheads, but some were fused to explode on impact, while others were set to explode in the air after reaching their target coordinates. The air-burst missiles were sent over aircraft parking areas, where the massive explosions destroyed anything and anyone for two hundred yards in all directions, while the impact missiles were targeted against buildings, weapon storage areas, fuel depots, and hangars. The OSOs could refine the missile's target using their real-time imaging infrared datalink, which gave the crews a picture of the target and allowed them to steer the missile precisely on target.

"Genesis, this is Fracture, clean sweep," Cazzotto radioed. "All weapons expended. How'd we do?"

"We'll get the next NIRTSat downloads in about an hour," Patrick replied, "but judging by the images I got from the JASSMs, you did outstanding. All Patriot radars are down; I show you clear to climb and RTB. Good show."

"See you . . . well, sometime, Genesis," Gia said.

"Looking forward to it, Fracture," Patrick said. And he really meant it.

EPILOGUE

Get mad. Then get over it.
—*Colin Powell*

THE OVAL OFFICE,
THE WHITE HOUSE, WASHINGTON, D.C.
The next morning

*W*hat in hell do you mean, the United States at-tacked Turkey last night?" President Joseph Gardner shouted. In the Oval Office with him was his chief of staff, Walter Kordus; National Security Adviser Conrad Carlyle; and Secretary of Defense Miller Turner. "I didn't order an attack! Who? Where . . . ?"

"The target was Diyarbakir, the main air base Turkey was using to launch air strikes into Iraq," Turner said. "Six B-1B Lancer bombers launched from the United Arab Emirates—"

"On whose authority?" the president thun-dered. "Who gave them the order?"

"We're not sure, sir . . ."

"*Not sure*? Six supersonic heavy bombers loaded with bombs take off from a base in the Middle East and bombs an air base in Turkey, and *no one* knows who authorized it? Who was the commander?"

"Her name is Cazzotto."

"*Her*? A woman bomber-wing commander?"

"It apparently is an engineering squadron, sir," Turner said. "They take planes out of mothballs and make them operational again. They were tasked with providing air support for operations in Afghanistan and Iraq."

"And they just blasted off and *bombed Turkey*? How is this even possible? Who ordered them to do it?"

"Colonel Cazzotto refuses to talk, except to say that the person that expedited the mission will make contact," Turner said.

"This is unacceptable, Miller," the president said. "Find that person and throw him in prison! This is insanity! I'm not going to allow six B-1 bombers to fly around anytime someone feels like taking out some buildings." He accepted a note from Kordus, read it, then crumpled it up and threw it on his desk. "So what did they hit?"

"They destroyed two Patriot radar sites on their way in," Turner said, "then they hit a variety of military targets at Diyarbakir, including parked and taxiing aircraft, hangars, fuel depots, and command and control centers. Very effective target selection. They used Joint Air to Surface Strike Missiles, which are high-precision subsonic conventionally armed cruise missiles. All the planes came back safely."

"And put in the stockade, I hope!"

"Yes, sir. It appears that the Turks were gearing up for a major air raid into Iraq. They had over a hundred tactical planes ready for takeoff at Diyarbakir. Looks like they were trying to get some licks in before we set up the no-fly zone in northern Iraq."

This somewhat mollified the president's rage, but he shook his head. "I want some answers, Miller, and I want some *butts*!" he shouted. Kordus answered the flashing phone, looked at the president until he looked back, then nodded toward the door to the president's private office, adjacent to the Oval Office. "Christ, just what I need when the shit starts flying—a VIP visitor."

"Who is it?" Carlyle asked.

"President Kevin Martindale."

"*Martindale*? What does he want?"

"Beats me, but he's been waiting for an hour," Gardner said. "I'll get rid of him. Get me some answers, Miller!" He entered his private study and closed the door. "I'm sorry, Mr. President," he said. "Something urgent came up."

"That happens a lot in this business, Mr. President," Kevin Martindale said, standing and shaking hands with his former secretary of defense. "I'm sorry for the unexpected visit, but there's something I had to run past you."

"Can it wait for lunch, Kevin?" Gardner asked. "You know, the whole Turkey thing is threatening to come off the hinges—"

"It has to do with Turkey," Martindale said.

"Oh? What about it?"

"The air strike on Diyarbakir last night."

Gardner's eyes bulged in shock. "The air strike . . . Jesus, Kevin, I just found out about it *two minutes ago*! How do you know about it?"

"Because I helped plan it," Martindale said.

Gardner's eyes bulged even farther. "I convinced the base commander at Minhad Air Base in the United Arab Emirates, General Omeir, to let the bombers go. He owed me." Gardner was absolutely dumbstruck. "Listen, Joe, you have to promise me not to pursue this thing," Martindale went on. "Don't investigate Cazzotto, Omeir, or anyone else."

"*Don't investigate*? A six-pack of American supersonic bombers attacked an air base in Turkey, and I'm not supposed to investigate?"

"It would be better if you didn't, Joe," Martindale said. "Besides, the air strike probably stopped a war between us and Turkey. From what I was told, we took out a fourth of Turkey's tactical air force on that single raid. They were getting ready to hit Iraq again, probably destroy most of Irbil and Kirkuk."

"Kevin . . . how in the *hell* do you know all this stuff?" Gardner asked. "What have you been up to?"

Martindale looked at Gardner for a moment, then smiled and said quietly, "I am Scion Aviation International, Joe. Heard of them?"

The eye-bulging incredulous expression was back. "Scion Aviation? Scion . . . you mean, *McLanahan's outfit*?"

"My outfit, Joe."

"You . . . you have the robots . . . the Tin Man . . . ?"

"Fewer than we had before, thanks to Hirsiz and Cizek," Martindale said, "but we still have the rest." He looked at Gardner and remained silent until the president looked at him in return. "I know what you're thinking, Joe: you grab

McLanahan in Iraq and force him to reveal where the other robots are, then rendition him to Uzbekistan for the rest of his life. Don't do it."

"Why the hell shouldn't I?" Gardner said. "That's exactly what he deserves!"

"Joe, you need to do what I did: stop fighting the guy and learn to work with him," Martindale said. "The man went out there, planned an air strike against one of the most powerful countries in that region of the world, brought together the aircraft, weapons, and satellite support he needed, and succeeded. Isn't that the guy you want *working* for you?"

"The guy sent two of those Tin Men after me, *at Camp David*, and one of them had me by the neck . . . !"

"And I know why, Joe," Martindale said. "I have all the evidence, stored away, just in case. Now it's not just McLanahan you need to eliminate: now it's me and a small group of attorneys who know where all the copies of all that evidence are hidden." He put a hand on Gardner's arm. "But I'm not here to threaten you, Joe," he went on. "I'm telling you, McLanahan doesn't want to fight you, he wants to fight *for* you, for America. He's got the gift, man. He sees a problem and moves heaven and earth to fix it. Why wouldn't you want him on your side?"

He patted Gardner on the shoulder, then retrieved his coat. "Think about it, Joe, okay?" he said as he prepared to depart. "And lay off the investigation, or paper over it, or classify it, do whatever. If it gets the Turks to back down, it's all good. You can even take credit. I'll be looking in on you, Mr. President."

THE PALM JUMEIRAH, DUBAI, UNITED ARAB EMIRATES
Several days later

From the rooftop restaurant of the spectacular new Trump International Hotel and Tower in Dubai, Patrick McLanahan and Gia Cazzotto could see a lot of the incredible trunk, crown, fronds, and breakwater of the Palm Jumeirah, one of the three Palm Islands, artificial islands and reefs that form one of the most unusual and one-of-a-kind residential and recreational developments in the world. In the shape of a huge palm frond, it adds more than three hundred miles to the Persian Gulf coastline of the United Arab Emirates.

Gia raised her champagne glass to Patrick, and he touched his glass to hers. "So tell me, General," she asked, "how did you get a hotel for you, me, and your entire crew at the most exclusive and impossible-to-book hotel in the world?"

"A very appreciative boss," Patrick said.

"Ooh, very mysterious. Who is he? Or can't you say? Is he like a Charles Townsend character, rich and powerful but prefers to stay hidden in the shadows?"

"Something like that."

They stood and admired the view for a few moments; then she said, "When do you head back to the States?"

"Tomorrow morning."

"You can't stay any longer?"

"No." He looked at her, then asked, "When do you go back to Palmdale?"

"Day after tomorrow. I thought I was headed to Fort Leavenworth, but all that stuff suddenly went away." She looked at him carefully. "Wouldn't happen to know why all those State Department and Defense Intelligence Agency investigators suddenly disappeared, would you?"

"No."

"Perhaps your Charlie became my guardian angel?" Patrick said nothing. She gave him a mock frown. "You don't say much, do you, sir?" she asked.

"I asked you not to call me 'sir' or 'General.'"

"Sorry, can't help it." She took a sip of champagne, then laced her fingers between his. "But maybe if you did some not-so-general type stuff, I'd get the hang of it." Patrick smiled, leaned forward, and lightly kissed her on the lips.

"That's what I'm talking about, Patrick." She gave him a mischievous smile, pulled him closer, then said before kissing him again, "But that's not *all* I'm talking about."

ÇUKURCA BORDER CROSSING, HAKKARI PROVINCE, REPUBLIC OF TURKEY

That same evening

There was a small crowd of well-wishers along the road through the Çukurca border crossing post on the Turkey-Iraq border, waving Turkish flags and cheering as the lead vehicles of the Turkish Jandarma forces reentered their home country. Border guards held them back, and patrol dogs were led up and down the line.

It was a long, exhausting, and degrading trip home, thought General Bezir Ozek as he alighted from his armored car once he crossed the border, but this was making the whole embarrassing debacle somewhat worth it. The border post commander saluted, and a small ceremonial band played the Turkish national anthem. "Welcome home, General," the commander said.

"Thank you, Major," Ozek said, "and thank you for this reception."

"Don't thank me—thank the people," the major said. "They heard you were coming home, and they wanted to welcome you and your men back from a victorious campaign against the PKK."

Ozek nodded, not saying what he was really thinking: his campaign had been a failure, cut short by the coward Hasan Cizek. After the American air raid on Diyarbakir, Cizek completely disappeared, leaving the government wide open. Kurzat Hirsiz resigned and turned over power to Ayşe Akas, and the campaign to crush the PKK was over. He had spent the last week fighting off ambushes by PKK and *peshmerga* guerrillas as they made their way back home.

"Come, please, meet your well-wishers," the major said. He leaned toward Ozek and said, "All security precautions have been taken, sir."

"Thank you, Major," Ozek said. He turned to the crowd and waved, and the crowd let out a cheer. Well, he thought, *that* sounded real enough. He started shaking hands. Men and women looked google-eyed at him, as if he were some rock star. Hundreds of hands were reaching out to him.

He was just about at the end of the crowd

when he noticed one woman waving her right hand to him and carrying a baby in her left. She was most attractive, made even more so by the fact that she was nursing the baby, with only a light gauzy blanket over her bare breasts. He grasped her free hand. "Thank you, my dear, thank you for this welcome," he said.

"No, thank you, General," the woman said gleefully. "Thank you for your hard-fought battles."

"I do my best to serve the people of Turkey, and especially beautiful women like you." He took her hand and kissed it. "It is a job I treasure, just as I will treasure meeting you."

"Why, thank you, General." The gauzy blanket shifted slightly, and Ozek grinned as he peeked at her chest. Damn, he thought, he'd been out in the field *way* too long. "And," she said, batting her eyes at him, "I have a job to do as well."

The gauzy blanket dropped away, revealing beautifully firm sexy breasts . . . and a horribly mangled left shoulder, half a left arm . . . and a wooden stick with a rakelike end attached to the stump. "My job, to avenge the people of al-Amadiyah, is at an end, General, as is yours . . . courtesy of the Baz."

And with that, Zilar Azzawi released the dead man's trigger on the detonators connected to the twenty pounds of explosives hidden in the doll she carried like a baby, killing everyone within a radius of twenty feet.